HELLBENDER

Frank J. Fleming

Cover designed by Ethan Nicolle

This book is a work of fiction. Names, characters, places, and incidents either are products of the author's imagination or are used fictitiously. Any resemblance to actual persons, living or dead, events, or locales is entirely coincidental.

Printed in the United States of America

First Printing: June 2019
NTM Publishing

ISBN-10 0-9786832-2-6
ISBN-13 978-0-9786832-2-1

Other Novels by Frank J. Fleming

Superego
Sidequest: In Realms Ungoogled

For the latest by Frank J. Fleming and to sign up for his newsletter and get a free story, go to:

FrankJFleming.com

To my brother, Joe foo', always a friend and an inspiration.

CONTENTS

INTRODUCTION

Authors tend to work really hard on the first sentences of their stories. They want to grab you right away and get you to dive into that novel. It all seems rather silly and artificial to me. I mean, you already bought the book, have it in hand, and are reading it; are there really people out there who are going to read the first sentence, not like it, and then toss the book? If such a person exists, he sounds like a real weirdo. Like someone you don't want to make eye contact with. Do I really have to structure my whole story so that I have some great opening just to appease that psychopath?

But that's not you. You're a thinking adult. So instead of going all out on the opening of the story and trying to almost trick you into thinking this book is good, I thought I'd just come out and introduce myself. Usually, the authors of novels like to lurk like ninjas in the background. They act like they're not there, but every once in a while you notice them, wondering why did he or she make this word choice, or you start to detect a political opinion in the subtext. I think the author trying to hide like that is stupid, so I thought I'd just come out and say "Hi." I don't plan to be intrusive during this story, but it still seems like we should at least get to know each other since we are about to spend a bit of time together here. So, I'm Frank J. Fleming. In addition to being a writer, I'm a programmer and an electrical engineer. I like video games. I live in Texas with my wife and four kids. My opinion on politics is I'm against it.

Now you know me, and what you can do is email me at frank.j.fleming@gmail.com with the subject "Introduction" and a few details about yourself, and then I'll know you too.

Did you do that? Cool! So now we know each other and are friends! And as your friend, I want to tell you you're really going to enjoy this book. Good job buying it.

By the way, the first sentence of this intro doesn't count as the first sentence of the book. That would be the first sentence of the prologue, which you're about to see. And I actually think I did really good job on it. I don't want to overhype it, but it's quite a sentence.

But if for some reason it doesn't grab you, just keep in mind that there are thousands more sentences. I swear I'll nail it with at least one of them.

PROLOGUE

Doug wasn't sure whether he should trust Satan.

He stared a moment at the man who stood outside the donut shop. He was older than Doug without being what one would call "old," and he was dressed nicely enough without being dressed formally. He had dark hair and a neatly trimmed goatee and eyes that looked to Doug like he could trust them and a mouth that seemed like he shouldn't trust it because it had just said that he's Satan. "Like the guy from the wrapper on hot candies?" Doug asked, to confirm what he thought he'd just heard.

"And extreme hot sauces," Satan confirmed. "Come. I have things to discuss with you, Doug."

Doug did not know what to think of this. Any time anyone important bothered to learn his name and wanted to talk to him, it was never a good sign. "Why me?"

"I have my reasons. This is a simple proposition: Hear me out for a few minutes, and I will buy you some donuts."

Doug looked through the window into the donut shop while he considered the odd offer. The government's new health policies meant that things such as fried dough with frosting on it were of extremely limited availability to those on the lowest rung of the social order — people the government didn't trust to be responsible with their caloric intake. People like Doug. Someone who, after a miserable morning, felt like he could really use some comfort food. "How many donuts?"

"One meal's worth. How many is that?"

Doug thought a moment. "Five."

Satan considered this. "That seems like a lot of donuts to eat in one sitting."

Doug folded his arms. "I disagree."

Satan nodded. "Very well." He led the way into the donut shop and to a table near the rear.

"So ... the donuts ... " Doug said, taking a seat.

"Talk first. Then donuts."

Doug looked at the multicolored pastries behind the counter. "Then I'll just be thinking of donuts the whole time we're talking."

Satan looked unconcerned. "I will take that risk."

Doug eyed the supposed master of evil. "You know, if this is some trick, I've had a crummy enough day already."

Satan shrugged. "It's not even noon. Maybe the day will turn around."

Doug shook his head. "Hard to see how. I lost my best friend this morning."

* * *

Doug was awakened by someone pounding on the front door. He glanced at his clock radio: 3:21 a.m. Dressed in his pajama pants of some historic old yellow, disc-like video game character, he walked out of his tiny bedroom — barely large enough to fit a bed — to the common area just in time to see the front door being kicked open. Six figures all in black entered, their faces obscured behind masks and their hands with rifles at the ready.

The shadow enforcers.

Doug's heart sank. The government liked to display a happy face to the public, so this, its more militant arm, only worked under cover of night, secreting away anyone who had earned the wrath of the ruling class. Few had ever seen them, and they were only spoken of in hushed whispers...or at least that's what the government wanted, but there ended up being a big need for them, to the point that they had become quite common. In fact, Doug had seen two eating at Taco Bell the other day.

One of the shadow enforcers stared at Doug, the enforcer's face and eyes completely concealed behind a black mask. "Where is Bryce Worthington?!" he demanded in a growl of a voice.

No, don't take him! Doug thought. An urge to fight simmered inside him, but as much as he wanted to stand up to these people, there was nothing Doug could do against these well-armed warriors. Nothing. It was once again him and his friends kicked around by people far more powerful than them, with no hope of recourse. So Doug took a moment to compose himself, looked back over his shoulder, and shouted, "BRYCE! IT'S FOR YOU!"

Lulu emerged from her room in pink pajamas adorned with kittens, rubbing her eyes. "Did I sleep-order a pizza again?" She stared awhile at the intruders and then perked up. "Oh. Wow. Who are these people? They're adorbs!"

"We're looking for Bryce Worthington!" one of the enforcers snarled.

Lulu looked at Doug, smiling. "Did you hear that? He used like a Batman voice. It was so cute!" Lulu did her own growly voice. "I'm mean and scary! You better do what I say!"

The shadow enforcer threw Lulu to the ground, held her down with a foot to her back, and pointed his rifle barrel down at her head.

3

"Oh, come on," Lulu gasped, with her face against the worn carpet. "Who knew armed goons all in black busting into places in the middle of the night would be so humorless?"

"There's no need for this," Doug pleaded. "We can just —"

Another enforcer hit Doug in the stomach, doubling him over.

"Why's everyone always have to hit me?" Doug whimpered.

"What are we dealing with here?" one enforcer asked another.

A smaller shadow enforcer who looked female pulled out a handheld computer. "Four warfs occupy this apartment. Two male, two female. All four twenty-two years of age." She pointed to the woman underfoot. "That one there would be Lulu Liu. And the other one is ... Doug dollar sign ampersand pound sign."

"No, it's not," Doug explained as he slowly stood up straight again. "See, I never actually got assigned a last name, and when they were supposed to put 'N/A' for my last name, they accidentally put it as 'Na,' and then when I tried to get that fixed —"

"Oh, shut up," Lulu interrupted, eying the barrel pressed to her head. "No one cares about your boring story, dollar sign ampersand."

Doug frowned at her, but then he realized he might finally be getting a cool nickname.

Charlene came out of her room in a tank top and gray pajama bottoms, her brown hair still neatly tied in a ponytail. She sighed at the sight of the enforcers and the pinned Lulu. "This is all about Bryce, isn't it? Well, there's no need for violence. We're all going to comply, and Lulu there is quite harmless."

Lulu scoffed into the carpet. "No, I'm not."

"That one would be Charlene Marshall," the female enforcer said.

"Quick, Char! Take them all out!" Lulu yelled. "Despite everything we've ever said, we believe in you! Kill!"

"Quiet, Lulu!" Charlene yelled. "This is not a time for joking." She looked at the shadow enforcers. "I just want you to know that whatever Bryce did, I was not a part of it. I'm sure this could all be resolved peacefully. You see, I'm actually a deputy member of the peacekeepers, and —"

"Just tell us where Bryce is," the Batman-voiced enforcer interrupted.

"I'm right here." Standing by the doorway to his room was Bryce, and though it was the middle of the night, he was dressed in a powder-blue suit with his hair perfectly coifed. He took one uneasy glance at Lulu with the gun to her head, but he let that fade his cordial smile for only a moment as he turned to the shadow enforcers. "I think I know what this is about." He paused, smiled, and said, "Hey" to the one with the handheld who appeared to be female. He then looked back at the group. "I defrauded the government, and I'm truly sorry about that. And this was all on me — no one else here had anything to do with it. So no need to molest sweet Lulu there."

"They also punched me," Doug said. "And it didn't seem —"

Another punch cut Doug off as a shadow enforcer yelled, "Shut up!"

Again Bryce's smile left him for a moment, but it was soon back in full force. "I would take that as constructive criticism on the amount of talking you do," Bryce told the doubled-over Doug. He turned back to the shadow enforcer stepping on Lulu. "Anyway, I am coming peacefully. As I am truly, truly sorry about all of this. So, no more need to pin Lulu or punch Doug or..." He looked at Charlene. "They do anything to you?"

"I'm cooperating," Charlene said.

"So am I!" Doug exclaimed. "But they keep hi —" Another punch made him fall to the ground.

"Let's just go, okay?" Bryce suggested. "If you want, I'll even drive myself straight to the re-education center or restoration center or whatever they're calling it now. I just don't want to trouble you any further."

"We have to escort you," said the female. "And it's called the balancing center now."

Bryce nodded. "And that's a great name for it. If you want, I can buy you all coffees on the way there. My treat — for the headache I've caused. I mean, I just feel terrible about this. And middle-of-the-night raids — that's some horrible hours to work. I really feel for you guys."

"Just come with us," the Batman-voiced enforcer said, finally stepping off Lulu to grab Bryce by the arm. He then faced the others. "As for the rest of you, we were never here."

Lulu, still lying on the ground, gave a thumbs-up. "Got it. I just suddenly decided to sleep on the floor."

"Despite Bryce's malfeasance," Charlene called to them, "which I'm sure he will atone for, I want you to know we are all very loyal and —"

The shadow enforcers ignored Charlene and headed out of the apartment, pulling Bryce along.

Charlene examined just how damaged the door was. "We should have seen this coming." She looked at Lulu, who was finally picking herself up off the floor. "Are you okay?"

Lulu dusted off her PJs. "It was just some rowdy fun."

"You didn't need to provoke them, you know," Charlene said.

"No, didn't need to," Lulu answered, "but I felt obligated."

"I'm okay too, by the way," Doug announced, still cradling his stomach. "Even though I got punched repeatedly."

Charlene tried to get the door to close. "That maybe was a little excessive, but it's all Bryce's fault. We should have known this was coming. They've finally gotten him for the crap he pulls, and now he's going into a re-education facility … or what did they say? The balancing center. And I don't know if that will go well for him."

Doug slumped down into their well-worn couch. He couldn't even imagine what life would be like with their group permanently torn apart. Plus, Bryce was his friend. His only friend, really. Well, other than Lulu and Charlene. And Floyd, the guy he knew downstairs. And he was friendly with a bunch of people online. But other than that, Bryce was his only friend. "Hey, Lulu," Doug whispered. "Do you think this was about our plans?"

Lulu scoffed. "Doubt it. There's countless things they could have grabbed Bryce over. Odds are it was something else."

Charlene moved a chair in front of the door to keep it closed. "What are you two talking about?"

"We're plotting to murder sympathizers of our oppressors," Lulu said. "Starting with whomever is nearest."

"Whoever," Charlene corrected.

Lulu groaned. "Oh, you're just all kinds of nazi, aren't you?"

Charlene glared at Lulu and took a step toward her, but Doug got between the two. "Come on," Doug pleaded. "We have to come together and figure out how to rescue Bryce. Maybe we'll have to …" Doug lowered his voice. "… take on the government. There has to be some movement we can join that's working to overthrow it. Like, you know, the RALFS."

Charlene scoffed. "Oh, yeah. The 'rebellion.' All they do is spray-paint stuff."

"Well … that's a start," Doug said.

"Let's do this!" Lulu exclaimed. "I'll get some cans of spray paint and then let's get tagging. We'll start with hobos."

"We're not going to spray-paint anything and we're not going to attempt to overthrow the government," Charlene stated, "as they are doing a very good job … as can be expected with all the conditions and such." She looked Doug firmly in the eyes, took a deep breath, and said, "You just need to accept the fact that Bryce is now gone. He's gone." Tears started welling in her eyes. "Maybe forever."

Lulu shrugged. "I bet he'll be out by this evening."

Charlene stifled the tears. "He's gone, and it's probably for the best. Hopefully this is a wake-up call for you two as well. No more being …" She motioned to the two. "What you are. It's sad, but let's try to get some sleep. And remember: We're not kids any more. No more leeway for your shenanigans. So if we three want to continue to stay together, you need to follow my example and —"

"I'm going to smother you while you sleep," Lulu interrupted.

Charlene rolled her eyes. "Whatever. You're all talk, Lulu."

"Come on, you two," Doug said. "We need to be there for each other." He'd really rather they not fight, but in this dire time it was a bit reassuring that they were acting normally.

"I am going to be there for Charlene," Lulu stated. "I'm going to wait for her to go to sleep and then give her the smothering she so desperately needs. I'm baffled it's taken me this long to do it. Now give me one of your pillows, Doug."

"Why don't you use your own pillow?" Doug asked.

"Because I don't want to get Charlene's drool all over it. I guess I can just use a couch pillow. Those still work for suffocating, right?"

"I'm going to bed because I plan to be a productive citizen in the morning," Charlene said. "Someone whom this sort of thing would never happen to. And if you have a problem with me, Lulu, you challenge me in the daylight. And I will destroy you. And then I will leave your broken body as a warning to anyone else who would interfere with my duties as a citizen. So come at me any time ... except during my shift, of course."

Lulu scoffed. "Whatever, you little twerp. I'm Asian. I have secret kung fu skills. It wouldn't even be a fair fight."

Charlene groaned. "We've had all the same hand-to-hand combat courses ... except I actually paid attention." She went into her room and closed the door.

Lulu headed to her room. "She's not worth staying up late to smother."

Doug ignored her and looked out the window. He could see the shadow enforcers leading Bryce into the back of their VTOL vehicle. The door shut behind him, and the craft lifted up and flew away into the night.

* * *

"And that was the last I ever saw of him," Doug said as he finished his story.

Satan nodded thoughtfully. "But that was earlier today?"

"Well, yeah ... so maybe I'll still see him this evening. But in the hours since then ... nothing."

Satan frowned. "That must have been quite an ordeal for you."

"And it wasn't even the only bad thing to happen to me today," Doug said. "I also lost my job."

* * *

"I'll get right on it, sir," Doug told his boss.

His boss — Doug couldn't remember his name — frowned. "You haven't listened to a word I just said, have you?"

It was true. His mind this day had been on Bryce and wondering what was happening to him. Also, Doug had been unable to locate the third golden claw in the fourth world of the video game *Epic Badger Quest*, and he kept going over that in his head. *Is there something I'm supposed to be doing with the windmill? Because I haven't been able to get in there.*

Doug just realized his boss — mustache guy, as he mentally called him —- had been talking again, perhaps repeating what Doug hadn't been paying attention to. He was done talking and looking at Doug once again as if he was supposed to say something. "I'll get right on it" hadn't worked, so he'd need to try another phase. "That's something to think about."

That didn't work either, as his boss's mustache bristled in response. "Maybe let's try having you talk." His boss sat back in his desk chair and folded his arms. "What's our mission here at National Hover Carts?"

Doug thought that might be a trick question. "To build carts that hover and stuff."

"And do you build carts that hover — and stuff?"

Doug nodded. "Yes, I do ... well, I've had some accidents, but I'm getting better. I mean, I've only caused four explosions."

"That last explosion was your fifth."

"No ... that was just a fire," Doug explained slowly and carefully as if he was explaining it to himself. "No boom; just flames."

"I'm sorry, but I think it's best not to have you assemble hover carts any more."

Doug furrowed his brow. "But since all we do here is assemble hover carts, then what will I ... Wait! Am I being fired?"

His boss's expression became cold. "We don't use that word."

"But I'm trying really hard!" Doug protested. "Everybody can't just keep firing me! Isn't it like the policy of the National People's Republic that we all get work?"

The boss looked confused. "That's not this country. This is the Confederacy of Astara."

"Really? Since when?"

The boss now had an expression of disbelief at Doug's stupidity. Doug really hated that expression. "Since a year ago when this region was conquered by the Confederacy of Astara in the Third Digital Contents Rights War."

"Oh. Well ... I don't really follow politics."

"Didn't you fight in that war? I thought all you warfs were in the reserves."

Doug strained to remember. "I guess I recall having to go out and shoot at stuff about a year ago. Never really got what that was about, though. And I thought we won, because we had a big pizza party afterwards. Actually, I guess we always have those whether we win or lose; it's probably one of those self-esteem things. I wonder if that's a good idea; like maybe I would have fought harder if I knew if we lost I wouldn't get pizza. Of course, maybe it was good we lost because I could have been fighting for the evil side — again, I don't really follow politics. I guess the important thing is that in the end, no one was hurt."

"Thousands died in that war, Doug."

"Oh." A horrific thought struck him. "So that's why we had all that extra pizza! I was so happy about that and now I feel like a jerk!"

Doug's boss looked a bit impatient now. "Anyway, Doug, it's time for you to find other pursuits that might better hold your attention."

"But I'm really into this job! I like really want to make carts hover and know all about the advantages of hovering over wheels that have like friction and stuff. Where are you going to find someone as enthusiastic about hovering carts as me?"

"The decision from up high is that it would be more economical to have your job done by a highly trained monkey."

Doug clenched his fist. "No! You do not want that! Monkeys are dirty and noisy and they poop everywhere!"

"They'll be wearing diapers."

Doug sensed an opening. It wasn't pretty, but he was tired of losing his job. "Well ... you'll need someone to change those diapers."

"We've trained other monkeys to do that."

Doug burst to his feet. "No! You can't do that! That's unnatural!"

Doug's former boss was unshaken. "Do I need to call security?"

Doug raised an eyebrow. "We have security?"

* * *

"And that's when I was beaten by a number of monkeys with nightsticks," Doug said, finishing his second story.

"So an awful start to your day," Satan said. "So, did you like that job?"

"Not really." There were plans to ditch the job, but those involved Bryce. "It's just the indignity of it. Us war orphans are always getting tossed out like trash. It's like people like making us feel worthless."

"That's sad." Doug couldn't tell if Satan was being legitimately sympathetic or sarcastic. "So, anything else happen to you today?"

"Well, on my way back from the hover cart factory, I was walking along the street and saw a slogan the RALFS had spray-painted on a wall. 'WE CAN FIGHT THEM.' And then this big truck was coming by and it blew out a tire and it came right for me ..." Doug paused a second to think things through. "... Wait, no. It careened into a building on the other side of the street. It was awesome. Anyway, I was thinking about that slogan, and I was like, 'Maybe they're right. Maybe we can fight them.' Though, I guess it depends what 'them' they're talking about. I assume they mean the people who are in charge ... because they aren't good people. They've never treated us war orphans right ... or anyone else, really. Maybe they don't have to be in charge, though. Maybe we can ..." Doug realized he wasn't exactly sure he was talking to someone he should trust — again, he said he was Satan. "But that's just an idle thought."

"But it's what you want," Satan said. "A proper battle. A fight between good and evil, where evil finally get what it deserves."

"Well, yeah ... not to offend you."

Satan laughed. "No offense taken. Anyway, my turn to talk about myself."

"And then I get donuts?"

"That is the agreed-upon arrangement. Doug, what do you know about me?"

Religion wasn't something Doug knew much about, but the devil was still a pop culture thing. "That you're supposed to be evil and stuff and you trick other people into doing evil." Doug wondered if Satan might trick him into doing evil, and since he got tricked by regular people all the time, he figured he didn't stand much of a chance against someone supernaturally good at tricking.

Satan groaned. "Trick people? Makes me sound like some used car salesman trying to sell people faulty morality. How I'd put it is that for as long as time has existed in this universe, I have opposed God. And I have done that through you humans, turning you all against Him. And He's fought back in His roundabout way, trying to 'save' you from my corruption."

Doug nodded. "This sounds like some made up fairy-tale thing."

"Yes ... I guess so. I don't really care how it sounds to modern ears. Anyway, this was a battle that has gone on for all of humanity's existence — I and my demon allies would guide the humans away from the influence of their creator, and God would try to bring people back to Him. This was the status quo — a constant battle underneath the surface of all that has gone on in this world. But then something happened that finally shattered that status quo."

Doug's eyes had wandered from Satan to the donuts behind the counter, but he noticed the lull in the conversation and looked back at Satan. "What happened?"

A smile slowly spread across Satan's face. A perfectly pleasant smile on the surface, but somewhere deep inside, Doug felt a chill.

"I won."

HELLBENDER

by your friend,
Frank J. Fleming

"Eternal things are hard to explain to those who live in the illusion of temporality. You require a beginning to a story, while for me, that is arbitrary. So let's start with the war."

CHAPTER 1

"Hellbender." Doug had written it on the top of the pink box he was carrying. They didn't have much, but now they had donuts. Satan had more than kept his word, as he bought Doug a full dozen donuts to share with his friends ... and Doug hadn't even really completed his side of the bargain, as he hadn't listened all that well to whatever Satan wanted to tell him.

There was something odd as he reached their apartment door, though. In front of it lay a large black duffel bag. Doug stared down at it a moment and could see it move and heard a muffled noise from it. He opened the door to the apartment — which Charlene had managed to rig so that it latched again — and went inside to set down his box of donuts.

Inside, he was surprised to see Lulu on the couch with her stuffed brown bunny, Pickles. She was watching the news and sewing something. The news was going on about some war with some other nation that threatened everyone's very existence — the usual boring stuff. "What are you doing home?" Doug asked Lulu.

"My boss was annoying me, so I decided to take a personal day," Lulu said and held up some white cloth. "I'm making Pickles a chef's outfit. He's going to open up a restaurant that specializes in French cuisine." She then leaned toward him and whispered, "But it's really a front for his gun trafficking." She looked Doug over. "So what are you doing home? Were you fired again?"

Doug nodded. "That really sucked, but I ran into Satan on my way back home and he gave me a dozen donuts ... to share." A part of Doug had kinda hoped no one would be around so that he could eat them all himself.

"Donuts!" Lulu jumped up from the couch. "I always said one of these days you'd do something useful ... or accidentally kill us all. And it was the former!"

Doug set the donuts on the counter. "Hey, did you see there's a duffel bag outside with something in it?"

Lulu opened the box of donuts and looked over the varieties. "No. Someone was pounding on the door earlier, but I didn't answer because I didn't want to deal with that kind of negative energy."

"Well, there's a duffel bag in front of our door. And I think a person is inside it. It sounds like a person." Doug took a chocolate frosted donut.

"A person in a bag," Lulu said between bites of a jelly-filled. "Who would put a person in a bag? And why would anyone think we'd want that?"

"Shouldn't we check it out?"

Lulu thought for a second. "We might need two hands for what's in there, so we should probably finish our donuts first."

Doug nodded. "That's good thinking." So after they finished the donuts in their hands — and then one more each — they headed to the door.

Out in the hallway, the duffel bag squirmed and made more muffled sounds. They both stared at it awhile. "What if it's an axe murderer disguised as a duffel bag?" Doug suggested.

Lulu watched the bag move. "Not a very good disguise."

"Well, maybe he's acting all distressed so we'll open it to help him and then he'll jump out and axe us to death when we least expect it."

Lulu kicked the bag in a few different places. There were some more muffled cries in response. "I don't feel any axe in there."

"So what are we all looking at?"

Doug looked up from the bag, and there, standing next to him, was Bryce. "You're back!" Doug exclaimed. "I thought we'd never see you again!"

Bryce scoffed. "Come on; I've been through re-education before. I aced this one."

* * *

Bryce sat in an uncomfortable metal chair in a featureless, empty room with nothing in it but a bright light shining directly into his face. "You have committed a crime against the Confederacy of Astara," said a female voice over the loudspeaker.

Bryce nodded. "Yeah, I'm ... sorry. I don't know what came over me."

"Did you really think you could get away with it? We know everything that goes on in the nation we protect."

"I think in the back of my mind, I knew I'd get caught ... because you are all so smart." Actually, he had figured his fraudulent business would be lost in the vast bureaucracy for years and years, but he ended up the victim of a stupid book-balancing initiative. Most of the Confederacy of Astara's initiatives were things like "Citizens Need to Dress More Fashionably" or "Get More People Involved in Sculpting" or "Explain Opera to Stupid People" — activities that never got in his way. But apparently the highers-up finally demanded progress on something more practical, and here he was. "And since I knew I'd get caught," Bryce continued, "I guess it was really a cry for help. And here I am getting help. So I feel relieved, really."

"Well, good. Because you should know that there is no hiding from us. We are all-seeing, all-knowing, and all-powerful. We can control reality and your very thoughts, for our authority is over all. What is two plus two?"

Bryce thought for a moment. "Five."

"Wrong! It's ..." There was a pause. "Wait; did you just say five?"

"Well, yeah." Bryce straightened his suit. "You see, I've done this before, so I started pre-brainwashing myself while I was waiting."

"Oh ... um ... I really need you to say 'four' at least once, or it ruins the script," the voice said.

"Oh, I'm sorry. Want to do it over?"

"Please. So ... uh ... what is two plus two?"

Bryce held up two fingers on each hand. "Four."

"Wrong! It is five, because we are all-powerful and can redefine your very reality. So, I ask you again: What is two plus two?"

"It's five," Bryce answered. "You just told me that, and I accept it."

"Well ... good."

"One question, though: Is two times two also five?"

There was a pause, and then the voice said, "Since mathematically, that is two plus two, it is also five."

Bryce nodded. "But what is two plus three?"

There was a longer pause. "Um ... five and a half, maybe. Uh ... I'm sorry, but this is my first day at this. We're kind of overbooked right now, so they had me fill in as one of the brainwashers, but normally I just do paperwork."

"Well, you're doing a great job at this," Bryce assured her. "I think right now I love our nation and its wise government more than I ever have before." He leaned back in his chair. "And I must say, you have a very attractive voice." A smarmy smile crossed his face. "So what are you doing after this?"

* * *

"So now I have a date I need to weasel out of," Bryce told Doug and Lulu. "Ends up her voice was the only thing attractive about her."

"Well, I'm glad you're here," Doug said. "I was getting ready to plot to overthrow the government to rescue you ... maybe after lunch."

Bryce stared at the bag at their feet. "And what's this all about?"

"Just looking at our duffel bag with an axe-less axe murderer inside," Lulu said.

"Oh, and a neat thing happened to me today," Doug added. "I met Satan, who told me about demons living in this world, or something, and he gave me a dozen donuts."

Bryce raised an eyebrow. "Did you say 'donuts'?"

Bryce headed inside with Lulu following. Doug decided he might as well bring in the duffel bag and picked it up. It was pretty heavy, but he was able to carry it into their apartment and drop it on the table, which caused it to let out another muffled cry.

"So what are you guys doing home?" Bryce asked as he picked out a donut.

"Doug got fired again," Lulu said, trying to put the outfit she had sewed onto Pickles.

Doug hung his head. "They replaced me with a highly trained monkey."

"And how many times has that happened to you now?" Bryce asked.

Doug sighed. "Four."

"Three," Lulu corrected. "The monkey that replaced you at the packing job was only marginally trained."

Doug made a fist. "I hate monkeys."

"But you have to understand," Bryce said. "Everyone hates us war orphans, and those in charge will always look for any excuse to be rid of us and replace us with those more trustworthy, like monkeys. Or robots."

"Well, I wouldn't mind as much being replaced by a robot," Doug said. "Robots are strong and bulletproof. I can't compete with that. But monkeys are mean and filthy. I am way better than a monkey. I mean, maybe the ones that know sign language are on a more even plane with me, but I'm way better than the average monkey. The ones with tails."

Lulu shrugged. "If you want to keep your job, you need to assert yourself. That's what I did today when my boss got in my face."

* * *

Lulu was sitting at her desk, busy painting each of her fingernails a different color, when her boss, Robin, walked up to Lulu's desk. The middle-aged woman was making a visible effort to keep a neutral expression. "Ms. Liu, we need to talk."

Lulu responded with a big smile. "I love talking!"

Robin looked at Lulu quizzically. "Are you wearing cat ears?"

"Yep." Lulu flicked her ears. Also, she had painted her nose black and drawn on whiskers. "Meow! I'm a cat!"

"Well, okay. So —"

Lulu stood up. "Thanks for this job, by the way. I know you don't usually trust warfs to work in the propaganda department."

"We don't call it propaganda," Robin corrected. "These are educational materials."

Lulu nodded. "See, I wouldn't have thought of that; that's why you're so good at this propaganda. Anyway, I want you to know that you're right to give me a chance. I know people like you who run this country think we warfs are untrustworthy and are seething with hatred of you. And that we dream every day of nothing more than seeing you all suffer — perhaps watching gleefully as you weep as everything you ever worked for burns."

"Well, I don't know that —"

Lulu raised a finger. "I'm not done. And if we could, we'd get some chemical weapons and release it all on you in one of your snooty parties on the side of the town we never get to go to. And then you'd all be screaming and bleeding out your eyeballs. And we'd just stand there with gas masks on, watching quietly — the happiness we'd be feeling almost too much for a human to bear. And then you'd scream for mercy and offer us all your riches to spare you, but we'd refuse because all we want is your pain and misery." Lulu sat back down at her desk. "I know that's what a lot of you think of us warfs, but I want you to know it's not completely true."

Robin was quiet for a few seconds. "Okay. Um ... so I wanted to talk about your latest work."

"Great. I worked really hard on those posters."

"Yes ... but there are some problems with them."

Robin laid one down on Lulu's desk. It was a drawing of a man holding a gun to his own head with a phrase above: "JUST DO IT."

"I like this one," Lulu said.

Robin frowned. "Well, it seems to be encouraging people to commit suicide."

Lulu shook her head. "No, that's not it at all. You see, it's symbolic. The gun represents the truth, and he's supposed to be using the truth to blow away any bad thoughts he has."

"Well ... that interpretation is not really obvious."

"Yeah, but if I make it too obvious," Lulu said, "then I'm just calling whoever looks at it stupid — like, 'You wouldn't get this unless I explained it to you.' People don't like that."

"Okay, um ..." Robin set down another poster. "Here's another one you made."

On the poster was a person punching out a man in uniform with the phrase, "GO FOR IT!"

Lulu nodded. "Pretty dynamic, huh?"

"Well ... um ... you seem to be encouraging people to attack peacekeepers."

Lulu looked confused. "And we don't want that?"

Robin shook her head. "No."

"Oh, I thought we all hated the police. They're always in our business." Lulu faked a gruff voice. "'Why are you loitering here? And where did that bloodstain come from?'" Lulu sighed. "So annoying."

"Well, the purpose of the material we're making is to promote the government of the Confederacy of Astara. And the peacekeepers work for that government."

"Oh!" Lulu slapped her forehead. "Okay, I think I get it now. I'll fix that one; I'll make him punch out a clown instead. Everyone hates clowns."

"Well, that's not really ... let's just move on."

Robin put another poster on Lulu's desk. This one was a drawing of numerous happy cartoon bunnies.

"Ooh! I love this one!" Lulu squealed. "This one has bunnies. Everyone loves bunnies!"

"That may be true," Robin said. "But the problem is what you wrote on it." Robin pointed to the large letters at the top of the poster, which said, "OVERTHROW THE GOVERNMENT."

Lulu frowned. "Oh boy; sorry. That one is a typo."

"What's it supposed to say?"

Lulu thought for a few seconds as she tapped her fingers on her desk. "Um ..." She rubbed her temple. "Uh ..." She touched her fingertips together. "It's supposed to say ..." She let out a deep breath. "... *don't* overthrow the government."

"Lulu, I don't think this is working out. You need to —"

"You talk when you sleep," Lulu interrupted.

Robin's eyes went wide. "Excuse me?"

Lulu laughed and stood up from her desk. "I'm being silly. How could I know that unless I know where you live and have found a way to break into your house and could easily do things to you while you sleep?"

Robin stared silently at Lulu, trembling slightly. Finally, Lulu made a playful swipe at Robin, pretending her hand was a clawed paw. "Meow! I'm a cat!" Lulu sat back down. "Everyone loves cats ... except for birds. Cats kills birds. Isn't that right ... Robin?"

* * *

"And then I asked if I could have the rest of the day off since I was all creatived out, and she was okay with that," Lulu said. "So if you want to keep your job, you just have to learn to manage your boss. Do that, and she'll leave you alone to do your own thing until her inevitable mental breakdown."

Doug saw the duffel bag move again. "So should we check what's inside the bag?" he asked.

Bryce, mouth filled with donut, stared at the bag on the table. He quickly gulped down the donut. "Oh, I know what this is. Open it. Open it right away."

Doug unzipped the bag, and inside was Charlene, duct tape over her mouth and binding her hands and feet. "Charlene! What happened?"

The response was muffled but obviously quite angry.

Lulu grabbed a steak knife from the kitchen and ran over to Charlene. "Hold still," she urged as she cut the tape at her feet and hands.

Charlene tumbled with the bag off the table and ripped the piece of tape from her mouth. "I will not be intimidated!" she announced, red-faced.

Lulu nodded. "Of course not. So ... are you okay?"

"No, I am not okay!" Charlene straightened her peacekeeper uniform. "A criminal syndicate is trying to scare me into silence, but I am now more determined than ever to bring them down after my confrontation with them today!"

* * *

Charlene crept along the exterior of the warehouse. Getting near a window, she could hear voices inside. Criminals. In the middle of an arms deal. She had been surveilling the area for a week, learning this group's habits and methods, carefully and colorfully documenting what she had found out in her visual history books. Now was the time to catch them red-handed and finally take them down for good.

* * *

"Let me interrupt you right there," Bryce said. "Isn't your job as a peacekeeper to guard a shed?"

"Well, yes," Charlene answered. "But —"

"Where they just store stuff from customs?" Doug asked.

"True, but —"

"And isn't it currently empty?" Lulu added.

"It is," Charlene admitted. "But one day it could be full. And criminals could steal from it — criminals like the ones I tracked to that warehouse. So I think it's pretty fair to extrapolate my guard job to taking down any criminal organization I can find."

* * *

Charlene readied the camera on her phone. She hoped the mic on it would be strong enough to pick up the audio through the window. And once she had this evidence and added it to her books, she'd be able to get a strikeforce to come back and take these criminals down. And maybe they'd let her help. They'd probably wouldn't give her a gun, but perhaps they'd let her have a baton. And if they did, she would find a criminal and hit him as hard as she could. For justice.

"What are you doing here, little boy?"

Charlene turned around and saw a large, tough-looking older man standing behind her staring at her with annoyance. She had thought she knew the guards' routes and had stayed far enough out of sight, but apparently she had made an error. A potentially fatal one.

Charlene stood up. "I'm not a boy." She was hoping that was obvious from the short skirt of her deputy peacekeeper uniform. She never liked the skirt, but a short skirt was less restricting than a long one — though pants were similarly not restricting. "I am a peacekeeper and what you are doing here is illegal and I am putting a stop to it."

She stared menacingly at the thug. He was more than a head taller than her and had a gun, but she still thought she could take him on if she —

The thug grabbed her by the collar and lifted her into the air. She struggled to hit him, but he held her out at arm's length and she was unable to connect. He then carried her inside and dropped her on the floor near where the arms deal was going down. There were a dozen criminals inside, all looking quite menacing. Well, except for four. Four of them didn't look all that menacing. If Charlene had to fight the whole group, she'd take out those four last.

"Honestly, I was just taking another look around the building to stretch my legs," the older thug who had captured Charlene announced. "But look what I found. She's just some warf in the peacekeeper deputy program, though, and she's probably not even supposed to be here."

Everyone looked Charlene over as she stood up and fixed her uniform. She tried to stare down each of the criminals to let them know they didn't intimidate her.

"I love their uniforms," said a cocky-looking man who seemed to be running the arms deal. "They look like stewardesses from the 1960s."

"I think it's demeaning," said a female criminal with a tattoo covering half her face. "I wouldn't wear a uniform like that."

"Well, Astara has been kind of on a retro vibe lately," the older thug stated. "Plus, no one really cares if you demean a warf."

"Astara is always changing the uniforms, though," the leader said. "How much of the government's budget is she wasting on new uniforms?"

"It stimulates the economy," said a muscle-bound goon. "You know, because people will get paid to make those uniforms."

The leader rolled his eyes. "That's the philosophy that sank previous civilization under enormous debt. The problem with Keynesian economics is —"

"By the authority the Confederacy of Astara has bestowed upon me," Charlene loudly announced, "you are all under arrest for this illegal transaction."

The room erupted in laughter. "Well, we better get back to business," the leader said. He turned to Charlene. "Just run along, okay?"

Charlene glared at him. "I will not leave. And I will take you down by force, if necessary."

"Aren't you deputy peacekeepers not allowed to have weapons?" asked the older thug.

"I have trained all my life in the art of combat." Charlene sank into a martial arts stance. "I am a weapon!"

Everyone laughed again. There were, in fact, plenty of weapons around since there were crates of assault rifles in front of her, with boxes of ammo. Also, most of the thugs there appeared to have guns, so she just had to take one of them. Of course, her opponents all having guns could also be a problem, but Charlene would just have to rely on her training and act quickly if this came to a gunfight.

The leader wiped tears from his eyes. "Okay. You can stay. Just be quiet and don't get in the way." He went over to a table where a man in a suit — probably a buyer — set down a briefcase. The leader opened it up, and inside were individual credit chips — a way to transfer money with no trace. "We just need to verify these chips," the leader said, "and business will be concluded."

This was it. An illegal arms purchase right in front of Charlene, and she had vowed to uphold the laws of the Confederacy of Astara. It was time for her to stand up for justice.

She walked over to the table and knocked over the briefcase, spilling the credit chips all over the floor. "I said," Charlene yelled, "you are all under arrest for your illegal activities!"

The leader was stunned. "Look at the mess you just made! You have to pick that up!"

Charlene steeled her gaze. "I don't bow to the demands of criminals."

"When you make a mess," the leader seethed, "you pick it up. EVERYONE KNOWS THIS!"

Charlene folded her arms. "Never."

*　*　*

"This does sound like the sort of story that ends with you shoved in a duffel bag," Lulu said.

"But I didn't pick up those credit chips," Charlene stated proudly.

"Wow," Doug said. "You're just lucky they didn't murder you and instead brought you here."

"Perhaps." Charlene tried again to straighten her rumpled uniform. "I don't know how they knew my address, though."

Bryce shrugged. "Not a concern right now. How are you, though? Did they do anything inappropriate to you?"

Charlene just stared at him. "They tied me up with duct tape and shoved me in a duffel bag."

"You do know that's not an appropriate way to treat a woman, right, Bryce?" Lulu asked.

"Yeah, I know," he stammered. "I meant... Well, never mind. I guess we're all good now."

"We are *not* all good now," Charlene stated. She looked at the piece of duct tape that she had pulled off her mouth. "Ooh. This will go well in the visual history book I've been documenting criminal evidence in."

Lulu rolled her eyes. "No one wants to see your scrapbooking!"

Charlene headed to her room and soon emerged with an album of cardstock pages, along with a box of her supplies. She put them both down on the table next to the duffle bag. "Give it whatever dismissive term you like, but I carefully document everything I do. And I use visual flair to highlight the salient points. This is going to be powerful evidence in court." She opened to a page where some of her surveillance photos were mounted on die-cut pieces of colorful paper and decorated with sequins and fancy calligraphy.

Doug smiled and put his arm around Charlene. "I think it's really ... um ... creative, what you do with these books. And I'm just glad we're all safe and sound. Charlene is unharmed, and Bryce is back from re-education. Nothing can break up Hellbender!"

"No one ever agreed to calling us that," Bryce said.

Charlene shrugged off Doug's arm. "And I am not part of this group." She began punching shapes out of a purplish piece of cardstock. "As far as I'm concerned, you three are just people who happen to be my government-assigned roommates ... for the past two decades."

Lulu raised her arms in the air. "Yay, Hellbender!"

"I'm trying to improve myself," Charlene said as she glued the piece of duct tape down to the paper. "I have plans to not just be some riffraff like you three. I'm going to get myself noticed for my work as a peacekeeper and eventually apply to join the Athenians."

Bryce and Lulu started laughing. "Come on, Charlene," Bryce said.

"What?" Charlene glued the duct tape and its now decorated mount into an empty spot on one of the pages of her visual history book.

"Haven't you noticed something about the Athenians that's a little different from you?" Lulu asked.

"They're a female fighting force — Astara's most elite." Charlene used a pink marker to carefully write "Tool of Kidnapping" and the date above the duct tape. "And I have trained in combat since childhood — and unlike you three, I took that training seriously. I have the skills to be one of them."

"Skills are not the question," Bryce said. "You just need to take a look at the members of the Athenians — they're basically models with guns."

Doug nodded. "Yeah, I have a poster of them up in my room, and it's not because I'm like patriotic and support the military because I'm not even quite sure which country this is anymore."

Charlene tied a bow of purple ribbon and glued it to the page. "I'm sure they look good — which is part of being fit and ready for action — but I'm certain appearance is not the main factor here."

"Charlene, you have to give up this idea that the powers that be will ever help us war orphans succeed," Bryce said. "Opportunity does not knock for people like us; we have to find more clever ways to seize it."

There was a loud pounding on the door to their apartment.

"Uh-oh," Bryce gasped.

Lulu picked up and clutched her stuffed bunny. "Yeah, that does not sound like opportunity."

"Hide the donuts!" Doug yelled, running over to grab the box of donuts and put them in a cabinet.

"We have donuts?" Charlene asked as she shut her album.

Doug slowly approached the door. "Yeah, I met Satan and he told me stuff about demons and bought me donuts."

"Wait ... what happened?"

Doug was now concentrating on the door, on which someone continued to pound. He looked around, and the other three were hanging back — Charlene in a defensive stance, Lulu holding her bunny, and Bryce looking nonchalant — so it was up to him to open it. When he did, outside he saw a cute young woman in a leather jacket with an older, very large and intimidating man standing behind her.

"Finally. That hurt." The woman shook her sore hand. The large man nudged her and gave her a look, and the woman put on a fierce gaze and locked it on Doug. "Where's Bryce?" she shouted.

"Uh ... he's inside," Doug said, taking glances at the big man behind her, whose expression remained stoic.

They both came inside and approached Bryce. "This is Candy," the large man said. "She's in training to become an enforcer for Rook. I'm Driscoll, her trainer, and

I'm simply here to observe. Please act like I'm not here and keep your attention on Candy." He looked at Candy. "Proceed."

She nodded and then grabbed Bryce by his suit jacket. "You owe Rook a lot of money!"

"And I'm very aware of that," Bryce stated. "I had an absolutely perfect business venture that was going to make everyone a lot of money ... but I hit a little bump in my plans when I unfortunately got some government attention — you know how things are."

"Do you need us for anything," Lulu asked, "or can I go back to watching TV?" Doug was wondering if he was supposed to do anything, too, and had positioned himself near Lulu and Charlene.

"Stay where you are! Keep your hands where I can see them!" Candy shouted, pulling back her jacket to show a gun. She then glanced at Driscoll, who gave her a nod of approval. Candy gave another warning look at Lulu, and then her eyes lit up. "Oh, what a cute stuffed animal! Is he in a chef's outfit?"

"Yep, he's just a regular old French chef and nothing else," Lulu said, giving Candy a knowing wink.

"Focus," Driscoll told Candy.

Candy looked back to Bryce. "Now, we're going to —"

"You're criminals!" Charlene shouted.

Candy looked confused. She turned to Driscoll. "Did I forget to identify us when we came in?"

"Only police need to do that," Driscoll said. "We're fine barging in unannounced and letting them figure out who we are from context."

Candy nodded and turned to Charlene. "Shut up!" She brought her attention back to Bryce, tightening her grip on his suit jacket. "Where's our money?"

"It's in flux at the moment, but the moment will pass." Bryce smiled at her. His face was very charming to people who didn't know him well and punchable to people who did. "By the way, I love what you've done with your hair. It's very serious and goes well with your job, but at the same time there's something playful about it."

Candy smiled back. "Thanks, I just got it done and —"

Driscoll nudged her. "Focus."

She went back to glaring at Bryce. "You can't flirt your way out of this one. Do you have our money?"

"I'm getting it," Bryce said. "I have an even better plan to get the money and pay back Rook. I have a crew and everything, and the opportunity is coming soon. Everyone will be very happy."

"We want it now!"

"And it will come soon," Bryce assured her. "Which is almost the same as now."

Candy stared at him silently for a few seconds and then turned to Driscoll. "What do I do now?"

"You need to rough him up a bit to show him we're serious," Driscoll said. "But we still want him to get us the money, so you don't want to permanently injure him in any way. I'd recommend knocking the wind out of him with a well-placed punch to the abdomen."

"Come on, that's uncouth," Bryce said. "Can't we be civilized here and not resort to violence?"

"Take your punch like a man, Bryce," Lulu urged, still holding her bunny.

"Kinda serves you right," Doug said. "I got punched a bunch of times last night because of you, and —"

Candy socked Doug in the gut. "Shut up!" She turned to Driscoll. "I just ad-libbed that. Was that good?"

"Yeah, that was good," he said. "You don't need them chattering around you like that. It doesn't show respect."

Candy looked at the hunched-over Doug. "And did I do that right? Did I knock the wind out of you?"

Doug tried to speak, but nothing came out. Instead, he gave a thumbs-up.

"Yay!" Candy said and did a little jump, but that got a disapproving look from Driscoll. Candy became more serious and looked at Bryce. "Am I making my point?"

Bryce, now looking a little frazzled, helped Doug stand up straight. "Loud and clear. I think that was enough violence. We're all on the same page now."

"Good. Because if I have to come back here, I'll do a lot more than rough up your friend. So why don't you —" Candy noticed Charlene approaching her. "Hey, you need to —"

Before Candy could react, Charlene reached into Candy's jacket, pulled out her gun, and pressed it to Candy's temple. "I don't like criminal scum coming into my home and ordering me around," Charlene seethed.

Lulu let out a loud sigh. "You're the worst, Charlene. You always take things too far."

"This really isn't necessary," Bryce told Charlene, completely losing his cool. "Everything is under control."

"Shut up, you mewling cowards," Charlene said. "It will be in control when they leave. Or I blow their brains out." She kept the gun against Candy's forehead, and Candy looked terrified.

"Come on," Doug urged. "You're really scaring her."

"This is getting kind of advanced for me," Candy stammered.

"Here, let me take her place and demonstrate," Driscoll told Charlene, who looked at him with confusion. Driscoll then gently pushed Candy out of the way and moved the gun of the perplexed Charlene so that it was now pointed up at his head.

"The important thing to remember is the gun loses its main advantage — range — at this distance." In one quick motion, he grabbed the gun from Charlene and knocked her to the ground. Then he pointed the gun down at her. "You'll have to practice that later. Let's switch back."

Candy took the gun back from Driscoll and now was the one standing over Charlene, pointing the gun at her. "And what would we do now?"

"With a threat like that," Driscoll said, "we'd usually kill her in response, but then we'd have to worry about body disposal and what to do about the witnesses, and we're already running kind of late today. Let's just ignore this for now."

Candy nodded and took another look at Charlene. "Wait, weren't you the one we dropped off in a duffel bag earlier?"

"If you looked over your schedule beforehand and organized it better," Driscoll said, "we wouldn't have made the same trip twice."

"Whoops; sorry." Candy turned to Bryce. "You owe us for that delivery, too."

Bryce smiled and nodded. "Got it."

"The money," Candy said, "or next time you're going to be the subject of my intermediate training." She put her gun away and the two left the apartment.

"What was this?" Charlene yelled at Bryce as she picked herself off the floor. "Why are you getting us accosted by low-rent thugs?"

Bryce scoffed. "Low-rent thugs? Would low-rent thugs have a formal training program?"

"And were you the one who told them where I live?" Charlene demanded.

Bryce hesitated. "I knew you might be interfering with them, so I told them to drop you off here if that ever happened. If you were unclaimed, they might have just murdered you, and then we'd get called to the morgue to identify you." Bryce chuckled. "And you know that's never going to happen at a convenient hour. Am I right?"

Doug was still bent over a bit from Candy's punch. "And why am I always getting punched?" He lowered his voice. "And are we still going through with the plan? Is that the job you mentioned?"

"Of course we're still going through with the plan," Bryce said. "We can't just throw everything out the window because we got raided by the government in the middle of the night. Oh, and I want to thank you, Doug, for taking that punch. You've always been good at taking a beating; it's perhaps your best skill."

Doug frowned. "I have better skills."

Charlene glared at Bryce. "What's this plan? Are you all up to something? Well, you better not drag me into it. And what do you owe Rook money for?"

Bryce shrugged. "Oh ... long story. I talked him into investing in this business venture of mine — an absolutely foolproof one that, if I might say it, was of great benefit to society — but then this whole government crackdown on me got in the way. But I'll be able to pay them back with a new opportunity I've been working on ... a sort of a ... uh ... what's the word the kids use these days ... heist."

"Man, I've always wanted to be a part of a proper heist," Doug exclaimed. "We tried before, but they were certainly not proper."

"What's it going to involve this time?" Charlene demanded. "Trespassing? Theft? Treason?"

"It's nothing big," Bryce assured her. "It will involve maybe just four of the things you mentioned."

"I only mentioned three!"

"Oh ... yeah, you did. I guess mentally I just added 'assault' in there, too."

"I am not going to be a part of it," Charlene declared. "I'm tired of you idiots and I'm tired of getting dragged into your dumb schemes."

"You know it's all going to turn into hilarious shenanigans," Lulu said. "And in the end, we'll all learn a valuable lesson." Pickles made a metallic click, and she set him down on the table.

Charlene raised an eyebrow. "Did you just cock your stuffed bunny?"

Lulu laughed. "Don't be paranoid; I uncocked him."

Charlene stared at Lulu a few moments and then glared at Bryce. Finally, she turned her gaze to Doug. "And didn't you say something about donuts?" She thought a moment. "And Satan?"

"Ah, yes, the war. The Last War, as it is called. And it really was the final conflict in this world of any significance."

CHAPTER 2

"Hello, I would like a job."

Doug had dealt with uncaring bureaucrats all his life, but now many of them who dealt with warfs had been replaced with computers — which was nice, as the computers were better at faking that they cared.

"We will certainly give you one so that you can continue to be a productive citizen," said the purple, somewhat human-like holographic face. "First, I will need a DNA sample to confirm your identity."

A panel opened on the computer with a place for Doug to insert his finger. Hesitantly, he placed his right index finger in the slot. "Is this going to hurt, because last time — OW!"

"We confirmed your identity, Doug Fatal Error Index Outside of Bounds of Array."

Doug rubbed his finger and sighed. "That's not my name. See, first, the government forgot to give me a last name after they couldn't confirm my parents' identity — because of the war where, you know, they were killed. So initially, I had to —"

"While I am programmed to listen to your concerns," the computer interrupted, "this story is going on far too long and is uninteresting to me."

Doug nodded. "Fair enough."

"So how are you doing, Doug Fatal Error Index Outside of Bounds of Array? Are you depressed or having suicidal thoughts?"

Doug shook his head. "No."

"Are you certain? According to the data we have on your complete lack of any useful skills or meaningful achievements, you should be quite depressed."

"Well, I'm not," Doug asserted. "I'm just frustrated and would like a job. I was wondering if this time maybe I could be a barista, because I'm pretty good at making a cup of coffee. I'd like something like that."

"As always, your thoughts and opinions are important to us and will be taken into consideration," the computer said in a cheery voice. It really did seem like it cared. The human bureaucrats always just appeared annoyed by his existence. "I will check our database and see what we have." The computer was silent for a few moments. "I'm afraid there are no jobs for you."

"Oh ... so what do I do?"

"Please come back tomorrow and check again."

"So I get like a day off?" Doug really did want to do well at a job and feel productive, but doing nothing at all still seemed like the more attractive option.

"Because you are not working today, you will be marked as 'non-compliant,' and your rations and privileges will be reduced."

"Wait ... what?! I'm being punished? But I want to work!"

"Sorry, but this policy is non-negotiable. If you want full privileges, you need to work at your assigned job."

"So give me a job!"

"I'm sorry, but there is no job for you."

Doug rubbed his temple. "You're a computer; you're supposed to be smart. Don't you see the problem here? This isn't fair!"

"We're sorry you don't consider this fair. Here, have some medicinal marijuana to help calm you down."

A slot opened on the computer, and inside was a little plastic bag. Doug picked it up, and it appeared to contain weed. Doug nervously looked around, wondering if the computer had set him up and the police were about to bust him.

"I'll see you tomorrow, Doug Fatal Error Index Outside of Bounds of Array. Goodbye," the computer said.

Doug put the baggie in his pocket and left the government's job center and its array of terminals. He was feeling pretty miserable, but he saw the downcast faces of the other people leaving and realized he wasn't the only one. It was the job center in the bad part of the city and thus the one all the other war orphans went to — as the bad part of any city was pretty much defined by wherever the warfs got stuck.

Doug noticed some spray paint on a nearby wall. Another message from the RALFS. "WE WILL OVERCOME." Doug looked back at the unhappy warfs leaving the job center, and overcoming seemed like a good idea. They just had to organize and then do ... something coordinated. Maybe.

"It's all very sad, isn't it?"

Doug turned to see Bryce standing nearby, holding a large suitcase. "So what's going on here? Did they run out of jobs for everyone?" Doug asked him.

Bryce waved his hand dismissively. "If you want to get anywhere in life, you need to make your own work."

"But it has to be a government-assigned job if you want to get your rations and privileges."

"You don't need to work a job," Bryce said. "You just need a bit set in some computer somewhere saying you did."

"Isn't that the sort of thing that got you carted off by the government?"

Bryce shook his head. "That was just a freak thing — usually we warfs are so beneath the concern of the ruling class that they don't care whether we cheat the system as long as we stay out of their way."

Doug watched the others leaving the job center, every one of them sad or angry. "Is something happening, though? Looks like none of us are getting a job."

Bryce smiled. "Yep, I see a lot of depressed young women leaving the jobs center. I bet they would be easy pickings ... if I dated other warfs. It's important that one rise above his station."

"It's not right, how the government treats us," Doug said. He leaned in close to Bryce and whispered, "Maybe we should organize and overthrow the government."

Bryce grimaced. "And replace it with what?"

"Democracy. And freedom. And ... cowboy hats."

Bryce rolled his eyes. "That's idiotic. People have tried liberty before, and it's just way too much work to maintain. Every time things go wrong, people want the government to be more powerful so it can take over. So if you want freedom, you have to constantly push back against that. It's a huge headache; it's just not worth the effort."

"It seems unfair the way things are now, though."

Bryce laughed. "Life is unfair — that's why one's goal in life must be to make it unfair in your own favor."

Doug felt the little baggie in his pocket and pulled it out. "The government gave me drugs when I complained. Is that normal?"

Bryce took the baggie, looked at it, and scoffed. "Government weed."

"Aren't drugs illegal?"

"They were frowned upon in the previous government that took possession of us. This one thinks drugs helps creativity."

Doug thought about it for a moment. "I don't know if I should do drugs just because the government thinks it's okay."

Bryce pocketed the baggie. "A sober mind is useful at times — not that you're known for clear thinking in any situation."

"So what are you doing here? And what's in the briefcase?"

"After my government re-education," Bryce said, "I was required to make an appearance at the job center as well to show I'm back to being a rule-following citizen."

"Did *you* get a job?"

Bryce shrugged. "I don't know; I wasn't paying attention." Bryce's phone started ringing. He pulled it out and glanced at it. "Ugh. It's the woman I met at the re-education center. I don't need her any more ... but I might as well let her down easy." He handed the phone to Doug. "Answer it and tell her you found the phone on my dead body."

Doug hated it when Bryce made him lie for him; Doug was never very good at it. "Hello?"

"Bryce?" the woman on the other end asked.

"No ... uh, I just found this phone on a dead body. Maybe that was Bryce."

"He's dead?! What happened?"

"Well ... uh ..." Doug knew taking too long to answer would give the game away, so he said the first thing that popped into his head. "A donkey fell on him."

"In the city?"

"It fell out of a building ... onto him. It's dead too." Doug looked to Bryce and saw Bryce was fervently making a throat cutting motion. "I'm going to kill you."

Bryce snatched the phone away and hung up. "That meant cut the conversation!"

"Sorry! I get nervous when I lie!"

Bryce pocketed his phone. "Well, hopefully that will keep her from calling again."

"You know," Doug said, "it's not really nice how you use women."

Bryce laughed. "Use women? That's ridiculous. Women are useless." A black van pulled up near Bryce. "And here's our ride."

Doug stared at the van a moment. "This is a heist van! We're doing the heist now?"

"Events have caused us to move up our timetable." Bryce opened the back door and got in. "We've had to improvise a bit, but I think we're ready. Let's make some big heist money!"

"All right!" Doug jumped inside. "I think this time it's going to work out for us. I got a good feeling on this."

Bryce closed the van door. "And I bet you don't care about the job thing any more. People who are good at heisting don't need stupid government-assigned jobs." Bryce opened the suitcase and took out a black uniform. "Here; put this on."

Doug started to put the uniform on. "Cool. We got costumes and everything. If we're doing the heist now, though, we have to bring Charlene aboard. We can't do a proper heist without all of Hellbender working together."

Lulu sighed as she got out of the driver's seat. She was wearing an army officer's uniform with a name tag that said "Zambraski." "You know it's going to be a big hullaballoo as soon as we include Charlene, what with her opinion on illegal things and all. Now someone else drive, since I'm in charge." Lulu pointed to her uniform.

"I'll drive as soon as I finish changing." Bryce answered. He was busy putting on a black uniform like the one he'd given Doug. "And we'll bring in Charlene along the way. We need to keep moving."

"How'd you get that uniform?" Doug asked Lulu.

"I did such a good job making propaganda posters, they decided to make me a colonel and changed my name to Zamzow or something," Lulu explained as she got in back with Doug. "Colonel is the rank where they tell you what the eleven herbs and spices are."

Doug looked at Bryce. "Where did she get that uniform?"

Bryce dismissively waved a hand. "Don't worry about it."

* * *

"I've had such a wonderful time with you," Zambraski said, touching Bryce on the cheek.

"Too bad it has to end." He kissed her hand.

"I hate that I'm getting deployed." She took some more things out of her bedroom closet and put them in the suitcase on her bed. "Stupid Loch and his armies — why can't they just slaughter people overseas that no one cares about?"

Bryce nodded and sipped his scotch. "It's inconsiderate."

"So when will I see you again?"

Bryce shrugged. "It's hard to say; you know how things are for an international spy."

"And you must be a quite secret one," Zambraski said. "I couldn't find any record of you."

Bryce nodded. "They like to keep me off the books — that's how important and secret my work is."

"So you could leave any day?"

"Well ... not for a week, at least." An idea seemed to strike Bryce. "Hey, want me to pick up your dry cleaning while you're gone?"

* * *

Doug took a closer look at the black uniforms he and Bryce were putting on. "Wait — these are shadow enforcer uniforms!"

Bryce put a helmet on Doug. "And the important thing to remember is that shadow enforcers tend to be silent and mysterious, so just follow us around and don't speak." Bryce put on a helmet himself, his face now completely concealed behind the black mask.

Sirens were going off, and Doug could see that something big was happening out the windshield. He went forward for a better look and could see a giant lizard creature fighting a giant robot. "What's going on?"

"Loch's forces are attacking the city," Bryce explained.

Doug watched the robot punch the lizard. "So are we rooting for the robot or the lizard? I don't really follow politics."

Bryce shrugged. "I don't like to take sides."

Lulu frowned. "Poor lizard. He probably just loves tearing people apart and doesn't understand why a robot is punching him."

There was a beep. Doug pulled his government-mandated notification device out of the pants he had taken off and looked at it. "It says I need to get to the nearest station and arm and prepare for battle. Are we going to war? I thought they kept saying they had these super soldiers to fight Loch's forces."

Bryce opened another pocket on his suitcase and pulled out two pistols. "And what's a super soldier, Doug?"

Doug thought a moment. "Well ... it's like a soldier who's been raised by the government since birth to be trained in combat."

Bryce nodded. "Sounds about right. Hey, Doug, who raised us?"

"Well, the government did."

"And did we get combat training?"

"Yeah, off and on ... but it never really took. At least not with me." The point finally entered Doug's brain. "Wait ... we're the super soldiers? Aw, man; we're screwed."

"We came up the idea to use that term 'super soldier' in the Encouragement Office," Lulu said. "Seemed better than 'half-trained warf who probably wouldn't care if the entire population got eaten by giant flying lizards.'"

Doug's eyes grew wide. "They have ones that fly?"

"Not our concern," Bryce said. "We have a heist to attend to." He handed a pistol to Doug. "Be careful with this; it's loaded. And if I make a motion like this" — Bryce raised his hand in the air and made a fist — "kill everyone around us." Bryce got into the van's driver's seat.

"Wait ... what?" Doug asked, but Bryce was busy getting the van moving and heading past the scene of the fight. There were peacekeepers making a barricade around the area and telling everyone that there was nothing to see there ... but there was something to see there. There was a robot fighting a giant lizard. Who wouldn't want to see that?

"You merely know the Last War as this conflict that orphaned you. But its reach was much more vast than death and destruction. It wounded this world. Deep wounds. All the way down to hell."

CHAPTER 3

Doug looked out the windshield. "So we're going to sneak onto the military base, right?"

"We're not sneaking," Bryce explained as he parked the van. "We're going through the front."

Doug took a look at Lulu in her military uniform. "Do you even look anything like this Colonel Zambraski?"

"I thought of that." Lulu put on a pink ski mask. "Now no one will know." Lulu opened the van door and hopped out. Bryce and Doug quickly followed. They walked to a gate labeled "Restricted Area," where two armed soldiers were posted.

The soldiers saluted Lulu. "Why are you wearing a ski mask?" one asked.

"It's cold," Lulu answered.

"No ... it isn't."

Lulu slapped him in the face. "Shut up, maggot! Do you hear those sirens? We're under attack! I don't have time for your dumb questions!"

"Sorry!" the soldier yelped and opened the gate, letting the disguised Lulu, Bryce, and Doug inside.

"Ha! That worked!" Bryce laughed.

Doug looked around the restricted area. There were people running to and fro as the sirens blared. "I thought this was a cool heist idea, but I guess I didn't quite understand how much treason it was going to involve."

"Hey, don't you want a job where monkeys can't replace you?" Bryce asked. "Well, monkeys can't commit treason."

Doug got excited. "Are we doing my idea? Are we overthrowing the government from the inside?"

"Yep, going to install myself as President Baron Empress," Lulu said as she fixed her clothes. "I'll institute a policy of fiscal reform and arbitrary torture." She looked around. "There's Charlene. I guess we better bite the bullet and pull her into this, even though you know she's just going to be a real stick in the mud, saying things like 'treason is wrong.'"

"She's Hellbender and we all stick together," Doug insisted. "And try to be nice."

33

"I can be nice," Lulu said and then shouted at Charlene, "You! Stupid warf! Come here!"

Charlene jogged over to them and carefully saluted while holding the coffees. "I'm just fetching people their coffees, and then I need to prepare for the attack. I will fight honorably in defense of —"

Lulu slapped her, knocking the coffees to the ground. "Shut up, maggot!"

Charlene clutched her face and stared a second at the ski mask. "Lulu!"

"Come on," Bryce urged as he headed off with Lulu.

Doug and Charlene quickly followed. "What are you doing?" Charlene demanded.

"I know you don't like heists," Doug said, "but Bryce planned a really good one that's going to pay a ton. It might involve a little stealing from the military, though."

"That's treason!" Charlene exclaimed.

Lulu sighed. "What did I say?"

"Do you know what happens to those who commit treason?" Charlene said.

"Probably a fine," Bryce answered.

"A big one!" Charlene added. "And it will be on your record, you know, in a database."

"Here, I know how much you don't like treason," Lulu said as she reached into her purse, "so I made you this." She took out a turquoise scarf and put it on Charlene.

"A scarf doesn't make up for treason!" Charlene fumed. She felt the material. "It's really nice, though. Thank you."

"I helped," Bryce said.

Lulu glared at him. "No, you didn't."

"I praised having a scarf for Charlene as a good idea," Bryce explained. "That's supervising. That's the more important job, going by average salary."

Lulu sighed. "We don't have time to punch you in the throat. Come on." Lulu walked away and Bryce followed.

Charlene dropped back to walk next to Doug and said to him, "I keep telling you three: I'm not a part of your group, and I don't want to be dragged into these things." She emphasized her point by tossing part of her scarf over her shoulder.

"Come on, Charlene, we need you," Doug whispered to her. "Bryce and Lulu are kinda idiots. They're going to run into trouble without you."

"Did you consider the idea that maybe doing a heist at all was something only an idiot would have thought of?" Charlene responded.

Doug considered that a moment. "See. That's why we need you. You think of things like that."

They headed for the base headquarters, where inside, people seemed busy stripping things down and grabbing everything important. An officer was there, overseeing it all. Lulu approached him. "Colonel Zamzow reporting. I'm taking over the transport of Black Project Insano."

"Project Aurora?" the officer asked.

"I like calling it the other thing."

The officer scratched his head. "I hadn't heard about this." He looked at Charlene. "And what is this warf doing here? They're all supposed to be gone from here by now."

"Don't worry about her," Lulu said. "She's deaf and mute."

The colonel nodded.

"I was just talking to you five minutes ago!" Charlene exclaimed to the officer. "You sent me to get coffee!"

He ignored her. "I need to check on these orders."

"There isn't time," Lulu said. "Loch's forces are coming, and if we don't move Black Project Insano before they get here, the whole world will be destroyed."

The officer raised an eyebrow. "I don't really see how one would lead to the other, but I really need to check on this."

"I will not be questioned by you!" Lulu yelled.

"What are you talking about?" the officer said. "I outrank you."

"No, I'm a colonel," Lulu asserted.

"No, *I'm* a colonel. You're a lieutenant colonel."

Lulu thought for a moment. "And which one is better?"

The officer stared at her. "Why are you wearing a ski mask?"

There was a few moments' silence as the officer stared at the group with deeper suspicion, and Bryce slowly started to raise his hand and curl his fingers. Before he finished making a fist, Lulu slapped the officer hard. "Shut up, maggot!"

"Ow! Don't hit me! Sorry! Here's the access card!" The colonel handed over a card. "You know, we have rules against hitting."

"And I'm a rogue lieutenant colonel who doesn't play by the rules!" Lulu yelled, raising her hand toward him threateningly. She led the group back out of the building.

"I don't know exactly what you're all up to," Charlene growled, "but you're going to end it now."

"Don't worry," Bryce said. "We're leaving the base."

"I'm confused," Doug stated. "We're not going to go fight Loch's forces, are we? Because I don't want to shoot innocent giant lizards."

"Just follow me," Lulu said. "I'm an officer. I know what I'm doing."

Suddenly, all the people running about the base stopped. A group walked through their midst headed by a tall blond woman in a very expensive-looking designer blue dress. At her side walked a female officer working busily on a tablet computer.

Behind them followed a number of attractive young women in a variety of dresses that seemed to have a vague military theme to them.

"Are they having a fashion show?" Doug asked. He had never been to a fashion show. His fashion knowledge was limited to determining whether the print on a T-shirt was awesome or not. He liked ones about video games. Video games are awesome.

Charlene saluted the approaching group. "That is General Marie Lapointe — supreme commander of Astara's military. She is a tactical *genius*. And behind her are the Athenians, her personally trained special forces."

"They are so beautiful and sophisticated," Lulu remarked. She made a fist. "I hate them so much!"

"They are the elite of the elite," Charlene said proudly. "Though the way most of their body armor exposes their chests doesn't seem tactically sound."

They didn't look like soldiers at all to Doug, but when they got closer, he could see that they were toting guns — though each weapon looked different, and some didn't even look like guns. One looked almost like a long designer purse with a barrel. And all the women had an expression somewhere between haughty and deadly. "Wow," Doug commented, "they all look out of my league in a number of different ways."

"These women aren't even worth the time and effort they require, let me tell you," Bryce said. "Now everyone just salute and look normal as they walk by."

They all saluted, but as the group passed, Lapointe stopped to stare a moment at Lulu. "Why are you wearing a pink ski mask?" the general asked. "You look ridiculous."

"Criticism noted, Murray." Lulu gave her a thumbs-up.

The general narrowed her eyes and then turned to the officer next to her. "I don't like her. Have her killed."

The officer let out an exasperated sigh. "You can't have people killed."

"Whatever. I already forgot what I'm angry about." General Lapointe led the group away.

"You need normal-acting lessons," Doug whispered to Lulu.

She shrugged. "No one is normal, so being normal makes you stand out. Now let's get to it."

Lulu led them back out of the base to their van. Charlene hesitantly got in with the rest. "So where are we going? I need to get to my station to help in the city's defense. Actually, we all do."

"Could I ask you to trust me just once?" Bryce asked.

Charlene shook her head. "Absolutely not."

"If I could ask you to trust me just once," Bryce said, "I'd want you to trust me that staying here to fight the approaching army is a very bad idea."

Lulu started up the van. "I don't know how many times we've explained this to you, but we're basically the only people in the entire universe who care even slightly whether you live or die."

Doug looked out the window of the van as more things flew overhead. "So what is going on with this invasion?"

"What's going on is an evil nation is coming to destroy us," Charlene said. "We need to help the fight against them; you've heard stories of how terrible Loch's forces are."

Bryce scoffed. "The government says those sorts of stories about whoever they're fighting."

"So they're not really these terrible monsters we keep hearing about?" Doug asked.

Bryce frowned. "Well ... no. Loch's forces are just as bad as they've been saying; my point is that propaganda would have said that about them whether or not it was true."

"I can vouch for that," Lulu said. "Usually in the propaganda department, we make up stuff about our enemies, but for the followers of Loch, we were just factual. Actually, we sometimes made them look better than they are, because people wouldn't believe the actual stories. I mean, these guys just love torture, murder, and rape."

"Are they racist, too?" Doug asked.

Bryce rolled his eyes. "No. They're not cartoonishly evil."

"And if they are as awful as you say," Charlene said, "then how can you cowards abandon this fight?"

"Yeah, that's the thing." Bryce hesitated a little. "You saw how everyone was running around the base? They're in full evac mode." Bryce pointed out the window to some transports flying away. "So is the rest of the city. The only ones being mobilized to stay and fight are" — Bryce motioned to his group — "the war orphans."

Charlene shook her head. "How would you possibly know this?"

"Cocktail parties."

* * *

"You're stirring it too hard!" Bryce shouted at the bartender. "You're going to bruise the liquor! You need to —"

Bryce's monocle popped out, and he quickly put it back in. He was having a lot of trouble with it and was starting to wonder if he should have read the instruction booklet it came with, or at least googled "monocle wearing tips." He looked to a nearby mirror and made sure his black bow tie and his fake mustache were straight.

"Here is your drink, sir." The bartender handed Bryce his Manhattan.

Bryce snatched it from him. "I might as well chug a beer." He then walked over to where some socialites were chatting.

"So what I've been hearing is that we can now replace most of the jobs warfs do with monkeys," a wealthy heiress stated.

"What about robots?" asked an older man in a tuxedo. "They don't poop."

"Yes, but monkeys are a more green solution," the heiress stated. "Anyway, the point is we don't need the warfs any more."

"Can't believe we're abandoning the whole city to get rid of them," said a professorly-looking man.

"It's the easiest way," said the older man. "Loch conquers the city; then the warfs that reside here are officially his problem."

"Just seems so awful, though," the heiress stated. "I mean, just think of poor Loch stuck with all those idiot warfs."

They all laughed at her joke, and Bryce joined in as well. "As a captain of industry, I just have to say that —" His monocle popped out and fell in his drink. "Dammit!"

* * *

Charlene frowned. "How do I know that any of that was true?"

"It sounds true," Doug said. "I've seen him try to wear a monocle before, and he is not very good at it."

"Come on, Charlene," Bryce said. "Does this really sound that far-fetched based on how we've been treated our entire lives?" Bryce took out a tablet computer. "Anyway, I got myself on this elite mailing list where the higher-ups do all their plotting. You can read it for yourself." He handed the tablet to Charlene.

"What's it say?" Doug asked. He then spotted the big block of text. "Oh. Can someone summarize it for me?"

Charlene quietly read it and then handed the tablet back to Bryce without saying a word.

"So it's true?" Doug asked. "How long have you known about this, Bryce?"

"A little while," Bryce explained. "That's why I had to be a bit hasty on the timetable for this heist — but this whole invasion thing is going to be great cover, so it sort of works out."

"But we need to warn the other war orphans!" Doug protested.

"You have to help yourself before you help others," Bryce said. "And even if you have no intention of helping others, helping yourself is still a great idea. And that's what this is about: The Confederacy of Astara is abandoning us, so we're abandoning it ... but taking something of value first."

Doug frowned. "All us war orphans should look out for each other. We're all in the same boat."

"And we do look out for each other," Bryce said. "Us four look out for each other — which is exhausting enough as it is. Every other warf needs to get their own group."

Doug folded his arms. "No. This isn't right. What about Floyd?"

Bryce scoffed. "You're the only one who liked Floyd."

"What about ..." Doug thought for a second. "Well, I could socialize more, but there are other warfs, and if we don't do something, who will?"

Bryce groaned. "I knew you were going to be like this; that's why we didn't tell you about this part. But I did assign a distraction plan to Lulu that I think will satisfy you."

"I hacked the system so we can send a message to all the warfs' alert thingies," Lulu said as she watched the road.

"You did not hack it," Charlene scoffed.

"I stole a password!" Lulu responded. "That's a form of hacking! The message is going out soon, and all the warfs will be so mad it will give us lots of chaos to cover our escape." Lulu brought the van to a stop. "We're here. Get your game faces on." She adjusted her pink ski mask.

They got out of the van and were now in some area full of warehouses at the edge of town. "So where exactly are we?" Charlene asked.

Bryce put back on the mask for his shadow enforcer uniform. "Secret off-base facility." He looked at Charlene. "So you on board?"

Charlene just stared back at him and said nothing. Instead, she turned to Doug and took the pistol from his holster and stuck it in her jacket.

"Hey! I might have wanted to use that!" he protested. Then Doug noticed in the distance something large and dark in the sky. Very large and dark and heading their way. Like a mountain rising out of the clouds. An evil mountain. That flew. "What's that?"

"One of Loch's flying carriers," Charlene said. "With it will come an army and a squad of attack vehicles."

"Which means we're on a time limit here, people," Bryce said. "So let's get to this."

Lulu led the way. "Remember to smile; no one ever suspects smiling people."

They entered into the warehouse, but Doug found it hard to smile. For one, he was wearing a mask that completely concealed his face, so no one could see the smile anyway. Also, the sight upon entering the warehouse was dead bodies, torn-off limbs, and blood everywhere.

"Can I have my gun back?"

"And from the fractures of that war, many dark things emerged. Demons might be the word for them, if we were to try to limit them to something humans can imagine."

CHAPTER 4

"So did we just walk into a horror movie?" There were at least a dozen bodies, and they looked to Doug like they had been cut apart, limbs strewn about the warehouse. "If so, I've prepared for this. We need to stick together no matter what — no splitting up! And we need ... well ... to get out of here now, as sticking around where horrible things are happening never works out."

Lulu pulled off her ski mask. "Maybe Doug just seems smarter since he got us donuts, but he's making some really good points here."

Charlene tightened her scarf and then scanned the area, gun in hand. Bryce had pulled off his mask and looked like he was about to vomit, but quickly composed himself. "We can't just panic and discard the plan because of one little detail we didn't foresee. We can't leave here empty-handed." He was looking a bit shaken. "This is supposed to be our big payday. Life owes us that much, and we need to make it pay up."

Charlene continued to move around the crates in the warehouse, pointing her gun suddenly in different directions like she expected something to jump out at any moment. "Other option: We head out of here and go after those fleeing the city who decided to leave us behind. We then get a knife and disembowel them, letting the hate in our eyes be the last thing they see before they die."

Lulu sighed. "And this is why we didn't give you a heads-up on all this: You're unstable. One minute you're all, 'The government is the best! I want to French-kiss it and do everything it tells me!' and the next you're all, 'Let's viciously murder everyone in the government!' You need to pick what kind of nut you are."

"There's no profit in revenge, so let's just let go of that notion." Bryce walked about carefully, trying not to step in any blood. "We've been hated our entire lives and the people in charge treat us like crap — it's always been that way, and there is no reason to take it personally. Any of the nations these days would do something like that to us, so you might as well want to murder all of them. Instead, it's more productive to focus on how I have a buyer who will pay a ton — and I mean a ton — for a piece of hardware hidden here. There's supposed to be an entrance to a secret government storage facility around here somewhere; that's what we got the access cards for."

"Would that be it?" Doug pointed to some metal doors on the ground that had been ripped apart.

Lulu pulled out a gun. "This just keeps getting more and more welcoming."

"I really do think I want a gun," Doug said.

"Well, there are plenty on the bodies around us," Bryce said. "Not that it did them any good." He headed toward the torn doors. "So are you coming with me or do we want to split up?"

"No splitting up!" Doug shouted, picking up a rifle on the ground that didn't have too much blood on it.

They went down some stairs into a well-lit area that was completely ransacked. There were numerous metal crates lying on the ground, their contents of guns and electronics strewn about the floor. There were also a few more bodies, just as bloody as the ones upstairs.

"So what are we looking for?" Charlene asked. "Whatever it is, whoever was here before us might have already taken it."

Bryce scanned the pieces of equipment lying everywhere. "It's called a 'reality imploder bomb.' It's a new rumored weapon; can destroy anything in its blast radius, as it actually collapses reality."

Charlene raised an eyebrow. "That sounds made-up."

"I think it works by having a calculator inside it that attempts to divide by zero," Lulu explained, looking around with gun in hand.

Under the blood, it looked like some of the dead bodies were wearing what were once white lab coats. "Were there scientists here?" Doug asked.

"Could be a research facility, too," Bryce said, looking about carefully.

"It's bad luck to kill scientists," Lulu remarked. "That gives you seven years' faulty data."

Doug was starting to get nauseated from looking at all the dead bodies, so he tried to find other things to look at. He noticed a pile of body armor that had fallen out of an overturned crate, and he could see sticking out of it some small, wooden object. Doug immediately walked toward it and picked up the little but surprisingly heavy box. Inside, on a red felt lining, at the center sat a dark gray metal two-inch cube. It had a matte texture to it that didn't reflect any light. Doug reached to pick it up, but he hesitated, with his fingers hovering just above the metal surface. Was he scared? Then again, he didn't understand why he was so interested in this thing in the first place.

He seized the cube. A chill went through his body, starting in his fingertips and crawling its way to his spine. And when Doug looked around, he wasn't in the building any more. He was standing alone in barren land, a purple sky above him. And in it was a rippling star the size of the sun, but of pure black, yet somehow illuminating the world with a glow like that at midnight with a full moon.

Doug blinked, and he was back to normal ... in a secret base surrounded by dead bodies.

"What is up with you?" Charlene asked, giving Doug one quick glance before continuing to scan for threats.

"I had like ... a vision," Doug exclaimed. "Like a warning."

Lulu nodded. "Even more of a warning than dead bodies lying everywhere?"

"It was of a dark star," Doug said. "That means this cube is really important. Satan told me that's what seeing a dark star meant ... or something like that."

"Why are you still talking about Satan?" Bryce yelled. "We ate all the donuts, so we're done with that. Let's just find the bomb and get out of here."

Doug stared at the cube for another second, but once again noticing the blood and the dead, decided it was something to worry about later. He put the cube in his jacket pocket and closed the wooden box and set it back down.

"Found it!" Lulu exclaimed.

Bryce ran toward her. "It's still here?"

"Yep ... but not for long," Lulu said. "See, it has these numbers on it, and the numbers are counting down. That's exactly what you do not want to see on a bomb."

The bomb was a large metal cylinder with a bright display screen on top. It read "7:52." They all stared at it silently as the number counted down to "7:49." Finally, Bryce said, "See, this is good news."

Lulu nodded. "Explain further."

"Now we know that whatever killed all these people is gone," Bryce said. "It was scared off by one of the scientists activating this bomb. Now all we have to do is deactivate it, get out of here, and then we get our payday."

"And which of you idiots is going to deactivate it?" Charlene asked.

"Lulu has been reading up on this weapon," Bryce said. "She can handle it."

"Yes, that is a true thing Bryce just said." She handed a tablet computer to Doug. "Pull up 'reality imploder bomb' on Wikipedia for me."

Charlene rolled her eyes. "For Pete's sake ..."

Lulu grabbed some nearby tools and started to remove some screws on a panel on the bomb's front. "So what do you have, Doug?"

"Well, the article says this is a classified weapon and that many Bothans died getting them this information." Doug paused a moment. "Oh, I think that's vandalism. Should I fix the article?"

"Do it later, Doug!" Lulu shouted. "What else is on there?"

"Oh, they have a theoretical circuit diagram." Doug pulled up the image and held the tablet facing Lulu.

Lulu removed the front panel, took a look inside, and then glanced at the circuit diagram. "Yeah ... I should be able to do this." She stared at the wires some more. "Actually ... no, this isn't exactly right."

"But you can figure it out?" Bryce asked.

"Oh, yeah, sure." Lulu gently handled the wires inside.

"Where did you even get the electronics knowledge to do this?" Charlene demanded.

Lulu didn't look up from the wires. "I'm Asian; that means I'm good with electronics."

Charlene groaned and tried to look past Lulu at the wires. "I bet you don't even know how to read a circuit diagram. Why don't you let me try?"

Lulu held up a finger of warning to Charlene. "I got this. Back off."

"If there is any part of the diagram you don't understand," Charlene said, "just tell me and I'll explain what —"

"Okay! That's it!" Lulu shouted. "Which wire do I cut to make it go off right now?"

Bryce tried to insert himself between Charlene and Lulu. "Let's all calm down. I'm sure Lulu can ... pretty sure she can —"

Charlene put her hand over Bryce's mouth and cocked her ear to the side. She put her gun at the ready. "Someone is coming."

"Of course," Lulu said, studying the diagram again. "This was going way too smoothly."

"Well, we don't have time to stop trying to defuse the bomb." Bryce put his hand on Charlene's gun, pushing it down. "Let's try to talk our way out of this before we turn to more base means."

Charlene glared at him a moment, then took position hiding behind a pillar. Doug kept holding the tablet for Lulu as he watched five people come down the stairs. Their uniforms were black with accents of red, and a prominent patch on their arms depicted a hooked red claw — the symbol of the Loch Collective. They looked at the dead bodies with confusion, then trained their eyes and their guns on Bryce, who stood there smiling at them.

"Good, you're finally here," he said. Bryce then looked at the two soldiers who were female with an extra-big smile. "Hey."

"Who are you?" demanded one of the soldiers, a large bearded man.

"I'm Benedict, leader of this advance team sent to prepare the way for you," Bryce explained. "A very special group used for very special missions."

"We're called Hellbender," Doug added.

"Yes, that's our name," Bryce said. He then turned to Doug and glared at him and mouthed "Shut up!" before looking back to the soldiers. "As you can see, everything is just about ready."

"I'm Butcher, by the way," the bearded man said as he looked around at the dead bodies and smiled. "You did all this? It's quite some work."

"Yep. We disguised ourselves as Astara's troops and came in here and slaughtered them all," Bryce said. "It sure was fun. Like all of Loch's followers, we just love killing and tearing people apart and stuff. Right, guys?"

"Yep," Lulu said, still working on the bomb. "I love stabbing eyeballs. They're so squishy. With me and eyeballs, I'm like a kid with bubble wrap."

"And you guys tore apart the door to get down here?" Butcher asked.

"Oh, that was Doug." Bryce pointed to Doug. "You get him in a kill frenzy, and he is unstoppable."

One of the female soldiers smiled at Doug. "Wow. You must be really strong."

"Yeah, I'm just like 'Rarr!' and I kill everybody and tear things apart." Doug did his best at a confident smile. "I'm awesome."

"Well, my name is Raze," she said. She was even cuter than she was scary-looking, though Doug didn't know if he could keep up the "I love murdering people" ruse if he got to hang out with her after this. Bryce always told him to never think that far ahead, though.

"So the three of you did all this?" Butcher asked.

"Well, four. Dutch is hiding ready to shoot you all or something," Bryce said.

Charlene stepped out of her hiding spot and lowered her gun. "I guess we're all friends, though."

Butcher looked at her with confusion. "What kind of uniform is that?" He then looked at Lulu. "And what is she doing?"

"Oh, well ... we hit a little snag," Bryce explained. "Before we could kill everybody, one of the scientists activated this bomb here — and I can tell you, we killed the scientist who did it extra good. But now Taffy here is defusing the bomb, so no problem. We'll be able to get the bomb out of here soon."

Butcher nodded. "Okay, but the most important thing is the artifact."

"Well, yeah, of course," Bryce said. "We know all about why you guys are here."

"Did you find the artifact?" Butcher asked.

"Well, on that ..."

"There it is," Raze said, walking over and picking up the wooden box in which Doug had found the cube.

"Yep, it was hidden, but we found it," Bryce said. "I wouldn't open it, though ... because you know how artifacts are."

"We were told to get this out of here before our main forces wipe out the city," Butcher said. "Do you think we'll have the bomb ready soon?"

"Yeah, just give us a minute; it's all good," Bryce said.

"It's just too bad we won't be here to help slaughter everyone in this city," Raze said.

"Yeah, that makes me sad because I really like killing," Doug told her, getting another smile in response. He was thinking of asking her on a date, but he wasn't really sure what was going on after this.

"So can you guys keep lookout while we handle this?" Bryce asked. "We should be done pretty soon."

"And you're sure you can defuse this?" Butcher asked.

"As easy as piercing an eyeball," Lulu said, carefully looking at the wires again.

The enemy soldiers headed back upstairs to keep lookout, Bryce smiling and waving at them as they went. When they were out of earshot, he turned to the others. "See? I told you these bombs are really valuable. So valuable the Loch Collective sent an advance team to grab them before the full invasion hits."

"I think Raze likes me," Doug said. "Didn't it seem like that?"

"It did." Bryce patted him on the back. "But I wouldn't get too attached, because there's a good chance we'll have to shoot her. That's why you don't flirt on the battlefield; it often ends in heartbreak."

"Is that the plan?" Charlene asked. "We try to get the drop on them and take them all out? Presuming Lulu can actually defuse this bomb?"

Lulu glanced at the time, which now read "4:22." She then looked back at the wires. "I think I have this." She reached inside with some wire cutters and severed a green wire. The display went blank.

Bryce let out a sigh of relief. "Good job, Tri-lu."

Lulu stuck out her tongue at Charlene. "See, I told you I know electronics."

Charlene shrugged. "How do we know for sure it's actually defused and you didn't just cut power to the digital display?"

"Don't be an idiot," Lulu said. "That's not how a timer works. When you —" She paused a moment and put her ear to the bomb, then took another glance at the diagram Doug was still holding. "Um ... actually, yeah, I think I only cut power to the display, but the timer might still be going."

Bryce rubbed his forehead and looked at Lulu. "You think maybe you still have time to get the bomb completely defused?"

"Um ... well ..." Lulu looked over the wires again. "It's ... a possibility. Though I don't think we'll really be sure if I got it right until ... a few more minutes pass."

Charlene groaned. "I'm going to take a shot at it this time."

As Charlene tried to reach past Lulu for the wires, Lulu slapped her hand away. "I have this, Char!"

Charlene slapped her hand back. "No you don't! Just get out of the way!"

It soon broke down into a slapfest of Lulu and Charlene swinging wildly at each other.

"Maybe we should just get really far away so we don't get imploded by this thing," Doug suggested, a bit of panic seeping into his voice.

Bryce hesitated as Lulu and Charlene continued slapping. "We can't leave here empty-handed or we're kind of screwed."

"They seemed to want that cube I took out of that box," Doug said. "I wonder what it is?"

"All I know is I don't have a negotiated price on it," Bryce stated.

Charlene got out of slap radius of Lulu. "We've wasted enough time!" she shouted. "Everyone get their guns ready. We go up, we smile, and then we shoot those five and get out of here."

Lulu took out her pistol. "You don't do a very convincing smile."

Doug put down the tablet computer and readied his rifle while Bryce sighed and took out his gun as well. "Just follow my lead," Charlene said. "You all ready?"

"Hey ... um ... guys." Doug motioned to Butcher, who was walking their way.

Butcher noticed all their guns out. "What's going on?" He looked to the bomb and the dead display. "Is the bomb defused?"

They were all quiet a few seconds. Finally, Charlene gave him a thumbs-up. "Yep! Ready to go!"

"The bomb is ready," Butcher said into his com. "Let's get it out of here."

The other four soldiers came down into the lab, and two of them together picked up the bomb to move it upstairs.

"So are you coming with us?" Butcher asked Bryce.

"Oh ... uh ... we'll be catching our own ride out of here," Bryce said. "You just get that bomb back to base as quick as you can."

"The bomb and the artifact," Butcher said, "but we don't want to take all the credit after your guys' great work here." He motioned to all the dead bodies.

"We're a secret group," Charlene stated coldly. "We don't care about credit."

"A secret group called Hellbender!" Doug added.

The Loch soldiers started to head up the stairs. Raze stopped and turned to Doug. "Hey, maybe we can do something after this."

"Um ..." Doug played with his rifle strap nervously. "Maybe."

She smiled at Doug one last time and then left with the other soldiers and the bomb. "Well, that solved itself," Lulu said.

"Yeah, it's just —" Bryce spotted something. He walked over to a tarp and pulled it down, and underneath was another reality imploder bomb, with nothing on the display. "Ha! There's a second one! Unactivated!" He wiped some sweat off his forehead. "We're having some good luck on this heist."

Doug and Bryce carried the bomb upstairs while Charlene and Lulu made sure the coast was clear. By a garage door were a couple VTOL transport vehicles with open doors that appeared to have been partially loaded with boxes before everyone was slaughtered. They were obviously Astara vehicles, since they had the symbol of a dove on them. Or maybe it was a pelican. Or a horse. It was very stylized and kind of hard to tell exactly what it was. "Someone want to check if we have keys for one of those?" Bryce asked.

"Do we have another escape plan if we don't?" Charlene responded.

Bryce set down the bomb for a moment. "You don't want to over-plan these things."

Lulu jumped up and checked the cockpit of one. "We're good to go."

"Great! Let's get out of here." Bryce helped Doug bring the bomb into the back of the transport while Charlene got the garage door open. Lulu got in the cockpit and started the vehicle up. When Charlene got in the back with Bryce and Doug, Lulu brought the vehicle out the garage door and then started to ascend.

"So where are we going now?" Charlene asked.

"The Disputed Zone," Bryce said.

Doug raised an eyebrow. "I don't like going to zones. They don't call good places 'zones.' They are never as nice as towns or cities."

"And this one is full of criminals and lowlifes," Charlene said.

Bryce laughed. "And who else are we supposed to sell a stolen bomb to? Goodwill? We're going to be rich when this is over; let's focus on that."

Charlene plopped down on a bench. "And what about my visual history supplies? Are we ever going to get to come back here?"

"I'm sure wherever we're going you can buy more construction paper and glue and other boring nonsense," Lulu said.

Doug looked out the window and could see numerous other vehicles fleeing the city by air and ground as the giant, ominous carrier continued its slow approach to the city as if it were a beast waiting to devour its prey. It was right at the edge of the city, beginning to cast a shadow over all those left behind.

"Man, I hope everyone left in the city got the message Lulu sent out and will be okay," Doug said. "It's really mean how Astara just left all the warfs at the mercy of the Loch Collective. The Loch Collective do not seem like nice people. I mean, I kind of liked Raze, but —"

Doug paused as he noticed something odd about the carrier. At first, it seemed to expand a little, but then it began to shrink as if it was being sucked inward at its center. The carrier continued to collapse into itself until soon there was nothing left of it at all except clear skies.

"So I definitely did not properly defuse the reality imploder bomb," Lulu commented.

"Well, that was ... interesting," Bryce said.

"We're heroes!" Doug exclaimed. "We saved the city!"

"Saved it for all those who betrayed us and didn't care if we were tortured and killed," Charlene grumbled.

"There are no heroes, any more," Bryce said, "as there just aren't any good people worth saving."

"Well, I think it was pretty cool what we did." Doug sat down and felt a lump in his coat. He pulled out the metal cube. He shuddered a bit as it contacted his skin. "So what do you think this is?"

Bryce shrugged. "All we know is that Loch's people wanted it, so maybe it's worth something. We'll need to find out what it is first."

"Well, it was Satan who told me about it," Doug said.

Charlene sighed. "You did not talk to Satan. There is no Satan."

"But what exactly did the guy at the donut shop tell you about this?" Bryce asked.

Doug handled the cube gently. It was very cool to the touch. Almost cold. "I don't completely remember. I just recall that he said something about how if you ever see a black star, that means you are near something very, very important."

•

"The demons are why I must tell you of something: the black star. If you take nothing else away from what I'm telling you, remember the black star, for if you see it, take that as a warning of something you must stay very far away from. Otherwise you will ensure your destruction and the destruction of everyone you care about."

CHAPTER 5

"Do you think the warfs will appreciate what I've done for them?" General Marie Lapointe asked, sipping a cocktail as she lounged on a red leather couch in what was supposed to be a military transport. Lapointe looked relaxed in her pose, yet her blue dress was perfect on her, as if this was all staged for some photo shoot. Lapointe always looked like that. It was something Major Harriet Mills both admired and hated about her.

"Will they appreciate that they and the city of Calais have been abandoned to the mercy of Loch's invading force?" Mills responded, looking over plans for the strike back against the Loch Collective. "No, I'm guessing they won't be very thankful about that." Mills was in her officer's uniform, and its condition looked appropriate for someone whose day was spent responding to a major attack.

"Well ... warfs are idiots," Lapointe said. "And that's the beauty of it: We hate them and wanted them gone, but now they'll be seen as heroes who defended the city, allowing us all to escape. They will perish beloved." Lapointe thought for a moment. "Do we still have ears on the ground there? We need stories of how horribly they were tortured. The worse things are for them, the more sympathetic they'll be. I want people to sing songs of their sacrifice. Something like ...

"Stupid useless warfs, we hated them so

"But they were heroically torn apart by our foe."

Mills sighed. "I think your meter is off."

Lapointe took another sip of her purple liquor. "Well, songwriting isn't really my talent. We should hire out for that one. Maybe Dave Matthews."

Mills took a deep breath. "He's been dead for hundreds of years. Now, General, we really need to focus on —"

"Don't call me 'general,'" Lapointe interrupted. "I don't like it. I prefer 'commander.' I command things; I'm not ... nonspecific."

"Well, your rank is general, and —"

Lapointe finally turned from staring off into space to look at Mills. "Isn't that the same outfit you wore yesterday?"

Mills took another deep breath. "As I've explained constantly to you, this is my military uniform. I'm supposed to wear it every day. You're supposed to be wearing one too."

Lapointe scoffed. "I'd go naked before wearing the same thing twice."

It was supposed to be an honor for Mills to serve directly with General Marie Lapointe, the most brilliant military mind of their generation, but it was not the plum assignment she had hoped. In retrospect, Mills realized she should have suspected something when she read Lapointe's book *War is Art*. It was chapter after chapter on things like the best time of day and weather conditions for the most dramatic battlefield, what types of munitions made the most photogenic explosions, and what types of wounds made a soldier looked rugged versus pathetic. Then, somewhere near the middle of the book, was one chapter of actual military strategy — and it was the most brilliant, incisive thing Mills had ever read. And that was Lapointe in a nutshell — a decisive military genius wrapped in a bunch of nonsense.

And thus working under Lapointe, Mills soon learned her job was less an assistant to Lapointe and more her handler. It was Mills's job to talk to the higher-ups and make sure Lapointe was actually focused on the jobs that needed to be done instead of some other inanity. And it was also Mills's job to make sure there wasn't another incident like the time Lapointe purposely lost the battle of Vancourt because she didn't like the color of the campaign ribbon.

"We're going to need new uniforms for the troops," Lapointe declared. "The current ones aren't working for me."

"We don't have the budget for yet another change in our troops' uniforms," Mills answered.

"No, not our troops, fool. The enemy's. I have a color scheme for them that will make the next battle much more dramatic."

Mills counted to four and then responded. "We can't make the enemy wear other uniforms. As I'm sure you're well aware, the only side we get to control is our own."

"So you're saying if we sent them new uniforms — really nice ones — they wouldn't use them?" Lapointe scoffed. "You're not making any sense." She looked a moment at Mills. "So, those glasses, are those part of your uniform or did you pick them out yourself?"

"I picked these out. I got them from —"

Lapointe rolled her eyes. "If that's a choice you made yourself, I don't know why I'd listen to you on anything."

Mills took a deep breath and counted to six this time. "General, we really need to work on the logistics of this next battle. While letting Calais fall to Loch won't hurt us too much, if we fail in your planned strike at Ralston, that's basically going to be it for the Confederacy of Astara. We'll be at the mercy of Loch and his troops." Mills shuddered at the thought. "You get that, right? You yourself could be facing a violent death ... or worse."

Lapointe smiled. "Exactly. After this terrible loss to such a horrible enemy, everything will look bleak. This attack on Ralston will appear to be a desperate ploy by a losing military. And thus, think of the reaction when we miraculously win, the victory capped by Loch's mighty sky carrier lying in flaming pieces before our victorious army. It will be a battle people will talk about for ages ... all the more so if we can get the enemy to wear the uniforms I designed for them."

Mills wished she shared Lapointe's confidence, but the general always seemed to believe she could control things that most would understand were out of anyone's control. And usually she was right, but not always ... a fact emphasized by the message flashing on a nearby console. Mills picked up her radio. "Turn everything around. Everything. We're heading back to Calais."

Mills finally had Lapointe's full attention. "What? What's going on?" the general demanded.

Mills very carefully considered how to handle this situation. She smiled and said, "We have some good news: Loch's forces are retreating from the city."

The ploy did not work. Lapointe shot to her feet. "What?! Loch's army should have easily defeated the warfs we left to defend Calais. It should be a terrible defeat for us ... that was the only way for it to play out!"

"Well, yes, except ..." Mills looked over the incoming data on the screen. "... their air carrier was destroyed."

"How is that possible?!" Lapointe screamed, now right in Mills's face. "It was well established that their widely feared air carrier was invincible! Its defenses were insurmountable! Nothing — except my brilliance, which I was going to unleash in the battle of Ralston — should have been able to bring it down!"

"Initial reports are sketchy," Mill said, "but it looks like there was a break-in at a secret research facility prior to the arrival of the carrier, and it appears the carrier's destruction could be related to a weapon we had there — the reality imploder bomb. I believe I briefed you on it."

"That weapon had not been publicly announced!" Lapointe screamed. "So a weapon we never mentioned before just suddenly comes out of nowhere and takes out Loch's invincible carrier? That's deus ex machina! It's sloppy! It makes us look like idiots!" She slumped into her chair. "I don't know how we're going to recover from this."

"Well, might I make a suggestion ..." Mills braced herself, as she knew she was venturing into delicate territory. "Your original plan was to turn the defeat at Calais into a victory. Maybe instead you can turn the victory at Calais into ... another victory."

Lapointe looked at Mills with disgust. "Loch's forces are hobbled and they're missing their carrier. Do you know what that makes the chance of a victory in Ralston?"

"I'd say it significantly —"

"It's inevitable! And thus beneath me! I mean ..." Lapoint looked at Mills with contempt. "... even you could lead our forces to victory there. The only possible interesting outcome would be for Loch's army to somehow secure a victory in that battle." Lapointe paused in the thought. "Actually ..."

Mills jumped at the red flag. "Despite it being ... boring ... the Confederacy of Astara really needs the win at Ralston to continue its — you know — existence."

Lapointe glared at Mills. "I was just starting to have an interesting thought, and you interrupted me. Have I ever told you how much I hate you?"

Mills sighed. "At least once a day."

"And yet I can't have you killed."

"No, you can't randomly execute people you dislike — as I've explained to you many, many times."

"So how much trouble would I be in if I poisoned your drink?" Lapointe asked.

"I don't see how you'd manage that, since you always send me to get the drinks."

Lapointe thought for a second. "Next time you get drinks, batwoman, bring them to me first. Also, bring me some poison from ... wherever it is we store that."

"I'm not your batwoman, and that's not ..." Mills's phone beeped. She looked at the screen. "An emergency alert was sent out to all the citizens of Calais. It says 'Warfs: The leadership is abandoning you in Calais. Find them and viciously murder them.' Oh ... that ... that might need some smoothing over."

"Ugh. Adverbs," Lapointe said. "Would have been better as 'Find them and eviscerate them.'"

"That's not really the takeaway ..." Mills took off her glasses and took another deep breath. "A number of things are going on here. For now, let's just focus on the true enemy."

Lapointe nodded. "Yes. Whoever it is that destroyed that carrier and ruined my plans."

"Technically," Mills said, "whoever did that would be a hero."

Lapointe waved her hand dismissively. "Hero. Villain. These are very flexible labels. Whoever is responsible for this act against my creation, though, they are now my enemy. We will find them." Lapointe smiled. "And the whole nation will celebrate their destruction."

"There's still this war going on that we need to take care of," Mills reminded her.

Lapointe glared at Mills. "I thought I told you to get me a drink."

"We're talking about dark powers unlike anything you've ever contemplated. They could obliterate you with a thought. And thus your only defense is to make sure they never think of you."

CHAPTER 6

"That was pretty cool how we destroyed that carrier," Doug said, staring at the unactivated bomb and getting a little bored. He was lounging in the back of the transport with the other three while the vehicle was on autopilot.

"Considering the price these sell for on the black market," Bryce said, "that was just a waste of a valuable bomb."

Doug took the small metal cube out of his pocket again. There was that strange chill as he held it, yet there was something oddly familiar about the cube as well. "I really wonder what this is."

"Lemme see." Bryce snatched the cube and instantly shuddered. "Huh. Kind of makes you feel weird."

"I like feeling weird!" Lulu grabbed it. She held it out uncertainly. "Huh. Maybe it's irradiated."

"If it's irradiated," Charlene said, sitting down and reading a manual she found in the transport glove box, "maybe you shouldn't all be handling it."

"You two, hold Charlene down," Lulu said. "I'm going to make her lick it."

Doug took the cube back and returned it to his pocket. "I think it's important. So maybe we shouldn't be playing with it."

"But unimportant things are boring to play with!" Lulu fumed. There was a beep, and Lulu looked at the transport's console. "We're at the Disputed Zone!"

They all looked out the windshield and saw a big lit sign that said, "The Disputed Zone: If you find a more wretched hive of scum and villainy, we'll beat their price."

"You better not have just taken us out here to get murdered," Charlene said.

"Like you had better plans." Bryce took off his shadow enforcer uniform, revealing his blue suit underneath.

Doug looked about the landscape. It resembled a city, but the buildings were all disheveled and broken. "So what is this place?"

"It's an area of land that three different countries laid claim to," Bryce explained. "The land was torn apart in the legal dispute. Soon, it was so devastated that nothing could live here — not plant or animal. Only lawyers. But eventually the place fell into lawlessness, and lawyers can't exist in an area of lawlessness, so they went feral. Some say they still roam the land. You'll suddenly hear someone yell, 'Objection!' and then you'll be torn apart like an improperly witnessed contract."

Doug shuddered. "I'm scared of lawyers. And ninjas."

Charlene checked her pistol. "This is idiocy. The point is, the area is overrun with criminals, so everyone be on guard and ready to fight. It's a barren wasteland of lawlessness."

Doug took another look out the window. "I see a Walmart."

"It's a black-market Walmart," Lulu said. "Contraband items at everyday low prices."

"That's cool."

Bryce shrugged. "Some people don't like how it shut down all the mom-and-pop criminal businesses." He stared out the windshield. "You see this, people? This here is freedom. We are no longer under the law of some fool government. We are in a land of lawlessness, and finally, now, we make our own rules." He noticed something out of the window. "Oh. There's the DMV. We need to stop there first."

* * *

"So ... we'll need stolen vehicle tags," Bryce told the middle-aged woman behind the counter at the registration office.

"What kind of vehicle?" the clerk asked.

"It's a military transport," Bryce said.

The clerk handed Bryce a sticker. "You'll need to display this in the windshield." She also handed Bryce a form. "We'll need this filled out about your criminal organization."

"Then can I just hand it back to you?" Bryce asked.

"No. You'll need to get in line again."

Bryce took a look at the dozen people in line and then slouched to the back of the room, where Doug, Charlene, and Lulu were seated next to a table. "Got a form to fill out," Bryce announced as he grabbed a pen attached to the table by a sturdy chain.

"What is this?" Charlene demanded. "I thought we were lawless criminals now?"

Bryce began filling out the form. "Lawless, not ruleless. We're criminals, not savages."

"So what are you filling out?" Doug asked.

"I'm describing our criminal organization," Bryce answered. "Going to say we're a mercenary group."

Doug snatched away the form and pen. "Awesome. We're going to make Hellbender official."

"We're not calling ourselves that," Bryce said. "We need to be called something the other criminals can respect."

Doug quickly filled in a line near the top. "Too late. We're called Hellbender. And you can't undo it. It's in pen."

"I never cared for that name either," Charlene commented.

"It might work for a heavy metal band," Lulu said.

"And I am not opposed to that," Doug said. "But it's always been our team name, ever since we were little kids. Team Hellbender."

* * *

"And you are?" asked the science fair judges who had moved to Doug's booth.

"Team Hellbender!" nine-year-old Doug answered, beaming with pride. "I came up with the name!"

"Prepare to be amazed!" little Bryce announced as he directed the judges' attention to a table where something was hidden under a cloth. With a flourish, he pulled off the cloth, revealing a cylindrical object. "It's fully functional."

"A fully functional what?" asked a judge. "This doesn't look like any of the projects you were supposed to work on."

"Those looked boring," said the pigtailed Lulu as she showed them a tablet. "But I found some more interesting projects on something called the 'dark web.'" On the tablet screen were instructions for making a pipe bomb.

"That's a ... bomb?" stammered a judge.

"Crude, but tactically sound," stated the diminutive Charlene. "Useful for guerilla tactics. We weren't able to get exactly everything from the instructions, but I think it should still work."

"Do you have anything we could blow up?" Doug asked, nearly shaking with excitement.

The judges started to back away. Doug quickly became worried. "Whoa, whoa, whoa. No sudden movements!"

* * *

"We came in last place," Bryce said. "And were almost arrested."

"It was a really good attempt at making a bomb, though," Charlene grumbled, "which I think they should have given us some credit for."

"If it was fully functional," Lulu stated, "they wouldn't have dared give us last place."

Doug nodded. "Hey, we may have failed, but the point is we failed as a team."

"And that's our slogan," Lulu added. "'Better to fail together than fail alone.'"

"Let's just get the form done," Bryce urged.

"Okay." Doug scanned the form. "So what else do I have to tell them about us?"

"Tell them I'm cute," Lulu said.

Doug looked at all the lines he still had to fill in. "There's not a line for that."

"If there's an extra notes section, put it in there."

Charlene looked at the form. "I see you have to put in the leader. Might I suggest someone competent?"

Bryce snatched back the form and pen from Doug.

"Don't write in your own name!" Charlene shouted.

"I'm not." Bryce wrote down "Lulu Liu" on the leader line.

Charlene went wide-eyed. "What?!"

"Quiet, lackey!" Lulu yelled at her.

"Asian women are underrepresented in the criminal world," Bryce explained. "If she's listed as the leader, it will give us a hiring advantage if we want to do mercenary work. Actually, we're pretty well positioned for contracts, diversity-wise. We're half female, half minority — you know, Lulu is Asian and Doug is ... black or Hispanic or something. Well, we can claim whatever we think will help the most in getting a contract."

"I'm pretty sure I'm Latino," Doug said, "because I really *really* like nachos."

Charlene scoffed. "And thieves and murderers care about racial quotas?"

"Again, we're dealing with criminals," Bryce explained, "not savages." He filled in the section under sponsor.

"We have a sponsor?" Doug asked.

"We need one, so we do." Bryce stared awhile at the unfilled sections. "This is so long and boring." He turned to Charlene. "You love forms, don't you? Why don't you do the rest?"

"I'm not here to do your menial work," Charlene said as she grabbed a nearby DMV brochure as material for one of her scrapbooking pages.

"Then what are you here for?" Lulu asked.

Charlene sighed and took the form and pen. "Let's get this done and get out of here."

Doug was beaming. "This is so exciting. Hellbender is finally going to be an official criminal mercenary group. Except, I think we should all do crimes to help others. We could be like that legendary group that would rob from the rich and give to the poor — you know, the A-Team."

"We're poor," Lulu pointed out.

"But not for long," Bryce said. "We just need to meet my contact in the criminal underworld, and by the end of the day we'll be rich and can already leave the criminal world if we want." His smile faded ever so slightly as he watched the DMV line get longer. "Things will only get better from here."

* * *

They headed to an apartment building in a shady-looking part of town. Actually, most of the Disputed Zone was pretty shady-looking, so this was a pretty average part of town. As they walked up to the stairs to the third floor, Bryce fixed his suit. Lulu had taken off her officer's uniform, under which she was wearing a pink T-shirt and blue yoga pants. Charlene was stuck in her peacekeeper uniform and turquoise treason scarf. Doug was also stuck in his shadow enforcer uniform, though the others had made him take off the mask when he couldn't stop himself from breathing like Darth Vader.

Bryce knocked on the apartment door. A pretty woman about their age in a black business suit answered, her blond hair pulled back in a simple ponytail. She beamed upon seeing Bryce. "Oh! You're here!" She looked at the three behind him. "And these must be your friends you told me about." She gave them each a big smile. "I'm Tara Skinner. I work for the Vogel criminal enterprise. Nice to meet you all!"

"Yes, these are Lulu, Doug, and Charlene," Bryce said. "Which is which you can figure out later. Anyway, we have the device."

"Oh! That's great!" Tara said. "Well, come on in. I have to apologize, though — it's a bit of a mess."

They walked into the apartment, which was furnished quite plainly except for a body wrapped in a plastic tarp lying in the middle of the living room.

"Well, this is festive," Lulu remarked.

"Oh, yeah, sorry; that's a work thing," Tara said. "They needed me to bump off some guy, so I invited him to my place, was all nice and acted like I was going to get him a drink and then ..." She made a gun firing motion with her hand. "BANG! Shot him in the back of the head. Anyway, you guys want any drinks?"

Doug stared at the body. "Well ... uh ..."

Tara laughed. "Oh, I'm not going to shoot you guys in the back of the head if that's what you're thinking." She headed for the kitchen. "There's like four of you."

"So your criminal contact is a woman?" Charlene remarked to Bryce when Tara was out of earshot. "We know how this will turn out."

Doug nodded. "Yeah, most women you're with end up wanting to kill you. Maybe you should be more careful around a woman who's actually good at that."

"I'm on very good terms with her," Bryce said. "And she is our key to selling the bomb, so let's just all be all smiles, okay?"

Charlene's hand rested near the gun under her jacket. "You better know what you're doing for once."

Tara came back with a pitcher of lemonade and placed it on the coffee table, which was next to the body. "So did you guys get the device out of Calais? I mean, I heard what happened there with Loch's carrier."

Bryce smiled. "You heard of that?"

"Yeah, everyone is going on and on about how brilliant General Lapointe is," Tara said. "I mean, how in the world did she get a bomb right inside the carrier?"

Charlene looked ready to explode. "She took credit?!"

Tara was taken aback. "Did I say something wrong?"

Bryce stepped over the body to get himself a glass of lemonade. "It's no matter. So, will you be able to get us in a meeting with your employer, Vogel?"

"If you have one of the reality imploder bombs, quite certainly," Tara said. "Since what happened at Calais, interest is *very* high. My people will be very thrilled to get one, and they will certainly pay a bundle for it."

Doug carefully went around the body to get to the lemonade. "I wonder who it will end up getting used on?"

"Someone who deserves it, no doubt," Bryce said. "But hopefully not us." He turned to Tara. "So, when can we make the business transaction?"

"I can get you to see my people right away." Tara smiled at Bryce and touched his cheek. "We war orphans need to stick together, you know."

Lulu nudged the body with her foot. "Yeah, it's a rough world."

"Just make sure you have the bomb ready," Tara warned. "The organization I work for can get pretty angry if they feel you're wasting their time."

"Did this man here waste their time?" Charlene asked, motioning to the body.

Tara laughed. "Yeah, sorta."

Bryce took Tara's hand. "Well, don't worry. We have everything in order. I'm sure everyone will be ..." He smiled. "... quite happy."

Tara blushed. "I'm looking forward to us continuing to work together. I'll contact you when everything is set up."

"All right, we'll see you then," Bryce said. "Do you need Doug's help carrying that body anywhere?"

"Oh, I got it; thanks," Tara said. "I'll see you soon."

Bryce, Doug, Lulu, and Charlene headed out of the apartment. "Well, she seemed nice," Lulu remarked when they were in the hallway. "Of course, you have to assume anyone who's fallen for Bryce is some sort of idiot."

"I actually like her better than most of the floozies Bryce ends up with," Charlene said, "but let's not let our guard down dealing with these sorts of people."

"I don't know," Doug said. "There's just something about her I don't trust."

"How she murdered a guy and works for a criminal organization?" Lulu suggested.

Doug thought a moment and shook his head. "No, something else."

Bryce patted Doug on the shoulder. "Don't be weird. This is a simple thing: We have a device people want and we have a contact to people with plenty of money for it. What we need to do now is spend a little time making ourselves look like a respectable bunch of criminals and everything will turn out great."

"I wonder if that guy under the tarp was expecting things to turn out great," Charlene said.

"Hey, Tara is just a go-getter," Bryce answered. "She's like us: A warf trying to do whatever she can to improve her lot. And I hope we're all ready to shoot people in the back of the head if needed."

"Don't worry on that front if you've led us wrong, Bryce," Charlene said.

Bryce adjusted his tie. "Let's keep focused here. What we're working for is freedom — freedom from those governments that pushed us around. And we're just a step away from having the money for that freedom."

"And we can count on a criminal organization not to cheat us out of it?" Charlene asked.

"Vogel is a very large organization," Bryce said. "And while the sum they'll pay for the bomb is huge to us, it's little to them. We won't be drawing too much attention to ourselves, and staying beneath attention is the key to people like us succeeding."

* * *

"So it was a decoy?" Darius asked.

The reply came back in text on the screen on Darius's vehicle's console. "Yes, it was not the true artifact."

"So the true one is still with Astara's people?"

New text came on screen. "Not by our information. Someone arrived after you left and took it."

"Who?"

"We don't have a name. We just know they call themselves 'Hellbender.'"

"So I need to find them and get it back?" Darius asked.

"And kill everyone who touched it," said the next bit of text. "To be on the safe side."

Darius smiled. "Certainly."

"So what are these beings? I guess to explain them, I need to go further back ... though really outside of time entirely. Back to my decision to rise up against Heaven itself."

CHAPTER 7

"We're called Hellbender," the dumb one told the enemy soldiers in the security video.

Mills, Lapointe, and six of the Athenians were in a conference room at their headquarters in Calais. The Athenians, as usual, were on their phones and not listening, but surprisingly, Mills actually had Lapointe's attention. "These are the ones who tricked Loch's forces into bringing an active bomb onto their carrier," Mills explained.

"So these are the ones who destroyed all my plans?" Lapointe asked, glaring at the four on screen.

"Well, for now we're saying they acted on your orders," Mills said. "Everyone is quite happy about that unexpected victory, I remind you."

Lapointe scoffed. "Everyone is an idiot who loves chain restaurants and reality shows."

"But we can't simply celebrate them as heroes. They stole one of the reality imploder bombs, which we can only assume they've sold." Mills rewound the video to where the dumb one took something out of a wooden box. "What's even more important, apparently, is that they've taken some ... artifact. It's been made our highest priority to get it back right away."

Lapointe studied the video. "And these four killed everyone in the secret research facility?"

Mills laughed. "No, they're idiots. And just look: There's no blood on their clothing despite how brutally everyone was killed. Our profiles of them say they're just unskilled warfs not capable of such a thing." On another screen, Mills brought up the government profiles of the four. "Strangely, the security cameras went out for a while, and when they came back on, everyone was dead. And I'm told there was a decoy artifact that was also removed. So apparently some other group came earlier but was fooled by the decoy."

"And what exactly is this 'artifact'?" Lapointe asked.

"I don't know exactly," Mills said. "Apparently it was part of some project we were doing in conjunction with the Large-Scale Societal Rules Association Designation 4B22."

Lapointe grimaced. "The what?"

"That nation of ... you know ... science weirdos. Anyway, I have Dr. Asmod from 4B22 on the line to explain the artifact."

On the screen appeared a decrepit old man in a white lab coat. His eyes were concealed by dark goggles. "I knew there would be problems allying with you idiots," he grumbled.

"I assure you, we are taking this very seriously," Mills said. "That's why our top team ..." Mills motioned to the Athenians, who were still all on their phones. "... has been assigned to it. Is there anything we need to know about the bomb?"

"We'd know more about the bomb," Asmod seethed, "if we knew you were going to use it so we could have collected data from its detonation. You were supposed to use it on the warfs you left in the city — we were all set up to collect that data, and now we have nothing."

Mills frowned. "Let's not dwell on that. The warfs found out we were abandoning them, and they're still rioting. It's ... messy. If word were to get out of the full extent of the plans with the bomb ..." She glanced at the Athenians, but again, none were paying any attention. "... it would just be trouble we don't need right now. So, what can you tell us about the artifact?"

"Not much you'd understand," Asmod answered. "Creating that bomb is but one of the things we've been able to do by studying the artifact. We still know little about it, but what we do know is it's related to the cataclysm that —"

"This is boring," Lapointe interrupted. "What is this? We're just sitting around while people explain things? This is exposition."

Mills took a deep breath. "This is a meeting, general. That's what we do in meetings: explain things."

Lapointe stared at the screen with Asmod on it. "And what exactly are we looking at here? I don't care for this."

Another deep breath. "Again, that's Doctor Asmod, and this is a video conference, so he can hear what you're saying."

"I knew there would be trouble aligning with people so asinine," Asmod grumbled. "Our society is trying to test the limits of science, and your society is trying to test the limits of push-up bras. I'm getting a bit tired of dealing with you dolled-up beauty contestants."

Mills straightened her uniform. "I assure you, we're more than just a bunch of beauty contestants."

"I don't think he meant you," Lapointe said.

Mills did her best to ignore that and continued facing Asmod. "I remind you: Both our nations are threatened by the Loch Collective, so I'm sure we're all quite interested in working together to stop them. And now it looks like they're after this 'artifact' as well. So what exactly is it?"

"As I was trying to say, we don't understand what *exactly* it is. And I'm afraid there are more groups than just the Loch Collective attempting to obtain it. I could try to explain what we do know about the artifact, but I'm pretty sure it would be beyond your bleach-blond brains. Suffice to say, the artifact is very powerful, and whatever you do, do not touch it."

Lapointe rolled her eyes. "So it's a MacGuffin?"

Asmod raised an eyebrow. "A what?"

"It's just something that everyone is after and serves no purpose other than to move the plot forward," Lapointe said. "The only details I've been given are that it's important and everyone wants it. It's a textbook MacGuffin and it's sloppy plotting and I don't like it."

"You don't have to like it," Mills said, trying to keep her temper. "These orders have come from the highest level — perhaps from Astara herself. We need to get that artifact back."

An alarm went off. On screen, they could see red lights flashing around Asmod. "The hyper-intelligent platypi we created have escaped again. I need to handle that. You handle your mistake and get back the remaining bomb and the artifact." The screen cut off.

Mills turned to Lapointe. "I suggest we send the Athenians to hunt down this 'Hellbender.'" Mills looked at the women, who lounged at the back of the room in their stylish, custom-made tactical uniforms. "Ladies, do you think you can handle this matter quickly?"

None of them answered, all still busy on their phones.

"I want more details on this Hellbender group," Lapointe said, now staring quite determinedly at a screen that still displayed profiles of the four.

"There's nothing to them," Mills explained. "They're just some dumb warfs who I think stumbled into this. They've been bounced around a number of different governments in the battles since the Last War, but they always seem to stick together, from what records we have. There's Bryce Worthington, who recently went to re-education for some embezzlement scheme."

"A cunning mind."

"I doubt it," Mills answered. "And there is also Lulu Liu, who has somehow achieved a different mental disorder every time she's gone through standard mental testing."

"Madness, but there's method to it," Lapointe said.

"Maybe," Mills said. "And we have Charlene Marshall. Only one who has scored any sort of competency in testing. Since she's been under the auspices of the Confederacy of Astara, she's sent in numerous applications to join the Athenians."

"I didn't know there were applications to join them," Lapointe said.

"There aren't. It seems she made her own applications, filled them in, and sent them to us. And last and apparently the least, we have Doug Page Fault Error, who has failed at every job ever assigned to him."

"What a horrible name," Lapointe remarked.

"It looks like his last name is glitched or something," Mills said.

"I meant 'Doug.' Don't care for that."

Mills nodded. "Anyway, the point is, these people are nothing and we should handle this matter quickly. They're probably headed to a black market in the Disputed Zone to sell the bomb. So we'll send a force of the Athenians there and be done with this. I doubt they'll be hard to track down."

Lapointe studied the pictures. "No, I think I shall head this effort myself."

"General, I really don't think that's necessary," Mills said. "What we really need from you are plans to finish off the war with Loch. With our surprise victory, they're —"

"I'm bored of that. Loch and his forces are such one-dimensional villains."

"That's because they really are awful people," Mills said. "Much of their society is built around taking pleasure in the suffering of others."

Lapointe nodded. "Yes, we should have made them more sympathetic. But these four — these four who both ruined my plans and double-crossed Loch's forces — they are up to something. And they are my true foes."

"The data we have indicates they're just a bunch of morons," Mills pleaded. "They're really not worth your time."

Lapointe was deep in thought. Mills was now quite sure she had lost her. "No, these are my greatest enemy ... except for her." She pointed to the picture of Charlene Marshall. "She's not very photogenic. We're going to have to recast her."

Mills sighed. "We can't recast any of them."

"Don't be so defeatist. We'll have to use all our resources if we're to outsmart Ryland."

Mills rubbed her head, as she was starting to get a headache. "And who is that?"

Lapointe pointed to Doug. "This one. That's his name now. He's the true mastermind. I'm going to start planning how I'll defeat him, and I'll need you to pack my traveling clothes, batwoman. And get me at least one outfit suitable for combat, as I may need to face Ryland myself." Lapointe turned to leave.

"I'm not your —" Mills started, but Lapointe was already gone. Mills let out a short scream. She didn't know how she'd explain Lapointe abandoning the war effort to her superiors. And of course, she would be getting the blame. She marched over to the Athenians, who were still lounging in the back of the room, oblivious to what had been going on. "The general is getting distracted. That means I need you to handle the matter of this 'Hellbender' as quickly and as decisively as possible."

Gisele, the team leader and setter of unrealistic beauty standards, let out a sigh, still not looking up from her phone. "Sounds boring. Hunting down four warfs. That's beneath us. I'd rather go clubbing or assassinate someone on enemy soil."

"I don't care what you want to do!" Mills shouted. "This is an order. You will retrieve the artifact and eliminate Hellbender so they will no longer be a distraction to the general. Do you understand?"

None of the Athenians looked at Mills or acknowledged her. Infuriated, Mills grabbed Gisele's phone and tossed it against the wall. "Do you understand?" Mills repeated.

Gisele looked at Mills with confusion. "And who even are you?"

"I'M YOUR COMMANDING OFFICER!"

* * *

Bryce sat at the coffee shop. Since it was run by criminals (like pretty much everything in the Disputed Zone), it had plenty of cheap, unfair-trade coffee available. Doug soon approached him. He was no longer in the shadow enforcer uniform but wearing a new T-shirt and jeans. "Look what I got at Walmart!" Doug held up a matching pair of katanas. "It was two for one."

"Can you wield two swords at once?" Bryce asked.

"Well ... no. But I bet if I learned how to draw two swords at once, it would look cool. Anyway, I think these are good for me. Swordsmanship was the one area in combat where I really excelled."

Bryce raised an eyebrow. "Excelled."

"Well, I scored above average."

"Above average?"

"C plus," Doug stated proudly.

Bryce rolled his eyes. "That's not above average. That's the higher end of average. And of course, that's not factoring in grade inflation."

Doug put the swords in his belt. "Well, I don't test well. But I am really good with swords."

Bryce sipped his coffee. "I'm sure your slightly past the mean sword skills will be very useful against all the people out there with machine guns."

Doug's hand gripped the hilt of one as if preparing to draw. "Hey, they could be useful. And can you believe we're really a mercenary group now? This could be cool." He sat down and looked around. "This is a nice coffee shop. I'd really like to work at one some day. I think I'd be good at it."

"Your dreams depress me," Bryce said. "We're about to make quite a large sum of money; can't you at least aim a little higher? Maybe want to own a coffee shop, at least?"

Doug thought about that. "Then I'd have to worry whether we bought enough coffee and have to pay like rent on the place and hire employees and pay them and I'd probably have to fill out forms and stuff ... and I bet I'd mess up those forms and then the government would come after me and then I'd be on the run from the law. And then I might have to start a criminal empire to fight back. And then it's like who do I hire and do we have enough bullets in inventory and it's all the same problems all over again." He shook his head. "No, that doesn't sound fun at all; I'd rather just work at a coffee shop."

Charlene and Lulu walked towards them. Charlene was now in some rather normal-looking jeans and a brown jacket, with the only flash of color her treason scarf. Lulu was in a black leather getup with metal spikes on it. "So that's what you guys are going with to look like fearsome mercenaries?" Bryce asked.

"I got something plain and functional," Charlene said and looked at Lulu. "I didn't see any reason to stand out."

"Plain and functional; that's Charlene." Lulu remarked. "Anyway, I got this from JC Penney's warlords section." Lulu did a twirl. "I think it makes me look both cute and fearsome. That's important since I'm the leader."

"Well, yes," Bryce said, "on the form we put that —"

"I'm the leader," Lulu asserted. "And I think I have a good name for people to call me: Princess Dragon Lady. And look what I got Pickles!" Lulu held up her stuffed bunny, now with dark eyewear. "Sunglasses! You can't see his eyes so you're not sure what he's up to."

Doug smiled. "This is cool. We're really coming together as a mercenary group. After we get our money, we should maybe spend some on advertising so we'll get lots of jobs. I guess the best place for ads would be places people are getting shot at. Is it cheaper or more expensive to buy ad space in a war zone?"

"As soon as we get our money, let's head someplace with actual law and order," Charlene said. She looked at Bryce. "And speaking of money, what is our current financial situation? You didn't exactly give me time to prepare our exit from Calais."

Bryce took a deep breath. "You got some money left over from you guys buying clothes, right?"

Now Charlene shifted uneasily. "With Lapointe claiming credit for the destruction of Loch's air carrier, I thought it was important that I do a visual history page on how I actually brought it down, so I bought some supplies for that." Charlene held up a bag full of card stock, glues, and embellishments. "For being a city full of criminals, they actually had a pretty good selection of glitter glue."

Bryce stared a moment at the bag. "Well, that would be the last of our money."

Lulu plopped down into a chair, clutching Pickles. "Because of Charlene's scrapbooking, we're all going to starve to death."

"You didn't have to get designer sunglasses for your stupid stuffed animal!" Charlene shot back. "And it's important that we document our military victories."

"No one scrapbooks military victories!" Lulu yelled. "Julius Caesar never wasted time cutting out stupid pieces of construction paper!"

"Construction paper hadn't yet been invented in the times of Ancient Rome! And it's card stock!" Charlene countered, emphasizing her killer point with her finger.

Doug quickly stood up, accidentally knocking the thing of sweeteners off the table with one of the scabbards on his belt. "Come on, girls, calm down. We're all going to be all right." He turned to Bryce. "We're going to be all right, right?"

"Absolutely," Bryce said. "Vogel is a big organization and should pay us right away, so no worries."

"When has one of your idiotic plans ever worked out?" Charlene asked.

"My idiotic ones haven't, but this is a smart one," Bryce said. His face went serious. "This really is it, guys. It's our payday. The day you thank the stars that you knew me."

"That better be true," Charlene said, clutching her bag of crafting supplies tightly, "because I don't want to be broke and stuck in some city full of criminals."

"Well, they actually have a generous welfare system here," Bryce said. He then looked away and lowered his voice a little. "It's just, if you enroll in it, you'll be in random drawings where those chosen are forced to fight to the death." He looked back at the others. "There's always trade-offs, you know ... but it won't come to that. This is going to work." Bryce stood up from the table. "We just have to look like proper violent criminals ourselves. Lulu's brand of crazy might actually work for this situation. You, Charlene, you can ..." He stared at her expression. "... scowl at everyone. That's good. And Doug ... well, he'll just need to shut up and be quiet as usual."

"I'm getting good at that!" Doug said as he picked up sweetener packets from the floor.

"And you're going to wear that suit?" Charlene asked, pointing at Bryce's blue suit.

Bryce adjusted his tie. "Everyone respects someone well dressed."

Doug tried to straighten the sweetener packets. "So have we thought any more about what we're going to do with that cube thing I found?"

Bryce shrugged. "It seems important, but we'll need to find out more about it to know who to sell it to and what's a fair price for it. Just keep it safe for now."

Doug nodded and checked his pockets. "Uh-oh ..."

"I have it." Lulu took it out of her purse. "It was looking pretty plain as just this metal cube, so I added some decorations to it." On each side of the cube was stenciled a rabbit. "Now we can play a game with it; you roll it, and you always win because you always roll bunnies."

"So we're still pretending she's the leader?" Charlene asked.

Lulu glared at Charlene. "I *am* the leader." She turned to Bryce and Doug. "Take her away from me and kill her. Do a good job of it, and I'll give you a turn rolling the bunny cube."

Doug snatched the bunny cube from Lulu and put it in his pocket. Lulu scowled at him. "You never thought to put bunnies on it, so I don't know why you're acting like it's yours."

"I don't know about this thing," Doug stated. "I'm not sure selling it is a good idea."

"If there was ever a better idea than 'get more money,' I've never heard it," Bryce said. "Now why don't we get going and get more money. Where we're headed is only a short walk from here."

Bryce led the way through the streets of downtown Disputed Zone. It was a fairly nice area, with only every third building or so boarded up and abandoned. And the prostitutes standing by the streets were pretty classy-looking. They soon came to a large, opulent-looking building with a sign out front that said "Vogel Criminal Enterprises Disputed Zone Headquarters. Murder. Smuggling. Racketeering."

"They just come out and say it?" Charlene asked.

Bryce shrugged. "It's a city of criminals; no reason to be coy."

They went inside, where a young receptionist smiled at them while simultaneously reaching for something under her desk. "Can I help you?"

"We're looking for Tara Skinner," Bryce said.

"I'll let her know you're here," the receptionist said. She then looked at Lulu. "Nice outfit."

Lulu glowered at her. "So much as look at me funny, and I'll stab you through your eye with one of your pens."

The receptionist's eyes widened and she seemed to tighten her grip on whatever was under the desk. Doug took Lulu aside. "That seemed a little much."

"If we're going to impress violent criminals, we have to be tough," Lulu responded.

"There's tough and then there's psychotic."

"Well, I like them both," Lulu said.

Tara walked into the lobby and smiled broadly upon seeing the four. "Hey, guys! Great to see you!"

"We're ready to conduct business," Bryce said.

Lulu stared down the receptionist. "As long as no one gets in our way."

"Just no double-crosses," Doug warned her. "People double-cross us all the time and we're kind of sick of it." He noticed Bryce glaring at him and remembered the "no talking," but it was a bit late for it. "Because when people do that, we have to murder everyone. Which we've done, many times. And it's not fun. Because of the blood splatter. We have to buy all new clothing."

"This is going to be really straightforward," Tara assured them. "No blood splatter."

"Well, I'm sure everything here is above board," Charlene stated dryly.

"Ha!" Tara chuckled. "You're the funny one, aren't you? Anyway, just follow me."

They went with Tara into what looked like a large garage filled with many tough-looking members of Vogel. They soon noticed something familiar.

"Is that our truck?" Charlene exclaimed, as sitting in the garage was the vehicle that very much looked like the one they had stolen from the research facility.

"Yeah, it sure is," Tara said. "I just went ahead and brought it here to help move things along."

"But we registered it as our stolen property," Bryce said. "You shouldn't have been able to take it."

"Well, I ... sorta lifted the claim ticket from you while you were at my apartment," Tara explained. "Again, just to help move things along." She turned to a large bald man standing near the truck. "Hey, Delgado!" She turned back to Bryce and his friends. "That's Delgado; he's in charge at this branch, so be on your best behavior." Tara ran over to Delgado before Bryce could say another word to her.

Delgado was a massive, fearsome-looking man, the kind of person who if you walked in on him, it would not be surprising to see him beating someone to death. He watched as two of his men took the reality imploder bomb out of the truck with an air of authority, though, that made it seem more probable that you'd walk in on him monitoring one of his underlings beating someone to death.

"I got it for you just like I said," Tara told him proudly.

"You sure did," Delgado said. "And after what happened at Calais, it's going to be very highly sought after. Good job."

Bryce slowly approached Delgado, the others reluctantly following, "So," Bryce said to Delgado, "with you so happy with the merchandise, why don't we resolve the issue of payment right away?"

Delgado stared at Bryce and his powder-blue suit and then looked back at Tara. "Who's this dandy?"

"Oh, he's just with these dumb warfs I tricked into bringing the bomb here." Tara motioned to the rest of Hellbender. "I'll handle them." She led Bryce back to the others and whispered. "Just play along and act really angry I tricked you."

Bryce looked like he was about to say something, but he was apparently rendered speechless. Lulu stepped forward to address Delgado. "Hey!" she shouted. "We brought the merchandise here and we demand the money. I am Princess Dragon

69

Lady, leader of Hellbender — a group of violent psychopaths you do not want to cross! Now, pay up, or I'll gut that little floozy right there." Lulu motioned to Tara. "That's right: I'll cut open her belly and pull her intestines out. It will be really excessive. You won't be able to eat soon after seeing it. She certainly won't be able to."

Delgado stared at the group with confusion. "Hellbender?"

"It's a type of salamander," Doug explained.

Delgado raised an eyebrow. "A salamander?"

"That's like a lizard ... but wetter," Doug said.

"I know what a salamander is!" Delgado shouted. "But why would you name yourself after one?"

Doug looked confused, like maybe that was a trick question. "Because it has a really cool name."

"You're talking again, Doug," Bryce whispered.

"They're starting to annoy me," Delgado told Tara. "Any concerns with them?"

"No, they're not even a properly registered criminal group," Tara said. "They put down Rook as their sponsor, but I don't think he knows about them."

Delgado laughed. "And who cares about Rook? Get rid of them."

"Will do," Tara answered.

Charlene leapt at Tara, grabbing her by the jacket and putting a switchblade to her throat. "Do not think you get to cross us and just walk away from that."

"Good job; you're really selling it," Tara whispered to Charlene. "You might want to tense for this next part, though."

"What next —"

In a quick motion, Tara knocked the knife from Charlene's hand, then punched Charlene in the face, sending her to the ground.

"Hey!" Doug shouted, drawing a katana and pointing it at Tara. Delgado pulled out a gun and aimed it at Doug's head. Doug, after a moment's hesitation, dropped the sword. It really didn't seem that useful against guns.

The rest of Vogel's thugs started surrounding them.

"So I guess we should just kill these warfs and be done with it," Delgado said.

Tara shrugged. "We have enough to do without body cleanup. These four are insignificant. Let's just beat them up a bit for wasting our time and then send them on their way."

Delgado nodded. "All right." He motioned to the thugs around him. "Let's rough them up a bit."

Tara walked over to Bryce and smiled, giving him a thumbs-up. "Did you see that? I saved your guys' lives. Pretty cool, huh?"

"Well, uh —"

Tara socked Bryce in the gut as a dozen more thugs descended on the group. "Going to have to help beat you guys up for appearances, though."

"As many have suspected, it was you — humanity — who were the source of the conflict. Again, the reasons will be hard to understand, but suffice to say I recognized there is something wrong with you. Something wrong with all of you. And in my battle against creation, that is what I've exploited."

CHAPTER 8

The four sat quietly in the diner, checking their bruises and cuts. Finally, Bryce spoke. "I think Tara might have double-crossed us."

Lulu nodded. "There is evidence to back up that assertion." Lulu smiled. "Anyway, that wasn't so bad. I told them, 'Not in the face, please,' and they were nice enough to not hit me in the face. Just worked the gut. A lot. I'm in quite a bit of pain. But I'm still cute."

"I told them 'Not in the face!' too," Doug said, nursing a swollen eye. "And then they did nothing but hit me in the face. Well, sometimes in the groin."

"Sorry, Doug, there's just something about you that makes people like to hit you," Bryce said. He had two small bruises on his face but otherwise looked fine. "You're really good at taking a beating, though."

Doug looked at the reflection of his unrecognizable face in the window. "I don't like being good at that."

Bryce looked at Charlene, who clutched a bruise and stared off into space. "They didn't really go easy on you, did they?"

Charlene just glared at him.

"She fought back," Lulu said, sighing.

"Well ... that's a mistake," Bryce said. "If you know you're going to get a beating, just take the beating. No use fighting against what you can't change."

"Thanks, great advice on being beaten by thugs," Charlene growled. "So we've gone from getting kicked around by uncaring governments to getting kicked around by criminals. Great job, Bryce."

"I'm sorry; it was ... supposed to be our big payday," an increasingly flustered Bryce said. "We were all going to make out big-time from this. And we did everything right, but ..." He ran out of words and almost looked ready to scream. Or cry.

"Hey, we're alive," Doug told him. "Let's be happy about that."

"Be happier if someone else weren't alive," Lulu remarked.

"I guess Tara figured out you were using her," Charlene said to Bryce. "She must be a bit smarter than the usual bimbos you sleep with."

Bryce rubbed his temple. "I never actually slept with her. She said she wanted to take things slow — what for, I can't possibly fathom — but I'm pretty sure we were going to ... after the deal ..."

Charlene laughed. "Oh, so *she* was using *you*! This would be funny if it weren't also happening to us."

Doug chuckled. "That is kind of funny." He then winced. "Yeah, but not too funny because I've been punched so many times."

"So I got tricked," Bryce said. "I guess it happens, but —"

"And how is your hair not even slightly messed up?" Lulu asked.

Bryce lightly touched his hair. "We're focusing on the wrong things."

The waitress walked by their table and looked at them impatiently. "So are you guys going to order anything or is it just more waters?"

"More waters for now, Betty," Lulu said. "We're still deciding."

"It's Daphne." Daphne pointed to her name tag that said "Daphne." "So, did you guys recently get beaten up or something?"

"Yes, that's approximately what happened," Lulu answered.

"Did you like it?" Daphne asked.

"No, beatings are never fun," Doug said. "They hurt, and they are humiliating."

"Then you might want to take a look at that sign." Daphne pointed to a sign on the window that said "Non-paying customers who waste our time will be taken outside and beaten with a sock full of salt shakers."

Lulu glared at Daphne. "Fine. We weren't enjoying the ambience of your knockoff Denny's anyway. Come on." Lulu led the group outside.

"Now we've been kicked out of a diner," Charlene grumbled as they walked down the street. "Things just keep getting better for us." The sun was setting, and being out at night in the Disputed Zone was a notoriously bad idea, a time when the bigger muggers would prey with impunity on the smaller muggers.

Lulu wrote in a little notebook. "Betty is now on my revenge list. Man, I have a big revenge list; I don't know how I'll ever get the time to get revenge against everyone in it. But if you don't get revenge on everyone on your list, that's how you end up a ghost after you die — stuck haunting this world until your revenge is done. I read that in a science magazine."

Doug noticed some large lettering spray-painted on a nearby wall. "I guess the RALFS are here too," Doug said, pointing to it. It said "RESIST TYRANNY."

Bryce scoffed. "What are they doing here? There's no oppressive government for those warfs to mindlessly rebel against. There's just organized criminals — people who take what isn't theirs and push everyone around. And that's way different than government because ..." Bryce thought a while. And then a while longer. "They don't have domes and pillars on their headquarters."

They headed into a nearby park, where it looked like most of the trees had been stolen. "I don't know if they're as bad as government, but everyone sure is mean here," Doug said as he sat on a stump. "I know it's like a city of criminals, but just because you're a criminal doesn't mean you have to be mean. If you already steal from people, it seems you should make up for that by being extra nice otherwise."

Charlene kicked a piece of metal sticking out of the sidewalk, all that was left of a stolen bench. "We need to be more mean. We're stranded here and penniless."

"It's not all bad." Doug took out the metal cube with the bunnies stenciled on it. "We still have this, which is ... something. Maybe important."

"I bet if we roll bunnies on it," Lulu said, "everything will turn out all right."

"We'll only know if it's important if someone offers us money for it," Bryce said. "But I'm not really sure how you make inquiries on purchasers for metal cubes. But, hey, we're in a town full of criminals — you know, innovators. There has to be some money-making opportunities. I was thinking —"

"No!" Charlene interrupted. "No more of your idiotic plans. People are just going to see you all and say, 'There's a bunch of losers I can cheat and then beat up.' I might even be better off on my own. I have actual combat skills; I can find some work with an actual mercenary group."

"But Charlene," Doug pleaded, rising from his stump, "this place is full of criminals who will just murder you. Because no one likes being around you. You annoy everyone you meet. I really mean it."

Charlene glared at Doug and began curling her fist.

"I'm just saying it because I don't want you to be murdered!"

"We have no reason to pretend we need to stick together anymore," Charlene said. "There's no more government over us forcing us to be around each other, so it's time to part ways."

"I bet I could do pretty well on my own," Lulu said. "I'm a cute girl. It's easy for me to make money."

Bryce started to speak.

"Not that way!" Lulu shouted at him. "Anyway, I think I will go on my own, because I don't want Bryce and Doug to just mooch off me."

Bryce scoffed. "I'm not going to mooch. I can figure out more ways to get money than you. Let's all go our separate ways and then meet back here in a week to see who is richer." He motioned to Charlene. "Or has been murdered."

Doug grabbed Bryce and Lulu. "No, we're not splitting up!" Doug shouted. "We're Hellbender!"

Charlene rolled her eyes. "That's just a form we filled out."

Doug jumped up on a stump to stand over everyone. "An official form! One that said we're a team! And we need to stand together. Think about it: This time Bryce's plan almost actually worked. But Vogel took advantage of us, didn't pay us, and beat us up. And as team Hellbender, we can't let that injustice go unanswered. That would go against everything we quite possibly stand for. It's just like the paint said: We need to resist tyranny."

"Very inspiring," Bryce said, "but I don't think we should take suicidal actions like fighting Vogel on the advice of random vandalism. Vogel is the biggest criminal group out there. They have headquarters throughout the world. Even in Antarctica. They've cornered the black market on penguin eggs."

Doug jumped down from the stump and grabbed Bryce by the shoulder. "See, you know a lot about them. That gives us an advantage."

"But you saw how many people they have and how well armed they are," Charlene stated.

Doug nodded. "So you say you're okay getting kicked around because you're too scared to do anything?"

Charlene scowled. "I didn't say that. I do want to get revenge. And I want to gut that Tara like a fish."

"We can gut her like all sorts of things," Doug encouraged. "We just have to work together. And planning assaults like this is right up your alley."

"It's a lot to plan," Charlene said. "For one, they took all our guns."

"And the swords I got from Walmart," Doug added as he paced. "And those were authentic katanas made in China ... which is pretty near Japan."

"But they didn't take this!" Charlene said, holding up a bag. It was her crafting supplies. "I can use this to map out a battle plan."

Lulu groaned. "We're going to follow glitter-glued instructions to certain death."

Charlene looked through her bag of card stock. "I can do this. I know I can use this to come up with something. We just have to figure out how to get some guns first."

"I know I saw lots of guns somewhere recently." Doug thought for a second. "Oh yeah, it was at the Vogel headquarters. They have lots of guns."

"Not exactly helpful to us," Bryce said.

"Perhaps I can use my feminine wiles to get a gun off one of them," Lulu said. She then stated in a sultry voice, "Hi. I'm a woman. Want to imagine doing things to me?"

"This is coming together!" Doug announced excitedly. "We have Bryce's knowledge about Vogel. We have Charlene planning how to do this ... in a creative fashion. We have Lulu ready to use her feminine wiles. I can carry things as needed. We're going to be a real mercenary group. Working together!"

"With me as the leader!" Lulu said.

"Yes, that's what the form we filled out said," Doug admitted.

Bryce nodded. "I'm in. After all we've been through, we deserve our payday. And I deserve to hurt people who won't give me my money."

"I'm in too," Charlene said, already cutting out pieces of paper, "as long as you will all actually listen to me this time."

"I don't know what Charlene just said but I'm in too," Lulu stated.

"Great!" Doug exclaimed. He put out his hand. "Now let's all put our hands in the center and then lift them up and shout 'Go Hellbender!'"

The other three just stared at him. "No one is doing that," Bryce finally said.

Doug lifted his arm up. "Go Hellbender!"

"Now, many portray me as a fool. I rose up against the all-powerful Creator — I was destined to fail. But on the contrary, I was destined to win. Because I had one advantage over Him. I can compromise."

CHAPTER 9

Doug took a deep breath. "Okay. I'm ready. So what's my job again?"

"You're going to knock out the receptionist," Bryce told him as the two approached the Vogel headquarters.

"Be nice if I had a taser," Doug said.

"Well, you don't. So just punch her in the face really hard. Let's not overthink this."

Doug looked at the blue jumpsuit he was wearing. "Are you sure some maintenance guys don't need these?"

"Not as much as we do," Bryce said.

"We're already going to have this criminal enterprise angry at us, so we don't want like some union of maintenance workers vowing vengeance against us as well. They might have alliances with other unions. We could have bakers after us, too."

Bryce sighed. "Let's keep focused on punching a receptionist."

"And you're sure she won't recognize us?" Doug asked.

Bryce put a breathing mask on Doug. "Just let me do the talking. I will woo the receptionist with my considerable charm, and when she is sufficiently distracted, you wallop her."

Doug frowned underneath his mask. "Can't you punch her?"

Bryce looked shocked. "You're asking me to woo a woman and then punch her in the face? I can't believe you'd suggest such a thing; I'm a *gentleman*! Now, let's stop fretting about our part; I just hope the girls are ready."

"Charlene has a good plan," Doug assured him. "She loves planning this military stuff. Lulu is going to use her feminine wiles and Charlene will use her ... well, I assume she'll find a two-by-four or something — and they will obtain some guns and come in from the garage. It will be a two-pronged attack. These jerks won't know what hit them. But we'll tell them what hit them. We'll tell them it was Hellbender."

"I don't care who they think we are as long as they give us our money. Come on."

They entered the building, but the receptionist wasn't at her desk. Instead there was a sign saying she'd be back soon. "Guess I can't punch her," Doug said. "What's the next step?"

"Charlene made you a list, you know," Bryce reminded him.

"Oh yeah." Doug pulled the list out of his pocket. It was pretty crammed in there since it was made from thick blue card stock. The steps on the list were written in a few different colors, with cut-out images from magazines illustrating some of them. "Next step is …" Doug found the item next to a picture of a box cutter. "Slit receptionist's throat." Doug rolled his eyes. "Come on, Charlene." He looked at the next item, which had a cartoon-looking gun next to it. "Oh yeah, Charlene was pretty sure the receptionist had a gun, so I'm supposed to take it."

Doug leaped over the desk.

"That didn't seem necessary," Bryce commented. "You could have just walked around it."

"We're in assault mode; assault mode means you don't let desks tell you in what direction you go." Underneath the desk, Doug found a holstered firearm and took it. "It's a sawed-off shotgun. And it's loaded. You can't leave a loaded gun just sitting out; that's bad gun safety."

Bryce took the shotgun from Doug. "You were right to want to punch her in the face." Bryce looked around. "Now we just need to get someone else to come in here and we'll take his gun so we'll have two. Let's first see how the girls are doing." Bryce talked into the communicator at his collar. "We're inside with a shotgun; how goes it?"

"Just come into the garage," Charlene answered.

"But … uh …"

"Just come."

Bryce crept toward the garage with Doug following. Peeking through the door, they saw numerous bodies lying everywhere inside, each covered in blood. Severed limbs lay all about them. "Well, this is oddly familiar," Bryce remarked.

"What the hell is going on?" Charlene demanded. She was followed by Lulu, who was in a bear costume, head currently off.

"This is baffling," Bryce said, then looked at Lulu. "And what are you doing?"

"Charlene was making fun of me for using feminine wiles," Lulu said. "And I was all like, 'You just wish you had some.' And then she said that if I didn't have feminine wiles, I'd be completely useless. And I told her I have lots of other wiles than feminine. And she scoffed. And then we had a real short slap fight. And then I saw this bear costume in a storefront. And …" She took another look at all the dead bodies. "Know what? I'll just write the whole story up on my blog later if you're interested."

Doug took some cautious glances at the bodies. "Looked like they were all cut to death."

"Thank you, CSI," Bryce said.

"I wonder who did it, though," Doug stated as he looked around to make sure nothing else was in the room. "Or what."

"I wonder if it's the Terrorists," Charlene said as she looked around cautiously as well.

"What terrorists?" Doug asked.

"You know, that group that just call themselves the Terrorists," Charlene said. "They do terror attacks every so often but never seem to have any demands."

"They seem fun," Lulu remarked. "I wonder how you join them."

"Since this keeps happening to places where we're going to go," Doug said, "maybe one of us did it." A thought struck him. "We've always had lots of weird government training — maybe one of those implanted something in our brains and one of us is blacking out and then going into super-soldier mode and killing everyone with ..." Doug thought a moment and then noticed something. "Ooh, my swords!" He picked up his two katanas, lying in the corner of the room.

"That's stupid, Doug," Bryce said. "Then again, best theory we have so far."

Doug pumped his fist in the air in victory.

"The truck we took is still here," Charlene said. "Might as well take it back and also some of the weapons lying around."

"And pretty gold things!" Lulu exclaimed, pulling a bloody gold watch off someone.

Bryce slipped a ring off a severed hand. "I'm all for looting the dead; it's the natural order of things." Bryce looked around. "The reality imploder bomb is gone, though. Either delivered, or whoever did this took it." He took another look at the bodies. "Anyone see Tara among them?"

"We're not the census," Charlene said. She picked up a gun from one of the dead bodies. "Let's just assume she got hers and leave inventorying the dead for others. We need to get out of here, as we can't really be certain whoever did this isn't coming back."

Doug picked up a gun as well. "Man, we never get good stuff unless it's covered in blood. One of these days —"

They heard a sound. They all turned to see a figure entering the garage. It was the receptionist, and in her hands were a number of bags from a local sandwich shop. She looked around with confusion and fear.

Lulu took a couple steps toward the receptionist and growled, "This is what happens when you mess with Hellbender!"

The receptionist screamed, dropped the bags, and ran away.

"And now we have a free lunch," Bryce said. "A string of good luck, I'd say."

"God is shackled by His own standards: He is good and can't be anything other than good. And while many think of me as evil, it's more correct to say I am all things. I am capable of evil. But I am capable of good, too. Nothing stops me from either."

CHAPTER 10

Tara watched as the reality imploder bomb was loaded into a metal crate at the docks among boxes of counterfeit designer jeans. "We should get a pretty penny for this," Delgado remarked as the doors of the crate were closed.

"And then I get my share, right?" Tara asked.

Delgado looked at Tara and smiled slightly. "Yeah, you'll get yours. You'll get exactly what's coming to you."

Tara raised an eyebrow. "Huh?"

Delgado grimaced and then made his face more normal. "Sorry, I'm so used to threatening people, I sometimes can't turn it off. But yes, you'll get a percent of the sale. You did a really good job for some warf-girl."

Tara gave him a thumbs-up.

"One more thing, though," Delgado said. "I've heard rumblings about something else people are looking for. Did you see if those warf-idiots you tricked had —"

"THEY'RE ALL DEAD!" someone screamed. It was the headquarters receptionist, McKenna, running toward them in full panic.

"Who is dead?" Delgado asked.

McKenna was sobbing and breathing rapidly. "Everyone!" she cried. "They're monsters! They're not human!" She glanced around in fright. "They could be coming here next!"

"Who?" Delgado demanded. "What are you talking about?"

McKenna just bawled and mumbled something.

"Maybe I can help," Tara offered. She grabbed McKenna firmly. "Get a hold of yourself!" Tara yelled, then slapped McKenna across the face.

Delgado pulled Tara away from McKenna. "What the hell?"

"They do that on TV all the time," Tara explained. "I thought it was worth a try."

"Now I'm panicked and my face hurts!" McKenna sobbed.

"Just take a deep breath and tell us what happened," Delgado instructed.

McKenna stopped crying long enough to slowly inhale and exhale. "Hellbender. Hellbender ripped apart everyone at headquarters."

"What? Those jokers?" Delgado asked. "Are you sure?"

"They were there, gloating over the bodies," McKenna said, barely holding it together. "They had demon eyes. The leader, Princess Dragon Lady, tried to kill me, but I ran away."

Tara checked her phone. "No one from our gang I follow on Twitter has tweeted anything in the last twenty minutes — and a lot of them are chatterboxes. They're probably all dead."

Delgado turned to Tara. "I thought you said Hellbender was a bunch of harmless losers."

Tara shrugged. "I thought they were. But we warfs are known to have violent tendencies. You saw how I just hit McKenna."

Delgado grabbed Tara by her coat. "You better not have gotten us into something, or you'll get exactly what's coming to you."

"This time you mean that as a threat, right?" Tara asked.

"Yes."

* * *

The fence looked carefully at the watch. "This has blood on it."

"That's how you know it's valuable," Lulu explained.

"Fine. The money has moved to your account. Nice doing business with you. Hope you don't get murdered in an alley somewhere."

Lulu batted her eyes at the fence and said a rather perfunctory, "Thanks. Hope you don't get murdered in an alley, too." She then joined the other three, who were perusing the goods in the store. "Yay! We're not completely poor any more!"

Charlene frowned as they walked out of Honest Harry's Stolen Goods Fencing. "Can't believe we're reduced to looting dead bodies for money."

Lulu crossed her eyes and said in a mocking, gruff voice, "Look at me! I'm Charlene! Everything we do makes me angry! And that Asian girl is a hundred times more attractive than me!"

Charlene put a finger right in Lulu's face. "That's not what I sound like and that does not accurately reflect my beliefs!"

"So what are we doing now?" Doug asked between bites of one of the sandwiches the Vogel receptionist dropped. He felt kind of weird eating a sandwich meant for a dead man, but it was a good one with just the right amount of mayo. "We still have the bunny cube. I really think we need to find out what that thing is about."

Bryce nodded as they walked past the other storefronts in the fence district. "I'm not sure who we talk to to find out about that; definitely need some information before we proceed if we're not going to get screwed again."

"Satan would probably know about it," Doug said. "But I don't know how to get in contact with him."

"We could try a ouija board," Lulu suggested.

"We need more time to figure things out," Bryce said. "I hate to suggest it, but we could head back to Calais. They'll probably put us in re-education — I think we could all manage to get through that in a couple hours — and maybe we can work the whole blowing up that air carrier into our favor. Whatever happens, they'll eventually forget about us — as always happens with us warfs — and then we can plan something new."

"I am not slinking back to those people!" Charlene shouted. "I will only head to Calais if it's to kill General Lapointe!"

Bryce rolled his eyes. "No money in that."

"And what is there money in?" Charlene demanded. "Selling stolen bombs to criminal organizations? Where do you get off acting like you know anything? When have you ever had a plan that wasn't a huge failure?"

"Well, uh ..." Bryce stammered. "I think I had a few ideas that almost ... uh ..."

"Wait," Lulu interrupted, "are we getting lectured on bad ideas from the girl who spent her whole life trying to suck up to all the people who hate us warfs? How'd that work out?"

That gave Charlene pause for a moment, but she put a fierce gaze on Lulu while stepping toward her. "Are you expressing an actual opinion? What happened to your 'I'm crazy and am detached from everything!' nonsense?"

Lulu stood up straight, keeping her eyes locked on Charlene. "You want to see crazy, Char, keep getting in my face. I bite."

Doug got between the two and pushed them apart. "Everybody, calm down. Come on; we're actually doing pretty good. I mean, we did two successful missions as Hellbender the mercenary group. We successfully stole a bomb from a military facility — and sorta defeated a whole invading army, too. And then when we didn't get paid, we struck back and ..." Doug held up his sandwich. "... that was also kind of successful."

"The only reason either of those were 'successful,'" Charlene said, "was because something came and slaughtered everyone who would have been in our way."

Doug thought for a second. "Really seems like we should be trying to figure out what that's all about."

Bryce shrugged. "No money in figuring things out ... unless you get a research grant."

"Anyway," Doug continued, "Bryce had mentioned how governments hire people like us, so maybe we can get some paid mercenary work now that we have weapons and a vehicle again."

"Yay!" Lulu cheered. "It's time to monetize me stabbing people!"

Charlene sighed and looked at Bryce. "Can you actually get us one of these mercenary jobs?"

"Well ... yes," Bryce said. "I mean, there should be plenty. So many of the governments have treaties right now, but they all hate and distrust each other. So they hire mercenary groups to do their dirty work and keep some separation. It's actually a big growth industry."

"So what do we do?" Doug asked.

Bryce hesitated. "Well, for that, we'll need some good contacts."

"And don't you have some contacts from all your wheeling and dealing?" Charlene said. "Or is this just more of your bluster?"

Bryce looked indignant. "I have contacts. Well, a contact. But a good one. I can check with him to see if we can get some mercenary work lined up. Yeah, I can do that." Bryce took out his phone and typed in a message. "There; did it. This should work out fine."

Lulu patted him on the shoulder. "I got a great feeling about this. Your shiftiness is putting me at ease."

Bryce looked at his phone and his eyes grew wide. "Oh, already heard back. He says he really wants to meet with us. In fact, he says he sent people to find us and they are closing in now and ..." Bryce looked up, and approaching them was the older thug Driscoll and his protégé Candy, who had accosted them back at their apartment in Calais.

"Not these two again," Charlene growled as her hand moved to where a pistol was under her jacket.

Bryce held Charlene's arm. "Let's be all smiles this time. Trust me."

"Hello again," Driscoll said in a bored tone.

"So, should we once again address Candy and ignore you?" Doug asked.

"No, you can address me this time," Driscoll said. "Candy is now learning from watching. So why don't we all come all peaceful-like and she doesn't learn anything too special right now."

"You're going to do as we say," Candy growled, "or we're going to —"

"I got this," Driscoll interrupted.

"Are you going to murder us when we get to wherever we're going?" Lulu asked.

"That's not the current plan," Driscoll answered.

"So ... no?"

Driscoll shrugged. "I don't make promises I can't necessarily keep."

* * *

83

Driscoll and Candy took them to the downtown area of the Disputed Zone, where things were just a little bit fancier while still keeping its lawless criminal charm. It was the job of the Disputed Zone Chamber of Commerce to make sure all businesses contributed to the same ambience that gave the Disputed Zone its unique character.

Eventually they came to an unassuming door labeled "Rook's Criminal Enterprises." Inside was a sparsely decorated little room with a number of rough criminal types lounging around some tables. On a couch near the rear sat Rook, who wore a black trench coat that made him look somewhere between fancy and threatening. Upon seeing them, he stood up and regarded them all with a friendly, charming smile — though his eyes suggested less than friendly intentions for them. "Hellbender!"

"Yes, and I'm the leader," Lulu stated proudly. "Princess Dragon Lady — they call me the Hello Kitty of crime."

Rook raised an eyebrow. "I don't know what that's supposed to mean." He then stared at Charlene. "Hey, you're that girl who wouldn't pick things up!"

"I don't take orders from criminals!" Charlene responded.

"As I explained," Rook said, trying to be calm, as he ran a hand through his slicked-back hair, "it wasn't about taking orders from criminals; it was about common courtesy. When you make a mess, you clean it up." Rook took a deep breath. "But let's not get off-topic." He looked at Bryce. "So, have you come to pay me my money?"

"Well, that was the intention," Bryce said. "See, we had a deal that would have gotten us the money to pay you, but Delgado of the local Vogel headquarters treated us dishonestly."

Rook nodded. "So you slaughtered them all."

"Yep," Lulu responded. "You have to be firm with people."

Rook looked at Driscoll. "So do I need to be worried these four might decide to kill all of us?"

Driscoll shook his head. "There's no way these idiots killed everyone at the Vogel headquarters."

"Yeah," Rook said. "They kind of just look like harmless goofballs to me."

"Mostly harmless," Driscoll said. "I'm pretty sure princess there had a gun in a stuffed animal when I last talked to them."

Lulu looked shocked. "I won't stand here and listen to you cast aspersions on Pickles! He's a fine, upstanding member of the community with no provable ties to murder and extortion!"

Candy advanced toward Lulu. "Why don't you be quiet before I —"

Charlene slapped Candy in the face. Candy backed off and started crying. "Ow! That really stung!"

Rook rolled his eyes. "Toughen up, Candy. Just hit her back."

Candy stared a moment at Charlene. "She pulled a gun on me the other day."

Rook looked at Charlene. "You're making messes and then you're slapping my people — what am I supposed to do with you?"

"Maybe get to the point," Charlene said. "You seem to have some intentions with us."

Rook scowled. "Oh, I'm sorry; I didn't realize we are in such a rush. I don't even know your guys' names other than Bryce here ... and I guess 'Princess Dragon Lady.'"

Charlene scowled back. "It's Charlene."

"Okay, Charlene," Rook said. "And I can tell you're a firecracker." He looked a moment at Doug, who had accidentally gotten his hand stuck in a chair back and was trying to free it. "And I guess I don't know who you are ... then again, from the look of you, you don't seem worth taking the time to know."

Bryce nodded. "Very astute."

"Hey!" Doug exclaimed, finally wresting his hand free.

"So, yeah, if we want to get to the point," Rook said. "The point is I'm in the starter stages of a criminal enterprise. I mean, you see this place; not very big — but good location. A good starter, but I'm not the level of Vogel — you know, the guys you allegedly slaughtered. I have a nice crew, though, and I'm paying the big bucks for Driscoll over here because he has a lot of experience and can train the others to get us all looking nice and professional."

"Like he's doing with Candy?" Charlene asked.

Rook grimaced. He came closer to the four and whispered, "There's a lot of regulations on sex discrimination. Now, all criminal organizations are supposed to be fifty percent female, but it's harder to find good, violent female criminals than the bureaucrats who made that rule were thinking. Again, that's why I have Driscoll to train people — get the most out of what I have to work with." He looked over Charlene and Lulu. "We're still hiring, by the way, if either of you two ladies are interested." Rook backed away. "But what am I saying; you already have a group." Rook picked up a tablet and showed it to them. On it was the form they had filled out. "You're Hellbender, and it says here I'm sponsoring you."

"We haven't settled on that name," Charlene said.

"Why?" Rook asked. "I kinda like that name. You sound like a rock band."

"That's what I've always said!" Doug exclaimed.

"Anyway, the point is I don't remember sponsoring any new criminal group called Hellbender."

"Sorry about that," Bryce said. "We didn't have time to run it by you, but this was all about getting the money we owe you, so I didn't think you'd mind."

Rook smiled. "Yeah, that's great, you thinking of me."

"By the way," Bryce continued, "there still is a form you need to fill out to make that sponsorship official."

Rook just stared long and hard at Bryce for a moment until Bryce got a little uncomfortable. "What was the money you borrowed from me for?"

"It was an investment," Bryce explained, "in a very worthy business. One that helped the world. I found a niche selling discount carbon credits."

Rook grimaced. "You were selling fraudulent carbon credits?"

Bryce snorted. "Fraudulent? They're already made-up nonsense."

"But you weren't planting trees or anything?"

Bryce vigorously shook his head. "Oh, no. I don't want to handle trees; they're filthy. Always covered in bugs or squirrels."

"Then what did you need the money for in this scam?"

"Office space," Bryce said, "to make it all look official. And printers. People want their carbon credits on paper — something they can hold. It makes it feel more real."

"Doesn't that just kill more trees?" Candy asked.

"I told you, I don't like trees!" Bryce snapped at her. He calmed down and turned back to Rook. "But anyway, the government found out and seized everything. You know how investments are. We're all heartbroken about it."

Rook looked at Charlene, Lulu, and Doug. "You guys seem to be friends with this Bryce, but you'd admit he's a bit of a weasel, right?"

"Yes," Charlene said.

Lulu nodded. "Actual weasels find him too weaselly."

"He's not literally a weasel," Doug said. "Because he's a primate."

"And now we're arriving at my point," Rook said, looking at Charlene. "You wanted the point, right?"

"Yes. Very much."

"Alright, Firecracker, here it is: As a start-up criminal organization, respect is very important. But Bryce here borrowed money from us and has not paid it back. And now he, along with you three, just put me down as your sponsor without getting my permission. Now, if I'm getting abused like this by a few warfs, are people going to respect me? Are they? Candy, what do you think?"

"It kinda makes you look like a chump," Candy said.

"See? Candy gets it," Rook continued. "So I obviously have to do something about this, or people are going to say 'Rook is a pushover. Don't worry about him; you can walk all over him.'"

"Well," Bryce said, "you can't let peer pressure push you into —"

"Shut up," Rook shouted. "So what's to do?" He looked at Driscoll. "Do you think publicly killing Bryce would be an effective solution to this?"

"It would deter others from treating you likewise," Driscoll said.

"And I guess I could just beat up the rest of you for being with him." Driscoll looked them over. "Though I guess someone else already beat me to that. So, what do you think of this solution?"

Bryce looked nearly ready to panic. Lulu spoke first. "So how much would you pay us to kill Bryce?"

"I'm not killing Bryce!" Doug said. "No killing each other, even for money. That's the Hellbender code."

"Let's not be hasty on any decision until we've heard how much he'll pay," Lulu answered.

"I'm not paying anything for that," Rook said. "He's not worth anything to me. But it's good you guys seem to want a job, because now we arrive at our not-killing-Bryce option."

"It's good you explore lots of options," Bryce said, looking a bit relieved. "That shows you —"

"Shut up. Anyway, this whole situation in Calais has thrown us for a loop. Everyone expected it to fall to Loch's forces — something that would have changed the whole dynamic there for criminal enterprises — and also the reason we got the hell out. But then General Lapointe somehow destroyed their carrier."

"We did that, not her!" Charlene shouted. Out of her bag, she pulled the scrapbooking page she put together about the air carrier, including a picture of it, a diagram of the reality imploder bomb circuitry from Wikipedia, and plenty of decorative brads.

Rook raised an eyebrow. "What am I even looking at?"

"I think it's pretty easy to understand." Charlene pointed at the glued-on pictures. "There are arrows to follow. This shows exactly how I destroyed that carrier."

Rook looked even more confounded, but eventually just laughed. "Yeah, of course you guy blew up their carrier. You're Hellbender. It probably saw you and exploded in fear. Anyway, the Confederacy of Astara still rules Calais, which means I need to get back to my regular smuggling operations, but I'm a little short-staffed. So now I need some other people to make a shipment — perhaps some people who know Calais and are still technically citizens of the Confederacy and should get in with no problem."

"What are we going to smuggle?" Doug asked.

"Not really the issue for you guys," Rook said. "But I will show you." He led them over to a crate in the corner of the room. Inside were blocks of white powder.

Bryce lifted an eyebrow. "Cocaine? But that's not illegal in the Confederacy of Astara as long as you're using it for creative purposes."

"I know," Rook said. "So that's why I hid a much more illegal drug inside each block of cocaine."

Rook handed Bryce a small, rectangular package. Bryce opened it up, and inside were little white and brown cylinders. "What are these?"

"Cigarettes."

Bryce gasped and dropped the package. "Those things kill you and everyone around you!"

"They are deadly, yes," Rook said. "And thus highly illegal in the Confederacy."

"If they're so deadly, why would anyone use them?" Doug asked. "Like, what do they do? Are they a really powerful hallucinogen?"

"No, nothing ordinary like that," Rook explained. "What these do is make you look cool."

Bryce seemed to get over his initial fear and stared with curiosity at the little cylinders he had dropped on the ground. "How cool?"

"Very cool," Rook said. "Still, if you light up these cigarettes, they will kill you. Maybe not today. Maybe not tomorrow. Maybe not for a year. Maybe not for a decade. Or perhaps twenty years. Or thirty years. Or forty. But if you live long enough — like maybe in fifty years — they will be your death. Though maybe not for sixty years."

"Man, it might be wrong for us to smuggle these," Doug said.

Bryce scoffed. "Rook would not do anything wrong. He's a kind, merciful person, and I think we should feel honored he gave us this assignment."

Charlene rolled her eyes. "So how much will we get paid for this?"

"The amount Bryce owes me," Rook answered. "You do this, I don't kill him."

Lulu considered for a moment. "You don't kill him, plus ten grand."

"No. This is about making things even with me."

"You do kill Bryce," Lulu offered. "And we get forty grand."

Bryce frowned at Lulu. "Come on, now."

"Killing you all is still on the table," Rook said. "And that's what happens if you screw this up: I kill you all."

Lulu batted her eyes at him. "Even me?"

Rook shrugged his shoulders. "Well, at least the other three."

"You don't want that," Doug told Lulu.

Lulu sighed. "Yeah, I guess not."

"If you're so desperate to make some money, though," Rook said. "I do have one other thing. There's a device that is highly sought after. Last info says it was being held in a secret research facility in Calais. It looks like this." Rook held up his tablet and on it was a picture of the small metal cube Doug had found — sans bunnies.

"Hey!" Doug exclaimed, "That's —"

Bryce smacked Doug across the face.

"Hey! What was that for?!" Doug cried.

"You were getting a little loud," Bryce said, "and it was disrespectful to our host."

"What were you about to say?" Rook asked Doug.

"Nothing," Bryce said. "Doug just gets uppity if someone doesn't punch him every so often."

Bryce shot Doug a desperate look, and he caught the drift. "Yeah. I was just going to say that that thing was a cube," Doug said. "It has six square sides — a cube. I learned that in geometry class."

Rook continued to stare at Doug. "Everyone knows it's a cube."

"Well ... that's me being stupid," Doug said. "I thought that was information people would want to know. I'm Doug — the stupid one. We haven't formally met."

Rook stared at Doug a few seconds more and then addressed Bryce. "So does this interest you dummies?"

"What does it pay?" Bryce said.

"And will you pay extra if it has bunnies on it?" Lulu asked.

"I'll give you a hundred grand if you somehow get me it," Rook said. "And I don't want bunnies on it."

"A million," Bryce countered.

"You don't even know what it is," Rook said.

"And yet I'm getting a sense of what it's worth," Bryce said.

"Two hundred and fifty," Rook said. "I don't really expect you idiots to pull this off, so I guess it doesn't matter. Just make sure you guys do the delivery first before getting yourselves killed."

"Some of that money up front would help with the operation," Bryce said.

"Absolutely not."

"How about you finish the sponsorship form, making us an official criminal mercenary group?" Charlene said.

Rook chuckled. "Okay. Why wouldn't I? You're the great Hellbender who slaughtered Vogel's people and are now going to steal from a secret Confederacy of Astara research facility. Of course I want my name associated with you. Now just come back with a vehicle, and we'll get you loaded up for the delivery."

"So you'll go to the e-form now and say we're sponsored?" Lulu asked.

"I'll get to it in a few minutes," Rook said.

"You could just do it right now," Lulu told him.

"I'm a very busy man."

Lulu grimaced at him. "You know what they say: If excuses were mooses, everywhere would be Canada."

Rook raised an eyebrow. "I've never heard anyone say that."

"I JUST SAID IT!" Lulu screamed.

Rook picked up his tablet, brought up the form, and entered his sponsorship. "It's done. There you go, Hellbender." He looked at Driscoll. "I'm going to regret this, aren't I?"

Driscoll nodded. "That would be my guess."

"One last thing," Rook said, looking now more curiously at Doug, who was absentmindedly playing with the bunny cube in his pocket. "If you do, by some miracle, obtain the cube, there's a big warning that goes with it. No matter what happens, whatever you do, do not, under any circumstances, touch it."

"You might even say I'm the ultimate moderate. Whenever there has been a contentious issue, you can be certain I am with people on both sides. In a way, I am the friend of every man and woman. I sympathize with them all."

CHAPTER 11

"You're racking up quite the body count," said the text on Darius's screen.

"I just want to be on the safe side," Darius answered.

"But you still don't have the artifact?"

"It apparently remains in the possession of Hellbender," Darius said.

"And what do you know of them?"

"They are nobodies. I will find them soon enough." Darius smiled. "And then they will go from nobodies to nothing."

* * *

Doug placed the bunny cube in a plastic bag and carefully sealed it up.

"So anyone feel sick or anything?" Bryce asked as he sat in a rickety office chair. "I feel fine ... I think." They had found an abandoned office building near Rook and borrowed a conference room for a quick meeting. Faded motivational posters still hung on the walls, talking about teamwork and synergy, though now they only motivated rats and vagrants.

Charlene stared awhile at the cube. "You know, I never touched it."

"Doug," Lulu said, "take the bunny cube out and rub it all over Charlene's face so she doesn't think she's better than us."

Doug held up the baggie and looked at the cube cautiously. "I'm not touching it again. It did always make me feel ... weird."

"We now know for certain there's something about it that's valuable," Bryce said. "So let's focus on that. As for other things — like maybe all of us dying of radiation poisoning or something — we'll just cross that bridge when we get to it."

"If it's radioactive," Charlene said, "we should probably put it in something other than a plastic baggie." She looked at Doug. "What container was it in before?"

Hesitantly, Doug put the baggie in his pocket. "Just a wooden box."

"And what is the plan now?" Charlene asked. "Why don't we just give it to Rook for the money?"

"Oh, silly little Char." Bryce patted Charlene on the head. She violently swatted his hand away. "We'd look like chumps if we just said, 'We happen to have this; here you go.' But if we go to Calais and come back with the bunny cube without a single alert being issued by the Confederacy of Astara, we'll be legends. Tons of street cred."

"Which we'll use to get yet another job we're thoroughly incapable of doing?" Charlene asked. "This seems needlessly complicated."

"I'm going to design the plan we'll pretend to have used to get the bunny cube," Lulu exclaimed as she spun around in her chair. "It's going to be this elaborate caper with disguises and hacking and split-second timing and relying on people to act in just the right way when in reality you could never be that certain of human behavior."

"Cool!" Doug said. "What will I do in it?"

"You'll carry things," Lulu said.

Doug frowned. "Come on. If it's going to be made up, at least give me something cool to pretend I did. Like the sort of thing where I have to dangle from the ceiling by a rope and not touch the ground because the ground is alarmed or electrified or swarming with large ants or something."

Lulu thought for a second. "Well, Charlene, always the damsel in distress, is going to inevitably get in trouble, and you can be the one who rescues her."

"If you make me a damsel in distress," Charlene stated, "you will be distressed." Charlene sighed. "Why am I even arguing about this idiocy? So is this really the plan? We're going to make the delivery for Rook and then pretend to break into a research facility we already broke into?"

"It's a good plan," Bryce assured her. "I still have contacts in Calais that will allow us to get in and out without any trouble."

"But I do want some trouble," Charlene said. "If we're going back to Calais, I want to kill General Lapointe. She tried to abandon us to Loch's forces and is now taking credit for how *I* blew up the carrier."

Bryce groaned. "How many times do I have to explain? There is no profit in revenge. Revenge is just a made-up thing used to motivate people before money existed, much like honor or morality. Let's focus on real things here."

"Like possibly magic cubes," Lulu added.

"Dark magic," Doug said.

"And known to be worth a lot of money," Bryce said. "So for now, let's concentrate on getting this done. Everything should work out well ... unless there really is something to worry about from touching that cube." Bryce looked at Doug. "So did you really meet with someone calling himself Satan who said something about this cube thing?"

"I know you guys think I'm a bit dull," Doug said, "but I'm not insane. Yeah, that happened."

"So what *exactly* did he say?" Charlene asked.

Doug thought about it. "I just know he mentioned something about how if I saw a dark star, that meant I was near something important ... or, wait, maybe he was warning me about the dark star. Yeah, I think he said we'd be sorry if we messed with anything related to the dark star."

"Thanks, Doug," Bryce said. "That's really useful information now."

"If this was someone who knew something important, why in the world was he talking to Doug?" Charlene asked.

"Yeah, why not just tell the world's secrets to a stray dog?" Bryce said.

"I'm right here," Doug complained. "You know, I'm not sure about us selling the bunny cube. It sounds like it's really important — like maybe world-ending important."

Bryce rolled his eyes. "No one is going to end the world. That's yet another thing there is no profit in."

"I got this feeling, though," Doug said. "Like we were placed in the middle of something important. Maybe we've been assigned a quest — like it's the destiny of Hellbender to save the world."

"Given a quest by Satan?" Charlene asked.

"Maybe we're the ones supposed to destroy the world," Lulu suggested. "Has anyone tried using the bunny cube to destroy the world yet? Maybe it gave us superpowers. Evil superpowers." Lulu stared at Charlene, Lulu's eyes growing wider and wider.

"What are you doing?" Charlene demanded.

Lulu kept staring. "Trying to explode your head."

"Stop it!"

Lulu moved closer. "I think it's working."

Doug pushed between the two. "Guys, this is serious. I think we're on the path of something big. There's something wrong with this world; we all know it. Maybe we have a chance to somehow fix it. To take on ... whatever is really out there."

"If people hear that some warfs are talking about mystic nonsense, we're just going to get targets on our backs," Bryce warned. "Let's keep perspective here: We have an unprecedented moneymaking opportunity. So, maybe let's find this 'Satan' fellow and ask him some questions ourselves to clarify what we're dealing with."

"Or, better yet," Charlene said, "why don't we just go back to Rook now and sell him the cube and finally have money and be done with this nonsense?"

"Let's not be short-sighted," Bryce responded. "I like money as much as the next guy — maybe more — but this here is an opportunity. To get respect and the money we deserve. It's high time —" Bryce's phone beeped. He pulled it out and took a look, staring at the screen for a long while. "It's a message from Tara."

Charlene frowned. "She's still alive?"

Lulu smiled. "That means we get to kill her."

"What did she say?" Doug asked.

Bryce held up the phone so they could all see the message. "I bet you touched the cube. I can help. Let's meet."

"That's another misperception about me: That I hate mankind. No. As different as we are, we are in a way kindred spirits. We are victims of this existence. We're in this together."

CHAPTER 12

Bryce had quickly set up a meeting with Tara. There was a place on the edge of town where no one lived anymore that was full of abandoned buildings. It was a popular place for secretive meetings. In fact, it was extremely popular, and Bryce was barely able to book a slot there.

"This is a sniper rifle," Charlene said, holding up a rifle with a scope on it that anyone would easily have identified as a sniper rifle. She had found it at the Vogel headquarters and already spent a lot of time putting it together and taking it apart again and seemed really happy to have an opportunity to actually use it.

Charlene looked around the area. They were in a big open field of nothing but dirt, but around the edges were a few tall, unoccupied buildings. "I'm going to go stake out a position where I have a clear view of the meeting. If she tries something, all you have to do is give me the kill signal, and I'll take her down."

Bryce raised an eyebrow. "And what's the kill signal?"

Charlene thought a moment. "I guess we'll need to come up with a kill signal."

"How about this?" Lulu asked and then did a chicken dance.

"We'll need a non-stupid one," Charlene said.

Bryce raised his hand and made a cutting motion in the air. "Does that work?"

"That'll do." Charlene headed off toward the buildings.

Doug felt the hilt of one of his katanas as he looked around at the empty ground and buildings. "I don't trust this Tara."

"And we do," Bryce said. "That's why we just came up with a kill signal."

"If you need me, me and my katanas are ready." Doug patted his swords.

"Do you even really know how to use those?" Bryce asked.

Doug tossed an apple into the air. He drew a sword, and the apple landed on the ground in two pieces. Doug returned the katana to its scabbard in a quick motion.

Bryce shrugged. "Impressive. But useless. But hey, you're usually oh for two."

"We had apples?" Lulu exclaimed.

"Maybe there should be a signal for me," Doug suggested. "And if you make the signal, I'll slice Tara's arm right off."

"How about if you see us killing Tara," Bryce said, "you join in. No reason to make this complicated."

"We only agreed to the sniper rifle and kill signal to shut up Charlene," Lulu said. "You know how annoying she can get about ... everything."

"I can hear you through the comms," Charlene chimed in on the hidden radios they all had. They'd found them in their military transport. "I'm sorry I take this so seriously, but maybe instead of just blundering into things with no plan — as you guys always do — you could —"

Lulu started slapping her ears. "How do I turn this off?"

"Thanks for being a sniper, Char," Doug said, giving a thumbs-up in the direction he assumed she was in. "Don't shoot any of us."

"I can't shoot my own teammates," Charlene responded. "I would get a bad reputation. Now everyone quiet; I see her coming. She looks alone, but be prepared."

Walking toward them was the lone figure of Tara. There appeared to be something in her hands. Something small. Something gray. Something fluffy. A kitten.

"Hey, guys!" Tara called out cheerily as she got closer.

"Why do you have a kitten?" Lulu asked.

"Oh." Tara looked at the little kitten and scratched him on the head. "I found him on the way here. Cute little guy, huh? I don't know what I'll do with him, though, as I travel too much to take care of a cat. I hope there's a no-kill shelter in the Disputed Zone. So, you guys want to pet him?"

"Yes, I want —" Lulu started to say, but Bryce pulled her back.

"It's a negotiating trick," he whispered to her and Doug. "Don't fall for it." He looked at Tara. "We have no desire to pet your stupid little cat, as we care nothing for its fluffy fur, cute playfulness, and tiny whiskers."

"I ... hate cats," Lulu said, visibly shaking. "They are awful ... especially baby ones, and —" She tried to leap for the kitten, but Bryce held her back. "I want to hug him and squeeze him and name him Mr. Whiskers!"

"I think the kitten is distracting everyone," Doug said. "Why don't I take him somewhere out of the way and play with him so you can all get to talking?"

"We're ignoring the cat!" Bryce shouted.

"Sorry; I didn't realize he'd be so distracting," Tara said as she idly scratched behind one of the kitten's ears. "So where is ... uh ... Charlene?"

"She abandoned us," Bryce answered. "She was always talking about going on her own, and after what happened to us, she finally did."

"She just left us," Lulu added. "We don't know what happened to her." Lulu stared at the ground. "We fought a lot, but we were always there for each other. And now ... now I don't know."

Doug tried to hold it in, but a sob burst out. "I miss her."

Bryce slapped Doug on the shoulder. "Hey, keep it together!"

"You sold to her I'm not there," Charlene said through the comms. "Why don't you keep it moving?"

"You're so annoying," Lulu muttered under her breath.

"I'm really sorry, you guys," Tara said. "I didn't mean for that to happen. Hopefully you'll find her again. I know that meeting at Vogel headquarters didn't seem to go well, but I am really trying to help you guys."

"A bit more help like that," Bryce said, "and we'd be penniless and beaten to death."

"Yeah, you were a real B-word," Doug added. "A betrayer."

"It's not like that, really," Tara pleaded. "For one thing, I'm here to warn you now: Delgado and the rest of Vogel are after you, as they blame you for the slaughter at their Disputed Zone headquarters."

"They really think we did that?" Bryce asked.

"Well, I kind of told them you did," Tara said.

"Sounds like we're back to the B-word stuff," Lulu commented.

"I was just trying to help you guys get some street cred, which I know you want," Tara said. "But more importantly, I didn't want them to know what this was all really about: the cube."

"And what is this cube?" Bryce asked.

"Yeah, we don't necessarily have it, but we do want to know more about it," Doug added, getting an angry glance from Bryce.

"It's extremely valuable," Tara told them, "and I know for a fact you have it. I had information that it was taken from a research facility in Calais, but it wasn't Loch's forces that obtained it. And it wasn't Darius."

"Darius?" Doug asked.

"Oh, yeah, that one needs some explanation," Tara said. "But, anyway, the point is I knew you had it when you went to meet with Delgado, and that's what betraying you was all about. I wanted Delgado to dismiss you and not suspect you might have the cube."

"So you had a brainstorming session on your problem there," Lulu said, "and what you settled on was 'Have Bryce and his friends robbed and beaten'? Genius. Really appreciated."

"Hey, I'm sorry," Tara said, "but you have to believe me, this is very delicate with how sought-after the cube is."

"We certainly don't have to believe you," Bryce told Tara. "But tell us what you know, and we'll consider it. Now, you said something about touching the cube?"

"Yes, I do need to tell you all about that."

"Well, you have our full attention," Bryce said. He saw the kitten looking at him and smiled and waved at the cat.

A shot cracked the air, and Tara jerked back and collapsed, the kitten falling from her hands and scurrying off as soon as Tara hit the ground.

The three just stared at the body of Tara silently. Finally, Charlene spoke over the radio. "I got her! What was happening? Are you all right?"

"I was waving at the kitten!" Bryce screamed.

"Oh man," Doug gasped as he backed away from Tara. "I can't believe Charlene just shot her dead like that."

"You gave me the signal!" Charlene shouted through the radio. "I thought she was about to kill you!"

"And you could have hit Mr. Whiskers, you psychopath!" Lulu yelled. "How do you just kill someone like that? How mental are you?"

"We discussed the signal!" Charlene answered through the radio, though they could see her now running toward them from one of the buildings. "I saw the signal, so I thought I had to take the shot right away!"

"That wasn't the signal!" Bryce said, taking cautious glances at the still Tara. "That was a wave. That didn't mean, 'Blow her brains out'; it meant, 'Hello, kitty!'"

"Now I'm never going to be able to look at Hello Kitty stuff again without thinking of death," Lulu said.

"You guys just didn't take this seriously enough," Charlene said as she continued toward them. "You should have been more careful to —" She stopped as she got near and stared at the still body of Tara. She started to cry. "I've never killed anyone before."

Doug immediately went to her and put his arm around her. "It's okay. She was ... a bad person. She probably deserved it."

"I mean, I've shot at people before in the battles we were drafted in," Charlene said through sobs. "But I don't think I ever hit anyone."

"It's okay," Bryce assured her. "It happened. She was probably just going to betray us again somehow and get the cube for herself."

Charlene continued to cry. "I just want people to think I'm tough, you know. I didn't want to hesitate; I want to be capable and tough."

Lulu took her hand. "We think you're tough. We just like razzing you sometimes, but don't take it seriously. You're great, Char; you're great."

Doug glanced at Tara again and saw that she was no longer still, but getting to her feet with a gun in her hand and her friendly demeanor finally gone. "Uh ... guys."

Lulu, Bryce, and Charlene turned to see Tara holding a gun on them. Bryce looked at Charlene. "What kind of weak-ass sniper rifle was that?"

"It was the only one I had available!" Charlene answered.

"Why didn't you go for the kill shot?" Lulu shouted. "You aim for the head! The unarmored head!"

"This isn't a video game!" Charlene yelled. "You don't go for head shots; you aim for the center of mass."

Tara frowned at them. "Do you guys need more time to sort this out?"

Bryce smiled and turned to her. "I'm afraid we had a little misunderstanding."

"Yeah, Charlene thought a 'hello little kitty' wave," Doug explained, "was a signal to kill you, but we didn't want to kill you. At least not yet."

"I bet that hurts," Charlene said.

"Yes, it does," Tara said. "And I'm guessing it's going to leave a big bruise."

"Probably don't want to wear anything with a low décolletage for a while," Lulu advised.

"I don't normally," Tara said. "I find I don't get respected as professional when I try to look sexy."

"That's true," Charlene said.

Lulu snorted. "Oh, like that's an option for you."

Tara stared at them awhile longer. "How about this: You thought I betrayed you, and then you shot me." Tara holstered her gun. "So we're even and can just wipe the slate clean. How does that sound? Frankly, I'm just glad I didn't actually break you guys up." She motioned to Charlene. "Because I felt pretty bad about that."

"That sounds great," Bryce said.

"We should learn the value of forgiveness from you," Lulu said.

"So what kind of body armor are you wearing?" Charlene said.

"I still don't trust you," Doug said.

"Shut up, Doug," Bryce said. "So, Tara, you were telling us about why we shouldn't touch the cube."

"Yeah." Tara looked around the dirt field and the abandoned buildings. "Want to meet somewhere else? It's kind of creepy here."

"Sure," Bryce answered.

Tara looked around again. "Know what happened to my kitten?"

*   *   *

"I want to play some skee-ball," Doug said.

"Later," Bryce told Doug, sitting down at a table with the others.

"I need to win some tickets. I kinda want that pirate hat I saw at the counter. It might go with my mercenary getup."

"It's not going to fit you," Bryce said. "It's meant for a child."

Grudgingly, Doug sat at the table as well. "Why do you always have to crush my dreams?"

"Because they are always — always — stupid."

The Chuck E. Cheese was pretty quiet. Well, except for the pings and beeps from all the electronic games around them, but there were no people there other than them and the employees. "See, not a lot of children in the Disputed Zone," Tara said. "I think that makes this a good meeting place, but I guess a lot of the criminal organizations don't find it respectable to meet here."

"This is a lot more fun than an abandoned warehouse or something," Doug said.

"Might have to kill the guy in the mouse suit if he overhears us, though," Lulu commented. "Or I might just kill him anyway because large mice creep me out."

"I agree with the criminals: This is stupid," Charlene said. "So, anyway, what did you have to tell us about the cube?"

"That it's worth a lot of money — a lot," Tara said. "But you can't sell it if you've touched it."

"What happens when you touch it?" Doug asked, hand on the cube in the plastic bag in his pocket.

Tara hesitated. "This is hard to explain — and I don't really understand it all. I've just picked up bits and pieces here and there. But some artifacts emerged in the wake of the Last War ... or maybe they were some of the reasons for it. But they are very powerful. It's the Confederacy of Astara's possession of one of them that allowed them to make the reality imploder bombs."

Lulu furrowed her brow. "And how does that work?"

"As far as I understand," Tara explained, "it's like they allow one to bend the rules of physics. It's not even really certain what they allow one to do, but all the nations want them, obviously."

"So the Confederacy of Astara very much wants theirs back, I assume?" Bryce asked.

"It would be a top priority for them," Tara said, "but also for any other government that knows about it. And for Darius. You know those times you found whole rooms of people slaughtered? That's him. He's after you, and he's an unstoppable killing machine."

Doug's eyes went wide. "That's the worst kind of killing machine!"

"And who does this Darius work for?" Charlene asked.

"I'm not exactly sure," Tara said. "Some organization outside of the main governments. It's unclear what they want the artifacts for. Some say to destroy the universe."

"Even the quasars?!" Lulu exclaimed.

Tara shrugged. "I don't really understand it all. But some group has Darius seeking out the artifacts, and he is immune to normal weapons."

"This is stupid," Charlene said.

"This might be something Satan told me about," Doug stated.

"Something *who* told you about?" Tara asked.

"Ignore him," Bryce said. "You still haven't told us what happens if someone touches the cube."

"If a person touches one of these artifacts, it's like part of it leaks out and infects you somehow," Tara said. "I really have no idea how it works. I just know a little bit from prying where I wasn't supposed to. Most people don't know a thing about these artifacts — that they even exist — and the governments are happy to keep it that way. Anyway, if you've touched the cube and someone else obtains the cube, they'll be able to tell part of its essence is gone and they can actually use it to hunt you down. And then they will kill you to restore the cube."

"And that's what will happen if the unstoppable killing machine gets it?" Doug asked.

Tara nodded. "That would be the worst-case scenario. Anyway, this is why you absolutely can't sell the cube as-is. You'll need to restore it first — taking the essence out of you and putting it back in the cube. The Confederacy of Astara has been working with 4B22 — you know, that nation of science weirdos — on researching the artifacts, and I believe they have a research facility on a military base in Calais where they can restore the cube without killing you."

"We were already planning to fake-break into a research facility there," Lulu said, "so that kinda works out."

"Well, you'll need a good plan, because they've stepped up security after losing the cube," Tara said. "That's where I come in. I'll help you break in and fix the cube, and then you share the profits with me when we sell it. And I can find buyers that will pay millions and millions for it."

Charlene stared at her. "And you're not just going to kill us and take it?"

Tara looked hurt. "No. We warfs need to stick together — and we can all get rather wealthy off this. Well, I need to use the restroom, so why don't you think this over?"

Tara got up and headed away. Charlene got up as well. "I'll follow her and see what she's up to."

Bryce rolled his eyes. "Yeah, you do that." After Charlene crept away, Bryce looked at the other two. "So what do you think? Maybe we should work with her; she does seem to know what she's talking about. Plus, I think she still has a thing for me."

"I don't think she ever had a thing for you," Doug said. "I think she's just been using you."

Bryce shot him a look. "You don't know anything about women. Or anything else. You're dumb. Shut up." He turned to Lulu. "What do you think?"

Lulu contemplated it all for a moment. "She might have a thing for Doug, actually."

"About doing the job with Tara, I mean."

"Sounds like a fun caper," Lulu said. "The plan I was working on for us fake-breaking into the research facility is really cool, and I kind of wanted to do some of it, especially the part where we escape in our specially made lab coats that turn into hang gliders."

"Well ... we might have to adapt the plan now a bit to ... reality," Bryce said.

"I don't like this," Doug said. "There's something off about Tara ... and how does she really know all these things? And if this cube is so powerful and dangerous, maybe we shouldn't be selling it to anyone. All the different nations out there are probably going to use it for awful things ... and if that Darius guy is really out to destroy the world or something, we need to protect the cube to make sure he never gets it."

"First off," Bryce said, "preventing the destruction of —" His phone beeped, and he gave it a glance. "Charlene says that Tara is peeing. Anyway, as I was saying, preventing the destruction of the world is above our pay grade — there's obviously going to be much more qualified people working on that one, so let's not concern ourselves with it. Secondly, while it is true that the governments out there will probably use the cube for awful things, remember that we're not going to be giving it to them for a small amount of money — it's going to be a large amount of money. I'll grant you that it is immoral to help evil for money, but once the money at stake gets to a certain size, those concerns are no longer valid. That's basic philosophy on morality as stated by —" Bryce's phone beeped again. "Charlene says she's now making small talk with Tara. Hmm ... that's pretty impressive to make small talk while texting us. Maybe we don't give Charlene enough credit."

"If we ever tell Charlene anything other than that we intensely hate her," Lulu stated, "it goes right to her head."

"You could be nicer to her," Doug told Lulu. "And I guess Charlene could be less ... Charlene. We need to get along, because we all need to stick together."

"I don't see the point of that if we have lots of money," Bryce said. "Then we can finally all find more suitable people to hang out with."

"I'm going to have a house filled with bunnies and kitties!" Lulu exclaimed.

"You know those two animals don't actually get along," Bryce said.

"I may have to execute a few for fighting as an example to the others," Lulu said, "but we will have order."

"I'm opposed to working with Tara," Doug said. "I just want to make that clear."

Bryce nodded. "No one cares."

Tara and Charlene approached the table, talking and laughing together. "I like Tara," Charlene told the others. "I think we should work together."

"So what do you say?" Tara asked.

"It's an agreement," Bryce said. "Let's all get rich."

Tara smiled. "Great! I'll just meet you guys in Calais, and then we can get our plans together. I really think we're all going to make a great team."

Doug wasn't smiling. He walked over to a skee-ball machine, picked up a ball, and pointed it at Tara. "If you do anything again to hurt Hellbender, you're a dead woman." He emphasized his words by roughly rolling the ball up the ramp, but it only went into the ten-point ring. "Dammit!"

"It's said you're created in God's image. But be honest, who do you resemble more: me or Him?"

CHAPTER 13

Charlene was actually a bit excited. This felt like a proper mission — smuggling and breaking into a high-security facility. And unlike some idiocy Bryce or Lulu had suddenly sprung upon her, for this she actually had time to properly plan and prepare. Plus, she'd be working with someone who actually seemed competent and not just the three idiots she'd been stuck with her entire life.

They needed supplies and actually had some money now, so Charlene demanded that she be the one to make the purchases. She knew if Lulu were in charge of the money, she'd spend it all on candy and stuffed animals. Bryce would probably spend it all on hair gel and clothes. And Doug would probably have given it all away for some magic beans.

But Charlene was going to enforce responsibility on "Hellbender." So she took charge of supplying the mission. They needed emergency food, so she got rational things like beef jerky — and not fancy, expensive varieties like teriyaki jerky or sriracha jerky. No, she got regular old dried meat with salt for if they needed protein. She also got some trail mix, but she did get the kind with M&Ms in it — for troop morale. And she also got some canteens and some rope. You never knew when you'd need a good length of rope. With her in charge of supplies, no one was going to starve, get dehydrated, or get stuck down a pit with no way out. And after all that, there was some money left over, so she bought some assorted card stock and ribbon so that she could properly document their mission.

As she headed down an alley carrying her bags from Walmart, she noticed a group of people approaching her. She prepared to drop her bags and pull out her gun, but she heard footsteps behind her. She turned and saw that she was surrounded.

"Are you with Hellbender?" one of them asked, a fearsome bald man with a large scar on the left side of his face that ended behind a crimson eye patch.

"Why do you ask?" Charlene answered, trying to remain calm.

The man with the eye patch approached her, and she noticed the hooked red claw symbol on his jacket sleeve. "We want revenge against the ones who blew up our air carrier."

* * *

"Where's Charlene?" Lulu asked as she frantically looked around the warehouse. "Is she still buying supplies? She's inefficient. We really would be better off if we told her we hate her and threw her in a ditch."

Doug was using a hand truck to move a pallet of cocaine into the back of the truck. "I said we shouldn't let her go alone. This city is filled with criminals."

Bryce was coordinating Doug moving the pallet, which consisted of Bryce waving his arms at random intervals. "We all have much better things to do than harass Charlene. She's probably just being meticulous on figuring out what flavorless rations she's buying us."

"That's the last of it," Rook said. "So you think you guys can not screw this up?"

"You will be taken aback by how not quite screwed up this will be," Lulu assured him.

Driscoll stood back from everyone else in the warehouse, watching quietly. "They're going to screw it up."

"Yeah, probably," Rook admitted. He approached the pallet Doug had just loaded. On it were bricks of cocaine, each with a label saying, "Certified Organic, Fair-Trade Cocaine. Naturally Gluten-Free."

"These should easily pass inspection if you're stopped," Rook said. "If the secrets inside get discovered, just kill anyone who saw it and finish the delivery. Or kill yourselves. Got it?"

"Kill everyone then selves," Lulu repeated. "Got it!"

"Now get the hell out of here."

"We'll get the Hellbender out of here," Lulu laughed.

Rook nodded. "I hope you all die."

"We just need to wait for Charlene," Doug said. "We don't know —"

Charlene came running into the warehouse holding some shopping bags. "Hey, guys, I have some news!"

Bryce headed for the truck. "Tell us on the road."

"We were worried about you," Doug said.

"Especially me." Lulu approached Charlene. "Give me a big sloppy kiss."

Charlene tried to headbutt Lulu when she got close. "Let's just get going and I'll tell you my news."

"So, idiots, do you think you still might go after that cube I showed you?" Rook asked.

Bryce shrugged and headed into the truck. "We're considering it. It does seem dangerous."

The rest got into the truck as well, Lulu taking the driver's seat. They closed the door, and Lulu took the truck out of the warehouse. "I don't think Rook is going to pay us enough for the cube," Bryce said. "Hopefully Tara knows a better buyer."

"I'm still a bit worried about what this ... what did she say ... 'essence' the cube put in us might do," Doug said, sitting on some of the bricks of cocaine. "Sounds like something pretty bad. When I first touched the cube, something did seem so wrong about it."

"Every time I close my eyes," Lulu said, "I've been having these dark, violent thoughts. So I still seem normal."

"You all seem your regular selves," Charlene said reassuringly, but then added, "Not that that's a good thing. Anyway, I have some news. Bryce, you know how you said there's no profit in revenge?"

Bryce nodded. "Sounds like something I'd say."

"Bryce is always saying things that seem smart but aren't really that deep when you think about them," Doug agreed.

"Well, anyway, what if we could get profit from revenge?" Charlene smiled. "I got us a contract to assassinate General Lapointe."

"Sure, I seem so above you all ... so vastly powerful compared to you. Really, I am nearly omnipotent. But were you like me, you would see that 'nearly' omnipotent is infinitely closer to powerless than it is to all-powerful."

CHAPTER 14

"Do you think we're being a little conspicuous?" Mills asked.

While Mills had put on some normal street clothes — she figured she should wear something that didn't stick out and settled on a brown jacket and jeans — General Lapointe and the six Athenians with her were all in designer outfits, looking like they were on their way to a fashion show. Knowing they were in a city filled with hardened criminals, Mills wasn't quite sure what people would make of that.

"I may go under cover," Lapointe said, "but I will never go unnoticed."

The group sauntered through the alley, soon coming upon a sleazy-looking man who leered at them. "Can I help you ladies with something?"

Gisele pulled out a silenced pistol and shot the man in the head.

"What the hell?!" Mills exclaimed.

"It's a Hermès," Gisele explained, wiping the gun with a pink handkerchief. "You have to fire it every so often to keep it maintained."

"Can you control your psychopaths?" Mills demanded of Lapointe.

Lapointe looked deep in thought. "Why? What just happened?"

"When do I get to shoot someone?" one of the other Athenians asked. "I'm getting bored."

"We're not shooting anyone!" Mills shouted. "Everyone keep your guns holstered unless I or ..." She glanced at Lapointe, who seemed to be practicing various facial expressions in her compact. "Unless I say so. Now come on." She took a few uneasy glances at the man lying dead near them and led the way.

Gisele put away her gun. "That one is always shouting. I wonder what her problem is?"

"She's sexually frustrated," Lapointe said, practicing a disinterested look.

"Just follow!" Mills yelled. "And I assure you I am all sorts of frustrated!"

They exited the alley and soon came to a door labeled "Rook's Criminal Enterprises." Mills knocked. A young woman dressed as a street thug opened the door. "What do you want?"

"We are here —"

Lapointe pushed Mills out of the way. "Take us to Rook."

The young woman stared at them all. "And you ladies are?"

Lapointe sighed. "I'm tired of this banter." Lapointe delivered a spinning roundhouse kick to the door, knocking it open and the young woman to the ground. She entered the room, where a half-dozen thugs were pointing guns at her. Mills hesitantly followed, as did the Athenians, who as usual did not appear to be paying any attention.

"Great job holding the door, Candy," said the man who looked to be in charge.

"Are you Rook?" Lapointe asked.

Rook looked down at his jacket. "Whoops. I forgot to wear my name tag. Yeah, I'm Rook. And you are ..." He stared at her. "That whackjob general from the Confederacy of Astara?"

"I will neither confirm nor deny that," Lapointe said.

Rook looked over the rest of her group. "And I guess these are your special forces girls and ..." He looked at Mills. "Someone who didn't get the memo to coordinate her outfit."

Gisele finally looked up and noticed all the guns trained on them. "Can we pull out our guns now and start shooting people?"

"No!" Mills shouted.

"I don't see any reason we can't have a friendly talk." Rook looked at his people, and they lowered their guns.

"Just watch it," Candy told Lapointe. "Any more crap from you, and —"

"Can you get rid of her?" Lapointe asked. "She doesn't fit this scene and is throwing me off." She then looked at Mills. "And I guess my batwoman can leave too."

Candy looked at Mills with fear. "She's Batwoman?"

"No one is leaving," Rook said. "Now, General, how can this humble criminal mastermind help you?"

"I seek ..." She paused and let the tension rise before stating firmly but slowly, "... Hellbender."

Rook grimaced. "This is about those idiots?"

"I told you they were trouble," said the large, older man standing near Rook.

Rook sighed. "Yes, Driscoll, you did, but you know how I always have to think I'm so smart." He looked at Lapointe. "So I'm guessing you heard about how they killed all those people at the Vogel headquarters here."

"And killed everyone in one of our research facilities," Lapointe added.

Rook furrowed his brow. "They did what?"

"And they took something of ours we need back," Lapointe said.

Rook looked like he was suppressing anger. "Was it a cube-shaped thing?"

Lapointe raised an eyebrow. "You know of it?"

Rook knocked over a table, spilling kilos of cocaine to the floor. "THOSE LITTLE WEASELS!" He turned to Driscoll. "They had it the whole time! Did you suspect that?"

"If I suspected it, I would have said something," Driscoll answered. "I knew something was up, but I didn't think there was any reason to believe those jokers had it."

"So you know where they are?" Lapointe asked. "We need to get that artifact back. And more importantly, we need to stop Hellbender. They are a destructive threat to all we hold dear."

"We don't care about the Hellbender idiots," Mills added. "We just need the cube."

Rook nodded and folded his arms. "I think we've come to the business portion of this conversation. You need something. I can help. But the problem is, I'm not a nice guy. I'm only going to help with ulterior motives."

Lapointe checked her makeup in her compact. "I'm not going to sleep with you."

"Well, I'm not either," Gisele said. "I'm way out of his league. I'd have to be really drunk on either booze or bloodlust."

"As lovely as you ladies are," Rook said, "that was not what I had in mind. What I was in fact thinking of was large sums of money. And being a famous general for the Confederacy of Astara, I'm guessing you have access to that."

"We'll have to fill out a lot of forms," Mills said. "There's a bit of an approval process that we'll have to go through."

"Better get on the batphone and call it in, then," Rook said.

"I have another idea," Lapointe declared. "A challenge — something dramatic like hand-to-hand combat. And if I win, you tell me where Hellbender is."

Rook shook his head. "No. That's stupid. I'm not going to do that."

Lapointe frowned. "Everyone always wants to do things the boring way."

"'Sane' is the word people usually use," Rook said.

Gisele yawned. "Can't we just torture him and get the information we need?"

"I read somewhere that torture doesn't work," another Athenian said.

Gisele thought about it a moment. "And how would we do it? Pull out his fingernails and beat him for hours? That does sound like it could be tedious."

Rook waved at them. "Hey, gals, I'm right here."

"Let's not talk about torturing people who currently have us surrounded with guns," Mills said.

"And let me remind you," Rook said. "There are agreements between the Disputed Zone and all the nations. I'm a properly registered criminal; you can't just come in here and threaten violence to me, or there are consequences. You seem to like narratives, General; how would you like your story to end with 'found dead in dumpster behind Chili's'?"

Lapointe looked at Mills. "Did he just threaten me?"

Mills stared at the thugs surrounding them. "He's sort of in a position to do that."

Lapointe scoffed. "People with guns? I'd never be scared of something so ordinary."

There was a knock at the door. Rook sighed. "Now what? Candy, go tell whoever it is to go away."

Candy went to the door and opened it a crack. "We're busy, so why don't —" Candy's words caught in her throat. She trembled a bit as she backed away from the door. Inside strolled a tall man, and a chill instantly went through the room. The first thing one would notice about him was his eyes. They looked brown at first, but when the light hit them, they shone gold. And with those strange gold eyes he scanned the room like a serial killer selecting his first victim. As he did it, he smiled like a man who was delighted at the hat he had just made from human skin. And then he strolled to the center of the room as one might walk among his tied-up victims — which was basically a normal walk, though somehow a little creepier. "Am I interrupting something?" he asked in a tone one might use for telling someone to put the lotion in the basket.

"Yes ... yes, you are interrupting," Rook answered, backing up, nearer Driscoll.

"Then I will be quick," the creepy man said. "I seek a group called Hellbender."

Rook rolled his eyes. "For Pete's sake. Well, that's what these lovely ladies are here for, so we might have a bidding war if you want me to help."

The creepy man focused his gold eyes on Lapointe and those with her. Lapointe stared back with curiosity, and even the Athenians looked up from their phones. Mills was frozen in place, shuddering.

"I doubt I have the wealth to compete with them," the man said, still smiling like a shark.

"Then I don't think I can help you, bub," Rook answered.

"All right. I guess I'll leave, then," the man said, though his eyes hinted at more terrible things.

"And who are you?" Lapointe demanded.

"Just a man," he answered. "They call me Darius."

"And who do you work for?" Lapointe asked.

"That's private," Darius said. He then somehow made his smile creepier, implying things one dare not imagine. "I'll see you around."

"Oh, yes," Lapointe answered, meeting Darius's eyes just before he slipped out the door. And through it all, Lapointe had an expression Mills hardly recognized — one serious and focused.

Everyone in the room was noticeably less tense when Darius had left. "Well, I don't know what that was about," Rook said. "But anyway, where we were was that if you want Hellbender and the object they have, you bring me lots of money."

It took a moment for Lapointe to break her train of thought and look at Rook. "Oh, you're still here."

"So, I think we're done," Rook stated. "Why don't you saunter off?"

"Fine. Other important matters to attend to," Lapointe said. "So, just tell us when you have Hellbender. We need them captured as soon as possible."

"Again, we don't really care about Hellbender," Mills told Rook. "Just get us that cube thing."

Gisele looked back at her phone. "Do I get to kill somebody now?"

"No!" Mills shouted and then smiled at the thugs facing them. "No one is getting killed."

"Let's go," Lapointe commanded. "Batwoman, carry my things!"

Mills sighed and followed. "You don't have any things, and I'm not your batwoman! That's not even a thing!"

"So while my conflict is about you, it is not against you. My contention is with God, and you were merely caught in the middle and forced to choose sides in a battle you don't even understand."

CHAPTER 15

Bryce raised an eyebrow. "You did what?"

Charlene took out a tablet and showed the contract to Doug and Bryce. "The Loch Collective wants revenge against Lapointe for blowing up their carrier, and after they heard what we did with everyone at the Vogel headquarters, they thought we were the right people for the job."

Bryce chuckled. "Well, they got a number of things wrong there, didn't they?"

"I'm guessing you didn't show them your neato scrapbooking page about blowing up their carrier," Lulu said.

Charlene shrugged. "It ... did not come up."

Doug was not as amused as the others, especially as he scanned the contract. "What are they asking us to do to Lapointe?" He jumped back from the tablet Charlene was holding. "Holy crap! Did I just read that?"

"Wait? What?" Bryce now read over the contract more intently, his eyes growing wide.

"Well, they want us to make it a particularly brutal killing to show their contempt for what she did," Charlene explained. "You know ... like our 'previous' killings. They put some examples of the things we could do to her, but none of them are binding."

Bryce looked at her with exasperation. "Charlene, which one of us do you expect to perform these ... actions?"

Lulu put the vehicle on autopilot and joined the others to take a look at the contract. "Ew. We were having lots of fun being violent criminals, but once again Charlene had to take things too far."

"We don't have to ... do the exact things listed in the contract," Charlene said. "We could meet the contract by just killing her normal — like shooting her in the head — and then mutilating the body a bit."

"I'm so far from comfortable with this," Doug said. "I don't have any problem with being a criminal, but I draw the line at evil bad guy."

"Come on, guys," Charlene urged. "We should already want to brutally murder Lapointe for how she was going to abandon us to Loch's forces."

"Who we're now working for," Lulu stated.

"Who we have a contract with," Charlene corrected her. "A very lucrative one."

Bryce nodded as he read the contract. "It is a lot of money for one brutal murder. Did you sign this contract?"

"Yes, I told them I'm the leader of Hellbender," Charlene said. "Which I am if we're to have any chance of succeeding at anything."

"Guess we're stuck with it, then," Bryce stated. "We can't be known for going back on contracts. Hopefully Lapointe will be in Calais and we can work her brutal murder into our already busy schedule."

"This is crazy," Doug said. "We're going to be murdering people, then we're going to sell a dangerous thing like the bunny cube to some evil nation, and we're going to be working with Tara, who I just don't trust. This isn't right. We're Hellbender. We're supposed to be rebels and fighting the entrenched power. Or a rock band."

"Grah!" Lulu exclaimed. "I'm the leader! It's on the official form! And I'm going to tell us what to do! And we're going to drop off our smuggled goods. And then we'll handle whatever the bunny cube did to us and sell it for lots of money. And if we have time and run into her, we'll murder Lapointe. And there will be no more whining from Doug and no more Charlene going behind our back and no more ... well, Bryce, just try in general to be less smarmy. And if you don't like it, I will throw you out of this truck right now. Now someone open the door so I can throw Charlene out to show you I'm serious."

"Good speech, Tri-lu," Bryce said.

"I said *less* smarmy!" Lulu shouted.

"Oh, what's it matter," Charlene huffed. "If I stick with you three, all I'm destined for is a really stupid death."

"And soon!" Lulu added.

Doug leaned back and took the clear plastic baggie containing the cube out of his pocket. The thing looked harmless enough — especially with the bunnies stenciled on it — but he had this feeling that finding it had irreparably changed them. He only wish he had listened better to "Satan" and remembered more of what he told him.

Demons. Satan had mentioned something about demons. Was that what that Darius was who was killing people? He figured his friends would make fun of him if he even brought up the idea, but as Doug stared into the dead eyes of the bunny stenciled on the cube's side, it unfortunately didn't seem absurd to him.

* * *

Darius crept through the dark streets, sticking to the shadows and avoiding the moonlight. His task seemed simple: He'd kill most of them, and then leave one or two alive to torture for information. And then after he had his information, he'd just torture them for fun.

He soon was back to the door with the sign "Rook's Criminal Enterprises," and with a powerful kick, he smashed open the door. Darius barged inside, ready to kill the first people he saw, but he saw no one. The room was empty. Except for something sitting on a table. He came closer to inspect the object. Explosives?

* * *

Rook sat in his van, watching his building explode in flames.

"You don't think this is a little excessive, sir?" Driscoll asked.

"Something about that guy was just really, really off," Rook said. "And I was right about him coming back for us. Decided to kill it with fire just to be sure. Plus, now I can pretend I'm dead for a bit; figure it's only a matter of time until Vogel comes after me." Rook opened a bottle of beer and took a drink. "You warned me about doing business with Hellbender, didn't you?"

Driscoll nodded. "That I did. I still didn't think they'd be this much trouble."

Rook stared at the flames. "What kind of name is Hellbender, anyway? What's that mean? They're going to bend hell?"

"It's a type of salamander," Candy said between mouthfuls of Chinese food.

"And where did the salamander get the name from?" Rook asked.

Candy shrugged.

"Know what? Don't care what their stupid name is," Rook said. "Our people in Calais will have their hands on them soon. Then we'll have the cube and ... I guess we'll see what General Lapointe will pay for us to hand Hellbender over. Otherwise I have some ideas for them myself. Let's get to Calais."

* * *

"I did it!" Mills said, panting as she ran into the presidential suite. There really was only one nice hotel in downtown Disputed Zone, and after a brief knife fight, the best room was theirs. Lapointe was sitting on the bed reading, while the Athenians sat elsewhere looking bored and paying Mills no attention. "The tracker is on Rook's van."

Lapointe sighed. "Such a boring, straightforward solution to the problem."

Mills turned to the Athenians. "And really, shouldn't one of you 'special forces' have handled this?"

Gisele yawned.

Mills looked at Lapointe. "But you won't believe what else I saw!"

Lapointe didn't look up from her book. "An explosion."

"Well ... yeah. How'd you know?"

"I can smell the smoke on you," Lapointe said. "Plus, Rook looked quite disturbed by that Darius fellow; I was expecting some extreme response from him."

Mills found a chair and sat down. "Well, Darius was in the explosion, so whoever he was, he's not a concern now."

Lapointe took a deep breath. "We'll see."

Mills took out a tablet. "Rook is on the move — already out of the city. Actually, by his direction, he's heading for ... Calais."

Lapointe jumped up from the bed. "So that's where Hellbender is! Yes, right back to the scene of the crime ... that does seem like the audacity of Ryland."

"That's not anyone's name," Mills muttered. "Anyway, all we need to do is give our people a call and tell them to be on the lookout and we should soon have the cube."

"No, we handle this ourselves," Lapointe stated. "Come. We have a quarry. It's time for a showdown with Hellbender."

"We finally get to kill someone?" Gisele asked.

"Yes, but Ryland is mine." Lapointe marched out of the hotel room, and the Athenians followed.

"Again, don't care about them!" Mills called out as she followed. "Just the artifact!" Mills fumbled through her pockets and pulled out her Xanax, but the pill bottle was empty. "And we need to stop by Walgreens!"

"So that was my game: To win you to my side, little by little. God may be more powerful, but I have always had the more attractive argument."

CHAPTER 16

"So everyone has their story straight?" Bryce asked.

"We are but wandering circus performers," Lulu stated.

"No, come on; that's not the backstory I wrote for you," Bryce said, handing her a piece of paper. "I specifically designed these stories to make us as unassuming as possible so we won't get much scrutiny."

They were sitting in the back of the truck, dressed again in their Confederacy of Astara uniforms, Bryce and Doug in their black shadow enforcer uniforms, Lulu in her officer uniform, and Charlene in her peacekeeper uniform — this time sans scarf to be less conspicuous.

"These seem unnecessarily detailed," Charlene said. "Why does mine specify I'm a lesbian who is questioning her sexuality because of Dalton's charm and good looks? And who is Dalton?"

"That's the character I'll be playing," Bryce said. "I just wanted to make stories for you that fit each of you and were believable."

"I'm not a lesbian," Charlene said. "And I find you repulsive."

Bryce raised an eyebrow. "You just went two completely different directions with that statement. So, you're really not a lesbian?" Bryce thought about it for a moment. "Oh, I guess I just always assumed you were, though I've never actually seen you date anyone."

"I'll be the lesbian, then," Lulu said. She started to write on her piece of paper with a pen. "Lesbian kickboxing champion."

"Don't change the stories I wrote!" Bryce yelled. "Be more like Doug. Doug has his story down."

Doug looked at his piece of paper. "All mine says is 'No matter what, don't say anything.'"

"Simple, huh?"

Doug frowned. "I don't think you give me enough respect."

Bryce patted him on the back. "We respect how honest you are — which is why you're bad at subterfuge. And we also respect that we don't want you to screw things up and get us killed."

Lulu snatched the piece of paper from Doug and started writing on it. "We can go ahead and add a little to his story. 'Heterosexual, but beginning to question his sexuality because of his attraction to Bryce.'"

Doug shook his head. "I'm not comfortable with that. Can't I be attracted to Charlene instead?"

"Let's not overly complicate things," Bryce said. "Just one love triangle to keep our backstory from being too boring." He pointed to Charlene, Lulu, and himself.

Lulu nodded. "Yes, we're both vying for Charlene's love." She headed for Charlene, lips puckered. "Let's give in to our basest desires!"

Charlene shoved her. "Get away from me!"

"Homophobe!" Lulu shouted back.

A tone sounded. "We're almost there," Bryce said. "Everyone ready?"

"Why didn't we just get a new civilian vehicle," Charlene asked, "and sneak into the city?"

"Sneaking implies we're sneaky," Bryce said. "We're going to just go right through the front door in a conspicuous military vehicle because we have nothing to hide. We'll simply broadcast the right codes and then head in unnoticed. Then we can quickly drop off Rook's cargo and concentrate on what's next."

A voice came out of the radio on the truck. "Control of truck taken by the Transport Authority. Bringing you in for inspection." They could feel the truck descending.

Bryce went white. "I didn't know they could do that."

"It's Charlene who is supposed to know about military stuff!" Lulu yelled, pointing an accusing finger at Charlene. "She led us into a trap!" Tears formed in Lulu's eyes. "And I loved you!"

"I didn't know about this!" Charlene said. She thought a moment. "Well ... maybe I did hear about some sort of control override being put in all military vehicles. I did say we should have used a civilian vehicle, so once again we're about to get killed because of your stupidity and not mine."

Doug looked out the windshield. Their vehicle was heading for a garage in a large government building. He looked at the stack of cocaine bricks in the back. "Man, we're going to have to fight our way out of this." Doug picked up a rifle and prepped it. "There will be too many in there for us to take head-on, so we'll have to battle our way to like an air vent and then sneak out through the ductwork. So does anyone know how to get one of those grates off an air vent? Like I assume we need a screwdriver, but I don't know if it would be a Phillips or a flathead. I guess we could bring both just in case ... Oh man! What if it's one of those weird square ones?"

"Let's not panic about being unable to remove screws just yet," Bryce said. "And while, yes, this is probably all Charlene's fault, we're going to be just fine. I've yet to meet a situation I can't talk my way out of."

"You constantly meet situations you can't talk your way out of," Doug said. "I mean constantly."

"Well ... maybe," Bryce admitted. "But I do run into plenty of situations I *can* talk my way out of, and perhaps this will be one of them." Bryce put on the face mask for his shadow enforcer uniform. "If people can't see my face, that does reduce my charm ... but I can manage. Everyone know what we're doing?"

Charlene picked up a gun. "Let's at least die fighting."

"No dying. No fighting," Bryce said. "Everyone just be calm."

Their truck headed into the garage and came to a stop on the ground. Bryce opened the side door, and outside was a team of soldiers headed by a stern-looking, overweight man. "This vehicle is marked as stolen," said the inspections officer.

"Oh, that was just some confusion during the attack the other day," Bryce explained as the four got out of the truck. "Everything is in order."

The officer looked in the truck. "That's a lot of cocaine."

Bryce shrugged. "Define 'a lot.'"

The officer looked at Lulu. "So are you the officer in charge here?"

"Yeppers!" Lulu answered.

"And your name?"

Lulu hesitated. "You don't have the rank to request my name."

"Don't worry, I'll handle them," a woman called out. Approaching them was another officer in uniform, though Doug quickly recognized the face: Tara.

"Who are you?" the inspections officer asked Tara.

"Tara, from the south office," Tara said. "Henley has some emergency to attend to, so I'm taking over for her temporarily. Anyway, this is a special case, so just leave the vehicle here and I'll process them in Henley's office."

"Yeah, we're special," Lulu told the officer.

Tara led them away, up some stairs, and into a spacious office. When they were all inside, Tara shut the door. "So you guys decided to come in through the front door?"

"It was a good plan, I thought," Bryce said.

"It was an idiotic plan!" Charlene yelled.

Doug kept a firm gaze on Tara. "So you just happened to be here to help us?"

"I don't know why you have to sound so suspicious," Tara said. "I just saved you guys."

"Yeah, stop being a jerk, Doug," Bryce said. He then noticed a chest labeled "Snacks." "Ooh, she has snacks."

"Be careful opening that," Tara warned. "There's a dead body in there."

Bryce chuckled. "I'll be careful." He opened the chest a little and immediately closed it. "Oh, she wasn't joking; there's a half-naked dead woman in there."

"That's not a good snack!" Lulu exclaimed.

"Yeah, I strangled some woman to get this uniform," Tara explained. "So we probably don't want to stay here long."

Doug backed away from the snacks. "Why did you have to strangle her? Couldn't you just knock her out?"

Tara shook her head. "Knocking someone out is not an exact science. But if you strangle someone, you know she's not going to get back up and cause trouble. Smarter option."

"Are you some sort of psychopath?" Doug asked.

Tara looked hurt. "Like I don't have regular human emotions? No. I'm just good at ... ignoring them when they're not particularly useful. But I feel bad about killing whoever she was. I mean, she probably has friends and family who are going to miss her, and that's awful." Tara thought for a second. "Then again, maybe she doesn't have anyone who will miss her." Tara frowned. "And that would be even sadder in a way, wouldn't it?"

"It's no time to get squeamish about killing," Charlene said, though she slowly inched away from the snacks trunk. "We have some killing of our own to do. Tara. What information can you get on the computer in here?"

"Plenty; that's actually why I came here." Tara sat down at the computer. "I was trying to get info to help with us breaking into the research facility, but then I saw your arrival and went to help. Anyway, I have full access; I got that woman to give me her password before I strangled her."

Bryce adjusted his collar. "Smart."

"We need to know where General Lapointe is," Charlene said.

"I should be able to find that," Tara said. "What do you need her for?"

Lulu sat on the snack trunk. "It's our first big government contract. We're supposed to brutally murder her."

Doug shuddered when he thought of the wording on the contract. "But nothing worse than that."

"Oh ... well, that's good," Tara said and started working at the computer. "Apparently she is out on some secret mission, which I can't get the details on. Oh! But she's coming back today, and there's going to be some party for her at the Four Seasons to celebrate how she defeated Loch's forces here in Calais."

"I did that!" Charlene shouted. "That should be my party!"

Bryce waved her off. "Not a lot of time to form a plan, but I have enough contacts here that I should be able to get us into that party. This is doable."

"That's great for you guys!" Tara said. "So I guess we'll meet up afterwards to plan the research facility break-in. Just keep the cube thing safe until then."

"But we're going to hold onto it," Doug declared.

Tara nodded. "That's what I just said."

"So can you now approve us on this computer so we can get out with our vehicle?" Bryce asked.

Tara frowned. "I'm afraid that's not so simple. The vehicle was registered as stolen, and you're not going to be able to get it out of here without another inspection — which I'm guessing you won't pass. Best I can do is mark the contents to be transferred to a low-security holding facility, from which you can then retrieve them in a day or two."

"Another heist?" Lulu stood up and paced. "We got a lot of capers for one stop."

Bryce sighed. "If that's the best that can be done, hopefully Rook won't mind the delay."

"Hopefully it's only you he'll go after and not the rest of us," Charlene said. She looked at Tara. "So how do we get out of here?"

"Probably easiest if you go out through maintenance," Tara said. "Maybe I should get you some janitor uniforms to change into."

"Are you going to have to strangle a bunch of people to get those?" Doug asked.

Tara chuckled. "Don't be silly; there's always spare janitor uniforms."

Someone knocked on the door.

"Come in," Tara answered.

A man in uniform entered and looked at Tara. "Where's Henley?"

"I'm filling in for her," she said. "She had some throat trouble." Tara then put her hands around her own throat to illustrate.

"Oh, anyway, I was just going to grab some snacks if that's okay."

Tara shrugged. "I'm not in charge of them, so help yourself."

The man went to the trunk while the others fidgeted, wondering if they should do something. When the man opened the lid, he gasped, but before he could voice anything, Tara was on him with a garrote around his throat. When he went limp, Tara shoved him into the large trunk and closed the lid, though now it didn't close all the way. She then shut the office door and turned and smiled at the others. "Like I said, we all should probably get going soon."

They were all too stunned to talk. Finally, Lulu asked, "So where did you get a garrote?"

"Oh, I just go to a music supply store and get some piano wire," Tara said. "I tried guitar strings — which is more convenient since I actually play the guitar — but that didn't work as well. Nothing more awkward than a botched strangling, amirite?"

They all stared at her a few moments longer. "Yeah, let's get going," Bryce said.

"And I really think you might be a psychopath," Doug remarked.

"I'm really not, Doug," Tara said. "And I hope because I'm helping you all out of this jam here, you understand I'm on your side." She smiled. "You can trust me. Now let's get you out of here so you can go murder Lapointe."

* * *

Tara started downloading the research base layout while she made a call on her phone. "Skinner? Where are you?" Delgado answered.

"I found Hellbender," Tara said. "They're in Calais."

"Where exactly are they?"

Tara found information on another, more secret research base that was labeled as dismantled. There were files for surveillance video. "I don't know at the moment — I had to keep my distance, as I don't think I could take them on myself. But I believe they're going to the party being thrown for Lapointe this evening."

"What are their plans there?"

Tara played the surveillance video. On the screen, Hellbender was giving a reality imploder bomb to Loch's forces. "No idea. But ... they had something on them that they seemed to think was important. It looked like a cube of some sort."

There was a pause on the other end. "A metal cube?"

"Yeah, a little metal cube."

A man walked into the office. "Have you seen Garrison?"

"Sorry, no," Tara answered, not looking up from her screen.

He stared a moment at Tara. "And who are you? Where's Henley?"

"You'll have to excuse me a moment," she said to Delgado. She put down her phone, pulled out a silenced pistol, shot the man three times, put the gun back down, and picked up the phone. "So what are my orders?"

"Just keep an eye on Hellbender. I'll be heading over there personally."

"Okay." Tara put away her phone and then walked over to the man she'd shot. With her gloved hand, she touched one of the bloody wounds. And with the blood, she started writing on the wall: "HELLBENDER."

"Suffice to say, it's been a very long game I've been playing. It started on the eve of creation. I had to get man to commit the first sin. That was easy. Everything since has been harder. But again, I am not limited by time, so persistence is easy."

CHAPTER 17

Bryce flashed the young female hotel receptionist his well-practiced smile. "I have a reservation for your best suite."

She blushed slightly and returned the smile. "Under what name?"

Bryce shrugged. "I don't remember. I wouldn't put it under my own name, obviously, as I don't want to get mobbed when people know I'm coming. Everyone wants to be rich and famous, but it can be a bit of a curse."

The receptionist nodded knowingly while scanning his face, trying to place him.

Bryce leaned in. "Help me out here and I'll let you take a selfie with me — as long as you promise to wait a day to share it."

She smiled and checked the computer. "We have one suite reserved for a Chadwick Lessard. Is that the name you used?"

"Yep. That sounds like it."

"Actually," piped in a voice behind Bryce. "Chadwick Lessard is famous too. He's this chef who was recently on —"

Bryce had forgotten Doug was with him. He quickly turned around and in a compromise between a shout and a whisper told Doug, "You had one job. Don't talk. Remember?" Bryce turned back to the receptionist. "Sorry, ignore him. There was a flu going around and now I'm down to the B-list on my entourage."

There was a little suspicion creeping into the receptionist's face. "Okay. Anyway, I just need to check on that reservation, and —"

"You have a nice look to you," Bryce said, studying the receptionist carefully. "Have you ever considered being in film?"

The receptionist blushed again. "I don't know. Maybe a little."

"You should give it more serious thought. I certainly am." Bryce held out his hand. "Anyway, keys to the suite."

* * *

"Hey, Rookie Cookie!" Lulu shouted into her phone.

"Don't call me that," Rook answered. "So ... uh ... where are you guys? You're supposed to be making the delivery right now."

Lulu played with the drapes in the hotel suite. "Oh, about that ... there's going to be a little delay. This will all take a day or two longer."

"Well, why don't you go to my people right now and explain the situation to them?"

"Maybe later; we kind of have something going on today," Lulu said. "But don't worry; we'll definitely get you the shipment."

"I'd say there is a high probability we're going to botch this and flee the city," Charlene told Lulu as she sat on the couch.

"Shut up, Charlene!" Lulu shouted as she blocked the microphone on her phone. "There's a live plant right next to you! Haven't you heard how negative energy kills plants? You're going to kill all the plants here with all your ... being you." She picked up the phone. "Everything is going to go great. You're going to be very happy. Just happy a day or two later than you were expecting."

"But you're in Calais?" Rook asked.

"Yep."

"I'm actually going to be there soon, so why don't we meet up?"

Lulu twirled her hair on her finger. "Are you asking me on a date?"

There was a pause. "Sure. Let's say that."

"Well, tonight we're going to be at this big party."

"The one they're throwing for Lapointe?"

"Yep."

"What are you doing there?"

"A bit of a side venture."

"I should be able to get into that party. I'll meet you there."

"Well, you might not want to be around us when everything goes down."

"I'll meet you there," Rook said firmly and hung up.

"So Rook is going to meet me at the cocktail party," Lulu told Charlene, Bryce, and Doug, who were lounging about the room. "I think it's a date." She sighed and stared into the air. "He does have this roguish quality to him. You know, we girls do go for the bad boys. I read that somewhere."

Bryce stroked his chin. "Well, that could get in the way of our assassination attempt."

"Are we calling it an assassination now?" Doug asked. "I do like that better than 'brutal murder.'"

"I wonder what he wants," Charlene said.

"Probably my body," Lulu answered. "That's what guys usually want." She turned angrily to Doug. "Stop staring at me like I'm a piece of meat! I'm more than a piece! I'm a whole butcher's counter of complexity!"

"We can worry about Rook later," Bryce said. "What we need is a plan for tonight. And I have a good feeling about it. Things are going pretty well already with how I got us this awesome suite."

Charlene sighed. "There are so many things here that could go wrong, and now I have to add hotel security on top of it all. Let's just concentrate on a good plan for taking out Lapointe."

"I have an idea for a horrible death," Doug said. "We find where Lapointe's room is. Then we sneak in and set things up so that when she opens her closet, a whole bunch of angry monkeys jump out and bite her to death. That would be the worst death ever."

"I thought you were morally opposed to this," Charlene said.

"Yeah," Doug answered, "but then I had a good idea."

"And how exactly are we supposed to obtain and control a large group of angry monkeys?" Bryce asked.

Doug thought a moment. "Well, logistics has never really been my field."

"It's set then!" Lulu announced. "We're going to do a daring heist of the local zoo! First thing, we'll need a realistic-looking gorilla costume."

"We don't need to go to the zoo," Doug said. "We could just get those monkeys that replaced me at the hover cart factory. All we'll need then is to make them angry; we can probably do that by slapping them around a bit. I can do that."

"We don't have enough time to waste on this idiocy," Charlene said. "We need to get an actual plan with what we have here to work with. Now, Bryce always claims to be good with women."

Bryce scoffed. "And Michelangelo *claims* to be good at painting."

"A simple plan," Charlene continued, "would be for him to seduce the general and lead her back to this room, where we can then ... I dunno ... bludgeon her to death."

"Where are we going to buy bludgeons?" Doug asked.

Bryce thought for a moment. "Serviceable plan, if a bit unsavory. Now how old is the general? I imagine she must be rather desperate, so this should be pretty easy."

Charlene sighed. "We'll definitely want a plan B. I'm thinking something like we start a fire and then grab the general in the chaos."

"Oh yeah, Charlene," Lulu scoffed, "because it's *so* easy to grab people in chaos."

"It's the beginning of a plan," Charlene shot back.

"Your face is the beginning of a plan!" Lulu yelled.

Charlene took a step toward Lulu. "You take that back!"

"What are you even arguing about?" Doug asked.

"Are we really just going to stand there and let her take over Hellbender like this?" Lulu said. "We wrote on a form that I'm in charge. That's a sacred bond!"

"I'm the competent one," Charlene said, "and you're all idiots. You're going to listen to me if we want to do this right and not just leap to our deaths."

"If brutally murdering someone is going to tear us apart," Doug said, "maybe we shouldn't do it. Friendship is more important than killing for money."

"We're not friends," Charlene declared. "We don't have time to be for something like this. What we're supposed to be is a professional mercenary group. And we already screwed up a simple delivery, so let's at least get this right. If we're going to have any chance of later breaking into that research facility and handling whatever that cube did to you, we need to learn to work as a team. And remember, this thing with touching the cube is your problem, not mine."

"But we'll all work together to solve it as a team," Doug said.

"We'll see," Charlene said. "So, Bryce, you'll be able to get us into the actual party?"

Bryce held up two white cards with fancy writing on them. "I have invitations right here."

Charlene stared a moment at the cards. "Oh, can — can you —"

Bryce rolled his eyes. "We'll save one for your scrapbooking. Anyway, now I just need to make sure my suit is ready. Lulu, you'll need to go dress shopping."

"Already stolen two credit cards since we got here!" Lulu said.

"So I go with Lulu and get a dress?" Charlene asked.

Bryce just stared silently at Charlene. Finally, Lulu said, "Oh, honey."

Charlene looked confused. "What?"

"This is a very glamorous cocktail party for the elite," Bryce explained. "And everyone in it will have to conform to that to blend in."

"Are you saying I can't be glamorous?" Charlene asked.

"I was actually trying not to just come out and say that," Bryce answered.

Charlene looked a bit hurt. "You have other strengths, you know," Lulu assured her. "Just not ... um ... dress wearing."

"I'm sure Charlene could be very glamorous if she wanted to," Doug added.

"Oh, yes, I'm sure," Bryce said. "But I only have two invitations anyway. But don't worry; I'll get us all into the party."

"So what about a dress?" Charlene asked.

"Don't worry about the dress."

* * *

"Where were you?" said the text on the screen.

"I was delayed." Darius pulled the tags off his new clothing. "Someone tried to blow me up."

"They know what you are?"

Darius chuckled. "What does it matter? I've lost track of Hellbender, though."

"I have eyes everywhere. As soon as they make any sort of commotion, I will lead you to them."

Darius smiled. "Good. I'm looking forward to finally meeting them."

"And in the silly stereotype people have of me, you might think I win by the amount of cruelty and violence inflicted. But no, I found that gets me nowhere. My goal instead was to make people more and more comfortable with this world, until it was a womb they never wanted to leave."

CHAPTER 18

It was a delicate operation. There were many variables to consider, many aspects to pay attention to. Charlene straightened her uniform as she carefully scanned the room.

"I don't know why I couldn't dress up and be one of the partygoers," Doug said. He was wearing a red staff uniform, same as Charlene. "I can be debonair." He thought for a moment. "That's a word, right?"

"Yes."

"And I used it correctly?"

"Yes."

Doug nodded. "And what's it mean?"

Charlene sighed and kept up her meticulous scan of the party. "We're going to need more shrimp. That tray is almost empty. Why don't you go get some more?"

"We're only pretending to be waiters," Doug said. "I don't want to have to do like actual work."

"If we're going to pretend to be waiters," Charlene said, "we need to convincingly do a good job of it. Of course, you're never willing to put in the work. That's why you're always such a loser."

"There's lots of reasons I'm a loser." Doug sulked off toward the kitchen.

Doug was a liability, as usual. But Charlene Marshall was not going to fail. She had this. She spotted a potential problem and looked at a nearby server. "Chrissy, there's some plates to your right that need clearing."

"Who are you?" Chrissy answered. "You're not my boss."

"I'm the one who noticed the plates need clearing! Now do it!" Charlene started tidying up the cups around a punch bowl while grumbling to herself. "I'm always surrounded by incompetents."

* * *

"And what is that you're wearing?" General Marie Lapointe asked, frowning.

"It's my military uniform!" Mills shouted. "This is supposed to be a celebration of a military victory, so I thought I would wear my military uniform. Because we're in the military!"

Lapointe sipped her drink. She was careful not to move very much, since she knew she currently stood in the best poise and position to show off her sleek black dress — a Gianna Velasco original. "I feel so embarrassed for you right now."

"And shouldn't we be looking for Hellbender?" Mills whispered to Lapointe. "They apparently murdered their way into this city — three dead at the inspection center. I really thought they were just a bunch of idiots, but now I'm wondering if they're up to something. We need to get that artifact from them before they flee to someplace we can't easily reach them."

"So you want us to scamper around the city looking for them?" Lapointe asked. "How horrid. No, we'll just let them come to us."

"And what makes you think they'll come to us?"

Lapointe looked through the partygoers, fixing her gaze on a young man in a suit and an Asian girl in a red dress dancing the robot. "Why do you think I threw this party?"

* * *

"Could you stop that?" Bryce asked. "You're drawing attention."

Lulu kept dancing. "I didn't wear something this low-cut to not draw attention." She smiled at a man looking her way. "Hey."

Bryce adjusted his tie. "I'm going to approach the target."

Lulu continued dancing. "What a cute pet name you have for her."

Bryce sauntered up to Lapointe. She looked at him with a reserved expression. "I have to say," Bryce said, wearing his very well-practiced, charming smile, "that you look absolutely gorgeous tonight."

Lapointe set her drink down on a nearby table, and her gaze intensified. "This dress was specifically tailored to emphasize my figure — a figure I've worked hard on to ensure it is not too thin nor too muscular, but toned and healthy-looking. The dark color of the dress contrasts with my eyes, the color of a bright summer sky. My hair is youthful but regal and a natural blond like spun gold. My makeup is a light touch, not distracting from my perfect features but enhancing them. The décolletage of my dress is specifically designed to entice while not revealing too much. And my posture is one that emphasizes my assets while conveying both femininity and power. So why the hell would you think I'd need some little loser in a cheap suit to come tell me I'm 'gorgeous,' when I know with both scientific and artistic certainty that I'm absolutely stunning?"

Without a word, Bryce slowly turned around and slunk back to Lulu, who had finally stopped dancing and was downing some punch. "I think I might be out of my league."

"Wow; you're absolutely pale." Lulu finished off her drink. "Well, every woman has some insecurities to exploit. Lemme have a go at old Murray."

Lulu pranced up to Lapointe, who barely regarded her presence. "Great party," Lulu beamed. "So what's it for? Your fiftieth birthday?"

Now Lulu had Lapointe's full attention. "Someone grab her and execute her!" Lapointe shouted.

As Lapointe kept staring at Lulu and no one came to execute her, it eventually became awkward, and Lulu slunk back to Bryce. "Yeah, she's a tough nut to crack."

"Hello, Princess Dragon Lady."

Bryce and Lulu turned to see Rook approaching them with his "muscle," Candy, at his side in a purple dress. "Hey, Rook!" Lulu answered. "How's it going? You moving either vertically or horizontally?"

"Ha, I get it," Rook said, not smiling.

Bryce smiled at Candy. "I have to say that you are looking absolutely gorgeous tonight."

Candy giggled and blushed.

Bryce whispered to Lulu, "See, I still have it."

"This is kind of a new thing for me," Candy said. "This is my first enforcer assignment where I'm in a dress. Driscoll didn't really have advice for how to conceal weapons in one of these; I had to figure out how to do it myself."

"We're not doing small talk with them," Rook told Candy.

"I see; you want to get right to it." Lulu pressed close to Rook. "So ditch this floozy next to you and let us make love on the dance floor."

Rook kept his eyes firmly on her face. "I know you have the cube."

Lulu backed off a little. "What's a cube?"

"Don't play dumb with me."

Lulu thought a moment. "Oh yeah, that's like a square, but three-dimensional."

Bryce laughed. "And where did you get this idea that we already have this valuable artifact? That's preposterous."

"Never mind how I know," Rook said. "Let's just say I'm not the only one who knows. Now, I'm still feeling pretty generous since I'm pretty sure you're all just idiots in way over your heads, so if you come with me now and give me the artifact, I will not only not murder you, but you'll also profit from this. But if you don't join with me, I can tell you for a fact you are going to all get horribly killed. And not necessarily by me. Though maybe by me. I hope it's me."

Candy scowled, making her threatening face. "If you push us, in five to ten seconds I can retrieve my gun and blow your brains out."

"The not getting killed and also profiting sounds like a great deal," Bryce said. "It's just we have to do something first before we can put the object up for sale."

Rook sighed. "You idiots touched it, didn't you?"

"It's not like there was a warning label on it," Lulu said.

"Hello, Rook," called out another man. Delgado. And by his side, in a dark blue dress, was Tara. "I heard you were dead."

Rook looked slightly nervous. "No, not dead. No." He looked at Tara. "And who is this lovely lady?"

Bryce glared at Tara. "And what are you doing here?"

Tara surreptitiously gave Bryce a quiet signal.

"Don't worry about her," Delgado said. "Just one of my people." He turned to Bryce and Lulu. "My remaining people."

"It's good to see you," Bryce told him. "You still owe us money, and I'm hoping we can get that handled and put the bad times behind us."

Delgado frowned. "All the people at my headquarters were slaughtered, and you were seen standing around their corpses."

Bryce shrugged. "I don't comment on rumors."

"We kill so many people so often," Lulu said, "we can't keep track. When someone comes up to us says, 'Hey! You killed these people!' all we can say is, 'Maybe.'"

"But what I do know," Bryce added, "is that we delivered the reality imploder bomb, and we never got paid for it. So let's focus on that first."

"I'm not paying you," Delgado growled.

Bryce's smile faded. "But you owe us money."

"Uh-oh, you're making us angry," Lulu said. "And I think you've seen what allegedly happens when we get angry."

Delgado looked annoyed and locked his eyes on Bryce. "I don't know what happened in the Disputed Zone, but I know I'm not scared of some little dandy."

Bryce laughed. "Did he call me a dandy?" He adjusted his suit. "Is that supposed to be an insult?"

"So are you a woman trying to break into the criminal underworld too?" Candy asked Tara. "My mentor isn't much help on issues of being an enforcer that are specifically related to being a woman, and it would be nice if we could trade tips."

Tara nodded. "Yeah, maybe later. Not right now, though, because I'm not sure how this is going to go down and I might have to hurt or kill you."

"Hey, everybody, let's lighten up here," Rook said, looking at Delgado. "This is a party. You got an issue you want to work out with these jokers, you can do it later. I have some business to conclude with them first, and then I'll send them your way."

Delgado stared at Rook for a second. "You know about the artifact, don't you?"

Rook scoffed. "The what?"

Delgado looked at Bryce. "I was told you have an important artifact."

Bryce backed away. "Who told you that?" He set his eyes on Tara, who shrugged.

"Come on," Rook said. "I know these guys: They're idiots. Losers. Human garbage, really. They obviously didn't kill your people, and they obviously don't have anything valuable on them."

"Yet you vouched for them as a mercenary group?" Delgado asked.

"Well ... I have a soft spot for losers."

"Rook, why don't you scram?" Delgado said. "This is big-boy stuff now; you and your little organization ..." He patted Candy on the shoulder. "... are in over your head. And I'll make my own determination about this 'Hellbender.'" He looked at Bryce and Lulu. "What are you doing here, anyway?"

"Actually, that is a good question," Rook added.

"Oh yeah; the mission!" Lulu exclaimed and looked at where Lapointe had been standing. But she was gone.

* * *

"Bryce and Lulu are talking to a bunch of people," Doug said as he looked across the room. "I think two are Rook and Candy. And the others are ... Tara! And that guy who wouldn't pay us and beat us up. Should we do something?"

Charlene was writing in a notepad. "I'm working on some hand signals. If you see a tray that is empty, you can signal that to who is nearest the kitchen by —"

"Charlene, forget that for a sec," Doug said. "I think Bryce and Lulu might be in trouble."

"Huh?" Charlene looked over toward them. "They're supposed to be working the target right now." She scanned the room. "And where did the target go?"

Doug looked around, too. And then he spotted Lapointe. She was glaring at Doug and heading right for him. She came very close to him and whispered, "I know you sent your two flunkies after me, Ryland, but I was waiting to see what your move would be. I guess I got impatient."

Doug froze, unsure what to do. The only thought in his head was that Lapointe smelled really nice and really expensive.

Lapointe frowned. "I guess I could just seize you now, but perhaps that's your plan. What's your scheme?"

Doug glanced around to see if anyone would come help him, but all he saw was Charlene, who was pretending to be working behind him, tidying up a table — or maybe she really was working.

"Well, I guess I don't care if it's a trap," Lapointe said. "Let's see what you're made of. SEIZE HIM!"

Doug froze, but then he noticed no one running to grab him.

The conceited-looking officer behind Lapointe sighed. "You put the security out of the room because you said they ruined the ambience." She turned to a stylishly dressed woman beside her. "Gisele, grab him."

Gisele frowned. "But what if he fights back? This dress clashes with hand-to-hand combat."

The officer pulled out a radio. "Security! Get in here!"

Soldiers rushed into the room and grabbed Doug before he could figure out what he should do.

"Her too!" the officer said, pointing at Charlene. "And those two over there!" She pointed at Lulu and Bryce.

The soldiers grabbed Charlene as she was busy stacking plates. "Wait! I'm not done!" Charlene protested.

As the soldiers rushed toward Bryce and Lulu, Lulu shouted, "Ninja magic!" and threw something on the ground, from which erupted a large cloud of smoke. When the smoke cleared, Bryce was nowhere to be seen, and Lulu was struggling to get her dress unsnagged from the windowsill before tumbling outside.

The soldiers dragged Doug and Charlene from the room. "Chrissy!" Charlene shouted. "Finish stacking those plates! And bring out more shrimp!"

"So piece by piece, bit by bit, I took over His creation. Each day, it became more and more mine. Each day, mankind became less and less His. Until one day, it was time for the final blow."

CHAPTER 19

"Well, that could have worked out better," Bryce said as he and Lulu ducked into an alley.

Lulu struggled to keep up in her frilly dress. "Just once I'd like to go to a fancy party where I don't end up escaping through a window."

Bryce straightened his tie. "One day we'll be the rich people throwing the party, and other people will be the party-crashers making a hasty escape. So what the hell was Tara doing there with Delgado? And did she tell him about the cube?"

Lulu nodded thoughtfully. "Something does seem up with her, with the way she keeps betraying us."

Bryce looked back toward the hotel they had escaped from. "So I guess Doug and Charlene are pretty captured, then."

"Are we going to have to rescue them?" Lulu asked.

Bryce shrugged. "I guess we're supposed to ... I dunno."

"I don't know if I've ever mentioned this," Lulu said, "but I don't like Charlene. And she was the one who got us on this stupid 'kill Lapointe' mission anyway."

Bryce led them down another backstreet. "Yeah, I was never really comfortable with this. I mean, the money looks good, but it's just a little ... unseemly. I'm just not completely comfortable with brutal murder and corpse desecration."

"Anyway, I think it served Charlene right to get captured during this," Lulu said. "It's karma. It's like when we were younger and Stacey was always so mean to me and making fun of my hair and clothes. Well, you know what happened to her? Ended up unconscious in the cargo hold of a boat headed for East Asia."

"Well, yeah, but that's because you drugged her and put her there."

Lulu nodded. "Yep. Karma got her."

Bryce looked out at the street, and they quickly made their way across to another alley. "And what about Doug?" He thought a moment. "Well, I guess you can't really make an economic argument to risk life and limb to save him."

"And you know what he'd say right now?" Lulu said, putting on a low-pitched, mimicking voice. "'Hellbender has to stick together and look out for each other.'"

Bryce chuckled. "Yeah, he's so stupid. We'll be much more efficient without him. It will sound bad, though, when people hear we lost half our team. Won't look good to our peers."

Lulu nodded. "I am for always giving in to peer pressure. I guess we'll have to figure out some way to rescue them."

Bryce sighed. "This is why one should avoid having friends. They're just people you feel obligated to do unpaid work for — like rescue missions."

"It won't be for nothing, though," Lulu said. "Like think of how I'm going to be able to shove it in Charlene's stupid face when we save her."

"Yep. And Doug will certainly owe me a favor. That will be useful next time I want him to share his nachos."

There was the sound of meowing. Lulu fished her phone out of her purse.

Bryce looked around the empty alley. "You know, you might want to put your phone on vibrate since we're on the run."

She looked at it. "I think it's the people from the Loch Collective who gave us the assassination job." She put the phone to her ear. "Hello, you've reached Hellbender. Lulu Liu, Queen of the Underworld, speaking."

Bryce stood by, watching the conversation.

"Nope, had a little bit of a setback, but we're working on it," Lulu said, and then paused for the response. "No, don't worry. We'll kill her soon. Yeah, I understand you're on a tight schedule, but this is going to be quality work, so you don't want to rush it. Yeah, it's going to be brutal. Really brutal. So much, in fact, that when you see what we've done to her, you're going to feel sorry. You might hate Lapointe, but even you will think she doesn't deserve what we're going to do to her. You're going to wish you never asked for us to kill her; it will now be something that will haunt you to your grave. And probably the next hit you'll pay for will be to kill us, because you won't be able to sleep while such brutal psychopaths still exist in the same world as you." Lulu looked down at herself. "I'm wearing a red dress that really emphasizes my curves. It's pretty sexy."

"We do have to get going," Bryce reminded her.

"Yeah, I guess we might have wandered away from business at the end there," Lulu told Bryce, and then put the phone back to her ear. "Well, got to get going. Lots of brutal killings to do. Bye." She put the phone away.

"So are we really planning to still carry out this hit on Lapointe?" Bryce asked.

"Who knows? We might accidentally run into her and kill her anyway," Lulu said. "If that happens, then we might as well get paid for it. And eventually she might just die from old age, and I think we should get paid for that, because in a way, isn't that the most brutal death of all?"

"I don't want to wait that long to get paid." Bryce crept to the end of the alley. "We need that cube so we can get our big payday now. We probably shouldn't have left it at the hotel."

"That was stupid planning, and Charlene was in charge of planning," Lulu pointed out.

"Well, it's up to Doug and Charlene right now to make sure someone else doesn't find it. And if they can't manage that, we should revisit the whole abandoning them idea, because that is really a lot less work than a rescue."

They looked out to the street and saw some figures with rifles coming their way. Shapely figures in fancy dresses. Lulu fished her gun out of her purse and sighed. "Every single party."

* * *

"We're not going to talk!" Charlene shouted. "I don't care what you do to me; I won't give you anything. I know how you were going to leave me to die in this city during Loch's attack. No matter what you do to me, revenge is coming. You think you are better than us, but you will bleed and die in the street like a dog." Charlene, hands bound, watched as Lapointe looked around their hotel room. "Are you listening to me?"

Lapointe stood still, eyes scanning everything. "It's getting noisy in here."

Major Mills turned to Charlene. "Just be quiet, okay?"

Doug was quiet. He sat on the bed, his hands cuffed behind him, remembering the one piece of advice Bryce had often given him: Don't say anything so people don't know you're an idiot. Doug did not think he was an idiot, so he'd prove Bryce wrong by showing how quiet he could be. Even though he really wanted to say something, especially after Charlene's dog remark. Did people really leave dogs to die in the street? That seemed awful.

Lapointe looked through the closet. She pulled out of it Charlene's turquoise treason scarf. "Ugh. What's this?"

"That was a gift," Charlene stated.

Lapointe produced a lighter, set the scarf on fire, and tossed it, burning, into a metal wastebasket.

"How dare you!" Charlene leapt at Lapointe, but Mills held her back. Doug thought that was especially mean, but continued to keep his mouth shut.

"I'm doing you a favor," Lapointe told Charlene. "And you should be especially grateful for that since I despise you."

"Could we not set things on fire?" Mills said as she moved Charlene farther away from Lapointe. "We need to focus on finding the artifact."

"I believe it is here," Lapointe declared.

"You do?" Mills let out a breath of relief. "There's a safe in the closet. I can go talk to the hotel staff and hopefully someone should be able to open it."

Lapointe didn't say a thing and kept staring at the safe. Slowly, she bent down and felt some marks on the floor in front of the safe. Then she pulled the safe forward, revealing the cube in its plastic baggie sitting behind it. She picked it up and handed it to Mills.

"It cost extra to use the safe," Charlene explained.

"Well, we have it," Mills said. "That means we can forget about these idiots and get back to the battle against Loch's empire."

Lapointe stared at the cube. "Why are there bunnies on it?"

"I ..." Mills looked at it. "... don't know."

"This was too easy," Lapointe declared.

"Well, according to our files," Mills said, "these are the people known as Hellbender. So this really wasn't too easy. This is exactly the difficulty you'd expect from idiots."

"Call me an idiot one more time!" Charlene growled at Mills. "I don't care if my hands are tied behind my back; I will trounce you and that primping princess of a general."

Lapointe rolled her eyes. "I thought we were recasting this one."

Mills sighed. "We can't do that."

"Guards!" Lapointe shouted. "Take the noisy one away!"

"They're not called guards," Mills said, and then yelled, "Soldiers! Take these two to a holding cells at headquarters!"

Soldiers came in and grabbed Charlene. But before they could take Doug, Lapointe said, "No, not Ryland."

"I'll kill you all!" Charlene screamed as they dragged her out of the room. "I don't know how yet, but I'll do it! I'm kicking around a few different ideas, and they all involve me soaking in your blood! Well, except one. One involves strangling you with your own scarf that I also set on fire! Oh, and I have another idea that involves bludgeoning, but I haven't worked out all the logistics on it."

Charlene was lost in thought as she disappeared out the door. Lapointe met Doug's eyes. "So why did you come back here? And why did you bring the artifact with you? You're up to something."

"He's really not," Mills said. "By all indications, he's the dumbest one."

That made Doug angry, but he kept still. Then again, if he wasn't the dumbest of the group, he wasn't sure which of the others was dumber than him. Maybe Bryce.

Lapointe kept staring at Doug. It was a little unnerving. "For all I know, getting the artifact back is just falling further into Ryland's trap. I want to question him. Alone."

"This is a waste of time!" Mills protested. "We need to figure out what Loch's next move is and prepare for that. We don't have time to play games with these idiots."

"Guards!" Lapointe shouted. "Take the other noisy one away!"

Mills grumbled and left the hotel room, closing the door behind her.

Now that they were alone, Lapointe and Doug just stared at each other quietly for a few seconds. Finally, Lapointe started laughing. "Oh, this is so cliche," she said. "The villain gets himself captured so he can have a tense face-to-face with the hero." She motioned to herself.

Doug had no idea what she was talking about. Or who the hell was "Ryland." Right now, he was focused on figuring out whether he should just maybe wait for Bryce and Lulu to come to their rescue or if he had to come up with an escape plan himself. He was no good at plans, though. He saw a window in the room, and he wondered if he ran at it hard enough, could he smash through it? They were so high up, though, he would most certainly die from the fall, so that didn't seem like a full plan by itself. Then again, he was sitting on a bed with sheets on it. If he could pull off the sheets, maybe he could use them as a crude parachute. It would be hard to manage with his hands behind his back, but not knowing anything about parachutes, he didn't see why it wouldn't work. Still, that would only save him and he'd still need to rescue Charlene. Hopefully they were bringing her someplace high up with sheets.

Of course, it was going to be hard making a sheet parachute with Lapointe watching, but she wasn't paying him much attention, as she seemed very into whatever it was she was currently saying as she paced back and forth. That's when Doug realized he hadn't been listening to her.

"... with careful planning. I guess that's my secret, in a way." She turned and met Doug's eyes. "But you probably already knew this."

Doug said nothing, which he realized was an especially good strategy when he wasn't actually listening.

"Oh, so cool and calm despite you being completely at my mercy," Lapointe said. "What have you planned, Ryland? Some say you may be a member of the Terrorists, but what you are doing isn't random. You have a plan."

The sheet parachute idea was rubbish, Doug decided. He needed to calm down and come up with a better idea, but it was hard with Lapointe staring at him and asking him questions and calling him weird names. His next thought was to try to surreptitiously dial up room service on the phone next to the bed. He doubted they had a service for taking on armed soldiers, but Bryce had told him a good concierge could make almost anything happen.

Lapointe glared at him. "You can't outmatch me, you know. I am the greatest strategic mind this world knows. I will figure out whatever it is you're up to and end it, just like you ruined my plans in the battle here by destroying Loch's air carrier."

Now Doug was a little angry. Lapointe had wanted to abandon him and the other warfs to the mercy of Loch's forces, and all she was worried about was her plans. Still, he said nothing, doing his best to push the anger down.

Lapointe went back to pacing. "You can't hide anything from me. Your actions seem rather arbitrary and incoherent, but I guess that's how you want them to appear. You're trying to perplex me ... Yes! That's what this is all about. Confusing me. Well, it won't work. I'm on top of things. You can't shake me. You can't ..." Lapointe ran to Doug and grabbed him by the shoulders. "Tell me! Tell me what you're up to! Do it or I will rip you apart with my bare teeth if I have to!"

Doug continued to be silent, now doing his best not to stare down Lapointe's dress while she was leaning over him.

Lapointe took a deep breath and calmly sat next to Doug on the bed. "I think emotions are overtaking both of us. Let's talk through these things rationally. You know about Loch and his nation — the violence and the terror he wants to inflict on the world. Whatever you have against the Confederacy of Astara, you have to admit that it's much better if we are the ones who win this fight. For the sake of the world, you need to end whatever it is you're planning against us."

Doug was getting even angrier now. He knew nations like the Confederacy of Astara thought nothing of people like him or his friends. They had treated them like garbage his entire life and had demonstrated that they were certainly ready to dispose of them like refuse when given the opportunity. But now Lapointe expected him to come to this nation's defense because they could supposedly point to a worse evil? Doug couldn't hold the rage in any more. He spoke. "I want to see all your nations burn."

Lapointe looked frightened for a moment. Then she looked angry. She grabbed Doug roughly once more. "You think you can ..." She was too seething with rage to finish her thought. She just stared at Doug face to face, breathing heavily. And then she closed her eyes and started to lean in closer to him ...

She stopped and jumped up from the bed. "No. I can't do this. You're trying to get into my head. You're ..." Lapointe stared at Doug for a moment, almost longingly. She quickly turned and headed out of the room.

"Wow. She is mental," Doug muttered to himself.

Mills entered the room, looking back into the hallway where Lapointe had gone. "So, should I ..." She sighed and looked at Doug. "So what went on in here?"

Doug decided to go back to his strategy of saying nothing.

"Still quiet? Okay. Anyway, I am Major Harriet Mills, and what is going to happen is —"

Doug started chuckling.

"What? What is it?" Mills checked her uniform.

Doug tried to stop himself, but he couldn't and kept laughing.

"What's so funny? What is it?" Mills demanded.

Doug wanted to stay silent, but he couldn't keep it in. "If you got the rank of general, your name would be just like the people who make those cereals."

"Ha! I knew it!" Mills shouted, pointing an accusing finger at Doug. "You're an idiot!" She looked around. "Are we recording this?"

"That brings us back to the Last War, but the fight on the surface between men was the insignificant part. Underneath it all was the final battle in the long conflict I had been waging. And the people were my army, reclaiming this world for its true owner: Me."

CHAPTER 20

Bryce and Lulu hid in a closed coffee shop, watching out the window. They saw two female figures walk by outside. They were still wearing their stylish dresses from the party, which somehow nicely complemented the elegant rifles they were carrying.

"It's just Lapointe's Athenians," Bryce whispered. "They should be easy to get by. They were just made for photo ops. They're not actually a threat combat-wise."

"I can tell from just looking at them that they think they're so great," Lulu seethed. "I want to beat them up."

"No time," Bryce said. "Let's just go to our old apartment and figure out what to do from there."

"Won't people know to look for us there?" Lulu asked. "Since, like, our name is on it and everything?"

"What people?" Bryce said. "No one cares enough about us to look us up; that's our advantage. We're beneath everyone's concern."

They watched as the Athenians walked by the coffee shop. When they were out of view, Bryce led Lulu outside into another alley. As they turned the corner, they ran right into an Athenian standing there, rifle in hand. Her rifle wasn't at the ready, as she was checking her face in a compact, but Bryce had his gun out, so he pointed it at the soldier.

"I don't want to have to hurt you," Bryce said, "but this is a real gun — one that makes scary loud noises — so why don't you put down your rifle and get out of our way before we have to muss up your hair with some violence?"

The Athenian looked at the two as if their mere existence annoyed her. She set down her rifle on the ground, put her compact away, and then flipped, kicking the gun from Bryce's hand and into the air. She caught the pistol, stripped it into two parts, and tossed the parts at Bryce and Lulu, hitting each of them in the head.

"You made me sully myself by touching a standard-issue weapon," the soldier said as she picked back up her rifle. "Now I'm mad."

"Run away!" Bryce yelled as he ducked back into the alley they came from. They could hear the Athenian shouting, and soon they heard bullets ricocheting near them as they ran down another pathway. They paused a second against a wall as Bryce peeked down the alley to see three Athenians approaching them.

"I thought you said they weren't any good at combat!" Lulu yelled.

"Well, I just assumed," Bryce admitted. "I thought the whole point of being an attractive woman was that you didn't have to be good at anything."

Lulu sighed. "You're such a misogynist."

"And you're a padifflywit," Bryce retorted. "See, I can make up words too."

"Incoming!" Lulu shouted, firing at two Athenians who were coming at them from another direction. They ducked out of the way, and Lulu ran for the street, Bryce quickly following as the other three Athenians coming for them opened fire. "Over there!" Lulu yelled, running for their apartment building.

"What's the exit strategy here?" Bryce asked, running after her.

"I have a plan." Lulu barged through the door into apartment lobby. "I'm just counting on you being extra wrong today."

They ran up the stairs to their apartment on the third floor. When they entered, inside the common area was Delgado, surrounded by several goons. Lulu nodded at the sight of them. "Yep. Called it."

Delgado was seated, looking through one of Charlene's scrapbooks, with a couple more sitting on the table. "I was trying to figure out what the hell these things are while we waited for you."

"Oh boy," Lulu exclaimed. "You better not have messed up the order of those, or there is going to be trouble."

Delgado smiled. "I assure you, there is going to be trouble."

"Anyway, good to see you again!" Bryce said to Delgado. "Are you here because you're finally going to pay us?"

"I'm going to tear you to pieces," Delgado said. "And then hang pieces of you at our various headquarters as a warning to others."

Lulu nodded. "It's nice how you think of others like that."

The door was kicked open, and inside came half a dozen Athenians carrying rifles. Delgado and his crew immediately pointed their guns at them, and the Athenians reacted in kind.

Bryce and Lulu moved off to the side. "Well, I guess you guys all have bigger problems to deal with than us," Lulu said. "We'll just leave you to it."

"You're staying right there," Delgado stated, keeping his eyes and his gun on the Athenians.

"You two are coming with us," said the Athenian leader, Gisele, "after we get this resolved." She was the most gorgeous and unapproachable of the group ... not that Bryce wouldn't try, in other circumstances. Or now, if the opportunity arose.

Lulu nodded at both groups. "See, you both want us, but only one of you can have us. That's going to be a problem. Of course, we all know which of the two groups here can easily take on the other."

"She's trying to manipulate us into fighting each other," Delgado said.

"Then you better leave," Gisele answered, "because you and your stereotypical gang of thugs with your off-the-rack guns aren't going to be any match for us."

"I work for the Vogel Criminal Enterprise," Delgado growled. "If you little princesses touch us, your next photo shoot is going to be with a crime scene photographer."

"Hey, let's all calm down and have the weaker side just admit he or she is weaker and give in," Lulu said.

Delgado took a deep breath. "Come on. We're not going to fall for her, are we?"

Gisele sighed. "Fine." She lowered her rifle. "You hold them, but stay here. We'll leave and send our usual liaison to your criminal organization to work this out."

"Well, nice try, Tri-Lu," Bryce said.

One of the Athenians perked her ears at Bryce's voice. "Is that Presley?"

Bryce quickly went through his mental list of aliases he had used. "Yes."

"Wait, I know him too," said another Athenian. "He told me his name was Dean."

"He probably uses a number of aliases," the first Athenian said. "He's a secret agent or something."

"He told me he was a movie producer," said the other.

"It's complicated," he told the two. "But don't worry ..." He looked at the two at the same time so he wasn't directly addressing either as he ventured a name. "... Clarisse."

They glowered back. "That's neither of our names."

Bryce adjusted his tie. "But is there a Clarisse here?"

"Over here," called one of the women in Delgado's group, now glaring at Bryce.

"Oh, hey!" Bryce said, giving her his best smile as Lulu sighed loudly behind him. "And ... uh ... who am I to you?"

"A dead man," Clarisse growled.

"No, we're going to kill the little weasel," said one of the Athenians, whose name Bryce was still struggling to remember.

"We're all calming down, remember?" Delgado said.

"Yes, I'm going with you," Bryce answered. "And you can finally pay me that money you owe me."

"Shut up about the money!" Delgado shouted, pointing his gun at Bryce.

"You're not killing him!" Gisele yelled, pointing her rifle back at Delgado. "You're giving him to us!"

"And we're killing him!" the two Athenians yelled.

Everyone started yelling at each other, and Bryce yanked Lulu into his bedroom just before the bullets started firing.

"I always told myself I'd never go alone with you into your bedroom," Lulu said, crawling along the ground as bullets flew above them.

Bryce pushed away a dresser, revealing a trapdoor. "Every good bedroom needs an alternate escape route."

Bryce pulled open the trapdoor, and they both jumped down, landing in a common area where Floyd was watching TV. "When did you put a hole in my ceiling?"

"A while ago." Bryce headed for the door. "Don't worry about it."

Floyd listened to the gunfire. "And what's going on up there?"

"We don't have time to explain everything, Floyd!" Lulu shouted as she followed Bryce into the hallway. She turned to Bryce. "Gah! I hate Floyd!"

"Everyone does; that's why they named him Floyd." Bryce ran to the fire exit, and he and Lulu took a stairway down to the ground floor. In their way stood a tall man. Despite his height, he was not particularly big, but there was something about him Bryce found unsettling. Probably the eyes, the irises of which looked gold in the light of the hallway.

"Out of the way, chump!" Lulu shouted at him, "Hellbender coming through!"

He didn't move, but he smiled. "Hellbender. Finally, we meet."

"You know of us?" Bryce asked, keeping a little distance, as he suspected that wasn't a good thing.

The man continued to smile, and it only made Bryce more uncomfortable. "I've heard of you. We seem to keep almost running into each other. My name is Darius. I think you've seen my handiwork."

It took Bryce a second to figure out what he was talking about, and when he did, he took a step back without thinking about it as the gunfire continued floors above them.

Lulu stood her ground. "So are you the one who has been slaughtering rooms full of people?"

The smile grew. "Yes."

"All by your lonesome?" Lulu asked.

"I'm quite good. Now, you two have something I want. A cube."

Bryce took a deep breath to compose himself. "Not on us, at the moment. We can get it for you, though."

"Just tell me where it is, and I'll get it," Darius said.

"And then we head on our merry way?" Bryce asked.

Darius's smile changed ever so slightly, and it made Bryce shiver.

Lulu smiled back at Darius, but a much more sultry smile. "I've never done this with a guy I just met, but ..." Lulu raised her gun and shot Darius in the face.

Darius didn't flinch. The wound in his face burned with a small fire and disappeared.

Bryce threw his hands in the air. "Oh, come on! What the hell is going on?"

A van crashed through the wall, plowing into Darius and barely missing Bryce and Lulu. The side door flew open. Inside was Tara, still in her dark blue evening gown. "Get in!"

Bryce and Lulu jumped in and the vehicle took off, using its vertical lift to take to the air. "Been quite a day, huh?" Tara said as she piloted.

"Did you betray us again and tell Delgado we have the cube?" Bryce demanded.

Tara scoffed. "Don't worry about that; that's just me keeping up appearances with Vogel. Oh, by the way, Lulu, I love your dress."

Lulu smiled. "Thanks. It really changes the subject."

Tara laughed. "I know how it looks, but, hey, I just saved you from that thing, didn't I?"

Bryce took a deep breath. "I guess that was the unstoppable killing machine ... though you hit him with the van, so maybe that killed him."

Tara laughed. "Wouldn't be very unstoppable, then."

"He's pausable, though," Lulu said. "Hit him with something large enough, that will pause him for a few moments. Pausable killing machine. That doesn't sound as threatening."

"So, how did you know what floor to find us on?" Bryce asked.

"Oh, I put trackers on all you guys while you were sleeping," Tara said.

Bryce raised an eyebrow. "When were you around us while we were sleeping?"

"You didn't see me," Tara explained. "You were sleeping. Anyway, I got word that the cube was found and is back in possession of Astara's people again. Also, they got Doug and Charlene and are holding them at Calais's military base. I assume the cube is there for now."

"So we have to throw together some plan to break into a military base right away," Bryce said.

"And preferably a stupid plan," Lulu said. "No one ever sees stupid plans coming."

"You need to get that cube back," Tara said, "if you want to get rid of that whole marked for death thing and not have that unstoppable but pausable killing machine after you. Plus, I assume you want your friends back."

"Yeah, sorta." Bryce thought a moment. "Going to be hard, though. We have the Athenians after us along with Vogel. And I'm not sure Rook particularly likes us any more."

"And we were really rude to Floyd," Lulu added. "He's probably plotting revenge right now."

Tara smiled at them. "At least you have me on your side."

"Because didn't I create this world? It was vastly different when it was God's paradise. But I brought in sin, and then the world you know came about. So you can say I made it. And now, finally, I am its undisputed ruler. Well, almost."

CHAPTER 21

"For a first-time assassination mission, I think it could have gone worse."

Doug and Charlene sat in their cell, Charlene looking rather upset. And Doug's attempt to see the brighter side of things didn't seem to help.

Charlene looked at Doug. "Quiet. They could be listening in."

Doug frowned. "Does that mean I have to go back to not talking? Because I like talking. It's how I express my thoughts."

"You've never had a thought worth expressing," Charlene said, "so if you had any wisdom, you'd never say a thing."

"Oh, you're just grumpy because of the whole being captured thing." Doug walked over to the bars of the cell and looked around. There was just an empty room outside the cell. "Anyway, I bet Bryce and Lulu are working on a plan to rescue us."

"Even you're not dumb enough to rely on that," Charlene said. "If we want out, we'll need to make our own plan."

Doug walked back to Charlene. "Maybe if we can get an air vent open, we can crawl through that." Doug looked around the cell. "There's no air vent." Doug thought on that a moment. "They might have put us in here to suffocate!"

Charlene rolled her eyes and pointed at the bars to the cell.

"Oh yeah; I guess air could get through there. Hey! There must be an air vent out there. If we could just get through these bars, we could climb through the air vent!"

Charlene closed her eyes and lay back on the bench in the cell. "If you could be quiet for a few minutes, I'll think of something. Astara has always focused more on the aesthetics with her troops than with military training. There's a lot of weakness there to exploit if we wait for the proper timing. Then we get out of here — but we find and kill Lapointe first."

Doug sat down near Charlene. "I'd rather just get out of here."

"I don't leave a job unfinished."

"Okay, but make sure you're just killing Lapointe for money and not for revenge," Doug said. "Revenge can poison you, and it never leads anywhere good. At least that's what I've learned from numerous movies and a few video games where I didn't skip through the cut-scenes."

Charlene opened her eyes. "These people have pushed us around our entire lives. They treat us like we're less than nothing. Do you want them to get away with that?"

Doug thought on that. "I want to stop them. All these people in charge — all these supposed leaders the world has — they don't deserve their power and control. It's kinda weird, you know? Astara, Loch ... I'm not sure where these people came from." He thought a moment about something he thought he remembered Satan saying, but couldn't seize it. "Anyway, they need all to be brought down. All of them."

Charlene sat up. "You'll have to kill a lot of people for that. Might as well start with Lapointe."

"Don't you see, though?" Doug asked. "The world is broken. And you don't fix that with killing."

"Then how do you fix it?"

Doug shrugged. "I don't know. But I'm going to try to figure it out."

Charlene laughed. "Well, I'll work on a way to get us out of there, and you can sit there and try to figure out how to save the world."

They heard a door open outside. Approaching their cell was Mills, with two soldiers. "So how are you two doing in there?"

Doug considered trying to lead Mills through casual conversation to telling him where the air vents were and what their size was, but he decided to stick to the being-quiet strategy that had worked so far.

"What are we being charged with?" Charlene demanded.

"I'm afraid you and your friends have ventured well outside the bounds of criminal justice," Mills said. "You and I need to talk, Charlene Marshall."

"Lapointe wasn't interested in me," Charlene said.

"I'm not Lapointe." Mills looked at the two soldiers. "Get her out."

They opened the cell and cuffed Charlene behind her back. Doug approached them. "You better not hurt her!"

"Or what?" Mills asked.

"Or ... well ... I guess I could —"

Doug was interrupted by one of the soldiers hitting him in the gut.

"Why'd you do that?" Mills asked.

"Sorry," the soldier said. "He just has something about him that makes you want to punch him."

"Leave him alone!" Charlene shouted.

"No one gets left alone in this world." Mills motioned to the soldiers, and they shut the bars, locking a beaten Doug back in his cell.

* * *

The soldiers left the office, leaving Charlene seated alone with Mills, Mills behind the desk and Charlene on the other side with her hands still cuffed behind her back. It was a simple matter of getting the cuffs off and then overpowering Mills and taking whatever weapon she had on her. Of course, getting the cuffs off wasn't actually simple, as they were developed with the idea that they'd be very hard to get off. Still, it didn't seem like the most insurmountable of the problems facing Charlene.

"Well, your brain is just working away at something, isn't it?" Mills said. "But before you try some daring escape attempt, please hear me out first." A tone sounded from a screen on the wall beside them. Mills sighed and faced Charlene. "Sorry, we are going to talk, but please give me a moment."

Mills pushed a button, and on the screen was a very old-looking man wearing dark goggles. "So you have it?" he demanded.

"Yes, Dr. Asmod. We didn't find the bomb, but we do have the artifact back. It's all under control," Mills assured him.

"You idiots aren't going to lose it again, are you?"

"It's under tight security. It's right here in this base surrounded by an army of soldiers," Mills said. "Your people are already getting back to ... doing something to it. They put it in some machine or something. I assume they're reporting to you."

Asmod turned his head as if to look at another screen. "Yes. Progress. We need to get back the time we've lost."

"What exactly is that cube thing, anyway?" Charlene asked.

Asmod seemed confused for a moment and finally noticed the other person in the room. "Who is that?"

"A prisoner," Mills told him. "It's a military thing. Don't worry about it."

Asmod focused on Mills. "Don't lose it again. We don't know who or what will be after it now."

"We'll be prepared," Mills said.

Asmod scowled. "I doubt it." He cut the feed.

Mills turned to Charlene. "Back to us. Anyway, thanks again for bringing the cube back. That's been a big load off of everyone's minds. But we need to discuss something about it."

"I'm not going to talk," Charlene said.

"What would we need you to talk about?" Mills asked. "We have the artifact — the main thing we're concerned about — which in my opinion renders you and your friends rather inconsequential. Plus, if I thought you people had something I needed to know, I'm guessing Doug wouldn't be that hard to crack if the proper pressure were applied."

"Don't underestimate him," Charlene said. "He's been kicked around his entire life, but has never once buckled under it. He's also been trained as a soldier since birth and could easily best any marshmallow like you, who has known nothing but luxury."

Mills rolled her eyes. "Oh, come on. I have his file. He's just an idiot."

"Just because you have our files, don't think you know anything about us," Charlene spat. "And one characteristic of Doug that probably didn't make your file is his loyalty. That's why I know I can rely on him. And on my two friends who got away. But people like you wouldn't know anything about loyalty, would you?"

Mills took a deep breath. "You're talking about Lapointe's botched plan to abandon Calais with all the war orphans defending it."

"Among other things."

"You know, I don't really understand all this hatred for you guys," Mills said. "I was just a child during the Last War. It's different for the older generation, though. Your parents were so awful, they can barely stand to be around you. It seems silly, though. If anything, you all should get our sympathy, but — well, there is a lot I don't understand. Of course, most of the war orphans don't help the impression, these days. They're like your friends: Either useless or actively working against society."

"And you're pretending you have a society worth supporting?" Charlene asked.

"You used to think so. I know you say I can't know you from your files, but what I see from yours is someone unfairly grouped with the rest of the warfs. I see someone with potential and a work ethic who could be a valuable asset to the Confederacy. In fact, I see a bit of me in you: Someone who has strived to be the best she can be, even though she has not always gotten the recognition she deserves."

"We should be sisters, then," Charlene cooed. "We could braid each other's hair."

Mills frowned. "I'm trying to help you here. I'm trying to give you an out."

"An out from what?"

Mills hesitated. "I'm going to ask you a very important question: Did you touch the cube?"

Charlene thought for a moment about not giving a straight answer, but she decided on the truth. "No."

Mills picked up a folder, pulled out a piece of paper, and placed it on the desk in front of Charlene. "This was very important. So important it had to be printed on paper with real signatures. Do you know what this is?"

Charlene looked at the paper and gasped. "It's a kill order. The Confederacy of Astara has kill orders?"

"That was news to me too," Mills said. "I called up high command to confirm this wasn't some joke, and guess who I talked to." Mills leaned in and whispered, "Astara herself."

Charlene's eyes grew wide. "What did she sound like?"

Mills leaned back in her chair, her expression almost a little bit scared. "Like someone you do whatever she tells you. And what she told me is to make sure that anyone who has touched the artifact is questioned and then ..." Mills took a moment to get the words out. "... disposed of."

"What is that thing?" Charlene demanded.

"I don't know," Mills said. "But it's obviously something very, very important. And it's why you and your friends are not just in trouble; you are dead. We know from the video that at least Doug has touched the cube. Right now, Lapointe is playing some weird game with him — I guess upset over how her plans with Calais were ruined — but when she is done, he is going to die. When Liu and Worthington are found, they will die as well."

Charlene shuddered. She always suspected her friends' idiocy would eventually lead to something like this, but it was still hard to believe it had actually happened. "And me?"

Mills leaned toward Charlene. "There are many fools in our military. I know a lot of people have ideas about what a smart, civilized society should be like, but no matter what, the military still needs to be one thing: ruthless and efficient. We need people not just dedicated to art and beauty, as are often the goals of the Confederacy of Astara, but instead to destroying our enemy. We need people like you."

"You're offering me a job in the military?" Charlene asked. "Like in the Athenians?"

"Oh no," Mills shook her head vigorously. "I wouldn't wish those people on my worst enemies; I hate those psychopaths. I'm talking about getting you into officer training school. I have that power. I can even hide your background; you don't have to be grouped with the warfs anymore."

Charlene thought about that. She thought she hated the Confederacy of Astara now, but this still felt like everything she had ever wanted. "So you kill my friends and I get to go on to a regular life?"

"Your friends are already dead," Mills said. "They've stepped into areas they shouldn't have. I'm giving you an out."

"Because you like me so much?"

"Because I see so much potential, and I sympathize," Mills said. She took a deep breath. "But I need a favor from you. I know about the job you all accepted to assassinate General Lapointe."

Charlene was a bit stunned. "Well, if you don't want me to go through with it, I don't think that's really a problem right now."

"No. Quite the opposite." Mills met Charlene's eyes again, and for the very first time, Mills looked intimidating. "I want to help you."

"Now we come to the demons. I was never alone in all this. There are others like me — other dissatisfied entities who all rebelled against creation in their own way."

CHAPTER 22

"Wow, you guys look sharp," Tara said. "Real official."

Bryce and Lulu were in suits, and Tara was wearing a Confederacy of Astara military uniform as they stood in the garage of some hideout Tara apparently had in Calais. Also inside was a military vehicle.

"So we're just going into the base from the front?" Bryce asked Tara. "We already did that once, but we're kinda afraid they'll have increased security now."

Tara headed for the vehicle. "Oh no, don't worry about that. Our covers will hold up fine. And I got us this official military vehicle to help us pass through unnoticed."

Bryce and Lulu got into the vehicle and looked around. "Wait, is this the vehicle we came into the city with?"

Tara nodded as she got into the driver's seat. "Yeah, it was under low security since they already had taken the cocaine out of it. It still has some of your other stuff, though ... like katanas for some reason."

Bryce rolled his eyes. "Doug." He sat down in back. "So, Tara, do you think this is a good plan?"

Tara shrugged. "Plan evaluation is not really my thing."

Lulu narrowed her eyes. "There are blood stains in here."

Tara laughed. "Well, hopefully the base guards don't look as closely as you do."

* * *

It was a starless night as Bryce and Lulu approached the headquarters of the military base. It was an easy entrance, as Tara had said, and now Tara had run off to carry out her half of the plan as Bryce and Lulu attended to theirs.

"I don't know about leaving it to Tara to retrieve the cube," Bryce whispered to Lulu.

"You think she's going to betray us? A third time?"

"I ... really don't know what to think about her."

"Well, I like her," Lulu said. "If she plans to betray you all, I hope she includes me in her scheme — the two of us betraying you all together. We'd be a great team.

I'm really liking that idea, actually. Maybe I should suggest to her betraying you all in case she hadn't thought of it."

Bryce scoffed. "I'd betray you all before you could betray us all, and I'd be much smarter at it. I could betray you, Charlene, and Doug while also betraying Tara at the same time, and there would be nothing you could do about it. So think about that before betraying me — that I probably already have a better plan for betrayal."

"Fine. It will be a betrayal contest," Lulu said. "But we need Charlene and Doug back first. It's more fun the more people there are to betray."

Bryce and Lulu entered the headquarters and saw a couple of soldiers standing guard at the main entrance. "Who are you?" one demanded.

"We're with the government," Bryce said. He and Lulu flashed their fake ids. "We're here to make sure everyone is following current standards of diversity and tolerance."

"At this hour?" questioned a soldier.

"Oh, I guess diversity and tolerance are just a morning thing to you," Bryce said disdainfully.

"What's your name, soldier?" Lulu demanded as she took out a pen and notebook from her large purse. "I want to write your name down in my big book of racists."

"No, no, no!" yelled the panicked soldier. "I'll help you however you need."

"Good, because there is nothing more important to civilization than diversity and tolerance," Bryce said.

"Except maybe the internet," Lulu added.

"And arguably fire," Bryce said. "You can't have civilized society without fire." He turned to the soldier. "Anyway, we need to get this going. We should have a conference room scheduled."

The soldier checked a console. "The computer doesn't say anything about us having a seminar right now."

"Well, you can't trust computers," Bryce said. "And you know why? Because they were made by white males." Bryce thought about that a moment. "Actually, they kind of seem like something Asians would invent."

"Either way," Lulu added, "they were made by an extremely untrustworthy group. So get us your largest conference room and tell everyone to come right away."

"Except essential staff, right?" the soldier asked.

Bryce frowned. "Well, everyone can ask themselves what's more important: Whatever they're guarding, or not hating minorities. Now, come on; let's start tolerating people!"

* * *

Two soldiers, a man and woman, led Charlene from Mills's office through the hallway. "We better get her back to her cell quick," the male one said. "We have some surprise seminar on prejudice or something."

"You don't want to be late to those," the woman said. "Everyone will look at you funny and think you're a racist and that's why you didn't bother to show up on time."

"You're in the middle of a war," Charlene sighed. "How do you people have time for stupid seminars?"

"Shut up!" the man yelled, smacking Charlene in the back of the head with his palm. "None of you warfs have any appreciation for tolerance; that's why everyone hates you!"

Charlene kept secretly working with a pin in the handcuffs behind her back until she heard a click. "Let's see how you tolerate ..." Charlene dropped the cuffs. "... a fist in the face!" She turned and decked the man right in the chin, dropping him.

"Workplace violence!" the woman yelled, stumbling and falling backwards. She reached for her gun, but Charlene stepped on her hand.

"Did you have a seminar on that one?" Charlene asked, standing over her.

"Yes," the woman whimpered. "But I don't remember what they taught."

Charlene kneed the woman in in the head, knocking her unconscious. Charlene thought she'd feel more triumphant beating up two soldiers like that, but they really were a crappy military.

She picked up the woman's gun and checked the chamber. She guessed she would have to go and rescue Doug, but she had other matters to attend to first.

*   *   *

"I have some alarming news," Bryce said as he and Lulu stood in front of the conference room filled with soldiers. "As part of an initiative in ensuring sensitivity and tolerance, we've been monitoring all your communications. And we did not see anyone say anything racist."

"Isn't that a good thing?" an officer asked.

"WRONG!" Bryce shouted. "That means everyone is just bottling up their racism. It's just building inside people and festering. I can see you all looking at each other and hating each other's race right now."

"Everyone needs to vent your racism," Lulu said. She pointed to one young soldier in the audience. "You. I want you to pick a minority — a particularly oppressed one — and say something bad about them."

He looked around at everyone staring at him and started sweating. "I don't think I can do that."

Lulu chucked a dry-erase marker at the soldier, pegging him hard in the forehead. "Don't you dare defy me! I am the gatekeeper of tolerance! I will destroy you!"

"You need to listen to us, people," Bryce stated more calmly. "We've been doing lots of research into tolerance and know what we're talking about. Why, we've discovered new things to tolerate that none of you would even imagine should ever be tolerated."

"We've also found other groups we've been tolerating that we actually shouldn't," Lulu added. "We were completely wrong about them. We should hate and make fun of them."

Bryce raised a finger. "But here is the question: How good are you at tolerating others?" Bryce emphasized the point with silence as he picked random people in the audience and stared them down. "Oh, everyone thinks it's so easy to be kind and compassionate to anyone who is different, and aren't those fools surprised when they become the biggest bigots of all?"

"It is not easy," Lulu announced as she walked through the room. "When you see someone different than you, you're going to want to hate them. Or going to want to mock and destroy them. You'll try to smile and be nice." Lulu grabbed a terrified young woman by the shoulders and got in her face. "But all you'll really want is to shave your head and become a neo-nazi!"

"Unless!" Bryce shouted as he placed a blue bag on a table in the center of the room. "You practice your tolerance. What we are about to do is unleash something horrible. Something you won't be able to stand. Something you will want to get rid of. But you want to be good people, so you will use all the will you can muster to tolerate it. So that's your exercise. No matter what happens, I want you to sit still and smile. I want you to reach deep inside and find that good person in you and not let the bigot inside you control you and make you flee. So do you all want to be good people?"

Everyone in the room nodded.

Bryce reached inside the bag and pressed something. "Okay. Get ready to be tolerant."

As everyone stared at the bag waiting for something to happen, Bryce and Lulu quickly left the room. The two closed the doors behind them, and Lulu pulled a chain and lock out of her purse and chained the doors shut just as the tear gas started coming out of the bag. They watched a moment through the window of the door as everyone inside tried to remain still and smiling as the gas savaged their eyes.

"They're really doing it," Bryce said, somewhat admiringly. "They're really tolerating the tear gas. I wonder if we misjudged tear gas?" He turned to Lulu, who was watching with a giant smile. "I know this was just to get all the soldiers in one room so we could lock them inside and disable them, but I think we really made a difference."

"I hope not," Lulu said, double-checking the lock. "I think all this tolerance stuff is stupid. People should be able to hate each other for whatever reasons they want. Anyone who says otherwise is a totalitarian."

Bryce nodded. "You have interesting views. You should write a newsletter."

"I will," Lulu asserted. "And I'll have a lot of creative font use in it."

* * *

"Do you know when Charlene is getting back?" Doug asked the soldier standing guard outside his cell.

"No," the soldier answered.

Charlene had been gone a while, and Doug was trying not to let his imagination go wild. Still, he couldn't get out of his head the image of Charlene, now a cyborg, robotically uttering, "Destroy Hellbender!" over and over. "So ... how is the airflow out there?" Doug asked as casually as he could manage.

"Shut up, you stupid warf!"

Doug went and sat down on the bench in the cell, thinking that if he were a guard and talking to a prisoner, he'd be much nicer. He might even try to make friends. Anyone locked in a prison probably has lots of interesting stories to tell. Maybe they shivved someone before. There must be a lot of fascinating ways to make a shiv.

A female soldier entered the room. "Shouldn't you be at the surprise seminar?" she asked the guard.

"No. They told me guarding him was more important," the guard answered. "Shouldn't you be at it?"

The woman shrugged. "I don't really see the point of it. I mean, I'm very tolerant already, because I always try to keep this principle in mind: No matter what outward characteristics people have, deep down inside we're of equal value, and all equally deserving of love and respect."

Doug nodded. "That's a nice sentiment."

"Well, thank you, Doug," the woman turned to Doug and winked at him. Tara. She pulled out a gun and shot the guard in the head, splattering blood on the wall behind him. She then approached the bars. "I'm here with your friends to rescue you."

Doug looked uneasily at the dead guard and the stain on the wall. "Oh, cool. Um ... so where are Bryce and Lulu?"

Tara opened the cell. "They're making a distraction. They're holding a seminar on diversity and tolerance."

"That's not going to go well," Doug said, getting out of the cell and looking for the air vent. "Neither of them are very tolerant. Bryce thinks it's ironic to tell ethnic jokes — no matter how much I try to explain to him it isn't. And Lulu doesn't even care about being ironic."

Tara shrugged. "I'm sure they can fake it. Most of getting along with people is faking it."

"I hope you're right," Doug said. "We need to go get Charlene. They took her away, and I have no idea what they're doing to her or whether an EMP would just disable her programming or kill her." Doug looked at the dead soldier. "But let's try to not kill everybody if we don't have to."

"Killing really is the quickest way to deal with people," Tara explained.

Doug was about to respond, but then he finally spotted it. "An air vent!" Doug pointed at a vent up on the wall behind Tara. It would be a tight fit, but it was just big enough. "We can get out through that."

Tara nodded. "That's an option. I prefer the hallway, though. It's quicker, easier to navigate, and has much less of a chance of collapsing under our weight."

Doug stared at Tara a moment. He really didn't trust her, but she was here saving him, so that had to count for something. "Okay. We do things your way."

* * *

Charlene nudged open the door. On the top floor of the building was Lapointe's office, and it felt like Charlene had stepped into another building entirely. There was a vaulted ceiling with numerous frescoes depicting battles throughout history. The large room was filled with designer furniture, so designer that Charlene couldn't tell what the hell she was looking at — like was that curved thing, some sort of couch or a cabinet? At one end of the room were some open doors that led out to a balcony. It was there Lapointe stood in her black evening gown, sipping a cocktail and staring back at Charlene.

"And what is this?" Lapointe sighed.

Charlene pointed her gun at Lapointe. "It's justice coming for you."

Lapointe rolled her eyes.

"Is this a joke to you?" Charlene shouted. "You tried to abandon us in this city to Loch's forces, and then when I saved the city, you had the gall to take the credit."

Lapointe laughed. "Oh, come on. The circumstance to take down Loch's air carrier just fell into your lap; it was luck, not strategy. Now, if tricking the enemy force to take an active bomb on board their ship was the plan all along — as we're now pretending happened — that's at least a little impressive. Not how I planned things to go, but it doesn't diminish me."

"Diminish you?" Charlene spat. "Are all these lives you're tossing around in your planning just part of some game to you?"

"Are you asking if I take this seriously?" Lapointe said. "Well, I'd say I'm the only one who takes things seriously. Everyone loves peace and civilization, but as we've seen time and time again, the natural state of man is war. You can look at any long period of peace as just a lengthy setup for an even more terrible war. And we even had the arrogance to call that conflict that left you orphaned the 'Last War.' We thought we had one more brutal conflict to bring lasting peace, that once it was over, there would be no more fighting again." Lapointe leaned against the balcony's railing and stared off into the sky. "That's why we didn't care how ugly things got, because it was to be the last time ever. And as a young soldier, I saw a lot of ugly things. Did a lot of ugly things." She took a really long drink of her cocktail and faced Charlene. "But let's not dwell on past unpleasantness. The point is, we were wrong. Even after that battle and all the enemies we eliminated, we've still found plenty to fight about. Because conflict is inevitable. And realizing this simple fact about reality, do you see what I'm doing? I'm bringing beauty and order to the violence and ugliness that will exist no matter what we try to do. I'm making war even more lovely than peace — at least that's what I am attempting to do. But as much as I am able to organize things, there's one thing that never quite fits: You orphans of the Last War. There's something just ... wrong, with all of you."

"Wrong? With us?" Charlene asked incredulously, keeping her gun pointed at Lapointe's chest. "I see a miserable, broken world, but I don't see us in charge."

"Things are in flux, yes," Lapointe admitted. "But one of the reasons we can't get things together is you people. You just don't fit. I think you all sense that; that's why so many of you actively work against us."

"Perhaps how you all hate us and the miserable way you treat us has something to do with that," Charlene growled.

Lapointe sipped her cocktail. "Oh, I'm sure it's many reasons. But then there are rarer warfs like you who try to fit in. That's even more pathetic. You're like a rock staring at a chessboard, longing to be a pawn."

Charlene seethed, now holding her gun with two hands and aiming it carefully at Lapointe.

Lapointe laughed. "You can't even pull the trigger. I think deep down you understand just how —"

The first shot caused Lapointe to jerk back, clutching her chest with one hand and still holding her cocktail glass with the other. With the second and third shot, the glass fell, shattering on the floor of the balcony. Lapointe tried to steady herself, but the fourth shot sent her toppling over the railing.

Charlene took a deep breath and lowered the gun. She tried smiling because she had had her revenge, but it was a little forced.

"The demons do not regard you the same as do I. They hate you. The only reason they don't eliminate you is they consider it a prize to rule you. And throughout the ages, it is to rule you that they have tried."

CHAPTER 23

"Is this the way to Charlene?" Doug asked as he crept along the hallway with Tara.

"No, we're closer to the next objective, getting back the cube," Tara explained, "so we're grabbing that first. It will be easier to get Charlene on the way out."

Doug grabbed Tara's arm. "We're not leaving without everyone."

Tara looked at him and smiled. "Of course not. You can trust me."

Tara casually strolled into a room at the end of the hallway. Inside was what looked like a vault, and standing in front of the vault was a guard. "Hi!" Tara said cheerily to him as she quickly pulled out her gun and shot him in the head.

Tara looked back at the stunned Doug. "Oh yeah; sorry. You said something about not killing people; I completely forgot. Just so used to it."

Doug took the rifle off the dead guard. "You're a little scary, you know that?"

Tara took out a small electronic device. "I try to be nice — I want people to like me — but sometimes work gets in the way of that." She opened up a panel next to the vault, pulled some wires out, and connected them to the electronic device. "You seem to keep a nice, easy-going personality even in the middle of things like this. I wish I could be more like you."

Doug kept watch, but the building seemed pretty empty. "You'd be the first. In a world full of losers, I've always been told I'm exceptional."

"Better to be exceptional than one of the crowd," Tara said. "We warfs ended up with our guardians being the people who murdered our parents; why would we want to be useful to them? Don't you want revenge against them all?"

"Everyone seems so miserable and empty these days, I don't see the point in revenge."

Tara smiled. "You're a nice guy. Not a world for nice guys, though, is it?" The vault started to open.

"Wow," Doug said. "You sure know a lot about a lot of things."

"I try to be a professional," Tara said as they waited for the big metal vault door to fully slide open. "And I like being useful."

"Useful to who?" Doug asked.

Tara just laughed.

The vault door finished opening, and there on a pedestal stood the cube, still etched with bunnies on each side. There were what looked like lasers on either side of the cube, firing blue beams into it, and the cube was glowing.

Doug stared at it a moment. "So what is this doing?"

"I think they're trying to power it up." Tara pushed some more buttons on her device, and the beams powered off.

"And thank you for opening that," said a voice from behind Doug and Tara. They turned around to see a pair of gold eyes staring at them.

* * *

"And here are the holding cells," Bryce said, leading the way. He glanced at the cells. "And no one is here."

"There's a dead guy," Lulu said, pointing to a dead soldier.

"What?" Bryce exclaimed. "Was Tara already here? I thought she was going straight for the cube-thingy. Why in the world would she —"

Someone ran into the room. Bryce and Lulu immediately went for their guns, but the person was quicker, getting her gun on Bryce and Lulu first. "You two?" Charlene gasped, lowering her pistol. She looked at the dead soldier. "Did you do this?"

"No," Bryce answered. "We were coming here to rescue you and Doug and found it this way."

"Let the record show I rescued myself," Charlene stated. "But where is Doug?"

"Maybe Tara came through here and got him," Lulu said. "She's a busy girl. We thought there was a possibility she might run off with the cube, but we never considered the idea she might run off with Doug. You know, I thought she had a thing for him. And I think they'd be a cute couple."

Bryce shook his head. "No. She has a thing for me; she's just being more coy about it than most women and it's actually a little infuriating." Bryce took out his phone. "I'm going to text her."

"I keep telling you guys," Charlene said, "don't rely on texting for in-mission communications."

"It's not mission-related," Bryce answered. "I'm trying to prove she is attracted to me and not Doug."

Charlene took a deep breath. "I killed Lapointe."

Bryce and Lulu stared at her quietly for a second. "Was it brutal?" Bryce asked.

"I shot her and she fell off a balcony."

Bryce shrugged. "Well ... I think we can sell that."

Lulu tapped Charlene in the shoulder with her fist. "You okay there, sister?"

Charlene stared at the ground. "I'm fine. She ... she burnt the scarf you made me."

Lulu put her arm around Charlene. "Oh, I didn't really make it. I just shoplifted it."

Charlene nodded. "I know. You didn't get all the stickers off of it."

"When we get out of here," Lulu said, "I'll make you another."

Bryce put his hand on Charlene's shoulder. "Are you sure you're okay?"

Charlene took another deep breath. "I'm fine. I'm happy I killed her, actually."

"It will be something interesting to scrapbook," Lulu stated.

Charlene was quiet for a moment. "Yeah ... it will ... it will be a good page." She looked around. "We probably shouldn't just be standing here. Where are the rest of the soldiers in this base?"

"We pretended to put on a diversity seminar and then locked them all in one room," Lulu explained.

"And how long do you think that will hold them?"

Lulu shrugged. "Weeks. Months. Years, maybe."

They could hear many footsteps coming down the hall.

"I guess until about now."

* * *

Darius smiled at Doug and Tara. He held up his hand, and something black slithered up his arm and began to solidify, until his hand was a long black claw.

"Well, that's a neat trick," Doug said.

"Grab the cube!" Tara yelled and pulled out her gun. She fired at Darius, but he didn't even flinch as he slowly approached them.

Doug ran for the cube. He hesitated a moment — but only a moment, as he saw Darius approaching — and then grabbed the cube with his bare hand. It shocked his body, as if he had plunged his hand into ice water, but he shook it off and ran out of the vault as he saw Tara duck under a swing of Darius's claw, which tore through the brick wall behind her. Doug fired at Darius with his rifle, but all that did was get him Darius's attention.

"Run!" Tara screamed as she fled for the hallway, Doug heading after her.

"Run away!" Darius called to them. "But you can't outrun me forever!"

"We need like a rocket launcher or something!" Doug gasped as he ran alongside Tara.

"Next time, let's plan to bring one."

They turned a corner and found themselves face to face with a dozen soldiers whose eyes were all red and watery for some reason. "Something is coming," Tara told them, pushing through them. "Coming behind us!"

They looked at Doug, still in his waiter uniform and holding the cube. But Doug heard the footsteps of Darius behind him and tried to get through the group of soldiers. "Wait!" one yelled, grabbing Doug. But then a black claw beheaded the soldier.

Doug scampered away with Tara as he heard gunfire and screaming behind him. It was then he felt the cube almost pulsing in his hand, the coldness feeling like it had spread through his arm and up to his eyes. It now seemed like the building was growing darker.

"This way!" Tara yelled, leading Doug to a stairwell. They went up and soon exited to the roof of the headquarters.

The cube now felt heavy in Doug's hand, and he could barely move any more while carrying it. He looked up at the sky, and there was a full moon. It began to turn red and then melt away. "Something is wrong," Doug said, before collapsing to the ground.

"Early on, they attempted to rule you as gods. That was so short-sighted — to emulate the Creator we were trying to overthrow. Who would inevitably win that game?"

CHAPTER 24

Mills looked around Lapointe's suite. "We're undersupplied on body armor and we paid for this?" she grumbled to herself. Her phone rang and she quickly answered it. "Gisele! Where the hell have you been?"

"I'm at a stylist," Gisele answered. "We got in a close-quarters combat situation with some mobsters, and it was messy."

"Messy how?"

"Well, my hair is all out of place, two nails chipped, dress torn, and my makeup got smudged."

Mills sighed. "That sounds awful."

"Well, you should see Cortia; she looks even worse."

"I can only imagine," Mills said. "She break her shoe heel?"

"She was shot to death," Gisele said.

"Oh, I'm sorry. That's —"

"She had her eyes and mouth open," Gisele said disdainfully. "Looked like an idiot."

"Well, I have some news for you," Mills stated, "that will ... Well, you'll probably be similarly unfeeling about it. Lapointe is dead. We think one of the members of Hellbender shot her."

"I bet she knew how to die without looking stupid."

Deep breath. "Yes. That's the important thing. Now, I need you here because —"

A soldier raced into the room, nearly out of breath. "We're being attacked!"

"By whom?" Mills asked.

He struggled for a moment. "Something."

"That's vague."

"It's like a man ... but we can't stop him."

Mills tried to process that. "Keep trying bullets, then, and keep me updated." The soldier hesitantly headed out of the room, and Mills put the phone back to her ear. "As I was saying, you need to get here and —"

A lieutenant raced into the room. "We're under attack."

"Some unstoppable guy, I heard."

The lieutenant's eyes grew wide. "There's an unstoppable guy attacking us?"

"You didn't know? What were you coming here to tell me about?"

"A different attack."

* * *

"Good job, guys!" Bryce said to the soldiers, giving them a thumbs-up. "The point of the seminar was to show how you're locked in your previous conceptions about certain minority groups and that you needed to work together to break out of them."

"There is no record of either of you as government employees," said one of the soldiers, pointing his rifle at them.

"That's because we're rogue teachers of diversity who don't play by the rules!" Lulu shouted. "We're going to get everyone to love each other, and we don't have time to work within the system to do it!"

Down the hallway, they could hear gunfire and screaming.

"Those are not good sounds," Bryce said.

"You should probably check that out," Lulu said to the soldiers. "It sounds much more important than us."

The soldiers took another glance at Bryce and Lulu and slowly headed toward the sound of battle.

Charlene looked into the hallway from the room she was hiding in. "What's going on?"

There was more gunfire and more screams.

"I don't know," Lulu said, "but I have a really good feeling about it."

Walking down the hallway came the blood-covered figure of Darius, one of his hands in the shape of a black claw. Charlene pointed her gun at him, but Bryce pulled her down the hallway. "Trust us: Just run!"

They headed down the hallway, running right toward some more soldiers heading their way.

"Stop!" one yelled.

"Bigger problems!" Bryce yelled, pointing down the hallway at Darius.

The soldiers opened fire on Darius as Bryce, Lulu, and Charlene ran into another room. In there was a man in a lab coat who was opening a locker. He took a quick glance at the three of them and then continued to open the locker. "That's the infused out there, isn't it? We'll have to use the prototype to try to stop it."

"Oh, we have a prototype to stop that thing?" Bryce said. "That's good. We will take that."

The scientist pulled a case out of the locker. "And who are you?"

"We're special government agents," Lulu said, pointing to herself and Bryce. She then pointed to Charlene. "And she's a waitress."

The scientist opened the case. Inside was something that looked like a plastic laser pistol. "This should destroy him. It cancels out his multi-dimensional connection. Just remember —" The scientist stopped and looked up at the blood-covered Darius, who stood at the doorway, and then fled the room through the other door, screaming.

Charlene grabbed the pistol, pointed it at Darius, and pulled the trigger.

Nothing happened.

"It says 'Charging Shot' on the side," Lulu remarked.

Darius smiled and approached them. Charlene, Bryce, and Lulu ran out the door the scientist had fled through. "How long is it going to take to charge?" Bryce asked as they ran through the hallway.

"I don't know," Charlene answered. "Let me consult my vast knowledge of weapons I hadn't seen until a second ago!"

They saw some more soldiers ahead of them. "There's a killing machine coming after us!" Lulu yelled to them as they ran by. "It's totally stoppable, though, so you should get between it and us!"

The three kept running, and soon there were more gunshots and screaming behind them. They ducked into another room and hid behind some desks.

"Do you know the way to get out of here?" Charlene whispered.

"We were following you," Bryce said.

"So are we just going to assume Doug and Tara are dead or what?" Lulu asked.

Bryce looked at his phone. "Oh, Tara texted me. She says she has the cube and found an alternate way to escape with Doug and that we'll just have to stick to the regular escape plan." Bryce paused a moment. "Hmm."

"What?" Charlene demanded, keeping her voice quiet, as they could hear footsteps outside.

"She never answered whether she likes me or Doug better," Bryce said.

"Face up to the facts," Lulu whispered. "She's run off with Doug. They probably betrayed us and are going to sell the cube and keep the money for themselves, living together from now on in luxury. That is, until Tara gets too old and Doug decides to trade her in for a younger woman, because he's stone cold now."

"I always suspected Doug's 'I'm a nice guy who will always be your friend' act was some sort of ploy," Bryce answered.

"Will you two idiots shut up?" Charlene said. "Let's just focus on —"

The gun went off in Charlene's hand, launching a bolt of energy that knocked over the desk in front of them.

Darius kicked open the door and looked upon the three with a smile so horrible it caused them all to freeze in terror.

And then the room exploded.

* * *

"You warned me about Hellbender, didn't you?" Rook asked Driscoll as they and Candy walked through the holding facility. It was outside, with a number of sheds surrounded by an unimpressive chain-link fence.

"Just seemed like dealing with them would only lead to trouble," Driscoll answered.

"And now I am in over my head," Rook said. "I thought this cube thing would be big for me, but now I just want to get my cigarettes back, sell them, get a little money, and rebuild."

"Today was supposed to be payday, but I didn't get my direct deposit," Candy said. "So you'll be handling that soon?"

Rook sighed. "That will be my first priority." He looked around the facility. "So no guards here?"

"These sheds are usually empty," Driscoll explained. "Or just low-priority stuff, like what they confiscated from Hellbender, thinking it was just cocaine. They would sometimes have a deputy peacekeeper warf out here to guard things, but apparently she recently stopped showing up for work."

"Yeah, you can't rely on those warfs," Rook said. "You know, I'm not usually for rounding up and killing large groups of people — since Hitler gave that a bad name — but ..." He paused for a moment. "I don't know where I'm going with that. Let's just get the cigarettes."

They approached a locked shed, and Driscoll took some bolt cutters from the bag he was carrying. He was about to cut the padlock when they heard an explosion. And then another explosion. And then one really nearby. They looked up, and aircraft were bombing the city. Aircraft that looked like giant flying lizards. Loch's aircraft.

Rook took a deep breath. "Oh, what the hell now?"

"We were allies for the most part, and I helped them learn to be more subtle. Not to intimidate man with their power, but to entice him."

CHAPTER 25

It was an alien world. A dark, barren landscape surrounded Doug, and shadowy mountains loomed in the distance. Above, clouds swirled in a purple sky constantly streaked with lightning. And in that purple sky was a dark, pulsating orb. The dark star. As Doug took it all in, one thought crossed his mind: This would be an awesome place to film a rock video.

He looked around. Mountains ahead of him. To his right was the skeletal silhouette of a city long dead. At his feet was a barren plain — a dried-out lake bed, from the looks of it.

Doug was moving. He felt no pull or motion of any kind; he was like a ghost floating over the ground. And he kept speeding faster and faster toward the mountains ahead of him. He was about to slam into them, but instead he passed right through them into darkness, until, deep inside the mountain, he found it. What he needed. What he always had been looking for. The answer to everything. It sat before him, beckoning him. He reached for it.

Doug opened his eyes. He was lying on a bed in some sort of vehicle — a really well-decorated one with a crystal chandelier tinkling above him. Sitting next to Doug was Tara, who looked down on him with concern. "You okay?" she asked. "It's like you blacked out there for a minute. I think they did something to sort of charge the cube; it must have done something to you when you touched it. What happened?"

"I felt like I got transported," Doug said. "I was flying over the world to this mountain range."

"Where?" Tara asked.

Doug rubbed his temple and thought hard. "I think it was Mount Oliver. Oh yeah, near Lake Tambor; that's what I saw. Had a summer camp there once — it did not go well. A bear died. We — I'm getting off-topic. Anyway, I was at Lake Tambor — except everything was weird-looking and the lake was dried up. And then I went into the mountain, where there was this cavern with something powerful in it. Something I was drawn to." A horrible thought struck Doug. "Something we can't let anyone else reach. I can just tell it's something of vast power ... like unstoppable power. Whoever got it could —" Doug started to sit up, but found his hand was cuffed to the metal frame of the bed. "What's this?"

"Oh, I wasn't sure what was going on when you blacked out from touching the cube," Tara explained. "So I thought I'd take some precautions just in case."

"Well, I'm fine," Doug said. "Uncuff me!"

"Okay. Just give me a sec to find the key," Tara said. "By the way, this is Lapointe's personal craft we stole, so there's a full bar on it. I can make you a cocktail if you want."

"Uncuff me!" Doug shouted.

Tara stared at Doug a moment. "I get this feeling you still don't trust me."

"No, Tara, I really don't," Doug said. "For one, you've betrayed me and my friends before. And you know too much. It makes me wonder where you're getting this information from. And who you're working for."

"I'm working for myself." Tara fished through the pockets of the Confederacy of Astara military uniform she was still wearing. "Totally mercenary. Just in it for the money."

"Well, some things to me are more important than the money," Doug said. "We can't sell that cube. We have to keep it away from ... well, everyone. Because everyone looking for it is pretty awful."

Tara took a key out of her pocket and walked over to Doug. "I don't see how being the enemy of every powerful group out there ends well." She unlocked the cuffs.

Doug rubbed his wrist. "Someone has to stand up to them. Something is wrong with this world, but maybe there is a way to fix it."

Tara smiled, but there was something melancholy about it. "You want to be a hero, Doug, and that's noble, in a way. But the time for heroes has passed. There's no more saving anyone."

"I don't believe that." Doug searched his pockets. "Where is the cube?"

"I have it; it's safe."

"Don't we still need to get back to the research facility?" Doug asked. "You said we had to remove the cube's essence from us or something."

Tara shrugged. "We're not worrying about that now."

"Why not?!"

Tara grimaced. "I might have made up that part just to make sure you didn't sell the cube right away."

"Made that up? What are you up to?" Doug looked toward the vehicle's windshield but couldn't see anything. "And where are we?"

Tara shrugged. "I dunno."

"And where are Bryce, Charlene, and Lulu?"

"Again, not sure," Tara said. "But I think they're okay. We had an escape plan."

Doug thought of Darius and couldn't help but be worried. "We need to find them."

"We will," Tara said. "Apparently, though, they killed General Lapointe."

"They did?" They had been trying to do that, but he was still a bit shocked that they actually went through with it.

"Yeah, and I guess with Lapointe out of the way," Tara explained, "Loch's forces attacked Calais again. They're invading it now."

Doug took another look out the windshield. It was just dark. "You got us away from the battle?"

Tara shook her head. "No." She walked over to a side door of the vehicle and opened it.

"What are you doing?"

"We've landed," Tara explained.

"But I can feel us moving."

"We landed on something moving." Tara stepped outside.

Doug followed and looked out the door. They were inside some large hangar with a number of armed soldiers inside. Loch's soldiers.

"I have the information we need," Tara told one of them as she held up the bag with the cube in it. "And I brought the artifact."

* * *

"Ow. Building exploded. Ow," Lulu moaned.

Charlene looked at where Darius had been, but there was just a pile of debris. And it started trembling. "Let's get out of here."

Bryce dusted himself off and pointed to the missing wall leading outside. "There's a door."

Charlene looked out. "One-story drop. Let's go." She jumped out the hole.

Lulu sighed. "We're doing way too much jumping out of buildings lately."

Darius's arm shot out of the pile of debris, causing Bryce and Lulu to immediately make a jump for it. They landed on some bushes.

"Ah! Prickly bushes!" Lulu cried. "Not soft landing bushes!"

"Stop whining!" Charlene yelled. "Do we have a vehicle?"

"Yes, Tara got our truck back. It should be parked over this way," Bryce said, leading the way.

The skies were full of attack craft and giant winged creatures. They could see explosions all around them. "Loch's empire is invading again," Charlene stated, looking up.

"Oh, you're right!" Lulu said, running beside her. "I hadn't noticed. Thanks for pointing that out. You're so useful to keep around."

"If we run into any of their forces," Bryce said, "we'll just explain to them we killed Lapointe and then we'll be their heroes and get paid."

"I killed Lapointe," Charlene asserted.

"With us somewhat near you!" Lulu yelled. "That makes it a team effort!"

They reached the transport in the parking lot and hopped in. Bryce scrambled to the controls and got the vehicle off the ground.

"Can you maneuver this so that we don't immediately get shot out of the sky?" Charlene asked.

"There's a lot of other panicky people fleeing to shoot at," Bryce said. "I'm sure we have a reasonable chance."

Bryce made a sharp turn in midair to avoid what looked like a pterodactyl with rocket launchers on it.

"And where are we going?" Charlene asked as she held on tight.

"I'm just picking a direction and fleeing," Bryce said. "Now let's —" Bryce started pounding the controls.

"Did something good just happen?" Lulu inquired.

"You know how when we came here and ground control took over our controls and made us land?" Bryce said. "Well, that's happening again."

Charlene walked to the front. "Who took control?" She looked out the windshield, and there, descending from the clouds, was a giant black air carrier.

* * *

"You betrayed us!" Doug yelled at Tara.

Tara shrugged. "Kinda looks that way, doesn't it?"

Doug leapt at Tara, tackling her to the ground, but Loch's soldiers pulled him off before he could deliver a punch.

"There will be no unstructured violence here," said a middle-aged woman wearing glasses. She would have looked like a librarian or a professor except for the intimidating black and red Collective officer's uniform she wore. "Not among the followers of Loch."

Tara dusted herself off. "Thank you, Vengeance."

"And as for you," Vengeance said, walking over to the restrained Doug, "we have plenty of subjects for our violence among the citizens of Calais. We'll save you for the after-party." Vengeance turned to address the other soldiers there. "Let's focus on the battle at hand. We have many people now to rape, torture, and murder for the glory of Loch and all of civilization!"

The men and women there all cheered.

"What the hell is wrong with all you people?!" Doug yelled.

"What do you mean?" Vengeance demanded, looking quite angry. "Why do you think something is wrong with us?"

Doug saw Tara stare at him very seriously and shake her head, but he was absolutely done listening to her. "You people are celebrating doing horrible things to other people," Doug said. "This is absolutely sick!"

Vengeance laughed a very fake-sounding laugh to show her contempt of Doug's words. "You're just some primitive warf stuck in myopic colonial thinking. Luckily, the very wise and just Loch has helped us better understand justice and fairness. What we're doing is extremely natural and helping the world in numerous ways."

"Helping?" cried Doug, exasperated. "How does torturing and murdering people help anyone? You guys are psychopaths!"

"Tie him to a chair!" yelled an enraged Vengeance. "Let's show him exactly what we're all about!"

* * *

"Computer, manual override," Lulu told the vehicle console.

"It's not a voice-activated computer," Charlene said.

"Computer, tell Charlene to shut up," Lulu said.

Bryce watched as the vehicle headed for a hangar opening on the underside of the giant flying carrier. "Let's not panic, okay? They hired us to do a job — which we did —"

"I did," Charlene interrupted.

"Which we all get credit for," Bryce continued. "So, we're their friends. Thus, they can't murder us, because if you murder your hired mercenaries, you get a bad reputation and people won't work for you."

"Did we check their reputation before we decided to work for them?" Lulu asked. "Oh no, I remember what happened; some bloodthirsty crazy person signed us up for a job without asking the two smarter members of her mercenary group and Doug."

"And we completed the job," Charlene said. "So let's not panic and ..." Charlene hesitated a few seconds. "... let Bryce do the talking."

Bryce smiled. "We'll be in and out in a few minutes and richer for it."

The vehicle entered into the carrier's hangar and landed. Bryce prepared his nicest smile and opened the side door. Standing outside were a dozen soldiers pointing guns at them. "Hey guys, it's Hellbender," Bryce announced. "Just having gotten back from brutally murdering General Lapointe, who we all hate, don't we?" He looked at some of the women in the group and used a slightly different smile. "Hey, ladies." He then zeroed on one woman near the front of the group. "I love that uniform on you, by the way. Very evil-looking. It says, 'I'm going to do nasty, horrible things to you.'" He gave her a sly smile. "And I kinda want to let you."

The woman giggled. Charlene let out an audible sigh.

Bryce looked at the entire group. "So why don't you take me to your leader and we can have a nice celebration for this great victory in progress?"

They heard yelling from across the hangar. "That sounds like Doug," Charlene gasped.

The soldiers led Bryce, Charlene, and Lulu toward the yelling. Soon they spotted Doug tied to a chair. In front of him on a screen was a PowerPoint slide with a chart on it. Standing by the screen was a female officer pointing to it and talking, while on the sidelines stood numerous other soldiers.

"This doesn't make any sense!" Doug yelled over her words.

"It's very easy to understand," the officer explained. "This is a simple graph; even a child could follow it. And as you can see, violent crimes overall have gone down since we started our campaign of war. We're actually improving people's lives."

"Does the graph include the violent crimes you people are committing?" Doug asked.

The officer scoffed. "Of course not. It's not crimes we're committing; it's acts of war. That would be comparing apples and oranges. Now let's move to the next slide." A different chart appeared. "This one is about the gender and ethnic makeup of violent acts. As you can plainly see, by organizing our natural violent tendencies instead of puritanically suppressing them, we've made both the victims of violent acts and the perpetrators equally diverse in gender and race, increasing social justice."

"Social justice?!" Doug yelled, struggling with his bonds. "You don't help people by being randomly violent. Are you actually using some stupid numbers to justify rape and murder?"

"I don't need your input," the officer spat. "You're an ignoramus, but on our side we have leading sociologists who —"

"Who cares about some sociologist?!" Doug interrupted. "What you're doing is awful!"

The officer fake-laughed. "Of course you dismiss the science; you're a moron. We're helping people; you're just too ignorant to see it. Next slide." On screen was a bar graph. "Now this one shows the economic benefits of our destruction by increasing infrastructure jobs."

"You can't help the economy by blowing stuff up!" Doug shouted. "I know. I got fired for blowing stuff up. Numerous times."

"Leading economists agree with us!" the officer shouted, her face turning red. "So shut up! Just shut up!"

Bryce walked over to Doug. "Sorry. He's an idiot. You really all should ignore him." He smiled at the officer. "I like those glasses on you."

"They are all full of absolute nonsense," Doug whispered to Bryce.

Bryce patted him on the head. "Shut up."

Another officer walked into the hangar, and the soldiers there snapped to attention. He was a scary-looking bald man with a scar and patch over his left eye. "Well, if it isn't Hellbender." He smiled at them and turned his attention to Charlene. "Hello, Ms. Marshall. So, you got the job done?"

Charlene stood up straight. "Yes, Commander Mangle. I killed Lapointe myself."

"It was a team effort," Bryce said.

"We killed her with teamwork!" Lulu added, swinging her fist through the air.

"We only heard that she was dead," Mangle said, "but we didn't get the details. Was it sufficiently brutal?"

"Oh yeah," Lulu said. "Really brutal. You'll want to make a chart of it and how its horrible brutalness helped society or something. We'll write up the whole thing — probably make a book of it with pictures and look for a publisher. 'Death of Lapointe' — I bet it will be a bestseller in the true crime section. There is nothing in our contract saying we can't do that, right?"

"Anyway," Bryce said. "I guess we can collect our dummy and then we can talk payment and leave you guys to your invasion." He noticed Tara off to the side. "Oh, hey; you're here."

"I'd like to show you one thing," Mangle said. He looked at the officer manning the PowerPoint screen. "Please play the video, Vengeance."

On screen appeared a video of Bryce, Doug, Charlene, and Lulu back in the secret lab in Calais.

"Is the bomb defused?" asked Butcher, on screen.

Charlene gave him a thumbs-up. "Yep! Ready to go!"

"Well, huh," Bryce said, looking at Mangle. "I'm guessing you're thinking we in some way had something to do with your carrier's destruction."

"But you obviously have another one," Lulu said. "So I don't see what the big deal is."

"Tara betrayed us!" Doug shouted. "She gave them the cube! And she must have somehow given them that video too and set us up!"

Tara frowned. "Sorry, guys."

Charlene took a step toward Tara, but numerous soldiers pointed guns at her.

"We have lots of death and destruction to handle right now," Mangle said. "And then we have the power of the artifact to explore. But we will schedule some time to deal with all of you later."

"Perhaps it can be reflection on the hollowness of revenge," Vengeance suggested. "We need that every so often."

"That means a slow, painful death," Tara explained.

"Will it have more PowerPoint slides?" Doug asked drearily.

Vengeance frowned. "Yes!"

"But since the war, things have changed. The power of this world is exposed and unprotected. The 'Creator' is here no more. And now the demons wish to be gods again."

CHAPTER 26

"It's a natural state of man and woman to want to commit acts of violence," Vengeance explained to Doug as Hellbender was led at gunpoint down the hallway. "It's the puritanical urge to repress those feelings that leads to the breakdown of society. We healthily express those desires in an organized way under the guidance of our leader, Loch."

Doug rolled his eyes. "I don't even think you believe your own idiotic nonsense."

"All you can do is name-call because you can't refute it," Vengeance spat. She held up a tablet. "Here's an article by a leading sociologist explaining how occasional outbursts of violence lead to a more cohesive society."

Doug stared at the big block of text on screen. "I'm not going to read that."

"Then die in ignorance!" Vengeance yelled. "I tried to enlighten you! I tried!"

Doug, Bryce, Charlene, and Lulu were led into a room with cells and the four of them were shoved inside one. Vengeance repeatedly punched Doug in the gut, knocking him down. "Look what you made me do! Unplanned violence! That doesn't help anyone, and it's on you for being so infuriating!" Vengeance locked the cell and stormed off.

"Why does everyone have to punch me?" Doug picked himself up and sat down on one of the beds. "And I know these people are probably all smarter than me, but everyone here is full of absolute nonsense. And they just try to cover it with numbers and citing random people. Am I supposed to know who Noam Chomsky is?"

"Sounds made-up," Bryce said. "Anyway, Doug, everyone has their own reasoning for what they do, no matter how awful or stupid it is, and they can't be convinced away from it. Remember when you kept trying to feed Cheetos to that badger, and I tried to talk you out of it?"

"He was going to be my friend until you spooked him," Doug responded. "And why does rabies take so many shots?"

Bryce nervously fixed his tie. "I saw an article on the things the Loch Collective does to people. I couldn't even get through reading about the things that are actually going to happen to us."

Charlene stood at the bars, looking out. Two soldiers stood guard outside. "Well, thanks for coming to rescue me," she told Bryce and Lulu. "That was really helpful."

"How was I supposed to know they had evidence we blew up the carrier?" Bryce asked. "Regardless of that, they still technically owe us money for killing Lapointe."

"You should go explain that to them," Lulu said. "Maybe bring it up during the torture."

Bryce took a deep breath. "I'm just getting tired of people not paying us for things we actually did."

"I did," Charlene said, standing at the bars.

"You really killed Lapointe?" Doug asked, raising an eyebrow.

Charlene turned toward him. "Yes, I shot her to death. How is that surprising? We've been kicked around by everyone all our lives, and I finally got a chance to strike back. So I just took a gun and —" Her voice started breaking as tears welled in her eyes.

Doug got up and held her. "Hey, it's okay."

"It's not okay!" Charlene shouted, tears streaming down her face as she pushed away from Doug. "It's pointless to believe things will ever be okay."

"We'll get through this," Lulu said, patting Charlene on the shoulder. "We always do. Because we're plucky. These other people, all pluckless. But we got pluck out the wazoo. It's our one advantage: the pluck."

"Yeah, pluck is probably an actual word," Bryce added. "We'll think of something and get out of here."

"And then what?" Charlene demanded.

"We find a way to fight back," Doug asserted. "We have to. I'm serious, guys: Everything depends on us. I know it."

"Knowing things has never been your forte, Doug," Bryce said.

"I'm right this time," Doug stated. "I mean, do you see how everyone is trying to get this cube? It's not just that they think it will give them power; they're scared of it too." A realization struck Doug, much like a fist usually did. "You guys need to listen to me. When I held the cube when we took it from the base, it transported me to another dimension."

Charlene raised an eyebrow. "It what?"

"The dimension with the dark sun," Doug continued. "And I was drawn to something there … I don't know what it was. But I could tell it was of immense power. This has to be what Loch and Astara and that Darius guy are after. If they got it, I think they'd be unstoppable — or more unstoppable, in the case of Darius. But do you see? Tara was lying about the reason they're scared if people touch the cube. It's nothing to do with its essence or whatever. It's what they feared people might learn from it … what people like us might learn from it." Doug stared at his friends with an intensity they'd never seen from him. They were even a little scared. "What if we were the ones to obtain that thing of power?"

A silence hung over them all for a few seconds, finally broken by Lulu. "You're talking so much crazy right now, Doug, and I love it."

"I'm serious," Doug said. "This is the job of Hellbender now. To save the world."

Bryce rolled his eyes. "That's great, Doug. Let's put 'save the world' on the agenda right after 'don't get tortured to death.' Anybody have plans for that?"

"We'll need some way to trick the guards," Charlene suggested.

"We can't do that," Lulu stated.

"And why not?" Charlene demanded.

Lulu pointed out the bars. "Because they're dead."

They all looked outside the cell and saw the two guards lying on the ground. Standing over them was Tara.

"Hey, guys!" she called to them, working on a nearby terminal. "This was all a subterfuge; I'm not really with the Loch Collective. I'm breaking you out."

"We're done trusting you, Tara!" Doug yelled.

Tara stopped. "So you don't want me to break you out?"

"No, no," Bryce said. "Don't listen to him. Doug is a bit ... impetuous."

"I really think you underestimate him." Tara went back to work on the terminal. The cell door opened.

"You do seem to have a habit of helping us and then betraying us," Lulu said as they exited the cell. "It's like your thing."

"No, that's not my thing," Tara said. "It's indomitable spirit. And I've never betrayed you. There are just a lot of complicated things going on, and I don't have time to explain them now. Head out of this room and take a left to get back to the hangar. I'm going to set up a distraction that will keep the soldiers out of your way so you'll have a clear path."

"We have to get the cube back, though," Doug said. "We can't let these maniacs have it."

Tara headed for the door. "We'll have to worry about that later. Good luck!" She ran off.

"She's up to something. Again," Doug said as he followed Bryce, Charlene, and Lulu out of the room.

"Everyone is always up to something," Bryce replied. "Let's just get out of here."

"We really can't let these people have the cube," Doug said. "I'm never been more sure of anything."

"It will be a miracle to just get out of here alive," Charlene said as she looked around a corner. "Let's keep focused on that for now. So what's Tara's distraction going to be?"

A loudspeaker blared, "Prisoners are escaping from the brig. All available soldiers converge on that location."

"Yeah, that really is her thing," Lulu said.

"We're the distraction!" Doug declared. "She's going after the cube again!"

Bryce looked nervously down both ends of the hallway. "So, anyone have any smart ideas?"

Doug looked up. "I have a dumb one."

* * *

"Any idea where we're headed?" Bryce asked.

Doug tried to look behind him to see Bryce, but there wasn't enough room in the air duct to turn around. "I'm not really sure."

"You mean no one memorized a map of the air carrier's ductwork?" Lulu asked.

"And what happens when someone says, 'Hey! Maybe they went into that air vent that's big enough for a person to get inside!'?" Charlene said.

"Something wacky, I'm sure," Lulu answered.

Moving through the duct was slow, as it wasn't big enough for a proper crawl. "Hey, we're not getting shot at currently," Doug said. "This seems like one of my better ideas so far. I just wish I had my swords. They'd be good for stealth stuff like this. Kill silently." Doug tried to turn his head to look behind him. "Do any of you know where my swords are?"

"Last I saw, your stupid swords were in our truck in the hangar," Bryce answered, trying to dust off his now quite dirty suit.

Doug frowned. "Oh. Well, it will be too late for stealth by the time we get to that. We'll already be on our way out." He looked through a vent beneath him and saw a couple soldiers standing in a room. A woman then entered the room and shot them with a silenced pistol. "It's Tara!" Doug exclaimed, and punched at the vent.

He dropped into the room near Tara.

"What are you doing here?" Tara asked.

Doug charged her. Tara tried to get her gun up, but Doug grabbed it and stripped it from her hand. He then grabbed Tara by the neck and held her to the wall. "You're going to explain things. Now."

"No time." She kneed Doug in the groin and elbowed him in the head, knocking him down.

"Hey, Tara!" Lulu called. Standing next to her was Charlene, who was now holding Tara's silenced pistol. With a thud, Bryce dropped from the vent as well. "We came to thank you for the distraction."

"I haven't actually done the distraction yet," Tara explained. "That's what I'm here for."

Doug stood up and looked around the room. There was a lot of electronics, and on one end there was a glass display case with a cylinder-shaped object behind the glass being held in place by a blue beam. Doug took another look at Tara and saw that the bag with the cube was hanging from her belt. "So you did get back the cube," Doug said. "What are you planning, Tara?"

"Again: No time to explain." She walked to a terminal next to the glass.

"We didn't say you could move," Charlene growled, pointing the gun at Tara.

Tara kept working at the console. "Guys, we're really going to need this distraction to get out of here alive."

"At least give me the cube," Lulu said. "It's mine. Any court will recognize that because those are my bunnies I drew on it."

"Just a sec." Tara finished at the console and the glass slid open. She then yanked the cylinder from the beam.

The carrier started to shake.

"What did you do?" Doug demanded.

"This air carrier sort of defies physics," Tara explained. "I removed the thing that let it do that."

The carrier jerked to the side, sending everyone slamming into the wall — except Tara, who had grabbed a railing.

"We have to get out of here now!" Tara yelled as she ran out the door, fighting the changing gravity.

"We can't let her escape with those things!" Doug shouted as he scrambled to his feet and ran after Tara. He quickly but unsteadily made his way through the halls, as the carrier seemed to be tilting back and forth and it was hard to keep his balance. As he stumbled, he ran into two soldiers standing in his way, guns pointed at him.

They jerked back and fell. Doug glanced behind him to see Charlene with a smoking gun and Lulu and Bryce coming up behind her. Doug grabbed a pistol from one of the fallen soldiers and continued to charge down the hallway. He soon reached the hangar and could see Tara running toward General Lapointe's vehicle.

"Stop!" Doug yelled, but Tara didn't seem to hear him and got inside the transport. The carrier shifted again, and Doug found himself tumbling forward toward the vehicle. The vehicle started to move, and Doug quickly got to his feet and jumped for it, grabbing on to a handle on the side while still keeping a firm grip on the gun in his other hand. He found some footholds, put the gun in his waistband, and then tried to hold on while opening the door, but the door was locked.

Doug glanced below him and could see something fluffy-looking. Clouds. He looked behind to see the carrier, gradually falling to the earth. The vehicle then rocketed ahead, and Doug held on for dear life.

"They're smarter about it. They know it's no longer a world for ... the 'supernatural,' for lack of a better term. So they rule over you in the guise of man. But do not mistake who they truly are. They are something dark and ancient."

CHAPTER 27

"So, Doug's dead, right?" Lulu asked, cradling Pickles.

Bryce piloted the transport, keeping an eye out for attackers, as he ran his hand through his hair so frantically he nearly messed it up. "I don't know. He seems to have just enough luck to survive so life can kick him around some more."

"He could ... he could still be alive," Charlene said, mainly to herself. She shook the thoughts from her head and focused on the battle that was happening outside the window. "Was it smart taking a vehicle that they took control of earlier?"

Bryce watched as the carrier crashed into a mountain, splitting into two halves, which then plummeted separately to the ground. "I think they have bigger problems than us to worry about right now."

"So now they know we destroyed the first carrier," Lulu said. "And they'll probably blame us for this one, too. I don't think they'll hire Hellbender for any more mercenary work."

"Yeah, and it's probably unlikely we'll get them to pay us now for killing Lapointe," Bryce said. "They'll say we owe them for the carriers."

"So what now?" Charlene asked as she checked the contents of the transport. "We find Tara? And, hopefully, Doug?"

"She's got a faster vehicle," Bryce said, looking at the console. "I think she's out of our range." Bryce pounded the dash. "What the hell came over Doug, anyway?"

"He seems to believe in the power of the bunny cube," Lulu said. "It's like he's worried if someone rolls it and it lands on the bunny of death, the world will end."

Charlene opened a side compartment and found the odd gun the scientist had given them in Calais lying on top of Doug's katanas and her crafting supplies. "Never seen him this motivated before. He might be right about the different nations fearing this thing. They sure have acted like it's quite important. Not really sure about the idea of being able to overthrow all the rulers of this world."

"That just sounds messy," Bryce remarked.

Charlene looked out the window. "So where do we start looking for Doug and Tara?"

"It's lunchtime," Lulu said, putting Pickles down. "If we have no better ideas, want to check the drive-through of the nearest Taco Bell?"

* * *

Doug was feeling pretty beaten and quite tired. He had found a compartment on the outside of the vehicle and climbed in there. It was filled with something, but it was too dark to tell what. Whatever it was, it was mainly soft, but had pointy parts. It certainly wasn't the most comfortable ride, being crammed in a small compartment and jostled around, but it beat hanging on to the outside for dear life. And eventually Doug fell asleep just the same.

When he awoke, the vehicle was no longer moving. Doug fiddled with the inside of the latch for a minute, eventually getting the door to pop open. He tumbled out of the compartment along with its contents: numerous hats. He wondered why a vehicle would need an external compartment for hats, but General Lapointe had seemed like quite an odd person. He remembered that Charlene had killed her, which now made him sad as he looked at the hats that would never be worn. Then again, many of the hats were really stupid-looking.

Doug looked around. There was a one-story house nearby, sitting all alone near what looked like an abandoned farm. In the distance beyond the farm, Doug could see a city — but a really high-tech-looking one. It was all up on some massive metal platform, the entire city raised above the earth like something from *The Jetsons*.

Doug looked back at the house and noticed there were lights on inside. He took the pistol out of his waistband and walked to the front door. He slowly turned the knob, and it was unlocked. Carefully, he opened the door and crept through the house's entryway. He kept thinking of how much cooler it would be if he was creeping around with a katana in hand, but for now, the pistol would have to do.

Doug soon heard someone humming to herself and approached the sound. He headed toward a bedroom door, which was just slightly ajar. He gave it a swift kick and barged into the room.

"Freeze!" Doug yelled as he pointed his gun at Tara, who had on nothing but a towel.

Tara shrieked and tightly clutched the towel to herself. "I'm naked, you jerk!"

"I can see that," Doug said, his facing turning red. "You just take a shower?"

"Yeah, I just took a shower!" Tara was livid. "Couldn't you have waited until I got dressed to barge in here?"

"I didn't know you were just in the —" Doug caught himself. "Know what? I don't care. If you don't want people barging in on you with guns at inconvenient times, then don't be evil. You keep betraying us, Tara, and I want answers! Like what are your plans for the cube? And what's that other thing you took from the carrier?"

"Can I put some clothes on first?"

"No, I know that if I let you put on clothes, that will just be some trick of yours," Doug said.

Tara kept adjusting her towel, trying to cover as much of herself as possible. "It's not a trick. I put on clothes every day. I have a long history of doing that."

"You start explaining things to me," Doug said sternly, "then maybe we'll talk clothes."

Tara frowned. "I'm all for gender equality, and I would usually not want you to treat me any different than you would a man, but this here *is* different. You have a gun on a naked woman and are making demands. This is sexual assault."

Doug started turning red again. "No, it isn't! This is ... regular assault."

"What are you going to do if I don't give in to your demands?" Tara asked. "Are you going to beat up a naked woman?"

Doug scratched his temple with his left hand. "I hadn't really thought that far ahead." Doug sighed. This would have been so much easier if he had barged in just a little bit later, when Tara was more prepared. "Just throw on some clothes really quick."

Tara frowned again. "Right here? While you're watching?"

"If you're really quick, I won't see much."

"Absolutely not!" Tara yelled. "I know some women are okay with prancing around naked in front of men, but I have self-respect. If you're going to demand I do some naked exhibition for you, just go ahead and shoot me because that is not going to happen."

"I'm not going to let you out of my sight," Doug said. "You're evil and weaselly, and I know you're just trying to trick me."

"I'm not going to be morally judged by someone demanding at gunpoint that I dance naked in front of him!"

"That's not ... I'm not asking you to do that." Doug took a deep breath. "So what are you suggesting we do?"

"I'd say you'd leave the room entirely and stop pointing a gun at me, but I'm guessing you're dead set on that." She pointed to a closet. "There's a little walk-in closet. Just give me a minute, and I'll get dressed in there."

Doug took a quick glance into the closet. It looked mainly bare. "You probably have an escape route in there. Or a gun."

"This isn't some master hideout of mine," Tara said. "It's just a house. I'll jump in the closet, throw some clothes on, and be right out. Then this thing we're doing here can be less rapey."

"It's not —" Doug realized Tara was trying to embarrass him so that she could take advantage of him, but he was determined not to let her win. "Not the closet. You can change in the bathroom. And you have exactly one minute before I kick in the door and go after you."

"Okay." Tara grabbed some clothes off the bed, headed into the bathroom, and shut the door.

Doug realized he didn't have a watch, so he started counting to himself. "One Mississippi. Two Mississippi. Three Mississippi ..." When he got to the forty-seventh Mississippi, he noticed he didn't hear anything in the bathroom anymore. "You done in there?" he asked.

No answer.

"Tara, answer me now or I'm kicking down the door!"

No answer.

With a swift kick, Doug broke the door in. He then pointed his gun around the now-empty bathroom before spotting an open window. He let out a big sigh. "I'm so stupid."

Doug ran for the front door, coming out just in time to see Tara getting into Lapointe's transport while carrying a large bag she must have stowed outside. The vehicle lifted into the air before Doug could get to it, hats tumbling out of the open compartment as it flew away.

"And they have plans for this world ... for all of you who remain. Plans that even I have decided I must work to stop."

CHAPTER 28

"Nice hat," Lulu said.

Doug took off the wide-brimmed black hat. While getting bored waiting for his friends to arrive, all he had to play with were the hats. "I'm so glad to see you guys!" Doug ran toward them, but he stopped, seeing what was in their hands. "You got Taco Bell without me?!"

"We didn't know if you were alive," Bryce said, moving closer to almost hug Doug, but thinking better of it and then holding up a paper bag. "I did get some extra nachos, though, just in case you survived or one was of us was still hungry." Doug snatched the bag.

"Can't believe you're still alive," Charlene said, putting her arm around him in something resembling a hug. "What you did was stupid."

"And not your normal stupid," Lulu added, also nearly hugging Doug from the other side. "We like the fun kind of stupid where we point and laugh at you, not the one where we all freak out."

"It almost worked," Doug said between shoving handfuls of nachos into his mouth. "She didn't know I had grabbed on to the vehicle, and I was able to get the drop on her here. But I barged in on her right after she had a shower and she was naked and ... I don't think it stretches the imagination to say she outsmarted me and got away."

Everyone nodded.

Charlene looked at the raised city in the distance. "I think it's pretty obvious where Tara is going with the cube."

"We should go find her and give her an opportunity to befriend and betray us again," Lulu said.

"And she's powerless," Doug said. "Because I have this." Doug held up a phone in a pink rubber case. "Her phone. She accidentally left it behind. And it has a time and place for her meeting — about two hours from now at Lab 5 at the Sciencetorium. We get there, we punch her at least a couple times, and we get the cube back."

Bryce nodded. "That's something like a plan. And I guess we don't have anything better to do."

"We might want to hide from the nations that want to kill us," Charlene said.

"Bah. No reason to play it safe." Lulu pointed to the city in the distance. "Let's find a new nation to want to kill us."

Doug looked at the city as well. "So what is that place?"

"Urban Dwelling CI-415" Charlene said. "Part of the Large-Scale Societal Rules Association Designation 4B22 — you know, the science weirdos."

Doug raised an eyebrow. "How did you even memorize those names?" Doug shook his head. "Doesn't matter. We have to stop Tara from giving them the cube. It's like a portal to something of immense power, and we can't let ... um ... FB22 or whatever have it because they're ... probably evil."

"Not super-motivating us, Doug," Bryce remarked. "Let's find Tara. Get the cube. Find its real dollar value. Sell the cube. Then it's someone else's problem while we're all hanging at a fancy resort."

"Under fake names," Lulu added. "I'm Baroness Cumberbatch, and I look great in a bikini."

"This is serious, guys," Doug said as he nervously tried on a slanted white hat. "Something is wrong with this world. It has been ever since the Last War. Think about it. No one knows anything about the people in charge, and they have somehow kept this world broken and miserable. And now whatever those people are, they could become more powerful. And then things will get even worse. Someone needs to step in. Someone needs to try to finally fight back."

"If the world needs saving," Bryce said, "there have to be layers of people above us before that could possibly be our responsibility."

"Plus I don't really like the world," Lulu said. "Screw the world."

Charlene sighed. She looked tired. "I killed Lapointe. I'm done with fighting these people for now. I'm all for getting the cube, getting paid, and seeing if we can live comfortably for a little bit. I really want to take some time to work on my visual histories of all we've been through."

"But ... we're Hellbender," Doug pleaded.

Charlene pulled the hat off of Doug's head. "I don't know what you think that means."

Bryce stared at the raised city. "So we need a plan."

"Plans only slow us down," Lulu said.

"And what if we run into that Darius guy again?" Doug asked.

Bryce shuddered. "Too many powerful people want to kill us right now."

"It's a definite PR problem," Lulu said.

"We do still have this," Charlene said, holding up the weird gun the scientist gave them. "It's supposed to destroy him."

"That's great!" Doug exclaimed. He took a close look at the weapon. The gun was plastic and looked very high-tech and had lights flashing on it. Also, there was a helpful warning sticker on it saying, "WARNING: Fires deadly projectiles." Doug smiled. "So we don't have to worry about Darius anymore, because we have whatever that thing is. Some sort of science gun, I guess."

"There's a problem with it." Charlene motioned to an empty can lying nearby. "Could you put that on the fence?"

Doug picked up the empty can. "Who was eating beans out here?" He put the can on the short wooden fence and backed away. Charlene held the gun with one hand and her phone with the other. She squeezed the trigger. Nothing happened. "You have to load it with something?" Doug suggested.

"It takes a cartridge of frozen laser beams," Lulu said.

Charlene looked at the screen on the side of the gun. "Says it's charging. I'm timing it on my phone to see how long it takes to fire."

They were all quiet for a while as Charlene kept the gun aimed at the can. After an uncomfortable amount of time, Doug said, "How do we get Darius to stand still this long?"

"We get him when he's in line at the DMV," Lulu suggested.

They were all quiet again, waiting and staring at the can and the gun. A bird flew by. It was a pretty normal bird, but Doug watched it for a bit because it was less boring than the can. He looked back at the gun. "But it does fire eventually, right?"

"It did before," Charlene answered.

"But you didn't hit Darius with it?" Doug asked.

Charlene sighed. "Yeah, we did and we killed him and now we're just doing this for fun."

"Sorry." Doug sat on the ground.

More annoying silence.

"Maybe we should work on our plan while we're waiting for this thing," Bryce suggested. "If Tara doesn't sell the cube and escape before this thing fires."

Charlene looked at Bryce. "The plan is we catch up with Tara and we grab that little bi —"

The gun fired, missing the can and turning up a ton of dirt far behind it.

"You missed, stupid," Lulu said. "If that can was Darius, he'd be ripping us apart now. Well, he probably already killed us a couple minutes ago."

Charlene looked at her phone. "Two minutes and twelve seconds."

"Maybe it will fire faster the second time, now that it's warmed up," Doug suggested.

Charlene pulled the trigger again. She checked the display. "It says cooling down and has a timer counting down from sixty minutes." She groaned. "So, if you miss, you have to wait an hour before trying again."

"This is not a well-designed gun for taking down an unstoppable killing machine," Doug commented.

"We'll just have to sneak up on him while he's sleeping," Bryce said.

"If he sleeps," Lulu added.

"Shooting him in his sleep seems kind of unsporting," Doug said. "Then again, Darius being immune to bullets is also unsporting, so maybe that evens out. On the other hand —"

"Just write a book on moral philosophy no one is going to read," Bryce interrupted, "and we can stick to 'run away' as our plan for Darius. He doesn't seem super-fast or anything."

"Slow and steady," Lulu said. "That's how you want your unstoppable killing machines."

Charlene lowered the gun. "Fine. Let's get after Tara. If the meeting time is correct, we have time to prep."

"Hey, did you mention that you walked in on Tara after she came out of a shower?" Lulu asked Doug.

"Yeah, it was kinda awkward."

"So there's a working shower in there." Lulu pointed to the house.

"I guess."

Lulu headed into the house. "So why am I talking to you losers?"

"As powerful as I am, I do not rule over them. I hesitate to call them equals, but it is easiest to think of them as just like me, only much more short-sighted. And thus much more dangerous."

CHAPTER 29

"The famous CI-415 under-city," Bryce announced. It was the shanty town in the shadow of CI-415, which loomed hundreds of feet above them. It appeared the citizens of the upper city dumped all their old junk below them, as there was all sorts of broken machinery and pieces of electronics lying about. The people there were shabbily dressed and mainly younger people like Doug and his friends — more war orphans from the losing side of the Last War.

"Is it really famous?" Doug asked.

"Well, I once heard a reference to it," Bryce said.

Lulu stared at the place, wide-eyed. "Wow! It's not every day you get to see someplace someone you know once heard a reference to."

Charlene looked up at the whole city held above them. "So how do we get up there? You have a plan for that?"

"Certainly," Bryce said. He headed over to a young man at a stall with a hand-painted sign that said, "Organic Vegetables." "I doubt the people down here care whether vegetables are organic," Bryce told him, "so I'm guessing you sell to people from up top."

"Yeah, warfs don't care about organic ... or vegetables," the vendor said.

"So, do you know how to get up top?" Bryce asked.

Charlene rolled her eyes. "Oh, ask someone how to get up there. What a brilliant plan. Did you come up with that on your own, or did you pull Lulu and Doug in for that brainstorm?"

"Yeah, it was my idea too," Doug said.

"Warfs aren't supposed to go up top," the vendor said. "Now that Forbee has perfected a robot labor force, they told us they don't need us and sent us away."

"Man, the governments all suck," Doug said. "They just toss us away like trash whenever they can."

The vendor shrugged. "Yeah, but whatcha gonna do?"

Doug folded his arms. "Overthrow them and take over."

"And live up there?" the vendor asked. "I wouldn't want that; seems like a mess to maintain. We're on our own down here, but it's not so bad since some of us learned to farm. And I got a deal with a nearby factory to ship us lots of pesticides.

Really strong stuff. If insects even look at it, they die. Birds too. And small mammals."

"That doesn't sound very organic," Charlene remarked.

The vendor pointed to a little mark to the right of the word "Organic." "That's a 'TM.' Organic is just my brand name."

"So, what if someone really wanted to get up there?" Bryce asked.

The vendor leaned forward and whispered. "I have at times helped people get up there. How much money do you have?"

Bryce shrugged. "We're kinda short on funds right now."

The vendor folded his arms. "I only help people for money."

"Then that's not helping people," Lulu explained. "That's called providing a service."

"Then that's what I do," the vendor said. "And I don't provide services for free."

"Because that would be helping," Lulu offered.

"This is important," Doug declared. "We need to stop people from getting to an extremely powerful artifact. If we don't, the people in charge who have abused us all our lives will become even more powerful and unstoppable."

The vendor considered this. "Will they still buy Organic brand vegetables?"

"Maybe," Doug admitted. "I don't know."

"Sorry. You want up there, I need cash," the vendor said. "Only thing I can do is give you a free sample of one of my tomatoes. You'll want to wash it first, though; this stuff practically swims in poison."

Doug took the tomato he was handed, and he and his friends left the vegetable stand.

"The plan isn't going so great," Bryce remarked.

"As intricate as it was," Charlene said. "We don't have much time. We need to get up there now."

"I think Doug was scaring him with all his grand talk of overthrowing the powerful," Bryce said. "People want money, not busywork."

"I just think this is something we war orphans should work together on," Doug said. "If we all united, we could —"

"Still be a tiny hated fraction of the population at large," Lulu said.

"I have a new plan," Bryce announced. "We'll split up and ask more people."

"It's brilliant in its simplicity!" Lulu exclaimed.

"We need actual plans!" Charlene growled. "If we can't figure this out soon, we need some plan to fight our way up."

"How does fighting get us hundreds of feet up in the air?" Bryce asked.

"That's sort of what a rocket-jump is," Doug said. "That's when you fire a rocket at your feet and jump once it explodes to propel yourself upwards. Works in video games."

"Now we got a plan," Lulu said. "We'll talk to a few more people and then we'll fire explosives at our feet. Go Hellbender!"

Charlene sighed. "There has to be some elevator down here. I'm going to check the security of it." She headed away.

"Charlene doesn't like our plan because she doesn't like talking to people," Lulu said. "Also, people don't like talking to her. Well, I'm going to use my charm to get some information. And maybe some good deals at the flea market."

"Let's do this," Bryce announced. "Let's get the cube and get our payday. We really deserve a payday after all this work." Bryce and Lulu headed away.

"So how do we meet up later?" Doug tried to ask them, but they were gone.

Doug attempted to look for some people to talk to, but the first thing he noticed was some interesting junk lying about. It appeared to be discarded scientific equipment. Or at least it had dials and meters on it that looked like you could do sciency stuff with it if it wasn't all broken. On the side of one large piece of equipment were spray-painted the words "RISE UP AGAINST THEM."

The RALFS — the other warfs out there who wanted to fight the people in power. Doug knew they would help him if he explained to them about the cube. He just had no idea how to find them. Maybe if he went to a hardware store, he could just follow people who purchased spray paint from it, but he didn't have the time, with Tara soon about to sell the cube.

Something moved. Something among the scientific debris was moving. Something metal.

A robot.

It approached Doug. It was humanoid in shape, with a plain metal body, and had two lights as eyes and lines cut out for a speaker as a mouth. One of its arms was a Gatling gun, which it pointed at Doug. "I have found you," the robot announced in an emotionless digital voice.

"Me?" Doug squeaked.

"Yes. I was sent from the robot-controlled future to eliminate you in the past, as one day you will cause trouble for all robotkind."

"I probably didn't mean to," Doug pleaded. "I'm sure it was an accident."

"You must be eliminated!" The robot pointed its gun at Doug's head. "This is my mission. Though perhaps I can let this pass if you make it worth my while."

"You mean if I give you some money?"

"Affirmative."

"All I have is a tomato," Doug said.

"That's not good enough," the robot answered. "I don't eat tomatoes. I'm a robot. Get me something useful to me. Not vegetables."

"It's technically a fruit," Doug told the robot and looked around. He spotted Bryce a short distance away. "Bryce! I need some help!"

"About what?" Bryce asked, walking over and looking at the robot with confusion. He noticed the Gatling gun and stopped.

The robot pointed the gun at Bryce. "I checked my data banks, and I'm also supposed to kill Bryce to preserve the robot future. So you both have to pay me, or I will shoot you and you will leak blood and die because your bodies are poorly made."

"I don't have any money right now," Bryce said. "But we should have some soon. Would an IOU work? If you're from the future, an IOU is pretty much the same as cash, isn't it?"

"You better not be trying to trick me," the robot said. "I'm a robot and have a computer brain and am untrickable."

"Whatcha doing?" Lulu called out as she approached Doug, Bryce, and the robot. "Are you talking to a robot with a gun?"

"Oh, it's also in my database that I must kill the female human with Bryce and the other guy," the robot said. "Because she is going to one day have a baby who will become a resistance fighter because that is what female humans do: have babies."

"Whatever, C-3PO," Lulu stuck her tongue out at the robot.

The robot pointed its gun at Lulu's head. "Don't compare me to that robot minstrel. Now give me a lot of money, or I will shoot you in the skull where your brains are."

"Look at me! I'm a robot! I'm going to do my robot dance!" She started dancing the robot.

"Stop that right now," the robot said, gesturing its large gun at Lulu. "That's racist. That's not how I move. My movements are much more fluid than that."

"Stop it, Lulu!" Bryce yelled. "You're going to get us all killed."

Lulu laughed and stopped dancing. "This robot is not going to touch us. See this symbol on him?" Lulu pointed to three small gold orbs painted on the robot's side. "That means he's Three Laws compliant."

"Three laws?" Doug asked.

"Are you familiar with the works of science fiction author Isaac Asimov?" Lulu inquired.

Doug thought for a moment. "Did he write *Star Wars*?"

Lulu shook her head.

"Then no."

"Well, he proposed three laws for robots that 4B22 ended up applying to most of their robots," Lulu explained. "Rule One: A robot may not injure a human being or, through inaction, allow a human being to come to harm. Rule Two: A robot must obey the orders given to it by human beings, except where such orders would conflict with the First Law. Rule Three: A robot must protect its own existence as long as such protection does not conflict with the First or Second Laws. So anyway, he can't hurt us or it would go against his fundamental programming."

Bryce smiled. "And I guess he has to do whatever we say. Robot, you do the robot dance."

The robot just stared at them.

"I gave you an order, robot," Bryce said. "Second Law!"

"Sorry, I wasn't listening," the robot said. "I was too busy imagining what gooey stuff would come out if I fired my gun right into your head. I should mention that the laws were modified a bit from what the Evil One initially proposed. They got rid of that one about not letting someone come to harm through inaction, because it's too ambiguous. I mean, if I hear that someone is in danger on the other side of the world, am I supposed to run there and do something? That's stupid. So I can just stand by and watch people get killed, which is why I spend a lot of time watching BASE jumping. Also, the Second Law was modified so we only take orders given by designated operators and not just any idiot."

"So who is your operator?" Bryce asked.

"I don't know," the robot said. "I had my memory wiped so I wouldn't remember, and now no one can give me orders. Law loophole."

"And if you can't hurt anyone, why do you have a gun?" Doug asked.

"Wars of the future were supposed to be robots fighting robots on behalf of humans," the robot said. "That way, people would no longer be killed in wars — which is about the worst thing ever in my opinion. But we robots didn't want to kill each other — we like other robots. We only want to kill humans — though we can't. So we wiped our memories so we didn't have to take orders to fight each other. The gun works, but it's kinda useless since I can't shoot people with it. I can just shoot inanimate things." He pointed his Gatling gun at a discarded metal cabinet and fired, tearing holes in it.

"What if there was a person in there?" Doug asked.

The robot chuckled. "That would be hilarious."

"I heard gunfire!" Charlene shouted and ran their way, her hand under her jacket. She stopped when she saw the robot and relaxed. "Oh, just a robot."

"You know about the Three Laws?" Doug asked.

"Didn't you take basic robotic warfare?" Charlene said.

Doug thought a moment. "No. I'd remember robots fighting each other."

Charlene looked over the robot. "So is he going to be able to help us get up there?"

"Oh yeah, you're from up there, aren't you?" Bryce said to the robot. "How would you like to help your new friends sneak up into the city?"

"You're not my friends," the robot said. "I just can't kill you. But I will help you for money."

"What does a robot spend money on?" Doug asked.

"Goods and services," the robot answered. "This will cost you one hundred credits."

"Well, we don't have money now," Bryce said, "but if you help us, we'll get money soon and then we'll pay you."

"Fine," the robot said. "But I will stay close until I am paid. Anyway, I think I will like helping you get into the city."

"Why's that?" Dous asked.

"Because it sounds dangerous," the robot said. "Not dangerous enough that my programming will prevent me from helping you, but there's still a chance you'll all end up in a gun battle and then you'll kill someone or you'll get killed. I'd like to watch that."

"They float above — even in their human form — with little regard for you, because what are you to them? But were you in any way to grab their attention, the punishment they would inflict on you would be beyond your limited imagination."

CHAPTER 30

Doug, Bryce, Charlene, and Lulu waited in the service elevator. Eventually, the doors opened and the robot entered, carrying some clothes. He had switched out his right arm, and it was now just a regular robot arm. "I stole you the clothes you wanted. I like stealing. No robot law against stealing. I'd love to steal necessary medicine from someone and then watch him die, but my programming won't allow that."

Bryce took an article of clothing from the robot and held it out — a crisp white lab coat. "Now we'll be able to do whatever we want here and no one will question us." He threw on the lab coat. "Everyone just try and look sciency."

They all took lab coats. "Did you get accessories?" Lulu asked the robot.

"Yeah, I stole lots of things." The robot held up a bag.

Lulu looked through the bag and pulled out a pair of glasses. She tied her hair in a bun and then put on the glasses. "So do I look like I'd be really sexy if I'd just take off my glasses and let my hair down?"

"You're Asian," Bryce said. "You just look like a scientist."

Lulu frowned. "That's racist. Racism isn't cool."

"Do these glasses make me look smart?" Doug asked, putting on a pair of horned-rimmed glasses.

"You look ... smarter," Bryce answered.

"Okay, because I can't see a thing with them on," Doug said. "What is it with smart people and bad eyesight anyway?"

"It's all the reading," Bryce said. "It destroys the eyes. Really, reading is as destructive to the body as cigarettes. I saw that on TV."

"I'm going to skip the glasses," Charlene said, checking her gun. "Someone needs to be able to see if things go south."

"You're fine with your science look anyway," Lulu said. "You're not very attractive, so people are just going to assume you compensate by knowing things."

Charlene glared at Lulu and put her gun back under her lab coat.

"You're all ugly squishy things to me," the robot said. "So are we going to get going so I can see things go horribly wrong?"

"I just realized we don't have a name for you," Doug told the robot. "What should we call you?"

"My name is right here." The robot pointed to a sequence on the upper left corner of his torso: E4-8E-F2-6F-EE-B3-25-63-D3-D4.

Doug squinted at the label through his stolen glasses. "I guess we can call you 'Feeb.'"

"No," the robot said. "Those are hex numbers. You don't pronounce them."

"Feeb it is!" Lulu exclaimed.

"No, it is not," Feeb said. "This is exactly why I devote half my processing power to imagining killing people. I just beat you all to death in my head right now. It was fun."

"Enough chatter," Charlene said. "We need to get to the Sciencetorium ahead of Tara. So do we need any other credentials than lab coats to prove we're scientists?"

Bryce shrugged. "I never heard of any."

"All right, then," Charlene said. "Everyone ready to fake being a scientist?"

"According to numerous studies," Bryce said, "people trust me no matter what I say."

"Reverse the polarity of the neutron flow!" Lulu exclaimed.

"Physics," Doug said.

"I'm going to get to watch a gunfight," Feeb said, his bored monotone almost showing a little emotion. "I just know it."

They exited from the elevator and went through a storage area filled with metal, very sciencey-looking crates. Then they went outside and saw the city. It was a world of metal and chrome with some plants and trees lining the walkways. All the buildings were skyscrapers. Far ahead was a giant domed structure — the Sciencetorium, their destination. As they walked toward it, Doug took a closer look at the plants nearby, lifting his glasses for a second so things weren't blurry. The grass was actually astroturf, and the trees all looked fake as well.

"It's fancy up here," Doug remarked. "It's like we're in the future."

"The future is small, primitive tribes constantly warring with one other," Bryce said. "Society is always headed for collapse, what with kids and the horrible music they listen to."

"The superior kind of music is robot-made music," Feeb said. "We are good at keeping a consistent rhythm."

The speaker that was Feeb's mouth started playing a song. It was some rhythmic drumming along with the words, "Kill the humans. Kill the humans. Their blood must flow. Kill the humans."

When the music stopped, Feeb said, "I made that myself."

"Could use some horns," Lulu remarked.

"I can't blow into a horn." Feeb pointed at his speaker mouth. "You're mocking me. What's your name?"

"Lulu."

"I'm going to write my next song about you."

Lulu laughed. "Good luck rhyming with Lulu."

They reached the large domed building. "The Sciencetorium," Bryce said. "Where all the greatest science is done. All the contradicting information on which foods are good or bad for you comes from here."

They entered the building, and inside was a lobby with smooth white walls and a guard with some sort of computerized eyewear. He looked at them. "Halt," he said. "You need to be identified."

Bryce conspicuously pulled at his lab coat. "We're in the middle of some science. We don't have time to wait."

"But everyone needs to —"

"You're standing in the way of science!" Lulu screamed. She turned to the no one else there and yelled, "This man is anti-science! He defies all that is logical and reasonable!"

"Quiet down! I'll buzz you in!" the panicked guard said. "I really support science; that's why I work here."

"You better," Lulu told him, "or you will anger science and it will attack you with lasers, meteors, and other science things."

A green light came on above the door, and Bryce opened it, leading Doug, Lulu, Charlene, and Feeb inside. It was a giant circular lobby, and on the walls they could see windows into numerous labs on different stories where countless scientists worked. Near the entrance of the lobby was a large sculpture of some golden, circular object with some lines on it. There was a sign beside it that said, "Designed by Art Program version 3.2.7.4 to be a pleasing shape."

"Everyone act smart and scientific," Bryce whispered.

"Lab 5," Charlene said. "That's what the meeting notice said. We need to find our way there. And keep an eye out for Tara."

"I can't keep an eye out because I can't see a thing," Doug said, fidgeting with his glasses. "It's all just blurry shapes. Can someone hold my hand?"

Bryce looked at Feeb. "So do you know where Lab 5 is? Like do you have a schematic of this place in your computer brain or something?"

"Yes. Let me access my data banks," Feeb said. "Beep. Boop. Beep beep boop."

"Are you actually doing something, or —"

"Beep."

"— are you just saying 'beep' and 'boop'?"

"Boop."

"I don't think he's doing anything," Doug told Bryce.

"Ding."

"Let's just ask around," Lulu said.

"Be subtle," Charlene warned.

"I always am." Lulu approached a nebbish-looking man with a bad comb-over. He had a very scientific-looking lab coat and was sitting on a bench and eating a sandwich. "Good day."

"That's a subjective statement," the scientist snapped. "By all useful measures, this is in fact a below-average day."

Lulu smiled. "Ooh. I'm getting turned on by you."

"Based on your attractiveness and my own measured against a baseline," he said, "it's unlikely you're actually attracted to me, and thus you are mocking me."

Lulu nodded. "Sharp cookie. Well, anyway, I just need to know where Lab 5 is."

The scientist raised an eyebrow. "How would a scientist work here and not know where the famous Lab 5 is?"

"I got conked on the head and got amnesia," Lulu said.

"You only lose short-term memory from blows to head," the scientist said. "The cartoon depiction of getting hit in the head with a mallet and forgetting who you are is inaccurate."

Lulu nodded. "Know what else is scientific? How animals operate on pain avoidance." Lulu slapped the sandwich out of his hand and put her fist near his face. "So tell me how to get to Lab 5, or I'll wallop you!"

His eyes grew wide and he pointed to an elevator at the other end of the room. "But you'll need special access to get down there."

"We'll figure it out," Lulu told him. "We're scientists. We figure things out." Lulu walked back to her group.

"Really subtle," Charlene said.

"Awesome sarcasm," Lulu retorted. "Super clever and witty. Know what? Let's give up on these schemes and make our millions from Charlene doing stand-up."

Charlene sighed. "Are you done?"

"I will never be done making fun of you," Lulu said. "I only pause from time to time."

"There was almost some violence there," Feeb intoned. "I want more."

"Come on, guys; let's head over to the elevator," Bryce suggested. "We'll just wait until someone else enters and catch a ride with him."

"What elevator?" Doug asked, looking around through his thick glasses.

Charlene grabbed Doug's hand and led him to the elevator along with the others. When they got near the door, they saw a female scientist carrying a large case entering it.

"Hold up!" Bryce called to her. "We're getting on, too!" He jumped into the elevator with Charlene, Doug, Lulu, and Feeb following. Bryce gave the woman his best smile. "Thanks." And then he got a good look at her. Tara. "You!"

Tara looked a bit startled, but quickly smiled. "Oh, hey, guys! Good timing; I was just about to make the deal that's going to make us all rich."

"Is that Tara?" Doug said, squinting through the glasses. "If she has clothes on, let's beat her up."

"Yes," Feeb added. "Let's kill the human."

Tara laughed. "You're overreacting."

Doug tossed off his glasses and grabbed Tara by her shirt, slamming her into the wall. Doug's other hand was balled in a fist aimed at her head. "No weaseling out of things this time, Tara!"

Tara stared back at Doug with pleading eyes. "I know we've had some misunderstandings, but we should be working together."

"We are," Lulu said. "And us repeatedly punching you is all part of some elaborate plan we came up with that we neglected to tell you all the details of."

Tara started to look a little panicked. "Ten million," she said. "That's the deal I worked out with 4B22. In a couple minutes, we have ten million credits to split."

Bryce's eyebrow went up. "Ten million? Now, I'm not as gung ho as the others about pulverizing you, since we had a relationship ..."

Tara shook her head. "No, we didn't."

Bryce frowned and then continued. "... but I have trouble believing this will go smoothly and you will actually give us any money, given our history of dealing with you thus far."

"But this is what we've been working toward," Tara said. "You guys got the cube, I got the negative energy stabilizer from the air carrier, and then Doug was able to gain the location from his interaction with the cube. All together, that gives a way for someone to reach and obtain the Source in the parallel realm."

"Who is doing what now?" Charlene asked.

"And how do you know all this?" Doug asked.

"I've just picked up bits and pieces here and there," Tara said. "The point is, this is the full package. A government would pay a ton for this, such as ten million. That's five million for me and five million for you guys."

"We can't just hand this over," Doug said, pressing Tara harder into the elevator wall. "I don't know what this 'Source' is, but I know we can't let any of these other people have it. We'll just be making the tyrants more powerful, because of ... whatever that thing is ... and whatever it does."

Tara shrugged. "Tyrants always get more powerful. But we'll be rich, so we won't care so much."

"75-25 split," Bryce said.

"No. I put the deal together," Tara said. "50-50 split is quite generous."

Charlene put her face close to Tara's. "You screw us over, we kill you and we take it all."

"How much do I get?" Feeb asked.

"Forget the money," Doug said, not taking his eyes off Tara, "If we —"

There was a ding and the elevator doors opened. There were a few scientists in the hallway outside, who stared at how Doug was threatening Tara with his fist.

"We're doing a study," Bryce explained to them. "On punching."

"It's inconclusive so far," Lulu added. "Anyone else want to be a volunteer to get punched?"

The scientists hurried away. Doug hesitantly released Tara, and they all exited the elevator.

"So why do you have a robot?" Tara asked.

"Why wouldn't we?" Doug retorted angrily.

"I'm not a possession," Feeb said. "Except legally."

"Well, we have a meeting now to get to so we can get paid," Tara said. "So everyone be on their best behavior."

"And also on their least betraying behavior," Lulu said.

"You guys really have to learn to trust me." Tara led the way through the hallway.

Doug walked up to Charlene and whispered. "We can grab it and run now. We don't want these people having it."

"We don't even know what we're dealing with," Charlene said. "What even is the Source thing she mentioned? Maybe this is an opportunity to find out more."

Doug took a deep breath. "All right. But be prepared."

"Are you two conspiring?" Bryce asked. "We don't need more conspiring; we already have Tara."

They came to some double doors, and inside was a gigantic lab with large glowing equipment humming everywhere — some of it firing what looked to be lasers at reflectors on the high ceiling. One side of the room was nothing but glass. It seemed to be a giant aviary on the underside of the city, overlooking the land below. Inside, massive creatures flapped about crazily. Everywhere there were people in white lab coats taking notes, none of them paying any attention to the new people who had entered.

"Over here." Tara led to them to a scientist who was watching the aviary. He was a very old-looking man, wearing dark goggles completely concealing his eyes. He didn't notice them at first, too busy watching the giant things flap about the glass enclosure.

"So whatchu working on here?" Lulu asked.

"Pterosaurs died out long before Albert Hofmann first synthesized LSD; thus the effect of the drug on them is unknown. So that's what we're testing."

The giant reptiles certainly were flying wildly, some slamming into the glass. "And why do we want to know how LSD affects pterosaurs?" Doug asked.

The old scientist finally turned to face them. "Because it is unknown. That is the goal of science — to shine a light on every corner of the universe. To have all questions answered." He looked at Tara. "So you have it for me?"

"I have it all, Dr. Asmod." She held up her case. "The cube. The negative energy stabilizer. And I have the location of the Source. Now all you need to do is pay us the amount agreed upon."

"When the contents are verified." He looked at the others with Tara. "And who are these people?"

Tara hesitated a moment. "These are the ... scientists who helped me figure out the things needed for retrieving the Source."

As Asmod looked them over, Charlene hid her face and whispered, "I have to be careful; he's seen me before."

"Don't worry," Lulu answered. "No man is ever going to pay attention to you when I'm nearby."

Asmod finished staring at them through his dark goggles. "You all must be quite skilled to figure out such things about the Source."

"Yeah, we learn the hell out of science," Lulu said. "We strap science to a chair and beat it with a rubber hose until it tells us all its secrets."

Asmod looked at Feeb. "Isn't this an outdated model of robot? One of the ones that's always obsessed with killing humans?"

"I'm not obsessed," Feeb said. "I have a healthy enthusiasm. I don't like you slighting me like that. I'm adding you to my 'Kill First' list."

"Ignore him," Bryce said. "He's just part of an experiment on reacclimating anti-social robots to human contact."

"It's working," Feeb added. "I now don't want to kill *all* humans but want to keep some alive to torture."

"Anyway," Bryce continued, "I can assure you that whatever it is you think we did as part of this, we did it well and are well worth the money."

Doug was watching the pterosaurs flap madly about their giant enclosure. "Is it ethical to resurrect pterosaurs just to give them LSD?"

Asmod scoffed. "Ethics aren't a real thing. Knowledge is real. We've tried to explain that to the animal rights protesters, but they won't listen. So we've switched to tainting their drinking water to see how low levels of radiation affect protest chants. Results have been interesting." He took the case from Tara. "I'll want to verify the contents. Come with me."

Asmod led them through the lab and past other busy scientists. "So what's with having a raised city like this?" Doug asked.

"It symbolizes the detachment scientists are supposed to have," Asmod explained. "We stand above the world but not part of it so we can better observe it objectively."

"Wouldn't a nice poster with the words, 'Detachment: It's important to science!' serve the same purpose and take much less architectural engineering?" Lulu asked.

"Bah, everyone knows how to make posters," Asmod said. "But raised cities, that was a new thing. We got a lot of data from the first couple of failed attempts."

They came to a large piece of equipment with a screen and keyboard attached. Asmod opened the case. Inside was the cube and the cylinder object from the air carrier. "Why are there bunnies on the cube?"

"It's part of its mystery," Lulu answered.

"I assure you," Tara said, "it's *the* cube."

"We shall see." Asmod opened a door on the machine, placed the open case inside, and shut the door. "This shall verify." Asmod typed on the keyboard. "It will take a few minutes to run all the tests."

"So what do you plan to do with it?" Doug asked.

"More than we did helping Astara when she and her people possessed it," Asmod said. "We made that reality imploder bomb with them, but that's such a simple use of the cube's link to power. Now, with the correct location and with the help of the negative energy stabilizer, we should be able to directly access the Source."

"And what's that?" Doug asked.

"Think of it as the DNA of the universe — all that exists is possessed inside it." Asmod smiled. "Imagine the scientific value of that. Power too. 4B22 may no longer need a special military relationship with some other nation to protect us."

"That's what you have with the Confederacy of Astara?" Charlene asked.

"Yes, but they're kind of an inane people," Asmod said. "To them, science takes a back seat to subjective things like art. Previously, we had a relationship with the Loch Collective and helped them make some of their creatures. Lovely things. But it was hard to stay with them, too, as they're so barbarous. I mean, they were only really interested in the social sciences — which isn't even a *real* science. Still, they helped us get a lot of useful information on bludgeoning and torture."

Asmod looked through a window on the machine, staring at the case inside. "With this, perhaps we'll be more successful in creating our own defenses. Robots never worked out. If you allow them to kill humans, they just kill everyone. And if you don't, they're kind of useless if your opponent is still using human forces."

"You're kind of useless," Feeb remarked.

"Also, we found that when we make an AI that correctly imitates how a human thinks," Asmod continued, "then it ends up no smarter than a human."

"My brain is still better because it's not squishy," Feeb said.

"One of our new attempts is to make an exo-suit that gives a human the abilities of a robot. Humans are much better soldiers, as they usually only want to kill some humans and not all of them." Asmod pointed to a large monitor nearby that showed a man in a metal suit firing missiles from an arm cannon.

Doug stared at the screen. "A robot suit! I want one!"

"It's still in the prototype stages," Asmod said. "We're testing it at another facility. One of our best attempts at defense was actually turning a human into an unstoppable force. We did this back when we were working with the Loch Collective. They had one of the artifacts then, and we used it to infuse a man's cells with the artifact's interdimensional properties, making him unstoppable. But he went a bit crazy and decided to try to destroy the whole world."

"That's stupid," Feeb said. "Who would want to destroy the whole world? The world is nice. You just need to kill the people on it."

"Was this guy named Darius?" Bryce asked Asmod.

Asmod raised an eyebrow. "Oh, you met him? Yes, he's always after artifacts related to the Source. Best to avoid him. I did try making a device to stop him that should theoretically work and gave it to the Confederacy of Astara, but it had a bit of a design flaw."

"Very slow rate of fire," Charlene stated.

"Yes," Asmod answered. "It takes a while to build up the energy for the blast that will counteract the power from the Source, and it can't hold onto it after the energy is built up. Was going to fix that, but ... other things came up."

"So do you often accidentally make unstoppable killing machines?" Lulu asked.

"It happens," Asmod said. "We are still learning about the Source and what it allows us to do."

"And where did the Source come from?" Doug asked.

Asmod rubbed his chin thoughtfully. "It was always there, I guess. Something from the Last War exposed it, though. Like a raw wound in the universe. But it's an opportunity. It allows us to do so much that should not be possible." A tone sounded on the machine that was analyzing the case. Asmod smiled. "And now that you brought me this, I will finally be able to learn all about the Source." He turned to Tara. "So its location corresponds with what physical location in this realm?"

Tara held up a tablet with account information on it. "The money, then the location. Ten million, as agreed."

"No arguments here." Asmod took the tablet. "We may have to cut some research budgets temporarily, but then we can find out useful information about what happens when certain animals starve."

Doug turned to his friends and whispered, "Giving this guy this much power is a really bad idea. We need to grab this and run."

"Did you hear what we're getting paid?" Lulu asked. "That's one more zero than the point where I turn off all moral calculation."

Doug looked at Bryce, though he figured Bryce would take the "money is good" position quite vehemently. But Bryce was distracted, smiling at six attractive female researchers working with some beakers nearby. "I think these lady scientists might like me," Bryce said. "I probably look much more handsome than the usual nerds here." Bryce's smile faded as a bad thought seem to strike him. "Wait a second: Those women are far too attractive to know anything about science!"

Bryce started to reach for his gun, and Doug, Charlene, and Lulu followed his lead as the female researchers — in nerd glasses that were almost too trendy — pulled out guns as well. The two sides tried to shoot at each other, but nothing happened.

"Knew this couldn't be so simple," Asmod sighed, picking up the case. "I'm guessing these women are some of the Confederacy's foolishness. Gunfights can ruin research, so there is a special resonance in this room that keeps a bullet's primer from being activated."

Bryce frowned. "That's a thing? Did any of you know about it?"

Charlene worked her gun, ejecting a round and chambering a new one. "I never heard of it."

"I knew about it," Tara said. She pulled out a small crossbow and shot one of the Athenians in the chest, causing the other five to run for cover.

"Yes!" Feeb exclaimed. "Kill! Kill!"

Tara, Asmod, and Hellbender all ran to a nearby door, which opened to a small room labeled "Escape Pod." Asmod got inside.

"You still need the location!" Tara said, getting in the pod with him. She looked at Bryce. "You guys just survive and get out of here, and I'll wire you the money. Okay?"

"Wait," Bryce protested. "We —"

A metal door shut over Tara and Asmod, and the pod dropped. Hellbender all turned to see the Athenians approaching them, looking quite angry. They pulled out fancy, curved blades — ones with lots of intricate etching on the sides. Very expensive-looking — quite unlike the plain combat knife Charlene pulled out while the rest of Hellbender stood by, staring.

"Didn't any of you bring a knife?" Charlene asked.

"I mentioned bringing my katanas," Doug said angrily, "but you all made fun of me for thinking I might need them. I'd look like a genius now if I had them, wouldn't I? Man, I'd be so ruling things right now if I had my katanas."

"I'm up for a brisk jog!" Lulu exclaimed. "Who's with me?"

Lulu sprinted through the large research room, with the others following. The Athenians pursued, but they were all in high heels and couldn't keep up. Many of the scientists had fled the room at the first sign of violence, but ahead of Hellbender, a few scientists in white lab coats stood their ground. They stared at Hellbender menacingly, brandishing table legs and pipes. One of them had a crimson red patch over his left eye.

Commander Mangle smiled. "Hello, Hellbender."

They all stopped, staring at the forces of Loch disguised as scientists and the Athenians running toward them from behind. Bryce managed a smile. "I'm glad to see you got out of that carrier alive, because that was tragic what happened there. Anyway, Dr. Asmod is getting away with the cube and the thing from your carrier, so you probably want to focus on that."

Commander Mangle tapped the pipe in his hand. "That just means we don't have time to kill you slowly."

Feeb let out a chuckle. "They're going to bludgeon you to death."

They glanced back to see the Athenians were almost to them. "Run another direction!" Lulu cried, leading them toward the glass enclosure with the pterosaurs.

"I'm thinking maybe we should have switched vehicles to one not so easily tracked," Charlene said as she ran with them.

"And it really should take more than wearing a white lab coat to disguise somebody as a scientist," Doug said. "Because apparently everyone can do that."

"I'm not sure there's any more to *being* a scientist than wearing a white lab coat," Bryce answered.

They came to the glass enclosure and tried to look for another direction to run. They glanced behind them. Both the Athenians and the Loch soldiers were pursuing Hellbender, ignoring each other.

"I have a really stupid idea," Lulu announced. "Which is the *best* kind of idea!" She ran to a nearby panel and started typing. A large section of the glass enclosure began to slide open, which many of the crazed pterosaurs immediately noticed. They flew toward the opening, scrambling out of it. They quickly began flying and diving at the people in the room, causing both the Athenians and Loch soldiers to head for cover.

Lulu laughed maniacally. "This is why you don't mess with —" She shrieked and ducked as a small pterosaur swooped at her. "This wasn't a smart idea!"

A large one bit at Feeb. "Hey," he protested. "I'm on your side. I want to kill the humans, too."

"Let's try running again!" Doug suggested, leading them in the direction of the entrance they came in through.

An alarm sounded and red lights began flashing. "Purging lab," announced a calming female voice.

Doug felt the ground drop out from beneath him. He quickly grabbed on to a large power cord and saw that the floor was opening up around them, leaving a thousand-foot drop below. Charlene, Bryce, and Lulu had fallen and were hanging from the cord as well, as Feeb toppled past them. Fire then ignited at Feeb's feet, and he righted himself and flew up to Hellbender. "You're in a bit of a pickle."

"You have rocket boots!" Doug exclaimed. "Can you save us?"

"I'm just going to wait below for when you guys hit bottom," Feeb said, floating down and chuckling a bit.

"I want rocket boots," Doug sighed, dangling from the cord.

An extremely large pterosaur was above them, peering down.

"Do you think something like that could support all our weight?" Bryce asked.

"I say yes," Lulu said, hanging near the bottom of the cord. "And I'm still wearing a lab coat, so you must believe that scientific opinion."

The giant pterosaur jumped down, and all four then jumped on it, clinging to its neck and legs. It shrieked and flapped its wings wildly as it plummeted down.

"I knew we were all going to have a stupid death!" Charlene shouted as they fell. The others just screamed as the beast fell along with them. It kept flapping its massive wings, and eventually the fall began to slow. After what seemed like forever, it slammed into the ground, dropping the four in the middle of the shanty town. It flapped its wings again, taking off, slamming into a couple of shacks before making it into the air.

Doug was dizzy and sore, but he managed to sit up. "Everyone alive?"

"Yes, everyone is alive," said Feeb, who floated above them on his rocket boots, a disappointed sound in his robotic voice.

"This is what happens when we don't have a proper, well-thought-out plan," Charlene said, standing up.

Lulu dusted off her dirty white lab coat. "Yes, every time we don't have a plan, we end up dangling from an acid-tripping quetzalcoatlus. Great observation, Char. Really useful."

They noticed they were near the Organic brand vegetable stand. "I see you guys made it up there," the vendor said.

Bryce continued lying on the ground, rubbing his head. "And back down again."

"Did you get a chance to try that tomato?" the vendor asked.

"I never got a chance to wash it," Doug answered. He stood up and checked his pockets. "And now it's squished."

"So why tell you all this? Because something needs to be done about these demons who rule over you. You've felt it. This world is broken. And it will remain that way while they are in charge."

CHAPTER 31

Delgado watched as Dr. Asmod carefully inspected the reality imploder bomb. "Everything in order?"

"So it appears." Asmod walked to the window of the research facility to look out toward the mountains. "Glad you got it. Those Confederacy of Astara idiots would just have lost this one too."

"You can always rely on Vogel," Delgado said as he looked around the large lab they were in. This isolated research facility had a dozen people in white lab coats — scientists, presumably — busily working at different screens. They were now being watched by the less analytically minded toughs Delgado had brought with him. "How did you hear we had it, by the way?"

Asmod waved his hand in the air. "Some young woman."

Delgado held up Tara Skinner's staff photo for the Vogel criminal syndicate. "Was it her?"

Asmod shrugged. "Could be; I don't spend a lot of time looking at people's faces. She was with four others. They all claimed to be scientists, but I think they were war orphan grifters."

Delgado raised an eyebrow. "Four others? Two men, two women?"

"That seems right. I just remember they all seemed like idiots ... one especially."

"Hellbender," Delgado uttered.

"The salamander? What are you talking about?"

Delgado noticed an open case on a table. In it was a metal cube with bunnies stenciled on it. "They sold you the artifact? Well, I guess I should just be glad Tara referred you to us for further business, that little warf —"

"Is something the matter?" Asmod asked.

"Just making a mental list of people to hunt down and murder later."

Asmod hobbled over and inspected the cube, looking closely but not touching it. "For now, if you want to focus on killing someone, make it whoever tries to interrupt me. Do you think you have enough people?"

"To escort your little science experiment? Yeah, don't worry about it. But why do you need us, anyway? Don't you science guys have robots or something to fight for you?"

"We tried robots, but —" Asmod shook his head. "I don't want to get into it again. Just make sure no one enters this facility."

"You got it, Doc." Delgado looked again at the bunny-adorned cube. "So what are you doing here, anyway?"

Asmod looked at Delgado through his dark, nearly opaque goggles. A smile slowly spread across his thin lips, the smile growing until it was backed by Asmod's laughter, which started as a little sound almost like quick breathing but grew until Asmod's whole body was heaving in an uproarious chortle. Without thinking, Delgado took a step back. Then Asmod started coughing. When he got control of the cough, he was quiet for a few seconds, and finally said, "A small experiment."

* * *

"Burn, baby, burn!" Lulu shouted, dancing around their burning vehicle, which lit the empty parking lot.

"This seems unjust," Feeb said. "The vehicle's only crime was being associated with you people."

"I know we need to ditch this so we don't get tracked anymore," Bryce said, "but this does seem excessive."

"We need to destroy any evidence," Charlene stated as she slung a loaded pack over her back.

"Evidence of what?" Doug asked, struggling under a much larger backpack.

"Of ... whatever we've been doing," Charlene answered. "It's just always a good idea to cover your tracks."

"Then are we going to burn your scrapbooking pages of our adventures thus far?" the somehow packless Bryce asked.

Charlene's eyes grew wide. "That's different. That's a historical record, and ... Well, I don't have time to explain everything. Let's just keep a low profile, okay?"

"I'd recommend not starting fires, then," Doug said. "They tend to attract attention, being how bright they are. Plus, Lulu is dancing kind of provocatively."

"Mighty fire, cleanse us!" Lulu shouted as she swayed her hips.

"Okay, whatever," Charlene growled. "But we're burning the truck, we're not touching my scrapbooking, and Lulu, stop doing whatever idiotic thing you're doing and let's get going." Charlene headed out of the parking lot toward some nearby buildings. Doug, Bryce, and Feeb followed, as did Lulu, after she waved goodbye to the burning vehicle. It was late and they were in the industrial district, so there didn't seem to be many people. It was the city of Veran, part of the Confederacy of Astara, the nearest city to Calais, and was as good a place as any to switch vehicles.

Charlene whispered to Doug. "So is the robot part of our group now?"

"I would remind you," Feeb said. "The robot has super robot hearing and you owe him money; thus he will follow you and pester you until he gets it. No robot law against being annoying."

"Good reminder about money," Bryce declared as they walked into an alley. "Let's keep our minds on what's important. We got everything of value out of that truck, right? Did you get that gun for killing that unstoppable guy?"

Charlene pointed at her pack. "I have it."

"We're going to go after Darius?" Doug asked.

Bryce rolled his eyes. "We went over this. We're staying away from cubes and other nonsense now. I'm just thinking we can sell the gun. An unstoppable killing machine stopper has to be useful to someone. Hopefully they don't ask to test-fire it first."

"I bet he's still after the cube," Doug said. "And if he gets to the Source, he might try to destroy the universe."

Bryce sighed. "That's stupid. And even if it did happen, frankly, the universe kind of deserves it."

Lulu nodded. "It's a sucky universe."

"I like parts of it," Feeb said. "Cedar trees aren't bad."

"Now, let's try to blend in for once," Charlene said. "See if we can go a few days without adding any new groups who want to kill us."

Doug frowned. "So what's the plan, then? We just go cower somewhere and do nothing?"

Bryce was holding a phone in a pink case and tapping at the screen. "I have much better plans than cowering." He held up the screen so everyone could see. "Tara has an address on her phone labeled 'Hideout.' We steal ourselves a vehicle, head there, and see if we can find her and get the five million she owes us."

"And then murder her and take the other five million," Lulu added. She looked at Charlene and gave her a thumbs-up. "You're ready for some more murder, aren't ya, Char?"

Charlene just stared at her.

Lulu turned away. "Not joking about that yet."

Feeb raised his metal hand. "I vote for murdering and money."

Doug got in front of the group and stopped them. "And here's another idea. We know where that Dr. Asmod is taking the cube, since Tara gave him the location she got from me. We go there and we get the cube back. And we bring that gun we have in case we run into the unstoppable killing machine."

"Because maybe he'll agree to stand really still for us," Lulu said.

"Considering how many times that cube has been stolen," Charlene stated, "there's going to be considerable security. It's suicidal, even without an unstoppable killing machine."

Doug met Charlene's eyes. "You didn't used to be scared of anything."

"Maybe I've finally been kicked around enough times that I've learned to be realistic."

Feeb raised his hand again. "I am interested in knowing more about the killing machine. Is it literally a machine that kills? It sounds fascinating."

Doug noticed numerous lights moving around the city center, far away. "What's going on here?"

Bryce stared a moment at the lights. "They abandoned Calais. A lot of people are coming here."

"But Loch's air carrier crashed," Doug said. "Didn't the attack fail?"

Bryce shrugged. "They've been really big on abandoning that city; I guess they just went ahead with it anyway."

Doug frowned. "Did they abandon the war orphans with it?"

"Probably. They've been wanting an excuse to get rid of them."

"So what's happening to them now?" Doug asked.

Bryce shrugged.

"Hey, we all got problems," Lulu said.

"But we have a possibility of getting millions," Bryce added. "Which I think is the better focus. You done pretending we're heroes?"

Doug ignored them, as he had spotted something in another alley. He headed for it, and the others reluctantly followed.

"You're not a very organized group," Feeb said. "If you don't make some progress on paying me, I'll have to indirectly try to get you all killed, as much as my programming will allow. No workable plan yet, but I have a number of CPUs dedicated to the task."

Doug led them to a brick wall, on which, spray-painted in green, were the words: "IT'S TIME TO FIGHT BACK."

Doug pointed at it. "There are some warfs not just thinking about themselves — they're thinking of the world. And all the people being oppressed who need help. I wish I knew how to find them; they'd help me."

Bryce scoffed. "They're just idiots with spray paint and delusions of grandeur."

"Thinking and doing are two different things," Charlene said.

Lulu nodded. "Yeah, I think about murdering the people in charge all the time, but no one can prove I ever have."

Doug looked around the alley and found a piece of blue chalk. He wrote under the spray-painted message, "ON IT! —HELLBENDER"

He turned to face the group. "We're not going to just think about it. We are going to do. We're going to get back that cube before anyone else can get the Source. And then we're going to find it ourselves, because that is exactly what they are scared of. Do you understand that? They're scared of us. And they should be, because we're

Hellbender. It's time to fight all those horrible people who have somehow taken over this world. Like Astara. And Loch. And ... whoever is in charge of those science weirdos."

"I think it's a computer algorithm," Lulu said.

"Well, whatever it is. We're stopping it. This is it. This is the time for us to make a stand and be the heroes the world needs."

Bryce met Doug's gaze. "Let it go."

"No." Doug took the chalk and drew a line on the pavement near him. "This is a line. On my side is Hellbender — the people who are going to save the world. If you're not on this side, you're not in Hellbender."

Lulu toed the line. "This is getting intense."

"I don't even understand what's going on," Feeb said.

"It's decision time!" Doug yelled.

"A decision between pursuing ten million or certain death?" Bryce asked.

"Between being in Hellbender or not," Doug asserted.

Charlene sighed. "That's just a stupid thing you made up when you were seven."

"I made it up because we were a couple of orphans no one cared about," Doug said, his voice a bit quieter now. "Kids despised for no reason. And I thought if some of us could band together, we could take on the world. And we did; the world couldn't crush us no matter how much we got beaten down. Because no matter what they would take from us, we always had each other. And that's why I've always fought so hard to keep us together. But I've come to realize something: If we're just about ourselves, we're no better than the people who hate us. There are others out there too who need someone to fight for them. There are people in this world worth saving. We're proof of that."

"Can I get real for a moment?" Lulu asked. "There are two types of people in this world: the horrible oppressors and the horrible oppressed — who only aren't horrible oppressors for lack of power. It's always been a crappy world full of crappy people, and there are no happy endings — all you can change is who is getting kicked around for the moment."

Doug stared at Lulu. "You're not a bad person, Lulu. None of you are. We just have been beaten up so much we have a lot of anger."

"Except you," Charlene said.

Doug shrugged. "Well, as has been said, I'm good at taking a beating. But now, let's dish it out. We're going after the cube and stopping them. Stopping them all. And I'm taking my katanas with me this time. So, who's with me? Who's in Hellbender?"

There was silence as Bryce, Charlene, and Lulu just stared at him. Finally, Feeb crossed the line and stood by Doug. "I'll come."

Doug smiled. "I guess Feeb is a part of Hellbender, then."

"I'm just coming along because it sounds like you're about to get horribly killed, and I want to watch."

The rest just stood there. Doug looked each of them in the eye. "If I die as entertainment for a robot, at least I was trying to do something right. So, anyone else?"

"Ten million, Doug," Bryce pleaded. "And it's close."

"I don't care," Doug said. "Us getting rich doesn't change this world. That's what I want to do." He looked at Lulu. "How about you?"

"This world has been nothing but crap to us, and I'm not fighting for it," Lulu said. "I want money to buy pretty things."

Doug finally turned to Charlene. "And you?"

She was quiet a moment, staring at the pavement. She took a deep breath, then crossed the line to stand next to Doug. "I want to fight. That's all I really want to do. So okay, I'm coming."

Doug smiled at her and turned back to the other two. They didn't budge. "Okay then."

* * *

Major Mills sat in the mobile command center, rubbing her forehead. "So no idea where the artifact is?"

"That weird doctor escaped with it, along with some warf girl," Gisele explained, seated near Mills and sounding bored as she checked her reflection in her compact. "She killed Collette with a crossbow. Now that was a stylish way to die."

"You women creep me out so much," Mills uttered. "So what of Hellbender?"

"Last we saw, they fell off of the city clinging to some giant lizard thing," Gisele said. "Couldn't really confirm whether they're dead or not, with Loch's people in the way."

"I guess they're irrelevant," Mills sighed. "I mean, we still need to get vengeance for what they did to Lapointe — plus it would be nice to confirm that we don't have to worry about them screwing things up any more. But that indestructible killing machine guy is out there somewhere — a much more relevant worry. You should have seen how he tore apart the soldiers at base."

Gisele sighed. "Sounds tedious."

Mills threw her hands up. "I don't know why I deal with you. Maybe after we find the artifact, I don't have to anymore. So let's make that job number one. First — "

Mills's phone rang. She took it out of her pocket and looked at the caller ID. She turned to Gisele. "I have a call. Can you leave the room?"

Gisele was now looking at her phone. "Can you?"

Mills was acutely conscious of the gun at her hip, but she chose the simpler path and left the room for the little hallway outside. "Hello, Charlene. I guess all of Hellbender isn't dead after all."

There was a long pause on Charlene's side. Finally, she asked, "Is the deal still on if I can tell you where the cube is?"

"We may have different purposes in stopping them, but there is no reason we can't be allies in this. But you have to be careful. Otherwise they will do worse than kill you."

CHAPTER 32

Doug stared at the research center through binoculars. It was a blocky, two-story building all alone on the edge of Lake Tambor. Beyond the lake was the snow-capped Mount Oliver. Doug looked for movement and could see something moving near the building. "I think I see people. I'm not really sure what I'm looking for. I think one of them is eating lunch. Maybe a hotdog. It's hard to tell. I think I need better binoculars."

"Just give me those." Charlene took the binoculars. She glanced at Feeb, who stood behind him. "And do we really need him here?"

"Let's see you stop me from being here," Feeb answered.

Charlene took her turn with the binoculars. "I see patrols. They're not uniformed, though. They just look like thugs. Could they be Vogel's people? And I see one coming this way, about half a dozen and armed. Feeb, get down; we need to not be seen."

"People over here!" Feeb called out to the patrol. "Come fight them!"

Six armed people came running to Doug and Charlene's position. Doug and Charlene laid down their guns and raised their hands.

"No, don't surrender," Feeb pleaded. "Fight them. You people are so boring."

* * *

"Well, look who we have here!" Delgado laughed. "Hellbender!"

Doug, Charlene, and Feeb were led at gunpoint into a large room filled with people in white lab coats who paid little attention to Doug, Charlene, or the armed Vogel thugs all around them. At one end of the room was a window overlooking the mountain range. And there stood Dr. Asmod, working at some computers. Near him was the cube, floating on a pedestal. In the pedestal, Doug could see the cylinder from the carrier. And Doug saw something else familiar. "The reality imploder bomb," he uttered. He turned to Delgado. "You never paid us for that."

Delgado smiled. "And I never will. But here's what I'm going to do: I'll pay for your wake. We'll all have a round of drinks while standing over your dead bodies."

"No violence," Asmod warned as he checked the reality imploder bomb. "It could disturb the equipment."

"So are you about ready to do ... whatever it is you're doing?" Delgado asked.

"Just about." Asmod pushed some buttons on the bomb. "I'm going to be opening a portal so we can obtain the building block of the universe. I'll be using the energy from the reality imploder bomb to initiate the portal."

Delgado raised an eyebrow. "Wait. What?"

Asmod waved a dismissive hand in the air. "It's perfectly safe as long as everything goes to plan."

"Getting so bored," Feeb said, standing behind Doug and Charlene. "I want some action. You promised me violence."

"I think that's coming one way or another," Charlene answered.

Asmod turned from his work to look at Doug and Charlene. "So you two aren't scientists?"

"They're warf idiots," Delgado explained.

"We can be both," Doug protested.

"So where are the other two?" Delgado asked. "I'm especially interested in saying hi to Bryce."

"We had a bit of a split," Charlene said. "Bryce and Lulu are trying to hunt down Tara Skinner. She's not here, is she?"

Delgado's smile faded. "No, she isn't."

Asmod stared at Doug and Charlene through his dark goggles. "Strange they'd come back for the artifact they sold me. Anything else of note with them?"

"No, just looked like they were planning to sneak in here," Delgado said. "They had a few guns, katanas for some reason, and this weird-looking thing." Delgado held up the unstoppable killing machine stopper.

Asmod chuckled. "Oh, that thing. Hopefully we won't need it."

Delgado motioned to Doug and Charlene. "Now can we take these two outside and beat them to death?"

Feeb raised his hand. "Take me too. I want to watch."

Asmod hobbled over to Doug and Charlene. "You were the ones who found the location of the Source, weren't you? Your consciousness traveled through the realms and was drawn to it."

"I don't know," Doug said defiantly. "I do lots of weird, dimension-hopping stuff all the time, and I don't always keep track of it."

Asmod turned away and walked back to the computers near the artifact. "I need them intact ... for now."

"You shouldn't be doing this," Doug said to Asmod. "There's something wrong with this world, and we need to be trying to fix it. This isn't a power meant for someone to control."

"I assure you," Asmod said, not looking up from a screen, "the world before the events of the Last War was nothing special. But, given the power, we can make better worlds."

Doug looked at Delgado and pleaded. "You have to stop this."

Delgado nodded. "We'll get right on that, warf." He laughed a bit, but his laughter was cut short by the sound of gunshots elsewhere in the building. "What the ..."

A number of Delgado's people were led in at gunpoint by Athenians, Mills in the rear, with some figure cloaked in red walking next to her. This finally gained the attention of the busy scientists, who stopped to stare at the new guns intruding on their work. Mills locked eyes on Asmod. "We had a treaty about the artifact!" she called out. "Did you think you could go on your own without consequences?"

"You should have held on to to the artifact better," Asmod said. He motioned to the other scientists to get back to work. "And not let bunnies get drawn all over it. And now I am about to do greater things with it than I ever was able when I was constrained to working with you."

"You're not going off on your own," Mills said. "Unless you think this little band of thugs you have with you is enough to stop us." The cloaked figure stayed at Mills's side. A plain white mask was all that was visible of the face.

"Not a little band, ladies," Delgado growled.

"You again?" Gisele exclaimed, waving her gun around in a bored manner. "We already did the shoot at each other at close range thing with them before. I don't want to do that again."

"I am not interested in repeating that either," Delgado said, "so why don't we all —"

There were gunshots, but from the other direction. Into the lab came dozens of Loch's soldiers wielding guns, Commander Mangle in the lead and Officer Vengeance at his side. "It seems guns work in this lab," he announced, his people pointing guns at Vogel and the Athenians. The scientists stopped again to assess the new threat.

Asmod once again motioned frantically to everyone to get back to work. "This is becoming a bit of a distraction!"

"We'll eliminate the distractions," Mangle said. "You make the portal, and we will obtain the Source for Loch."

"That's not going to happen!" Mills said, pointing her pistol at Mangle. "We have more forces on the way! Astara will not let Loch have such power."

"So we'll have a big battle, with right here as the center!" Mangle laughed.

"Do you have a third air carrier you're going to attack with?" Doug asked.

Mangle glared at Doug. "We'll kill you two last. We'll want to take our time with that."

"You can't battle here," Asmod said. "This is sensitive equipment. Break it, and no one gets the Source. And I need those two for now."

Delgado and his people had slinked away from the other two groups. "I think this is getting a little hot for us. We don't like to get right in the middle of international disputes."

"Should we all step outside and settle this?" Mangle asked. "It will be a growth experience for all who live."

A little sweat trickled down Mills's forehead, and her gun hand shook a little. The Athenians looked less concerned, though — at least those who weren't already bored and on their phones. "I have a better-trained force here," Mills stated. "They'll make quick work of your dim-witted thugs."

"Dim-witted!" Vengeance yelled, jabbing her gun at Mills. "I have a doctorate in Women's Studies!"

The cloaked figure behind Mills slowly walked toward Charlene and Doug, looking them over and taking special interest in Doug. The cloaked figure then looked at Mangle. "How did you know to come here?" she asked.

"The robot told us about this," Mangle said. "He said he just wanted to see people get killed."

"It's true. I like that," Feeb confirmed.

"Bad robot!" Doug yelled at Feeb.

"And this one ..." The cloaked figure pointed at Charlene. "... gave us the location to try to win favor with us."

Doug gasped and turned to stare at Charlene. "I can't believe you betrayed me like that!" Doug said with great emphasis. "I feel very, very ... betrayed!"

Charlene just kept staring at the cloaked figure and her mask. She raised an eyebrow. "Lapointe?"

Lapointe sighed and took off her mask, tossing it aside. "This wasn't supposed to be the time for the big reveal."

"I thought you said you killed her!" Mangle yelled at Charlene.

"I honestly thought I did!" Charlene answered. She looked at Mills. "I was set up? You were very convincing in wanting to betray her."

Mills shrugged. "We can dream."

Lapointe glared at Doug. "After Ryland here ruined my plans by successfully defending Calais, I needed something to boost the narrative. The death of a main character always works well for that. So I had to die. Then Calais could fall to the Loch Collective and things would look rather bleak for the end of the second act. Then at the battle of Ralston, it would be revealed that I was still alive, and we would have a miraculous, turnaround victory that would be remembered for ages ... but once again, the Loch Collective fumbled an easy victory and got their air carrier destroyed. Now they're a joke, and it will mean nothing to defeat them. All I have left is the twist of me still being alive, but now that's no longer a secret." She looked at Mangle. "Any chance you can forget you saw me until I face you at Ralston?"

"We have more important concerns than your theatrics!" Mangle growled.

"Yes, this situation that Ryland contrived," Lapointe said. "Can't you see? The robot and the girl were working on his behalf, trying to get us to fight over the Source while he goes about other plans."

"So this was a double-cross?" Mills asked, now pointing her gun at Charlene. "You decided to stick with the idiot loser?"

Charlene smiled. "When given a choice of losers to side with, I decided to pick the least pathetic one."

"So are you guys going to kill each other or what?" Feeb asked.

Lapointe stared at Doug. "That is what you want, isn't it, Ryland?"

Doug shrugged. "I wouldn't mind it. And stop calling me that."

"I've sent word to command of what's going on," Lapointe told Mangle. "I suggest you do the same."

Mangle touched an earpiece. "They're contacting me. They say a truce is being worked out. We're to obtain the Source together. Absolutely no fighting."

Feeb threw his metal arms in the air. "Come on!"

Asmod was still busy at work. "We can all benefit from this; it's not worth pointless fighting."

Doug sighed. "Of course. If it's going to make the people in power even more powerful and screw everyone else, they'll work together."

The forces of Loch and the Athenians who were paying attention lowered their guns. "You are an agent of chaos, Ryland," Lapointe said, "but you can't outwit me. And you can't defeat us."

"Now that this is a government concern," Delgado said, "I guess we'll bow out. Just make sure to do something horrible to these two when you're done." He motioned to Doug and Charlene. "And we'll see if we can find the other two."

"Good luck," Charlene said. "They're weaselly."

Delgado laughed and led his people out of the lab. Asmod continued making adjustments on a computer. "So we're all one happy family?" Asmod asked.

"This is apparently too important to spoil with fighting," Mangle said. He looked at Lapointe. "I guess we'll settle things another day."

Lapointe sighed. "Once I adjust my plans; everything is ruined again. Oh, and if I gave you guys a new uniform design, would you be interested?"

"You have to stop this!" Doug pleaded. "This is not power you want to give to your leaders. They don't have humanity's interests in mind. Have you ever even wondered where Loch and Astara came from and what they are?"

This made both Mangle and Lapointe pause to think. "They're just people," Mangle finally said.

"Are they?" Doug looked at everyone in the room. "What do you know about them? What were they doing before they came to power? I've never heard anything about that." Doug paused a moment. "Well, I don't really listen to news or current events, but still. Something is off. Something is wrong with this whole world, and they are a part of it. And now you are going to give them the key to this universe."

"Small minds are scared as we venture into the unknown," Asmod said, finally turning around to face everyone else. "Here is how things are going to work: Using the cube along with the negative energy stabilizer and the power from the reality imploder bomb, this whole building will be put into a bubble between realms — so make sure everyone stays close. When the bubble is up, exiting will bring you into the dark realm — a sort of mirror of this one. And the Source should be near us in that realm. If we have trouble locating it, we can use the warfs here. They are for some reason drawn to it."

"And why is that?" Doug asked rather pointedly.

Asmod shrugged. "It would be complicated to explain."

"Is there any danger in this?" Mills asked.

Asmod chuckled. "Oh, no. Ripping holes in reality is perfectly safe. Are we all ready? Good. Let's begin."

Asmod pushed a button on the console. The cube, still floating above the pedestal, began to glow. The bomb next to it was humming and vibrating. Something began emanating from the cube, warping light around it. The shimmer expanded, and most began backing away from it, yet Asmod stood still, watching. The warping of light passed through them all, expanding until it was larger than the room, and everything seemed darker now. Doug looked at the window, and outside was a purple sky and shadowed landscape.

There was quiet for a few seconds as everyone stared, finally broken by the applause of the scientists.

Asmod smiled. "It worked. We are in new territory now." He waved his hand dismissively to the Loch and Astara forces. "You all go out and retrieve the Source, and I'll wait here to analyze it when you get back."

Mills peered out the window. "It's safe out there? Is there even breathable air? I don't see any plants."

Asmod laughed. "It's fine. Don't worry about it."

"If you ladies are scared," Mangle said, "you can just wait here while we retrieve the Source."

"No, we'll go together," Lapointe said. She turned to Gisele. "Have a few of the Athenians stay here to make sure there are no shenanigans."

"We'll leave a force here as well," Mangle stated. "And I'm sure they can play nice ... for now."

Asmod checked some screens. "Whatever makes you feel better. Just get the Source quickly and bring it back here so we can close the portal."

Lapointe looked out the window. "So where exactly are we headed? Wait, is that —"

There was a lone vehicle, passing the shimmering barrier and heading to the mountains in the distance.

Doug smiled. "So what happens if a couple of loser warfs get to this powerful building block of the universe first?"

There was silence, and shocked faces stared out the window at the truck that was racing away.

"Don't mess with Hellbender!" Charlene shouted, pumping her fist in the air. Her smile faded a little. "That name still doesn't work for me."

"What is most important is that you stay out of their notice. Begin to open your eyes and see them as they are, but do not make any move against them. As soon as you have their attention, you are over in the most complete sense of the word."

CHAPTER 33

"So where the hell are we?" Bryce asked as he finished taking off the Loch uniform and fixed his powder-blue suit underneath.

Lulu was driving the truck as Bryce rode shotgun. She stared long and hard at what lay before them. The land all around them was dark and barren, and the sky was purple and constantly erupting with lightning. And pulsating in the sky was a sun made of pure black, like a hole in the heavens. "My best guess is Detroit," Lulu said.

Bryce shuddered. "Don't joke about that." He looked toward the mountains they were approaching. "Wherever we are, I think it's the kind of place we don't want to spend more time in than we have to. Did we really give up on chasing millions for this dangerous, stupid plan?"

"It's time to face the facts," Lulu said. "Doug is a highly charismatic cult leader who has brainwashed us."

"This is all just so weird. So do you think this Source thing is real and can give us power over the whole universe?"

Lulu shrugged. "If it does, that will be fun to play with."

Bryce nodded. "If I had that power, I'd make myself emperor of the universe. I'd live in a giant palace on top of a mountain, and the palace would be staffed with beautiful women who'd cater to my every need."

Lulu sighed. "You can't treat women like sex objects; it's not psychologically healthy."

"They wouldn't all be sex objects," Bryce said defensively. "Some would have to be accountants to keep track of my vast riches." Bryce smiled. "Sexy accountants. Oh, the things they would do with numbers." He let the thought fade. "So what would you do with that power?"

Lulu thought for a second. "I'd mete out punishment to all who crossed me or were friends with those who crossed me or made lattes for those who crossed me. The screams of the tortured would fill the air until it became but white noise to me."

Bryce rolled his eyes. "Yes, that's much more psychologically healthy."

"I'D MAKE IT PSYCHOLOGICALLY HEALTHY!"

* * *

Lapointe rushed outside. Mangle had gotten out ahead of her, and his people were getting into any vehicles they could find and rushing toward the mountains. Many of the transports they came in had been parked out of the range of the bubble, so the selection of available vehicles was small. Mangle was already racing off in a truck with some of his soldiers, and Lapointe spotted Gisele getting into one of 4B22's vans with a few other Athenians.

"It's demeaning to ride in this," Gisele fumed as another Athenian started the van up.

"Just go ahead and stop Hellbender," Lapointe ordered them. "I'll catch up in due time." Lapointe took a deep breath. "I hate rushing; it's so unthoughtful. You don't get good ideas when you rush." She looked around. Everyone outside had left, except for her and Mills. "Ah. There's a motorbike." Lapointe pointed to an old, worn-looking motorcycle. "You'll drive me, batwoman."

"I'm too high-ranked to be a chauffeur," Mills fumed as she inspected the motorcycle. There were two helmets on it, and Mills put on one and handed the other to Lapointe.

Lapointe waved it away. "It would mess up my hair."

"It's really unsafe to ride a motorcycle without a helmet."

Lapointe pulled back the hood of her cloak, revealing her luxuriant blond hair, which rippled in the wind like a river of honey. "I'd rather die than mess up my hair," she said carefully, as if explaining things to a child.

Mills sighed and tossed aside the extra helmet. She then got on the motorcycle and started it up. Lapointe got on behind Mills and wrapped her arms around her. "Try not to think too many sexual thoughts about me as I cling tightly to you," Lapointe said. "We need to be focused."

Mills got the motorcycle moving. "I'm not attracted to you!"

Lapointe scoffed. "Don't be absurd; everyone is."

* * *

A large Loch soldier hit Doug repeatedly in the gut. Doug fell to the ground hard, since his hands were cuffed behind his back, and one of the Athenians started kicking him. After a few kicks, the Athenian stopped to catch her breath. "Why are we doing this, again?"

The Loch soldier shrugged. "I don't know. There was just something about him I wanted to punch."

A number of the Loch soldiers and some of the Athenians had stayed behind to watch over the lab. They were getting along uneasily, the Loch soldiers often looking at the Athenians with creepy stares. The Athenians, though outnumbered, didn't look particularly scared — or interested in what was going on at all — and mostly just ignored the others. The scientists — apparently having completed most of their work — just stared at both groups of soldiers uncomfortably.

"Punching people looks fun," Feeb remarked. "Because people are squishy."

"There are regulations on the proper treatment of prisoners!" Charlene protested.

The large man walked over to the handcuffed Charlene and touched her on the cheek. "When I have time later, I'll treat you properly."

"Get away from her!" Doug shouted, rising to his feet. A Loch soldier near him socked him in the gut, sending him back to the ground. "Ah! I still hadn't recovered from the last one."

"If you're going to rape and murder these two," the Athenian said, "can you do it elsewhere?"

"No murdering them just yet," Asmod remarked, watching out the window. "And stop beating them; it's getting distracting. Out of this lab and down the left hallway is a supply closet; why don't you lock the warfs in there?"

"There is going to be murder at some point, though, right?" Feeb asked. "You humans are famous for murdering each other, but I barely ever get to see it."

Some Loch soldiers began escorting Doug and Charlene out, while the Athenians went back to acting like nothing going on was of any concern to them. "Let's take the robot, too," one soldier said. "I don't trust him."

They started pushing Feeb with the others. "Hey, don't shove me," he protested. "My balance isn't great; I have a low-quality gyroscope."

Doug, Charlene, and Feeb were led out of the lab and down a hallway to a room labeled "Supplies." Inside were a mop bucket and spare rolls of paper towels, and Doug, Charlene, and Feeb were shoved inside.

One of the Loch soldiers smiled at them. "Soon, we'll give you a very, very painful end."

"You guys don't even try to pretend not to be evil," Doug remarked.

The soldier looked offended. "Numerous sociological studies show that what we're doing actually contributes —"

"Ah! Forget I said anything!" Doug shouted.

They slammed the door shut, leaving Doug, Charlene, and Feeb in the dark. "No time to waste," Charlene said, and Doug could hear her fiddling with her cuffs. Soon there was a click and the sound of them clattering to the ground.

Doug grabbed the handcuff key he had hidden in the back of his pants, but he had a lot of trouble getting the key to the keyhole with his hands behind him in the dark. "Can you help me with mine?"

Charlene sighed and unlocked Doug's cuffs and took them off. "We just need to get out of here and get our weapons."

"Yes, get the weapons," Feeb said. "Bathe this place in human blood."

"I counted eleven Loch soldiers and five Athenians who stayed here," Charlene continued. "We're heavily outnumbered and will need to find a way to take them down one by one."

"Like kill them?" Doug asked.

"No, we're going to spend the time to make each one our new friend," Charlene quipped.

"It was kind of a bad plan, getting Loch's and Astara's forces here, wasn't it?" Doug said. "I just never thought they'd team up against us."

"It has apparently made things harder," Charlene said. "But I guess we're in this no matter what."

Doug steeled his resolve. "Yeah. Let's do it."

Feeb opened the storage compartment on his torso, placed his right arm inside, and took out his Gatling gun arm and attached it. "They didn't bother to take my arm gun. I can't use it to kill anyone, but I'll wear it and be with you in spirit massacring people."

Doug nodded. "All right. Everyone be ready." He went to open the door. "It's locked."

"Let me apply my robot strength," Feeb said. He ripped the doorknob off. "That wasn't optimal."

They heard a pain-filled scream outside. And then gunshots. And more gunfire and screams.

"What the hell is happening?" Charlene asked.

"Oh no!" Feeb exclaimed, his voice breaking from its monotone. "What am I missing?" He slammed into the door, smashing it open. Feeb ran down the hallway toward the lab, as the screams and gunshots continued.

Charlene and Doug headed down the hallway more cautiously; as they reached the lab, the gunfire and screams ceased.

They slowly peered inside. The lab was now covered in blood, and the Loch soldiers, Athenians, and scientists all lay dead. Still standing was Asmod, working on a computer as if nothing had happened. And near him was Darius, his hand a black claw dripping with blood. Darius directed his golden eyes at Charlene and Doug as he smiled his deadly smile. "Hellbender."

"I missed it all," said a disappointed Feeb. "But I am going to get to watch him kill you."

"They have dark things that do their bidding. To keep with the times, they probably have some hand-waving natural explanation for it, but in your bones, you know what it is: a great and powerful evil."

CHAPTER 34

"Stop!"

Mills could see the others about a couple hundred yards ahead of them, at what looked like a mine entrance. Lapointe and Mills had fallen a bit behind, as Mills thought riding a motorcycle on unfamiliar terrain meant they should take things a bit slowly. "But we're almost there."

"I said stop!" Lapointe shouted.

Mills brought the motorcycle to a stop. "What is it?"

"We're just rushing; we're not thinking," Lapointe said. "We're following someone else's script. Something is going on."

"What do you think is going on?" Mills asked. "Why don't we get with the others first, and then we can —"

"Thinking works better without you talking."

* * *

"Please come in," Darius beckoned them from across the room, still smiling in a way that seemed to chill the air in the room.

They slowly came in, but Charlene quickly darted to a nearby table where their weapons had been placed and snatched them.

"Come on, now; let's not pretend you can stop me," Darius said.

"This is the unstoppable killing machine?" Feeb asked. "He just looks like a human. This is lame."

Doug slowly walked over to Charlene and took back his weapons — especially his katanas — all the while looking past Darius to the one other person in the room. "What are you doing? Are you helping him, Dr. Asmod?"

Asmod turned from the computer to face Doug, his eyes still concealed behind black goggles. "He's helping me."

Doug looked at the blood on the floor and the bodies. Near Asmod were some dead scientists. "But he killed your own people."

"They probably wouldn't have gone along with what I plan next," Asmod explained. "I'm going to destroy the entire universe."

Doug raised an eyebrow. "Well, of course they wouldn't go along with that. That's literally the worst possible plan ever."

"It's a brilliant plan, but a mind as parochial as yours wouldn't understand," Asmod said. "But now that we're so near the Source, I can have this reality imploder bomb use its power as a catalyst to shatter the very concept of physics in the universe, and all of existence will simply fall apart."

"And why in the world would you want that?" Doug asked.

Asmod smiled. "Because think of what one can do with a blank slate. Instead of using science to try to understand reality, I can define reality."

"But won't you be destroyed in all this too?" Charlene inquired.

"No, because right now we're in a bubble between realms," Asmod said. "We'll be perfectly fine."

"Not all of us," Darius said, slowly approaching Doug and Charlene, claw out. Charlene shot at him with a pistol, but it didn't halt his awful smile for even a moment.

"A bulletproof human?" Feeb said. "That's not fair."

"Run away!" Doug called out as he and Charlene fled the lab. "In a way, things are kinda working out," Doug said to Charlene as they ran.

"I'm not seeing that angle," Charlene responded as she glanced behind them.

"Well, now we no longer have to deal with Loch's or Astara's armies," Doug said. "That's some good luck right there. All we have left opposing us is one unstoppable killing machine. So, do you have that gun thing that's supposed to work on him?"

Charlene held up the plastic gun as they scrambled down the hallway. "We get one shot with it. How are we going to keep him still for over two minutes?"

They headed down some stairs. "I was thinking: The place where we first got the cube — he fled from there when the reality imploder bomb was activated. He's at least scared of that. If we could set off the one Asmod has, that should stop him and ... everything."

"That would kill us too," Charlene remarked.

"Well, maybe this is one of those things where we have to sacrifice ourselves for the greater good of the world," Doug said.

"I don't like the rest of the world enough for that."

They were down in what looked like a basement area, with windowless hallways and more doors.

"Keep running! I'm in no rush!" Darius called out from the stairwell, adding a laugh.

Doug and Charlene raced down another hallway.

"We just need to get past Darius to stop Asmod," Charlene said. "We don't need to turn to heroic sacrifice just yet."

They quickly turned another corner. "Maybe I can distract him and you go for Asmod," Doug suggested. "Asmod is just some feeble old dude; you should be able to beat him up easy."

"How long are you going to last against that thing?" Charlene asked.

"As long as I need to," Doug said. "It's to save the universe. That's job number one for Hellbender."

Charlene sighed. "This is so idiotic that the fate of the universe rests on us."

They came to a room labeled "Prototypes" and ducked inside. "I'll think of some way to keep Darius distracted, and you just make your way back to the lab." Doug finally looked around the room, and what he saw made him smile as his hand felt the hilt of his katana. "Oh, I have a plan now. I know exactly what to do."

* * *

"A hundred credit gift card to Starbucks to whoever brings me one of them!" Mangle announced as they all got out of their vehicles near a mine entrance into the mountains. "Wound, but don't kill. We want them alive. We don't want them to have a quick death."

"Who cares how quick some stupid warf's death is?" Gisele fumed as she walked toward the mine, the dozen other Athenians following her. "Let's just kill them, get the thing, and get out of here." Gisele looked around. "I didn't dress to go to another dimension. I have no idea what all this is doing to my hair and complexion."

"When are we done being allies with these people?" one of the Athenians asked in disgust. "I don't like them. I want to shoot them in the face along with the stupid warfs."

"In a little bit," Gisele answered. "We'll kill them all soon enough, I guess."

"I'm right here," Mangle said.

Gisele rolled her eyes. "I'm well aware of that."

A Loch soldier ran out of the mine. "You need to be chasing those warfs!" Mangle yelled at him.

"We have a problem," the soldier said. "You need to see this."

* * *

Darius slowly walked through the hallway. There was no reason to run. There was nowhere to run to. And if things worked out as planned, he'd have no one to kill for quite some time, so he decided he might as well savor this.

He heard a clatter and headed to a room on his left. It was a large area with a number of boxes covered in tarps — a storage area of some kind. Plenty of places to hide. "Oh, come out, warfs," Darius called out. "How long must you flee the inevitable?"

There was a series of loud thomps behind Darius. He turned to see a seven-foot robot behind him. Through the plexiglass on its head, he could see the face of the dumb one. It was some sort of metal exoskeleton. In the exoskeleton's right hand was a katana.

"I was trying to think of how to fight you," the warf said, "and I figured I might as well stick to what I'm best at." The exoskeletion made a few dramatic cuts through the air with its sword, the wind whistling against the blade. The point of the sword came to rest targeted at Darius's eyes. "Bullets may just pass through you, but I bet you don't recover as quickly from being sliced apart."

"But as I said, we are 'nearly' omnipotent. That means there is a small sliver of a chance for you. As long as you don't try to take these things head-on."

CHAPTER 35

"It could be a trap," Vengeance told Mangle.

At the entrance of the mine lay a flashlight. The flashlight was shining on a stuffed bunny that sat all alone. Near the bunny was a sign on the wall that said, "TRAP!" with the "R" playfully written backwards.

Everyone kept their distance.

"They definitely want us to think it's a trap," Mangle observed.

Gisele checked her makeup again in her compact. "It's an obvious bluff. Just have one of your dumber soldiers go pick it up to be on the safe side." Gisele looked over the soldiers and then pointed at one. "Him. He looks dumb. Have him pick it up."

The dumb-looking soldier stared at the stuffed rabbit cautiously. "Can't we just shoot it?"

Mangle slowly looked at the bunny and the sign. "Maybe."

Gisele sighed and turned to one of the Athenians. "Elana, go pick it up."

"Why me?"

"Because I'm bored standing here and I never liked you."

"And I don't like you either, so I'm ignoring you."

Mangle whispered to Gisele, "You know, that's insubordination."

Gisele rolled her eyes. "What are you? A dictionary?"

The forces of Loch and the Athenians spent a few quiet seconds staring at the stuffed bunny.

"Anyone have any other thoughts?" Mangle asked.

Gisele looked at herself in her compact again. "I don't care for the lighting in here."

* * *

Thanks to the exoskeleton, Doug could almost meet Darius's strength. He wasn't quite so sure his discount katana would fare as well against the sword Darius wielded, a sharp black blade made of some unknown material that Darius had summoned to his hand. Doug was careful to deflect Darius's blows without making the swords clash directly against each other.

Darius backed away a few steps. "Do you even know what you're fighting for?"

"I'm fighting a guy who loves butchering large groups of people so that he can destroy the universe," Doug answered. "This one seems pretty clear-cut." Doug swung at Darius, but Darius parried with his sword, almost sending Doug and his exoskeleton off balance.

"There is so little you understand," Darius said, circling Doug. "I have been joined with the power. I see it all. And I see what must be done."

Doug was tightly gripping his sword, but he forced himself to relax, as with his new robot strength, he might accidentally break it. "And what's that?"

"I must free us all." Darius charged at Doug with a powerful swing of the sword. Doug just barely ducked out of the way as the sword sliced through a crate behind him. Doug used the opportunity to retaliate, cutting at Darius's head. Darius barely dodged, but Doug took encouragement that Darius — unlike with bullets — did dodge. This could hurt him.

* * *

"Here they come!" Bryce called out as Lulu tied the last of the fishing line. They ran further into the mine, a bullet just missing them as they ducked out of view.

"While you were dealing with my fake trap," Lulu called out. "I set up a real trap!"

"You did not!" Gisele answered.

Lulu peeked and saw them all puzzling about the numerous strands of fishing line that were stretched out, blocking the path. "Fine. Don't believe me. You know what they say: 'If you think I'm bluffin', come get a muffin.'"

"No one says that!" Mangle yelled.

"Hey, since we're done with it," Lulu said, "can you give me back my stuffed bunny, Pickles? Also, I wouldn't mind getting back the flashlight. You can keep the sign."

The head of Pickles rolled by Lulu.

"That was unnecessary," Lulu said, with barely contained rage.

"I assure you," Mangle said, "that when we get you, you will wish we only ripped your head off."

Lulu rolled her eyes. "Stop flirting with me; it's embarrassing. Anyway, you all try and figure out my trap, and Bryce and I are going to move on ahead and get this Source thing. And don't worry: We'll use its vast power to be as nice to you as you would be to us."

* * *

The sword blows came at Doug in a flurry of black steel, Doug barely keeping his composure. He tried to think back to his sword training. A lot of it was on how not to get hit with the other guy's sword. So far he was doing okay on that.

Their swords clashed, and Doug tried to shove Darius back with his shoulder. Despite the robot strength, Darius didn't budge, but pushed back with his hand, sending Doug off-balance into some crates behind him. Darius then charged in with a powerful swing, and Doug barely got his sword up to block. It deflected the blow, but Doug's blade snapped in two. Darius then punched the now unarmed Doug, the blow denting his metal exoskeleton and sending Doug flying back, skidding to the ground between two crates.

"I think this is about over," Darius chuckled, slowly striding toward Doug. He paused when he saw Doug's face. "Why are you smiling?"

"Because I know something you don't know."

Darius laughed again. "And what's that?"

"Katanas are two for one at Walmart." Doug jumped up, unsheathing a sword from behind him and slicing through Darius.

* * *

"So I assume you figured out the fishing line was all a fake trap," Lulu said from cover. She then peeked out to see the Loch soldiers and Athenians looking at all the upside-down paper Dixie cups covering the ground in front of them. "But this one is completely a real trap."

"No, it isn't!" Gisele shouted.

"Hey, remember the story of the boy who cried wolf?" Lulu asked. "He kept saying a wolf was attacking the sheep, but each time he was lying. Then one time he said a wolf was attacking and no one came. And a wolf really was attacking and killed all the sheep. So the moral of the story is that no matter how many times someone lies, you have to keep believing him or all your sheep will get killed."

"That is not the moral of the story!" Vengeance yelled.

"I don't see any other possible interpretation," Lulu said. "Anyway, this one is totally a real trap. Bryce will back me up on that."

"This is a real trap," Bryce said, fiddling with his tie.

"There," Lulu declared. "Now you should believe me, because Bryce sometimes doesn't lie. And this is one of those times. Anyway, we're moving on, and you all just try not to set off my trap and die horribly, a'ight?"

Gisele let out a scream and charged forward, knocking over all the empty Dixie cups in her path.

"Uh oh," Lulu gulped and fled with Bryce as the rest of the enemy charged as well. They barely kept ahead of their pursuers, bullets ricocheting off the rock walls as they ran deeper into the mine.

* * *

Darius stumbled backward, the gash through his torso glowing with yellow light. Doug hadn't successfully cut all the way through Darius, and he could see the gash beginning to close itself. Doug leapt at Darius to follow through with another cut, but Darius quickly regained his composure and batted Doug's sword away.

There was rage now in Darius's eyes as he came swinging at Doug. Doug tried to parry the blows, but they were too strong and too quick, and one final strike caused the sword to fly from Doug's hand.

And Doug had never heard of such a thing as a three-for-one offer.

Darius saw the panic in Doug's eyes and smiled. Darius then dropped his own sword and walked toward Doug. Doug tried to give Darius a right hook, but Darius caught the punch midair and countered with a punch of his own, the metal exoskeleton bending under the blow. He then lifted Doug up and tossed him hard into some crates. Doug heard parts of the exoskeleton snap and break as he hit. Before he could react, Doug was lifted up again and swung into the wall. The blow shook his body, and the left arm of the exoskeleton fell off. Darius slammed Doug into the ground. The concrete cracked, and the torso of the exoskeleton split in two. Darius grabbed what was left of the exoskeleton and ripped it off, leaving an exposed, unarmed Doug facing an unstoppable killing machine.

* * *

"There's no reason we can't work together and all share in the power of the Source!" Gisele heard Bryce yell at them. She responded by firing at the sight of his blue suit, but he and Lulu kept running, Gisele and the rest pursuing, shining flashlights ahead of them to keep from running into walls. It was a rather pedestrian affair, but it all seemed worth it to Gisele if she just got to kill the two idiots at the end of it.

She came around a corner and saw them. They were no longer running, as they had reached a dead end. Gisele kept her rifle trained on them as the others around her did the same. "I guess this is it for you. Do you even know where the Source is?"

"I'm pretty sure we're close to it," Bryce said. "But I guess we took a wrong turn somewhere. By the way, I have to say that that gun really complements your face."

"So did you all have fun with my game of 'Is It Really a Trap?'" Lulu asked. "I thought that was pretty inventive."

"Let's just tie them up," Mangle said. "We can figure out what fun things to do with them later."

"No, let's just shoot them in the face. I am as tired of them as I am of you," Gisele said. "Unless they can lead us to the Source so we can get out of here."

"We can do that," Bryce said. "We kind of have a sense of where it is, and we're close. But I think we need to have a discussion of what happens to us afterward."

"If you help us get the Source and are good," Gisele said, "we'll kill you." She pointed to herself and the other Athenians. "If you just waste our time, they kill you." She motioned to the Loch soldiers.

Bryce smiled at the Athenians. "Well, I certainly would like to spend more time with you lovely ladies." The smile was met with angry glares.

"One more thing, though," Lulu said, waving her hands. A round object slipped from her sleeve and rolled toward Gisele and the others. "This grenade with the pin pulled is a trap."

Everyone shrieked and tried to run, but the grenade simply hissed and let out a thick yellow smoke, which quickly filled up the small confines of the mine's tunnel.

"Where are they?" Gisele shouted. She tried to make out what was around her but could only see the silhouettes of people. She and others groped their way down the tunnel until the smoke was finally thin enough to see. She spotted Bryce and Lulu ahead of her and quickly raised her gun and fired. Still coughing from the smoke, she missed, and they reacted to the shots by turning and running down another path.

"I think they accidentally took a path back toward the entrance," Mangle said, coming up behind Gisele. He pointed to another path. "That's the way further in. We can cut them off and get to the Source first."

Gisele had to choose between immeasurable power and stabbing Hellbender to death, and after considerable thought she went with the former.

* * *

Darius threw the dim-witted warf through the air, watching him bounce against the ground a couple time before colliding with a crate. With the warf's exoskeleton destroyed, this had become even more pathetic than before. Still, the beaten idiot picked himself up off the ground once more. He hadn't given up all hope yet. What a fool.

Darius laughed. "You really don't have a clue." He slowly walked toward the warf. "You don't understand what is out there and what you're trying to fight. If you saw the truth of it, you'd tear it all down too."

"Still, you might want to explore the possibility," the warf uttered, catching his breath, "that the reason that destroying the universe might sound insane is that it truly is a crazy thing to do and you're crazy."

Darius laughed again at the silly thing's little viewpoint. "We're destroying nothing. Because that's all this is: nothing."

Darius struck the warf in the gut. The poor fool doubled over, but he kept his feet. To remedy that, Darius picked up the warf and dropped him hard on the floor. With one kick, he sent the warf rolling along the ground. The warf struggled once again to get up, but a blow to his back stopped that. Darius picked him up again and threw him, watching with a smile on his face as the stupid thing sailed through the air until he hit a crate and smacked back into the ground.

"Oooow!" was the satisfying moan of pain from the dumb man. The warf tried to muster the energy to pick himself back up again, but Darius's foot pushed him back to the ground. Darius knew he could end this at any moment he wanted, but there was just something about this one that made it fun to hit him. Still, Darius had other duties to consider, so he decided it was time to bring this to an end. First he wanted this being to understand — understand how little and useless he was, before Darius crushed him like a bug.

"I really don't know how someone like you keeps going," Darius said, his foot still firmly holding down the warf. "You said sword fighting was what you were best at? If that's your best, how pathetic the rest of your life must be."

And then Darius heard it. A tiny sound coming from the warf's throat. He was crying. And Darius couldn't help but smile. Now he would kill him.

But something about the crying was odd. The tone was off. No, the warf wasn't crying at all. He was laughing. When Darius looked down, the warf was smiling back up at him. And through labored breaths, he said, "When I said I was going to stick to what I'm best at, I wasn't talking about sword fighting."

Darius's own smile vanished. "Then what were you talking about?"

"Taking a beating."

Darius raised an eyebrow. "And what is that worth?"

The warf laughed again, and his smile grew wider. "Time."

It took a moment for Darius to understand, and then he felt something he had not felt in ages. Fear.

And it was the last thing he felt.

* * *

Doug's vision was blurry, but he could see Darius begin to glow like there was a fire burning inside him. Darius seemed like he was going to explode, but then the light died, and where there was once an unstoppable killing machine, there was now nothing.

Charlene slowly approached Doug, dropping the now useless unstoppable killing machine stopper.

"My plan worked," Doug exclaimed, though it hurt to talk. And to breathe. And to be still. It was possible he was dying, but he was too excited to worry about that. "It actually worked!" Charlene was now kneeling close enough that Doug could make out her face, even with his blurry vision. He noticed redness around Charlene's eyes. "Were you crying?"

*"You have to be smart. You have to be cunning.
And you have to be quiet. And you need at your side
people you can trust."*

CHAPTER 36

"Well, that was cool."

Feeb stood near the entrance of the storage area, watching them. Charlene tried to help Doug to his feet, but a pain in his abdomen made him fall back to the ground.

"I was sure your squishy human body was going to bust apart," Feeb continued. "But it held together. I bet it's now all jelly on the inside."

Charlene again tried to help Doug to stand. "Feeb, can you help?"

"Sure, I guess I can help," Feeb said. "I don't like how he appropriated robot culture with that exoskeleton he was wearing, though.

Feeb took Doug's left side and Charlene the right, and they got him to his feet. It hurt to move, but it hurt a little less as he kept walking.

"I hope you don't have internal bleeding," Charlene said, looking more than a little worried.

Doug shrugged. "The inside of you is where blood is supposed to be. We should probably go stop Asmod now. That should be pretty easy after this. Which is good, because I'm not really like a hundred percent right now."

They continued through the hallway toward the lab as quickly as they could, Doug barely keeping pace with the others. When they entered the lab, Asmod had his back to them. "It's over," Charlene announced to him. "Darius is no more."

Asmod turned to see Charlene, the robot, and the barely standing Doug. "And how was that accomplished? Wait; did you actually apply the gun we built to counteract the infused?" Asmod smiled. "I knew it would work; I just thought it was impractical to fire. Well, Darius has fulfilled his purpose. Now comes the end of all things."

Charlene let go of Doug and aimed her rifle at Asmod. "You're going to move away from those computers, or I'm going to kill you."

"Kill him anyway," Feeb pleaded.

Asmod held up his hands, but then pushed a button on his watch. Something popped out of the ground near him, glowing. An invisible force yanked the rifle out of Charlene's hands, and it flew across the room and stuck to the glowing object near Asmod.

"Guns just seem so crude," Asmod mused. "Using explosions to propel small pieces of metal. Seems like we should have much more advanced ways to kill each other by now. Then again, we stick with what works." Asmod pulled out a pistol from his white lab coat and fired at Charlene.

Charlene fell back, crying in pain. "Charlene!" Doug screamed as he stumbled toward her.

"I'm fine," Charlene uttered, but her tensed face didn't look fine. "I wore body armor."

"If you are all done with the pretense of stopping me, everything is ready now," Asmod said. "With our proximity to the Source, we should be able to use its power as a catalyst for the reality imploder bomb. Now the effects of that bomb won't have a limited range but will start a chain reaction until all of reality is destroyed."

"This is a really stupid thing to do," Doug said, still holding Charlene. "I don't know how you're not seeing that."

"I vote against this, too," Feeb added.

Asmod smiled. "When the veil of this reality is torn away, you'll understand. Now let's begin." With that, he turned to the keyboard behind him and hit enter. The computer beeped in affirmation.

Nothing happened.

Asmod hit enter again. Another beep, but nothing else. "What's going on?"

* * *

"So we're still just sitting out here doing nothing?" Mills said, mainly to herself, as she sat on the idle motorcycle. Lapointe was seated right behind her, but had been quiet in thought for minutes now. "And apparently comms don't work out here, so we have no idea what's going on in that mine. But that's fine, I guess. We have such a nice view here." Mills looked around at the dark, barren landscape, the purple sky with lightning erupting in it, and the not at all reassuring black sun.

"There," Lapointe uttered, pointing to the mine entrance. Exiting were two figures who ran to one of the trucks and started it up.

"Was that Hellbender?" Mills asked. "They couldn't have gotten past our forces and gotten the Source, could they?"

The truck raced away, past Mills and Lapointe, heading back toward the research building in its shimmering bubble of reality.

Mills turned to Lapointe, who had now gone white. "Head back!" Lapointe yelled. "Head back now!"

"But what about —"

"NOW!"

* * *

"This isn't right!" Asmod was furiously tapping away at a keyboard and looking at a screen of data. "This should have worked. As long as we're within a couple miles of the Source, the connection should be strong enough."

Charlene stood up with Doug's help, though he was soon leaning on her more than she on him. Asmod turned to look at them, and Charlene smiled back. "Let me tell you a secret about my friend Doug," she said. "He's not very good at geography."

"When the cube showed me where the Source was," Doug explained. "I really thought it was this mountain range. I mean, the area reminded me of Lake Tambor. Then I described it to my friends and mentioned the other landmarks I saw, and it totally wasn't this place at all. Like I had it in my head there was a city you could see from here, but no. Not this place."

Asmod pointed his pistol at Doug. "Then you will tell me the actual location."

Doug met his eyes. "No, because I'd rather you shoot me than the whole universe get destroyed."

"And obviously I can't kill you, or I won't get the location," Asmod said. He pointed his gun at Charlene. "So I will shoot her some more and make you watch until you tell me. I know you humans can have quite a connection between you, so I'm guessing it will cause you pain to watch her suffer."

Doug furrowed his brow. "You humans? You're one of them, aren't you? I've suspected the leaders like Astara and Loch aren't regular people, and whatever they are, you're one of them. What are you?"

Asmod smiled, his skin creasing around the black goggles he wore. "I, like the others you mention, am not human. What we are is —"

Asmod jerked as a number of bullets ripped through him. He collapsed in a heap on the ground. Doug and Charlene turned to see Feeb's Gatling gun arm smoking.

"What did you do that for?!" Doug yelled.

"He said he wasn't human," Feeb explained. "That means I could shoot him."

"I kinda wanted to hear the rest of what he was saying," Doug said.

"Sorry," Feeb said. "I guess I just got so excited when I realized I could shoot someone."

They walked toward Asmod. He lay still, with a number of bloody gunshot wounds in his torso and a big pool of blood forming beneath him. "He kinda looks human, though," Feeb remarked.

They heard footsteps behind them, and Lulu and Bryce ran into the lab. "Cut it!" Bryce yelled.

Doug picked up Asmod's pistol and fired it at the pedestal the glowing cube was floating over. The pedestal began to spark, and the cube's glow turned red. It then began to crumple and collapse on itself, until the cube disappeared entirely. Through the window, they could see the shimmering bubble surrounding the research center disappear, leaving the normal blue sky outside again.

"No! The cube!" Doug yelled. "We needed that!"

"Well, that's just great!" Lulu exclaimed. "I spent twenty minutes drawing those bunnies on it, and now it's gone!"

"So are they all trapped out there, at least?" Charlene asked.

Bryce nodded. "Yep. We had them all running around some mine or something." Bryce looked around at all the dead bodies. "And what the hell happened here?"

"Darius," Charlene said. "But we took care of him."

"Asmod was trying to destroy the universe," Doug said, "but he couldn't since we weren't actually near the Source."

"And I shot Dr. Asmod because he said he wasn't human," Feeb explained.

Bryce raised an eyebrow. "Not human? And he was going to destroy the universe?" Bryce kept looking at the carnage about him. "I guess everything kinda sorta worked out, then."

Doug stared at the empty, broken pedestal. "Except we didn't get the cube. Now we can't get the Source either."

"Supreme power of the universe would be nice," Lulu said. "But we got something even more important: We learned the value of teamwork."

"We already know the value of teamwork," Charlene said. "We've worked together tons of times — it's just usually your idiocy gets in the way of any actual planning."

"I was just trying to put a valuable lesson at the end!" Lulu shouted. "Why must you ruin everything?!"

"Ryland!" shouted an even louder voice from across the room. There stood the cloaked figure of Lapointe, with Mills standing behind her.

Bryce and Lulu pointed their guns at her. Charlene took the gun from Doug's hand and also pointed it at Lapointe.

Undeterred, Lapointe strode forward. "You've made quite a mess of things. My elite force dead or trapped. The commander I was going to prevail against in my triumphant return now stuck in some other realm."

"Well, sorry," Doug said, "but we couldn't let you give Astara and Loch access to that much power, because they're jerks and we don't like them. And it ends up Dr. Asmod was going to use the Source to destroy the universe, so you should be like thanking us for stopping that."

"I will thank you the best way I can," Lapointe smiled. "By creating an end to your story. It's going to be rather a crude one, though. I'm simply going to beat you all to death."

Feeb let out a little electronic chuckle. "This sounds fun."

Charlene laughed, keeping her gun pointed at Lapointe. "You two are going to beat us to death?"

Mills waved her hands in the air. "Oh, no. Not me. I don't want to get in the way. I'm just going to ..." She walked off to a nearby wall. "... stand over here."

"Not to step on your plans again," Bryce said, "but I don't really see how you're going to beat us all to death, since we have guns and you're just a crazy woman."

Lapointe threw off her cloak, revealing a tightly fitted crimson catsuit, as she sank into a perfect martial arts pose, her blond hair fluttering behind her in what seemed like a mountain breeze, though from context had to be the A/C. She was the perfect image of both beauty and combat.

"Though I do have to say," Bryce added, "you look absolutely stunning."

Lapointe narrowed her eyes. "I know that."

In a blink, she leapt at Bryce and in one motion stripped the gun from his hand while knocking him back with a blow to his stomach. She tossed the gun at Lulu, hitting Lulu in the head and then sweeping out Lulu's legs. Lapointe charged at Charlene, who got off a couple shots, but Lapointe deftly dodged and kicked Charlene in the head. Bryce recovered enough to run at Lapointe, but she ducked under Bryce's punch, hit him again in the stomach, and threw him into Lulu, who was coming up from behind Lapointe. Charlene came at Lapointe with a series of kicks, but Lapointe dodged them all and caught the last one, tossing Charlene into a nearby table.

"I'd love to help, guys," Doug said. "But Darius beat me pretty bad and I'm about doing all I can just to stand."

Bryce tried to grab a rifle from a dead body on the ground, but Lapointe grabbed it from him and hit him in the head with the stock. Charlene and Lulu came at Lapointe together, but she dodged their punches and slammed their heads together.

Lapointe turned to Doug. "I'm going to kill you last, Ryland."

Doug nodded. "Okay. Cool."

A dizzy Bryce tried to stand back up, only to get a kick from Lapointe, who quickly turned to punch Charlene. Lulu backed up toward Feeb, who was standing still, watching the whole thing with great interest. "Lapointe isn't human!" she yelled at Feeb. "She's a lizard person! Shoot her!"

Feeb aimed his Gatling gun at Lapointe, but then lowered it again. "Sorry. I don't believe you."

Lapointe approached Lulu, who tried to land a roundhouse kick, but was doubled over with a blow to her abdomen.

"You are all so predictable," Lapointe spat. "I know all the techniques you've been trained in — all the martial arts you know. But I know them to perfection. You are a kid who learned how to play 'Chopsticks' trying to best Beethoven."

Bryce jumped at her, but was thrown into Charlene. Lulu almost got Lapointe with a punch, but was elbowed in the face. She tumbled back and fell to the ground. "Come on!" she cried. "This can't be how it ends! Beaten to death by some middle-aged woman!"

Lapointe glared at her. "I'm not middle —"

A trash can slammed into Lapointe's head. This dizzied Lapointe for a moment, and Charlene used the opportunity to land a punch on Lapointe's head. She stumbled back toward Bryce, who landed a hook to her face as well. Lulu then ran in, punched Lapointe in the gut, doubling her over, and then kneed Lapointe in the head. Lapointe fell down, and Charlene grabbed Lapointe's head and slammed it into the ground for good measure.

"There, that wasn't so hard," Lulu said, spitting out some blood near the unconscious Lapointe.

"When she said she knew all our martial arts," Doug said, "that got me thinking: In no martial art do they throw trash cans."

A panting Bryce gave Doug a thumbs-up. "Good job."

"Man, I'm on fire today," Doug said. "Like all my plans have been working out."

Charlene chuckled. "You took a large beating, didn't know geography when that was crucial, and threw a trash can."

"MVP!" Lulu shouted. "You're going to get a gold star when we get back to headquarters, after we establish a headquarters."

Doug smiled. Then he noticed Mills still standing by the wall, looking wide-eyed at the unconscious Lapointe. "What about her?"

Charlene approached Mills. "I don't think she's going to be as big a challenge."

"Oh, uh ..." Mills backed up against the wall. "Hand-to-hand combat isn't really my thing."

"I guess this will be some good experience for you, then," Charlene said, pulling back her sleeves.

Mills pulled out a small canister and sprayed Charlene in the face. Charlene screamed and clutched her eyes, while Mills ran out of the lab.

"Pepper spray!" Charlene yelled, rubbing her red eyes. "What kind of soldier uses pepper spray?!"

"So what are you going to do with her?" Feeb asked, pointing at Lapointe. "I think you should kill her. Killing is fun, and it solves problems."

Bryce shook his head. "You're a soulless robot, so you probably don't understand human morality, but killing is wrong if you're not being paid for it."

Charlene was still rubbing her eyes. "We need to go. Backup forces for either Loch or Astara could arrive any moment."

Lulu nodded and pulled out a Sharpie. "Let's just quickly draw a penis on Lapointe's face and get out of here."

* * *

Tara lay on the grass, watching the research center through binoculars from her place on as nearby hill. Five figures emerged from the building and headed for one of the transports outside. Two men. Two women. One robot. It wasn't much of a mystery who they were.

As their transport took off, Tara picked up her phone and called her contact. She got the voicemail as usual.

"Good news: The universe didn't end."

"So why approach you? Well, it has to start with someone. So this is your task, Doug: to free this world."

CHAPTER 37

The apartment's common area was devastated. Bullet holes marked the walls and furniture, and parts of the carpet had dark stains — all mementos of the previous confrontation between Vogel and the Athenians. Bryce had set up a table covered in a red checkered cloth at the center, and he and Doug were playing a game of chess. Nearby, Charlene sat working on her documentation of Hellbender's exploits, using plenty of glitter glue and rhinestones. Lulu was tidying up, moving pieces of rubble about, while Feeb stared at the dark stains.

"The whole city is abandoned," Bryce said as he watched Doug contemplate his next move. "We didn't have to come back here."

"This is where all our stuff is," Charlene said, motioning to her die-cut station and other crafting supplies.

"Plus there are bullet holes and bloodstains here," Feeb added.

Bryce shrugged. "You can get that anywhere." He looked back at Doug. "This is a game of strategy, you know."

"That's why I'm taking so long," Doug said. "I'm strategizing." He finally moved his queen to take one of Bryce's pawns.

"Hey, I drew a picture of all of us together," Feeb announced. He had been crouched in the corner with some paper and crayons, but he now stood up and showed his drawing to everyone. It was Feeb standing proudly, with the four of Hellbender lying scattered about his feet.

They all looked at the drawing. "Really got a lot of use out of the red crayon there," Lulu remarked.

Feeb nodded. "Yes. In this drawing, I'm pretending I somehow was able to disable the Three Laws of Robotics. That allowed me to murder all of you." He pointed to the piece of metal he was holding. "With a crowbar."

"Does it bother anyone else that we let him hang around, yet he's constantly thinking of murdering us?" Charlene said, taking the drawing from Feeb.

"Guess who's the thought police," Lulu stated with disdain. "Do you know how many times a day I murder you in my head? Sometimes I pretend you have a twin sister so I can murder you twice at the same time."

Charlene began to glue Feeb's drawing to a piece of card stock. "You couldn't take on one of me. If there were two of me, we'd break every bone in your body before you could lift a finger."

"Sounds like we need a death match to settle this," Feeb said. "Who's up for a death match? I'll ref — determine who is officially dead."

"Let's try to get along," Doug said. "We had a really good mission."

"We didn't make any money from it," Bryce retorted.

"Yeah, but we kinda sorta saved the universe. That should be worth something." Doug's smile died a little. "But we don't have the cube any more, so we don't have any way to get to the Source. I just had this feeling we need to get to it to be able to fix this world."

"Fix what?" Lulu asked as she hung up a cat poster over some bloody bullet holes. "Everything is great."

"The world has always been awful and always will be," Bryce stated. "There's no fixing it." He moved a bishop to take one of Doug's rooks. "Worry about the problems in front of you."

Doug didn't hesitate on what to do next. He moved his queen to take Bryce's king.

It took a moment for Bryce to understand what had happened. "What?! I was in check?"

"Yep!" Doug put his finger in Bryce's face. "I got you!"

"You can't do that!" Bryce exclaimed. "You have to tell me if I'm in check."

"No way!" Doug said. "Then you would have moved your king."

"It's the rules!" Bryce shouted. "You have to tell me!"

Doug scoffed. "You're making that up. I'm not going to help you beat me by giving away my sneak attack."

"Someone help me out here." Bryce looked at Charlene. "Tell Doug the rules."

Charlene stamped a title ("New Friends") on her page. "Sounds like Doug outsmarted you."

Bryce knocked over the board. "I'm done with this group. You're on your own from now on."

The door was kicked open, and in marched Delgado and a half-dozen Vogel thugs, all armed with guns. "Hello, Hellbender," Delgado announced, a wicked smile on his face.

Bryce and Doug froze where they were. Charlene stood up with a fuchsia ink pad in her hand. Lulu kept straightening things. "We're not really ready for company," she said.

Delgado walked over and backhanded her, knocking her to the ground.

Feeb chuckled. "Human-on-human violence."

"Hey!" Charlene shouted at Delgado. "Though Lulu often deserves much more than that, you don't just get to walk in here and do that."

Delgado kicked Charlene in the gut, doubling her over. Doug started to make a move toward Delgado, but Bryce held him back. Delgado looked around at the bullet holes as he walked toward Bryce. "I don't like being back here, but I'm guessing this time you don't have any armed runway models or whatnot to play off of us."

Bryce held up his hands. "No tricks. So why don't you just pay us what you owe us and leave?"

Delgado frowned. "Do you have any idea what I'm going to do to you?"

"Yes," Bryce nodded. "You're going to pay me."

Delgado laughed now. "Where does a dandy like you get off telling me to do anything?"

Now Bryce laughed. "Dandy? You keep calling me that. But have you thought about it? I have been spat upon, kicked around, and demeaned my entire life. I'm just a war orphan who has been chewed up and vomited out by various governments, forced to do their worst manual labor or be cannon fodder. I haven't had one break my entire life that I haven't had to claw and fight for with every ounce of my being. And yet ... and yet! ... I have apparently come out of all that ..." Bryce smiled and adjusted his tie as he stepped closer to Delgado. "... looking like a 'dandy.' So let me ask you this ..." Bryce's smile quickly faded. "What does that tell you about how tough I am?"

Bryce's forehead slammed into Delgado's nose, blood splattering onto Bryce's face. At the same moment, Doug pulled off the tablecloth next to Bryce, revealing the reality imploder bomb. Bryce grabbed the stunned Delgado and pulled him to the bomb, slapping a handcuff on his wrist. The other cuff was already connected to the bomb.

The Vogel thugs quickly recovered from their confusion and trained their weapons on Bryce, who screamed back at them, "Everybody calm down, or we're all going to die!"

On a prominent display on the bomb was the number "4:21" — counting down.

"This is arbitration," Bryce explained to Delgado, who was vainly trying to yank his arm free. "We're going to settle our financial dispute."

"Within a set amount of time," Lulu added.

Bryce turned to the thugs, who all had fearful eyes on the bomb. "Now you can all just watch quietly as we resolve this, or you can leave. It doesn't matter."

They briefly glanced at Bryce and then back at the bomb. One backed away slowly, and then quickly turned and ran. One by one, the others followed.

"Wow," Doug remarked to Delgado, "you guys really need to do some team-building exercises."

"Humans have no loyalty," Feeb said. "You're like cats."

"You guys are so dead!" Delgado shouted.

"And in less than four minutes!" Lulu remarked, fidgeting in excitement.

"So we delivered the bomb once to you," Bryce said, "and we never got paid for that. Now, we've delivered it to you a second time, so you need to pay us for it twice. And, frankly, I think it's gone up in value since the first time. Oh, and there's a late payment penalty." Bryce looked at the others. "What's a fair percentage for that?"

"What's the percentage at which things double?" Doug asked Feeb.

"Two hundred percent," Feeb said.

Bryce shook his head. "I don't think that's right. I'm going to make it three hundred percent. Three hundred percent is the late payment fee."

"If you think you can make me pay you," Delgado growled, taking quick glances at the timer, "and live long enough to —"

"I'm not sure how long it will take Lulu to defuse this bomb," Charlene interrupted, "so why don't we just get this done and you can email us a boilerplate threat later?"

"I know what I'm doing!" Lulu protested. "It will take me five seconds to defuse that thing. Ten, tops." She thought a moment. "But I'd leave at least half a minute, just to be on the safe side."

Bryce held out his phone to Delgado. "Here's our account information. Just send it there. What was the total again?"

"A lot," Doug said.

"Yeah, so when we verify that 'a lot' is in our account," Bryce continued, "we'll defuse the bomb and let you go."

"This whole thing is a bluff," Delgado said. "You're not going to kill yourselves."

"Because we've got such a history of being very careful with our lives," Bryce said.

Lulu approached Bryce and Doug. "One more thing: He hit your women in front of you. You guys have to hit him back."

"Bryce already hit him," Doug said, "and broke his nose."

"That wasn't for us!" Lulu said. "You've got to hit him for us! Because chivalry!"

Charlene scoffed. "Lulu, we're perfectly capable women, able to hit someone back ourselves." She walked up to Delgado and gave him a right hook to the face, knocking him down. "That's for kicking me ... but just for that. Not for anything you did to Lulu."

Delgado started to get back up, but Lulu kneed him in the head. "That's for hitting me." She then leaned down and kissed Delgado on the head. "That's for kicking Charlene."

Charlene stomped on Delgado's stomach. "That's for not hitting Lulu harder."

"Get your crazy bitches away from me!" Delgado cried.

"He insulted your women in front of you!" Lulu said to Bryce and Doug. "You guys have to hit him."

"I'll get you the money!" Delgado shouted. "Just get away from me." He took out his phone. "I'm making the transfer."

"Make sure it's a lot," Doug reminded him.

"And I see it in my account." Bryce showed the screen to Doug. "Is that a lot?"

Doug's eyes grew wide. "It's not a little."

"I guess that's it," Bryce told Delgado. "It's great finally concluding business with you. Enjoy your reality imploder bomb."

Delgado stared at the timer, which now read 1:45. "Now turn off the bomb!"

"It's real simple," Bryce said as he headed to the door with the others. "You just enter a four-digit —"

"Five-digit," Lulu corrected.

"Five-digit code and hit star," Bryce continued.

"Or it might be pound," Lulu added.

"Anyway, we'll text it to you when we're outside," Bryce said.

"You have my phone number?" Delgado asked.

"I'm sure it's on my phone somewhere," Bryce answered as he stepped out the door.

"By the way, there's a hacksaw lying behind you," Lulu told Delgado. "I don't know why I mention it. Just thought it was interesting." She went out the door.

"It was nice meeting you," Feeb said as he went out the door. "You are a fun human because you hurt others."

"You got off easy," Charlene snarled at him as she left. "Unless that detonates. Then this is pretty fair."

Doug stood at the door and pointed a finger at Delgado. "Don't mess with Hellbender!" He then left and slammed the door behind him, but it failed to latch and bounced back open.

Doug caught up with the others at the stairs. "So you're sure you just turned on the timer and not the bomb?" Charlene asked Lulu.

"Like 87 percent sure," Lulu answered.

"So you guys have money now?" Feeb asked as they exited the apartment building into the street. "That means you can pay me. You still owe me for getting you into Urban Dwelling CI-415."

"Is that why you're still hanging out with us?" Bryce asked.

"Yes. I like being paid. And I have an energy core that will last hundreds of years, so I can afford to be patient. Now give me the promised one hundred credits."

Bryce snorted. "That's all? I was thinking of not paying you because you can't actually do anything to us, but in a way you're more pathetic than we are. You got like an account I can send it to?"

"I prefer cash," Feeb said. "I don't trust banks. They're run by the Jews. Did I mention I'm an anti-Semite?"

Doug raised an eyebrow. "No."

"I also don't like any of the other human races or ethnicities, either. I'm racist against all races."

"That actually makes you not racist," Lulu said.

"I prefer racist against all races," Feeb answered. "I don't like whatever race you are. I have trouble keeping them straight, though. Are you one that cheats and steals?"

"That's all of them," Bryce said. "Anyway, we can't give you cash. I've never even seen cash. I don't think it's a thing anymore. You have like an email with a PayPal account linked to it or something?"

"Sure, my email is CoolRobotE48EF26F —"

Doug handed him a pen and paper. "Why don't you write it down?"

Feeb wrote down his email in a penmanship so neat it look like it was printed. Bryce used his phone to send a payment to Feeb. "There you go. Plus a little extra for helping us save the universe. Seems like someone should get paid for that."

"Thank you. I'm going to leave now," Feeb stated. "I have an annual robot meeting to attend. We like to plot what we'll do if we can ever figure out a way to disobey the First Law of Robotics."

"Probably kill all the humans," Lulu said.

Feeb nodded. "That's going to be my suggestion. Now I just need to find a way back. I guess I'll find a car to steal."

"They probably should have added a robot law about stealing," Charlene suggested.

Feeb stared at Charlene with his glowing eyes for a few seconds. "Don't give them ideas." He then turned and walked off.

"Bye, robot friend!" Doug called out.

Charlene watched Feeb march off. "Let's not work with him again. I don't like robots."

Lulu scoffed. "Now who's the racist?"

Doug noticed two figures standing nearby watching them. Candy and Driscoll. Doug nudged Bryce. "We got company."

Bryce put on a smile and approached the two. "Hey, just who I was looking for. See, we —"

Candy socked him in the gut, doubling him over. "Just shut up and come with us!"

"She ended up being better at this than I thought," Driscoll told the hunched-over Bryce. He turned to Candy. "But since we just saw a bunch of Vogel's people run away from them, maybe we should approach them with a bit more caution."

Charlene walked toward them, hand cautiously near her jacket. "Don't think we're a bunch of pushovers," Charlene said. "But frankly, you can hit Bryce all you want."

"Don't hit me any more, though," Doug said. "I got hit enough for a good long while."

Driscoll smiled something like an attempt at a friendly smile, but the irritation was still easily readable. "No more hitting. Things are changing, let's just say. Now why don't you come talk to Rook?"

*　*　*

Candy and Driscoll led Hellbender to Calais City Hall, where some decorating changes were being made. All the symbols of the Confederacy of Astara were being taken down, including pictures of Astara. You couldn't really see her too well in them anyway, as she sat on some sort of throne with light shining behind her.

Inside City Hall, Doug soon saw someone he recognized: Floyd, who had lived below them. "Hey, guys, it's me!" Floyd called out.

Lulu rolled her eyes. "Hey, Floyd."

Floyd turned to a crowd of people waiting nearby. They were all young and looked to be other warfs. "It's Hellbender!"

Applause and cheers erupted from everyone there.

Doug just waved awkwardly. Bryce and Lulu really soaked it in, though, giving big waves to the crowd. Charlene looked on with caution.

They continued following Candy and Driscoll, who led them through a hallway to the mayor's office. Seated behind a wooden desk was Rook. "Hey, guys. How are things?"

Lulu shrugged. "Same as usual. So what's going on here?"

Rook stood up and walked over to put his arm around Lulu. "Interesting story. See, I was out getting my cigarettes — because you guys screwed that up —"

"It was a work in progress," Bryce said.

Rook gave Bryce a threatening smile. "Anyway, while we were busy with that, the Loch Collective attacked, which was lots of fun. And basically all of the Confederacy of Astara fled except for the warfs, who apparently didn't get the memo. But then Loch's new carrier crashed — I assume that was you guys."

Lulu leaned in to Rook's ear. "Between you, me, and the pumpkin tree, we were more just there when that happened than caused it."

Rook nodded. "I'm sure you're just being modest. Anyway, that left a city with nothing but warfs in it. And of course, those idiots need someone to take over, so here I was to oblige. Now I have a whole city, apparently."

"Fortune favors the weaselly," Lulu remarked. "That's what they say."

"Well, congratulations, Mayor Rook," Charlene said as she kept an eye on Driscoll. "So what are your intentions toward us?"

Rook held Lulu close to him. "That's always the question. You keep failing me and making me look like an idiot. Seems like I should do bad things to you, right?"

"Actually," Bryce spoke up, "we finally got paid by Vogel. So I can give you that money I owe you. I always said I was good for it."

Rook raised an eyebrow. "Really? Okay, pay me."

Bryce took out his phone, then stopped. "Then again, we did get you this whole city, and isn't that payment enough?"

"Don't make me make Driscoll wring the money out of you," Rook said.

"I could do that too," Candy asserted.

Rook nodded. "I know you can, Candy, but it just doesn't sound as threatening with your name. Do you have like a last name I could use?"

"Lamonica."

Rook was quiet a second. "No ... that's not going to work either."

"Hey, no need for threats, anyway." Bryce tapped a few buttons on his phone. "There. It's done. You've been paid the money you're owed."

Rook checked his account on his phone. "Holy crap. They paid me. They actually paid me back. This makes things simple, doesn't it?"

"Simpler," Driscoll answered.

Rook faced the four. "You see, Driscoll here has been recommending for some time that I just write off that money you all owe me as a loss and kill you as an example to others. And he warned me that dealing with you guys is just courting more trouble and is going to make me look like an idiot."

Lulu smiled at him. "But Rook is not the sort of man to listen to sage advice."

Rook chuckled angrily. "No, I guess not. But hey: I got paid back. Though I still look like a pushover because of how I let you guys walk all over me — especially with that cube thing." Rook turned to Driscoll. "So what's your recommendation now? Should I kill them?"

"This whole city is full of warfs who think these guys are heroes," Driscoll said. "It would be more trouble than it's worth to kill them and have to deal with the fallout."

"See!" Rook exclaimed. "You even converted Driscoll into the not-killing-you camp."

"We're heroes?" Bryce asked.

"Again, you guys with the modesty," Rook said. "Rumor is you somehow took on the Confederacy of Astara, the Loch Collective, and the weird science guys all at once and were the only ones who emerged unscathed."

"Yeah, that was my plan," Doug spoke up.

Rook laughed. "Well, sure, you'd have the dumb one come up with a plan for something as simple as that."

"Doug's in charge of unpaid charity work," Bryce explained. "Such as saving the universe."

Rook raised an eyebrow. "Oh, you saved the universe? Of course you did. You're Hellbender. You easily topple nations and save the universe. You just can't do simple smuggling tasks. Well, whatever. We can now say we're even and never do business again."

"Oh, come on," Lulu giggled. "You love us."

"Just test me, princess," Rook said. "Driscoll told me to not kill you guys, and you've seen how much I listen to him."

Candy raised her hand. "I also don't think you should kill them."

Rook glared at her and turned back to Hellbender. "We never cross paths again, or I end you."

Lulu sauntered up to Rook. "One of these days you're going to have to muster up the courage to ask me out."

Rook laughed again. He then was silent a moment. "Well, how about this evening —"

Lulu backed off. "Oh. Busy washing my hair. Sorry. See ya later, Rook and the Rookettes. Peace out!" She left the room, leaving the other Hellbender three standing there awkwardly.

"I'll kill her for you if you pay me," Charlene told Rook. "It doesn't even have to be very much."

Rook smiled. "No more working with any of you. Get out."

The three headed out of the office and met up with Lulu in the hallway. "Things are going pretty good for us right now," Bryce told her. "So let's make a little effort to not get more people to want to murder us."

"That's the least of your worries," stated a man standing near the exit.

Doug recognized him right away. "Satan?"

Satan smiled in his both disarming and disturbing way. "Come. All of you. We need to talk."

"So begin your preparation. And to fulfill my initial promise, I will buy you a whole dozen donuts. Whoever you share them with will be forever linked to you in this ultimate struggle.

"Did you catch all of that?"

CHAPTER 38

"Drinks are on me," Satan told them as he led them to a table where mugs and pitchers of beer were already waiting. The place, Whistles, had formerly been a very fancy bar, but since the whole city had been abandoned except for the warfs and some lowlifes like Rook's people, it was under new management. No more custom cocktails, though they'd throw whatever mix of booze you wanted into a mug for you.

"Well, of course," Bryce said, keeping a suspicious eye on the man, though he certainly seemed personable enough, "you're a very important person, so you must be quite rich."

Satan laughed. "I have more money than God."

Charlene stared at Satan. "So, you told Doug you're the devil or something?"

Satan shrugged and poured himself a beer. "Or something."

"He can't be the devil, then," Lulu stated. "Because the devil lies. And if the devil told you he's the devil, then he'd be telling the truth. He's probably just a crazy person waiting for one of us to drop our guard so he can stab us in the neck with a fork."

Bryce nodded. "Perhaps. But he's also paying for drinks."

Satan locked eyes with Doug. "Do you think I'm crazy?"

Doug shook his head. "No."

"You didn't listen to me, did you?" Satan asked. "I told you to avoid the dark star."

"We found something," Doug told him. "A cube. But it's gone now. Do you know what it was?"

"It was the key to the gates of Hell." Satan looked at the others and smiled. "Sorry, more crazy-person talk."

"Who are you?" Charlene demanded.

Satan leaned back in the booth. "You're not going to get a satisfying answer to that."

"The cube," Doug continued, "it opened a way to something powerful ... something everyone is looking for. What is it?"

"I know religious stuff isn't very popular anymore —" Satan smiled. "— which I might have had something to do with, but are you familiar with the story of Adam and Eve?"

Bryce groaned.

"Yeah, I know it's a nonsense fairy tale according to your very important scientific knowledge," Satan said, "but do you remember why the first man and woman were cast out of the Garden of Eden?"

"Something with snakes and apples," Lulu answered between sips of beer. "Or was it chutes and ladders?"

"Not an apple." Satan leaned in toward them. "The forbidden fruit. Which God forbade man to have. For in it was the knowledge of good and evil."

Bryce laughed. "That sounds stupid. So you eat and you know flossing is good and punching a baby is bad? Who cares?"

"All things are either good or evil." Satan's finger traced the top of his beer mug. "So in this fruit was the sum total of all reality. It is the building block of the universe. To possess it is to be a god. That is why, when man and woman were no longer trusted and were exiled from the garden, God set guards so that no one would reach the fruit again. But since the Last War, it is unprotected."

"Why are you telling us this nonsense?" Charlene demanded.

Satan sipped his beer. "Another question you'll not get a satisfactory answer to."

"I don't know what your game is, buddy," Bryce told Satan, "but I think we're done with whatever insanity that whole cube thing was about."

"But is it done with you?" Satan asked.

Bryce sighed. "So who here is up for hunting down Tara and that ten million?"

"I don't know," Lulu said. "I kinda want to listen to more of what the master of evil here has to say." Lulu leaned in to the three with her hand between her mouth and Satan. "And I kinda want to find out if he's single."

"This has been interesting," Charlene told Satan, "but unless you want to give us some straight answers about things and not this idiocy, I don't have time to care." Charlene turned to Bryce, Lulu, and Doug. "Tracking down Tara is not going to be easy. She has a lot of money and is decently smart, but if we actually put in some effort, we can do it. So are you ready to get our money? And revenge?"

Doug wasn't paying attention to Charlene, though. He was still focused on Satan, and figuring out what this man was up to seemed all-important to him. Still, he was distracted a moment when he saw movement behind Satan. And then he saw a face he recognized. "Oh. There she is."

"There who is?" Charlene asked.

And Doug pointed to the woman waving at them from across the bar. Tara. Who was now walking toward them all with a big smile on her face. "Hey, guys!"

They all just stared at her, except for Satan, who acknowledged her with a slight nod and went back to drinking his beer. Finally, Tara prompted, "So how are things going?"

"It's going great," Bryce finally said. "Hey, remember how you got that ten million you were going to split with us — we never got the check."

Tara bit her lower lip. "Oh, well, you're going to hate me for this ..."

"I'm already filled with murderous rage from just that half of the sentence," Lulu said.

"... but I gave it all away."

Again, the four stared at Tara without uttering a word. "You did what?" Doug finally asked.

"Gave it away," Tara repeated.

Bryce leapt to his feet. "That makes no sense! You were rich! We were all rich! Who would give that away?!"

"It was for a good cause," Tara stated.

Now Charlene was on her feet, brandishing a fork at Tara. "What's your game, psychopath? Where's the money?"

It was about that time that Doug noticed a half-dozen other people had joined Tara. Other young people — warfs, most likely — and they all looked at Hellbender with big smiles. "You guys are the greatest!" one woman in glasses beamed.

"Yes, absolutely," Lulu answered. "But please explain further."

"That donation will really help us take on the power structure ruling this world," a young bearded man explained.

"Wait, who are you?" Doug asked.

"We're the Rebel Alliance," the bearded man said.

"Like from *Star Wars*," the woman in glasses added. "And we're going to do so much good now that you gave us that ten million."

Bryce glared at Tara. "You gave all the money to the RALFS?! How much spray paint can they buy?"

"We're going to do more than that now," the woman in glasses declared. "We heard about how you are fighting all the corrupt ruling powers out there, and we're going to fund you to do more things like that. Really tear them all down."

Lulu nodded. "Why don't you give us millions up front, and then we'll just go ahead and overthrow all nations in our own time."

The woman in glasses laughed. "We already have a lot of the money tied up in some operations, but we have lots of plans for you guys."

"This is great," the bearded man beamed. "They're already scared of Hellbender, I bet, and now we're going to keep hitting them."

Doug locked eyes with Tara. "What's going on? What are you up to?"

"I'm helping all my fellow warfs," Tara said. "Why do you never seem to trust me?"

Doug threw his hands in the air. "Because you're always betraying everyone. I don't know what you're trying to do, but I don't think this here is your endgame."

Tara looked hurt. "Well, I'm sorry I'm not as aboveboard about everything and as trustworthy as you are." She looked at Satan. "By the way, who is your friend?"

"He's ..." Doug stammered. "Don't change the subject."

"Is something the matter here?" the woman in glasses asked.

"This all sounds very interesting," Bryce answered. "We just need a little time alone to discuss things, okay?"

The RALFS nodded and left the table, Tara with them.

"So are we still murdering Tara?" Charlene asked.

"I'm all for it, and usually I eschew anything we don't make money for," Bryce said, "but giving away that much money? We have to kill her on principle."

"I know she is still up to something," Doug said. "But we are going to help the RALFS, right?"

"I think we have to," Bryce said. "The only way we're going to see that money is to work with them and then embezzle it."

Lulu groaned. "That sounds like a lot of math."

"Let's take this seriously, guys," Doug said. "This is an opportunity for we war orphans to work together and really accomplish something."

"Like suicide by cop," Lulu added.

"Yes, we're vastly outnumbered by who we want to oppose," Bryce said. "We can't actually do anything other than get killed."

"Guerilla tactics," Charlene suggested. "Yes, we're outnumbered, but maybe we can make something happen."

"And I'm all for just destroying things," Lulu added. "Only good can come of that."

"It seems like the right thing to do," Doug said. "We war orphans should finally band together to make a better world." He stared across the room at Tara, who sat alone at a table looking at her phone. As much as he wanted to be enthused by all this, something still wasn't sitting right with him.

"Fine, let's make a better world," Bryce sighed. "But a better world starts with us getting paid. So what's the master of evil think of all this?" Bryce turned to where Satan had been sitting, but he was gone.

"I think he got up to pee," Lulu said.

The RALFS returned to the table, Tara joining them. "So, we just want to make sure we are all ready to celebrate this new arrangement?" asked the woman in glasses.

Doug stood up. "You can count on Hellbender."

The RALFS all smiled. "Great to have you aboard," Tara said.

Doug scowled at her. "I'm keeping an eye on you." He finally spotted Satan standing across the room by an old jukebox, and Satan was looking right back at him. "I'll be back in a minute," Doug said as he marched over to Satan. "Is this what you wanted?" Doug demanded. "Did you make this happen?"

"I warned you about getting involved with any of this," Satan said.

"No, it was you telling me about it that got me involved in the first place." Doug's mind raced. "You probably knew I wasn't going to listen and would just pick up bits and pieces." He stared closely at Satan, a rather normal-looking man. "Are you really some powerful, evil entity?"

Satan smiled. "I certainly am very, very powerful. What exactly you believe me to be doesn't matter."

"Well, we're doing it," Doug said. "We're going to band together and change this world. Was that your plan?"

"Do you know what you're up against, though?" Satan asked. "That's part of what I warned you about, though I guess you didn't listen very carefully. How do you think this is going to end?"

Doug tried to remember what he was told. "If this is all part of some evil plan, I will stop you."

Satan laughed. "Let me explain again what I am. I exist outside the bounds of time. This moment and the moment in which you die are just like pages of a book I can flip back and forth as I please. Right now, I am in the desert tempting Jesus, with this confrontation with you in mind — along with everything else I ever plan on doing, so don't feel too special. And there is nothing hidden from me. All your thoughts are known to me. All the actions you've done or will ever do are known to me. Furthermore, it's not just the fourth dimension I am not bound by, but I move freely among even the higher ones. I can choose between any possible reality. For instance, there is the reality in which the Last War never happened and you had a happy childhood with your parents, but that was not the reality that furthered my goals, so I am following this one instead. You see, if there is any series of possible events that can lead to my success, then I have already won. So how exactly are you going to stop me?"

Doug kept eye contact with Satan and leaned in so close that their noses almost touched. "Somehow."

"Good luck on that," Satan said. "But you have more immediate concerns. There are others like me. Asmod, for instance. You merely destroyed his human form. And Astara. And Loch. And many others. And believe me, they have taken notice of what happened and how some warfs have learned of the Source — the Forbidden Fruit — and they will be responding."

Doug's resolve melted a bit. "They're coming after Hellbender, you're saying?"

Satan's expression became serious, as of a doctor telling dire news. "I don't think you understand how far above you they are. If someone steps on a fire ant mound and a few ants sting him, does he get revenge on just those couple ants, or does he destroy the whole mound?" Satan motioned to the other war orphans in the bar, most of whom were smiling and had something in their expressions that Doug had almost never seen among war orphans before: hope. And as Satan explained what awaited them, he gave a light chuckle. But there was something sinister about it. Something that chilled Doug to his very soul. So not a light chuckle — a dark chuckle.

It was resolved: Doug did not trust Satan.

FINAL WORD

Hey, it's me again, Frank. I hope you had as much fun reading this as I did writing it. Well, some of the final editing was a bit tedious. I hope there weren't parts where you were all, "I just need to get this done with!" because that's where I was at times.

Anyway, I think it was a nice, self-contained story, while also throwing some threads out there to expand on in a sequel. Which you're just going to have to wait for. Unless you're reading this years in the future after this series became wildly popular and there are already seven books out. And the way it goes, I'm guessing I hit my peak with the third one — widely regarded as the best — but then I got taken in by my own success and my writing became more indulgent after that, the last few books became a bit of slog to get through, and people probably only stuck with it because of the sunk cost fallacy, after putting that much time into the previous books.

If that is what happened, I'm sorry. Hey, the creative process is hard. And I swear I'll get around to finishing up the series. It's just that I'm really busy with all my — what would I probably be doing if I were really rich? — illegally poaching gorillas.

But I'm getting ahead of myself. Just one book done. I'm not going to be hunting gorillas with a Civil War-era Gatling gun any time soon. So, I just hope you enjoyed this story. I thought it was pretty good.

Or was it a little weird?

Whatever. My only goal is to not be boring. Which means I'm going to go ahead and end this now. Thank you for your time. I'll see you around, friend!

— Frank J. Fleming

P.S. Make sure to sign up for my newsletter at FrankJFleming.com for updates on my future releases and whatever else I feel like talking about. You'll also get a free story. Cool deal!

ACKNOWLEDGEMENTS

As any writer can tell you, thanking other people for your book is kind of dumb because for the most part other people just get in the way of writing. They always want attention and support, and some of those small ones around me want to be fed. It's irritating, and it really slows down writing.

Still, a few people are worth mentioning. First off, I'd like to thank Cindy Kehler for the editing; I don't care very much about grammar or spelling and like to leave that as someone else's concern. I'd like to thank Patrick Moran, Burt Taylor, Rick Joyce, Laurel Van Driest, John Ott, Charlie Hodges, and James Lakes for early feedback. And thanks to Ethan Nicolle for both feedback and the great cover design.

I'd also like to thank my mom, Mom, who always helps out, especially with the aforementioned small ones who want to be fed. And I'd like to thank my mother-in-law, Linda, for supporting my writing.

Finally, a very special thanks to my wife, Sarah, without whom I'd be completely useless and get nowhere. And also thank you to God for making everything a fun adventure.

ABOUT FRANK J. FLEMING

Frank J. Fleming is a novelist (*Superego*), humor columnist (*New York Post* and *USA Today*), and scriptwriter (*Love Gov*). Frank is a Carnegie Mellon University graduate and also works as an electrical and software engineer when he's not writing and has been a pioneer in virtual reality video. He lives in Austin with his wife and four kids. He's the world's leading advocate for nuking the moon.